P9-DBU-239

HOLLOWGIRL
A Twinmaker Novel

Also by Sean Williams

Twinmaker

Crashland

HOLLOWGIRL

A TWINMAKER NOVEL

SEAN WILLIAMS

BALZER + BRAY
An Imprint of HarperCollins*Publishers*

Balzer + Bray is an imprint of HarperCollins Publishers.

Hollowgirl
Copyright © 2015 by Sean Williams
All rights reserved. Printed in the United States of America.
No part of this book may be used or reproduced in any manner
whatsoever without written permission except in the case of brief
quotations embodied in critical articles and reviews. For information
address HarperCollins Children's Books, a division of HarperCollins
Publishers, 195 Broadway, New York, NY 10007.
www.epicreads.com

Library of Congress Cataloging-in-Publication Data
Williams, Sean, date
Hollowgirl : a Twinmaker novel / Sean Williams. — First edition.
        pages   cm
Sequel to: Crashland.
Summary: "In the final book in the Twinmaker series, Clair, Q, and
Kari Sargent must enter the Yard, a digital landscape created by their
enemy, in order to save the world"— Provided by publisher.
        ISBN 978-0-06-220327-4 (hardback)
        [1. Science fiction. 2. Cloning—Fiction. 3. Space and time—
Fiction.] I. Title.
PZ7.W6681739Ho 2015   2015006514
[Fic]—dc23   CIP
                                                    AC

Typography by Erin Fitzsimmons
15 16 17 18 19 CG/RRDH 10 9 8 7 6 5 4 3 2 1
❖
First Edition

The wheels on the bus don't go round and round
Titanium wings don't keep planes off the ground
What price the mirror, the box, and the wire?
Everywhere is anywhere is nowhere
Now

Lyrics by Nana Healey © 2059

[I]

CLAIR WAS TWELVE the first time a story about d-mat truly scared her. She was at a sleepover with Libby and a girl named Jude, a friend who later drifted away after getting into sports. They had been whispering long past their bedtime when Libby said in an almost gleeful voice, "Did you hear the one about the girl who used d-mat to lose weight . . . and died?"

Jude threw a pillow. "That's not true. You can check it out on the Air. It's all made up."

"It's true. You know Mei from school? Her cousin was the girl's sister's best friend."

"Yeah, sure," said Jude, "if you say so."

"I *do* say so."

More to forestall an argument than anything else, Clair asked, "What happened to her?"

It was simple. The girl in the story had had an abusive boyfriend who thought she was overweight. He hacked into the network and made it so she lost a certain percentage of the fat in her body every time she went through d-mat. She shed weight, sure, but he didn't realize that fats were everywhere in the body, in every cell, every nerve.

Eventually, she just . . . stopped. When they opened her up to see what had gone wrong, they discovered that the girl's skull was completely empty. Her boyfriend's selfish hack had hollowed her out from the inside.

The thought chilled young Clair to the core. D-mat was supposed to be completely safe. The very suggestion that it might not be threatened to bring her world crumbling down.

Just as it crumbled down five years later. She knew now that some urban myths were true.

"We didn't dream it, did we?" Clair's voice echoed from the buildings around her.

They seemed to be standing in an empty square in the middle of a city. But Clair knew that couldn't be real. The world was dust now. When Jesse and Trevin had shot down the satellite that was supposed to contain the Yard—attempting to bring Ant Wallace to justice and rescue everyone he had illegally copied—they had unleashed a terrible chain reaction that dissolved everything that had ever been through d-mat. Clair had fled with Peace-keeper Sargent and Q into the actual Yard, which she now knew was really deep under a frozen lake in Russia.

Where they *appeared* to be was in San Francisco, according to the Yard's version of the Air, which her lenses accessed just as they always did. They told her that she was in the southwest corner of Union Square near a gallery that specialized in rare manga. The Air also provided the date, time, and temperature. It told her that no one was currently following her—which was a relief after the intense scrutiny of recent days—and which of her friends were connected and where they were. She could even hear them talking through the chat she had open.

"Are you *sure* this is the right place for a crashlander ball?" Tash was saying.

"Positive." Ronnie's voice had a shiver to it. "Could be warmer, though."

"That'll change when everyone gets here," said Libby.

The only jarring note was the sound of her own voice when she herself wasn't speaking. . . .

"I feel like I've just woken up," said Kari Sargent. The tall peacekeeper was standing nearby, turning around in a circle with her arms held out from her body, palms raised to the sun.

"That's my fault," said Q. Her voice came over Clair's augs as clearly as it used to, but Clair cocked her head, not entirely reassured by Q's presence in her ears. For days Q had been hiding in Kari's head, operating her body like one of Ant Wallace's dupes. It seemed that Clair had passed Q's test of friendship, but she was now unsure what that meant for the two of them.

"In order to pretend to be you, I had to temporarily suppress you," Q said to Kari. "That was hard. You're very strong."

Kari shrugged. She didn't seem bothered by what Q had done to her. Shouldn't she have been angry? Clair would have been.

"You gotta do what you gotta do," Kari said. "That's what you were thinking before we came here. You had to break into the Yard just like you broke into me."

"In some ways the situation is very similar," said Q. "The Yard is as complex as a living thing. We don't really belong here."

"What *is* 'here,' exactly?" asked Clair, waving a hand to take in the square, the city, the world. Her fingernails were chipped. She could hear the sound of wind rustling through nearby trees. "It feels so real—but it can't be, can it?"

"That depends on your definition of 'real,'" said Q. "What you are experiencing is a simulation that is as exactly detailed as the real world, re-created from the data stored in the Air—the Air that used to exist, I mean, outside this simulation. Every measurement and every property of every single thing on Earth has been copied and re-created in the Yard, using the same physical laws that scientists use to understand the world outside. The only difference is that instead of being built on subatomic particles and forces, the Yard is built on data, and this has implications . . . that I am investigating. It is *very* complicated. . . ."

She trailed off, lost in the thought.

"So the Yard can feel real even though it's not?" Clair pressed.

"It *is* real, for all intents and purposes. Simply a different kind of real."

"And the outside . . . ?"

"There is no communication with the outside."

"Because it's forbidden by the simulation," asked Kari, "or because there's no one to communicate with?"

"Perhaps both."

Clair wrapped her arms around her stomach, feeling her ribs jutting into her elbows. This was bad. For a moment she had hoped that Wallace's terrible chain reaction might have somehow spared San Francisco, maybe other cities as well, but if Q was saying what Clair thought she was saying . . .

"They're all really dead," Clair said, remembering the blue dawn sweeping around the globe.

"Yes," said Q. "Every d-mat user who couldn't get somewhere safe in time."

"The Stainers will be happy." Kari's face was twisted in a way that indicated the joke wasn't supposed to be funny. "That's . . . so bad I don't think there are words for it."

Clair agreed. She could barely hold the thought in her head.

The world was gone.

And yet it was right here, too, seemingly the same as it had ever been, inside the Yard.

Clair could still hear her friends talking over the open chat. They had no idea what was happening. To them, the world they were in was precisely as real as it appeared to be. They were going to a party together. No one they loved had died.

Feeling overwhelmed, Clair put the chat on mute. She took a deep breath and shuddered it out.

Real.

Cool sunlight reflected off a windowpane, blinding her when she inadvisably glanced at it.

Real.

A creeping sickness in her gut was one part hunger, one part dread, and a large part self-blame.

Real.

"Libby and the others are in Switzerland," she said. Jesse wasn't among them, which worried her. She couldn't hear his voice or locate him anywhere in the Yard, not on a search through the Air. Perhaps a deeper search would find him, later. "We should join them."

"Are you sure that's what you want to do?" Kari asked. "*She's* there too."

Clair winced. "She" was a copy of herself. Clair had accidentally broken parity again by allowing two of herself to exist at once—and if what Q had told them earlier was correct, this other Clair was also real, not a dupe.

And now she was with her friends . . . with Tash and Ronnie, and Libby, and Zep . . .

At least two people on that list were supposed to be dead.

Clair felt dizzy. She crouched down with her arms around her shins, face pressed firmly into her knees. Her eyes closed so tightly she saw bursts of colors.

Real.

"Make it stop," she said. "I can't take any more."

A hand came down on her shoulder. Up close, Kari Sargent smelled of ash and blood and fear.

"I know how you feel," Kari said. "Are we dead or alive? Or are they? Maybe that's the better question. What if Billie really is in here? I grieved for her when I was dreaming that Q was me. Would I feel the same way about her now because she's not allowed to exist?"

Billie was Kari's girlfriend, lost in the crash caused by Clair's first breaking of parity, when d-mat had stopped working all over the world. There had been lots of deaths. At the time, that had seemed like the worst thing imaginable.

Clair rose up to Kari as the older woman stooped to her level. For a moment they just held on to each other and cried. They were alive. So many weren't. Some were confusingly in between. But at least the two of them had each other.

"Screw the law, and screw philosophy, too," Clair said

through ragged gulps for air. "We have to accept them, don't we? Or else we're worse than the people who copied them."

"Yes, yes." Kari sounded relieved. "You're right, of course. What was I going to do—*arrest* everyone for being an illegal duplicate?"

She laughed and pulled away, wiping her eyes with one hand.

"We can go to them," Kari said. "If you want to. But we should move quickly. Wallace will be in here. This is his place, his artificial Earth. If he finds us before we find him, it's all over."

They stood, Clair telling herself to ignore the confusion and press on. Kari was right. They couldn't afford to drag their heels.

"Q, is it safe to use d-mat in here?" she asked through the Air, then repeated the question when Q didn't immediately respond.

"Sorry, Clair. I was thinking about something. You know, although it seems impossible, I actually recognize many of the algorithms used to maintain conceptual continuity across the nodes—"

"Right now I just need to know about d-mat."

"Oh yes, d-mat will function normally. I will monitor your transmissions and make sure nothing interferes. I will also create a mask, so your passage will not be noted."

"Thanks. Really. We couldn't do this without you, Q."

Q didn't respond at all. Clair was used to Q getting lost in technobabble, but she didn't normally ignore people.

"Where are we going?" asked Kari.

"To the Sphinx Observatory," Clair said, shaking herself out of her concerns. "Where this whole thing started."

[2]

CLAIR GAVE THE booth the destination and the mirrored door slid shut, surrounding them with infinite reflections. Whereas in the real world, d-mat used complex fields to take matter apart, particle by particle, and then put it back together exactly as it had been, in the Yard, Clair supposed, simulations of complex fields would do the same thing to simulations of particles. She wondered what would happen if she told it to take them outside the Yard. An error message? Or would it send them nowhere at all . . . ? *An experiment for later*, she thought.

Distantly, at the far reach of her many reflections, Clair caught a flash of a face that was neither dark like hers nor light like Kari's, but something in between: a young woman with tan skin and bright purple hair, someone Clair had never seen before.

In an eyeblink, it was gone. Clair recoiled, and Kari caught her arm.

"Another dupe?"

Clair felt her pulse race in her throat. Had she seen it at all? Jumping at shadows or mental glitches wasn't going to help anyone.

"Q said there weren't any dupes in the Yard," she reminded herself as much as Kari. "Everyone was reset. Besides, she's watching over us now. We'll be okay."

Kari touched her brow. "Oh yeah, right. I forget she can do that now that she's not in here. . . ."

Clair wondered if that was why Kari wasn't angry. She and Q had spent several days in the same body, after all. What had they learned about each other in that time?

sssssss—

Clair looked up at the ceiling, listening.

"It sounds exactly the same," she said.

"I know." Kari grinned, all her reflections grinning with her. "So weird to hear it again."

—*pop*

The booth shrank, pressing them close together. They had arrived. In the second before the door opened, Clair's resolve faltered. Her heart held such a chaotic mix of emotions she couldn't begin to describe how or what she felt. "Intense" was one word. "Everything" another.

When the door opened, Clair took a step backward, unconsciously placing Kari's larger form between her and the space beyond. Cold air flooded the booth, making her shiver. The observatory sat atop a mountain over eleven thousand feet high: she should have asked the booth to fab her a parka.

Kari walked out into the cavernous space and glanced at the darkened windows directly opposite the booth, then to her right.

"Have you come for the party?" said someone.

"Welcome!" said another. "You're the first ones here."

Clair hugged herself tighter. She knew those voices.

"No, I haven't," said Kari. She glanced behind her, into the booth, where Clair was hiding from more than just the cold. Then she turned back. "Libby and Clair, isn't it? I'm PK Sargent. And you must be Ronnie, Tash, and Zep."

Kari walked out of view. Clair heard footsteps coming to meet her across the dusty floor. It was gloomy out there, with dawn still hours away. She knew exactly what the space would look like. The observatory had the echoing ambience of an empty factory, with thick iron beams studded with rivets and lots of space, its only furniture a boxy four-door booth that had seen better days. Observation decks provided uninterrupted views of the surrounding mountains. The glass would need a clean before the ball began. . . .

"Who called the peacekeepers?" asked Zep. "Talk about a buzzkill."

"It wasn't me," said Ronnie. "And anyway, what buzz is there to kill?"

"Do you know where everyone went?" asked Tash, her voice tinkling in the reverberant air.

"No, I don't," said Kari. "There was no one where we came from either."

That struck Clair as odd too, now that she thought about it. A moment ago they had been in central San Francisco during daylight hours, yet there hadn't been anyone around except them.

"Who's 'we'?" asked Libby. "I don't see anyone else."

This was Clair's cue. It was either come out now or run away forever. She wondered why she felt so ashamed, like she was hiding something or lying to them, when in fact she was as much a victim of circumstances as they were. But what circumstances they were—illegal copying, murder, the end of the world . . .

Mentally slapping herself, she opened her eyes again and stepped out of the booth.

"It's me."

They each reacted differently.

Libby gasped. If she had gone any paler, she would have been transparent.

Tash's eyes went wide, her mouth moving in a silent *Oh my God.*

Ronnie said, "This isn't allowed. What's going on?"

Zep looked from one Clair to the other and back again, then kept shaking his head in denial.

The other Clair retreated a step, her hand flying to her

mouth as though she was about to throw up.

"Who *are* you?" she asked.

Clair didn't shrink away from their reactions. Now that there was no going back, she felt more committed.

"I'm you," she said, staring right at her double. The other Clair wasn't exactly the same: her hair was shorter; her face was clean. "I'm not a dupe."

"What's a dupe?" asked Tash.

The question took her by surprise. "A copy of a person with someone else's mind inside. Don't you remember?"

"That's just an urban myth," said Ronnie, her eyebrows meeting in a frown behind the frame of her glasses, "like Improvement."

"Improvement isn't a myth," said Clair and Libby at the same time.

They looked at each other, then away.

Clair began to understand then. Libby was wearing a silver dress with white tights and red boots. The other Clair was wearing blue plaid and a navy headband. Zep had on a red checked shirt and tight blue jeans. Tash and Ronnie had dressed in their best party gear too. *Clair knew these outfits.* They had worn them to the ball. But it wasn't only their clothes that dated back two weeks or more.

"You've just used Improvement, haven't you?" she said to Libby. "That's when you were copied, and everyone else with you, because you used Improvement on the way to the ball. I remember you telling us about it there."

"Telling us about what?" asked the other Clair.

"I didn't tell anyone anything," said Libby. She was flushed now, a carnation pink that was anything but delicate.

"You did, only it wasn't this version of you." Clair wished there was an easy way to explain, and someone else to do it for her, since she doubted they would take her word for it.

Then she remembered that there *was* someone else.

"Q? Can you help me out here? Are you listening?"

"I am listening, Clair," said Q. By the way the others reacted, Clair knew that they were hearing the voice too. No more asking for permission to open chats; Q was much cleverer now that she knew what she was.

"My name is Q," she said, her tone more measured than when she talked to Clair. "I am not human, but I am Clair's friend and I want to help her help you. I will explain what has happened, and afterward I will answer your questions as best as I can."

"Wait," said the other Clair, who Clair was beginning to think of as Clair 1.0: the Clair she had been before the crashlander ball. "First tell me why there's a copy of me but not of anyone else."

"It's not deliberate," Clair said. "That's just how it worked out."

"Why?" A flash of anxiety crossed her double's face. "What did I do to deserve this?"

Again, a flash of unwarranted but irrepressible shame. "Q will explain, if you let her."

"I want to hear it from you."

Clair tightened her lips. They had the same genes. They were equally stubborn. If Clair 1.0 wanted to force the issue, Clair 6.0 was happy to push back, but what was the point?

"I'm not the copy," she said bluntly. "You are. You're a backup saved when Libby used Improvement, the same as everyone else here." She hesitated, then pressed on, knowing that this would be as hard for them to hear as it was for her to say. "The reason why there's only one of *them* is because their originals are dead."

That provoked another shocked reaction, more of disbelief than anything else.

"*I'm* not a copy," said Tash.

"And neither am I," said Clair 1.0, narrowing her eyes. "I'm me and I'm real, and if this is some kind of stupid crashlander hazing, then screw you and whoever's behind it. We don't want to belong to your clique anymore."

Clair understood. They didn't trust this new Clair, and looking at it from their point of view, who could blame them?

"It's hard to explain," she said in a softer tone. "I made a mistake. I made lots of mistakes. If you just let Q talk, she'll tell you all about it."

"But first," said Q, "a correction. Not all of you are dead.

It is quite likely that Tash has survived, outside."

"Well, that's a huge relief to the rest of us," said Zep.

"Outside where?" asked Libby.

"What's *inside*?" asked Ronnie.

At least, thought Clair, they had moved on to different questions.

———————————————————[3]

Q LAID IT out in a way that probably seemed matter-of-fact to her.

"The Improvement meme was designed by Ant Wallace to select candidates from the broader population, specifically young adults between fifteen and twenty years of age . . ."

Clair thought of it as a net designed to catch a particular sort of person, one willing to try an impossible meme to illegally make themselves *better*. Using his powers as head of VIA, the regulatory body in charge of keeping d-mat safe, Wallace created Improvement in order to find new bodies for geniuses considered too valuable to die. It was later misused by lawmakers who wanted to create a secret army of illegal dupes to take over the world.

"Once Improvement found a suitable candidate," Q said, "their pattern was modified before being put back into the world, containing a different mind. Sometimes people who hadn't used Improvement were copied. Those secondary patterns were stored in the Yard for future retrieval, to be used as blackmail. Those secondary patterns are you."

Clair had personally seen Zep and Jesse's father used this way, in Ant Wallace's space station. She had never thought to consider when, exactly, those patterns had been taken. The answer wasn't hard to work out now. Libby knew about Improvement but Clair 1.0 didn't. That put them in a narrow window of time just before the crashlander ball.

If Clair had any doubts about the timing of the copies, all she had to do was look at the way Clair 1.0 and Zep kept shooting glances at each other. They never stood too close but they never strayed too far away, either.

That feeling . . . of being entranced and entrapped at the same time . . . Clair 6.0 remembered it well.

Now, though, it came with a yawning sensation deep in her gut. She couldn't go looking for Jesse right now, she told herself. She had to do this first.

Clair fabbed a parka while Q brought the others up to speed, encouraging her occasionally to skip parts of the story in order to keep it simple. If her friends knew the world was a wasteland of ash, they might just give up hope on the spot.

"So Ant Wallace, the man in charge of keeping d-mat safe for everyone, tried to take over the world," said

Ronnie. She, too, had fabbed a parka and was holding it closed around her throat with one long-fingered hand. *Real.*

"That wasn't entirely Wallace," said Kari. "He was working for the lawmakers. *Ex*-lawmakers, I should say. LM Kingdon was arrested right before the end, when her conspiracy was exposed. She'll be in here too, I expect. She'll still be trying to take over, and Wallace will still be helping her. Clair and I are committed to keeping the peace by stopping them as soon as we can."

"Who says you're actually a peacekeeper?" asked Tash. "You don't look like one."

Kari glanced down at her filthy armor. "Extenuating circumstances."

"You could just be saying that," said Clair 1.0, with a suspicious look at Clair 6.0. "You could both be dupes."

"I'm not a dupe," Clair snapped, irritated by the accusation.

"Just saying it doesn't help."

"If I were a dupe there would be someone else inside me. Someone who isn't *you.*"

"Are you me, though? You don't even look like me. You look . . ."

"Older," said Tash.

"Harder," said Ronnie.

"Angrier," said Zep.

"Damaged," said Libby.

"Exactly." Clair 1.0 came right up to Clair 6.0 and folded her arms. "So prove it. Prove you're me."

Clair fought the urge to curl into a ball again. She knew she had changed. Like Kari, she was dirty, tired, and desperate, wearing clothes that didn't belong to her. She was covered in the ashes of friends this other version of her had never met. But could she really have changed so much?

She knew she hadn't.

Clair leaned in close and whispered into Clair 1.0's ear so no one else would hear.

"I know how you feel about Zep," she said, grabbing at Clair 1.0's arm when she tried to pull away. "I kissed him. That was my first mistake."

Clair 1.0 wrenched out of her grip, glancing at Libby and then back at her. There was guilt in her eyes as well as acceptance, alarm, and something that might have been jealousy.

"Do you believe me now?"

"I can't believe that there are two of you," said Tash. She had a lock of bright blue hair wrapped around one finger and was pulling it tight, like she did when she was worried. "Isn't that supposed to be impossible?"

"You make copies of things in a fabber," said Ronnie. "Why not people in a booth?"

"But people aren't just the stuff they're made of."

"Who says?" said Zep. "Otherwise d-mat wouldn't work,

and the Stainers would be right."

He mimed a zombie attack that Tash batted away.

"If I *were* a dupe," Clair declared, "there's no way I'd just appear to you like this. I'd try to replace my other me, not argue with her in front of you."

Libby was watching both Clairs closely, as though trying to figure out what had passed between them a moment ago.

"How do you know *I'm* not a dupe?" she asked.

Because you're not a psychotic bitch with a death wish named Mallory, she almost said.

"Your birthmark," Clair said. "It's still there."

Libby's hand came up to touch her cheek, where the purplish blotch was faintly visible under her foundation.

"Right," she said with a decisive nod. "That's what I asked Improvement to change. Did it work?"

"Yes. It disappeared."

"But there's no such thing as a free lunch," said Ronnie. "We're getting that."

"And now none of us is really real, apparently," said Zep. "How does *that* work?"

"This simulation we occupy is accurate to the highest degree," said Q. "If you had the right instruments, you could see the faintest stars or the tiniest particles known to humanity. The Yard's reality is not built on matter— it is built on information—but the way it is *perceived* remains the same. There's a word for this: 'qualia.' That's a name as well, interestingly. . . ."

"I'm getting a headache," said Tash."

"Q does that to you sometimes," said Kari.

"The Yard has been active ever since Ant Wallace's unstable-matter bomb went off," Q went on, ignoring them. "When that trap was triggered—"

By Jesse, Clair thought with a snap in her heart so painful she was amazed the others didn't hear it.

"—the Yard . . . woke. Before, it was inert. There was no anything. Then an emergency protocol resurrected the backup of Ant Wallace, and of course Wallace needed an environment in which to exist. I am still analyzing the way the Yard did that—what makes it work, and possibly *who*—and I believe that I am close to an answer. . . ."

She wandered off into silence again, the third time Clair had noticed Q's attention drift. Clair hoped it wasn't something they should be worried about.

"Sounds like the entire world needs rescuing, inside and outside the Yard," said Ronnie.

"We are the rescue party," said Clair, wishing it weren't true. "What you see is what you get."

[4]

"WELL, THE FIRST thing we have to do," said Libby, pushing forward, "is to decide what to call you two. Clair One and

Clair Two? Clair A and Clair B?"

"One and Two," said Ronnie.

"All right, but who's One?"

"You can be," Clair told the other version of herself. She was already thinking of her as Clair 1.0 anyway. "It doesn't matter to me."

"How can it not matter to you?" Clair One asked. "This is all so wrong."

Once it would have bothered Clair to be one of two. But, unexpectedly, talking to Clair One didn't make her feel uncomfortable. It wasn't a fundamental attack on *her*. It was just confusing, and there were more important things to worry about.

"The first thing I want to do," she said, "is get out of the Yard before someone finds us."

"Can't we just use d-mat, like the way you came in?" Zep asked Clair.

"What do you say, Q?" Clair asked, remembering the experiment she had thought of trying earlier. "Can we do that?"

"Impossible," said Q. "The network is completely degraded now. The data would vanish if I tried to send you to a booth outside—if there is one."

So much for that, Clair thought.

"You should also know," Q said, "that just being here, Clair, you and I are causing . . . disturbances . . . you because of the break in parity, me because I'm me."

"What kind of disturbances?"

"Causality errors, topological defects, continuity strains . . . It's hard to explain. But it is likely our presence has been noted."

That was an ominous thought. Wallace would do everything in his power to hunt her down if he knew she was there. She had already killed him once.

"We need to get somewhere else," Clair said, "somewhere safe, inside the Yard. Somewhere we can think about how to escape."

"We could go back to my place," said Ronnie. "My olds have guns."

"Too dangerous," said Kari. "It's the obvious thing to do, too easy to anticipate."

"I agree," said Clair One. "But there's no point rushing off anywhere until we know where Wallace is. I mean, he could have a hideout anywhere."

"Q can help—"

"Q's not all-powerful, or you wouldn't be in here with us," said Clair One.

"So how do we do this?" asked Tash. "Where do we even start?"

"One step at a time," said Ronnie.

Clair was grateful for Ronnie's calming, levelheaded approach. She had always been the practical, science-y one among her friends.

"You're good at this," whispered Jesse's voice in her ear.

"You've missed your true calling."

Clair startled out of her thoughts, her heart leaping with the hope that he had found them.

She looked behind her, but there was no one there.

"What is it?" asked Kari, noticing again.

Clair shook her head. She was certain she hadn't imagined it. But what could she say? If she tried to tell anyone that she was hearing voices, they would laugh at her for glitching. But if she didn't . . . What if this was like Devin and Trevin's whispering to each other, or if it had something to do with the disturbances to the Yard Q had mentioned?

"It's not safe here," she said. "Let's go."

"Why go anywhere until we know what we're doing?" asked Clair One.

"You have no idea what we're dealing with."

"What do any of us know? Running might take us right to them."

"She has a point, Two," said Zep.

Of course you'd agree with her, Clair wanted to say. But she was too worried to patiently explain it to them. Her mind was full of horrible images: dupes coming at her without care for their own disposable lives; Nobody—the worst of them—identical in appearance to Jesse's father. How could she convince someone who had never seen dupes in action that they should run while they had the chance?

[26]

Her thoughts were interrupted by the sound of a booth activating. Clair left the others to see what was going on. The door she had emerged from was shut. The other doors were shutting too.

"Shit," she said. "Q, are you there? Can you tell who that is?"

Q's reply came immediately. "Four people, their names protected by peacekeeper protocols. I can't tell you who they are without drawing attention to myself."

Lawmakers and peacekeepers had worked with Wallace in the real world. Anyone could be traveling under those protocols.

"I told you. We have to get out of here," she said, turning back to the others. *"Now."*

"Whoa," said Zep, raising his hands. "Is that necessary?"

Clair looked down and discovered that her pistol was in her hand. She didn't remember drawing it. Covering her surprise with a brusque nod, she said, "It might well be. Ronnie, check the floor plans of this place. I remember reading about an elevator somewhere, the last time I was here. If it's working, we can take it to the bottom of the mountain. There might be other booths there. Q, is there anything you can do to delay their arrival?"

"Nothing that won't alert them to my presence."

"Don't do that. You're our only advantage." Clair worried at her brow with her free hand, jiggling her right heel on the spot, wanting to run but not knowing how to.

"Ronnie, how are you coming along with those floor plans?" asked Kari.

"Got them. The elevator is locked, but maybe Q can deal with that?"

"I can."

"Great," said Clair, relieved that they would finally be moving. "Let's go. Which way?"

"Wait up!" Clair One stood in their way. "What if I told you it wasn't Wallace or anyone who worked for him? Would that make you slow down a second?"

"Yes," said Kari, "but how could you possibly know who it is?"

"They're using peacekeeper protocols because they're PKs," Clair One said, her chin raised. "I know that because I called them."

_____ [5]

"YOU DID *WHAT*?" asked Clair.

"This is all too weird," Clair One said, "and you just expect us to take your word for it. I want a second opinion. That's not unreasonable."

Clair had to bite the inside of her lip to curb an impulse to scream. No, it wasn't unreasonable at all, which only made her frustration even worse. She knew exactly why

Clair One had made that call, because the first thing she herself had tried to do on being confronted with WHOLE and Jesse's father's death was call the PKs. She couldn't blame Clair One for doing what she, too, would have done.

Only this wasn't a week ago. It wasn't even the real world. There was no way of knowing who in the Yard was actually on the end of a call to the PKs, be it people or dupes or more corrupt lawmakers. . . . She supposed they were about to find out.

So much for running.

"All right," she said. "We stay, but the rest of you hide while I see who it is."

"I'm with you," said Kari.

"You're both being paranoid," said Clair One.

"If what we're telling you is true, we have good reason to be." Clair forced herself to moderate her tone. "And if we're wrong, I won't argue anymore."

Clair One hesitated, then nodded.

"Through here," said Tash, tugging at the door leading to the next chamber, where Clair knew they would find the ladders up to the roof. "Quick, or they'll see us."

Glad that at least one of her friends was picking up on her sense of urgency, Clair ushered the rest out of sight. When they were concealed, Clair turned back to the booth. Kari was circling it, tapping each door with the barrel of her gun.

"Which one first?" Kari asked Q.

"The one you will tap next. It will open in ten seconds. The remainder will open in the subsequent thirty seconds."

Half a minute, thought Clair, *and if they come out with guns blazing it could be all over. Because Clair One tried to do the right thing . . .*

Kari slipped around the side of the booth, where she would be out of sight when the first person emerged. Clair stood front and center, waiting with her pistol behind her back.

The ancient booth hissed. The door opened.

Inside was a PK wearing a perfectly ordinary blue uniform. No armor. No camouflage. No weapons drawn.

Clair might have relaxed had she not recognized him. Gripping the pistol even more tightly, she pointed it at his chest and crouched behind it like she would a shield.

"Stop," she told PK Drader, and her voice caught for an instant, "right there."

He raised his hands. PK Drader had an open face and a relaxed manner that had always grated on her. He seemed to be trying too hard. To cover up his lies, she had learned later.

"You're Clair?" he said in a friendly voice, as though they had never met. "I don't think you called us here to shoot anyone. Tell me what's going on."

"You betrayed us," she said, not bothering to dissemble. He was a member of the conspiracy trying to take over the world. "You're working for the lawmakers."

He grinned as though she'd said something stupid. "All peacekeepers work for the lawmakers."

"You know what I mean."

"I'm afraid I don't."

"LM Kingdon? The seastead? The muster?"

He tilted his head, a picture of innocence. "No idea what you're talking about, Clair. I only know your name because of the call you just made. Why don't you put down the gun and we'll talk?"

Clair bit her lip and thought fast. This could be an old copy of PK Drader, innocent of his crimes in the real world. But even if he honestly didn't know what had happened before the blue dawn, that didn't mean he was on her side. He could have been working for Kingdon all along. He could still be the enemy.

Another door hissed open, the one on the far side of the booth. There was an *oof* of surprise, and Clair's attention darted to where she had last seen Kari, but there was no one there now. When she looked back at Drader, he, too, was holding a pistol, aimed squarely at her midriff.

"It's over," he said, all pretense gone. "You're done. Come quietly and no one will get hurt."

Clair's heart lurched midbeat, then steadied. "No," she said. She wasn't going to give in, not after everything she had been through. She wasn't going to fall into Wallace's or Kingdon's hands so easily, even if she had to fight them every second she was inside the Yard. Wherever they were, whatever they were doing, she had to find them and stop them so she and her friends would be safe.

To Clair's left another door opened. She saw Kari grab the person who emerged from it—a wiry woman with close-cropped white hair, dressed in a tight black thermal camouflage suit. They scuffled, and this time it was PK Drader whose attention strayed.

Clair jerked her pistol higher so it pointed at his face.

"You're the one who's coming quietly," she said. "You're going to put your gun down, and then you're going to tell me everything you know about the Yard and how to get out."

He didn't flinch. His gaze remained coolly superior.

"I'm not afraid of you, Clair. You won't shoot."

"Then you don't know me." She didn't want to shoot anyone, but a progression of mental images undermined any reservations she had in his case: dupes dying in droves outside the muster, the failure of Devin and Trevin's plan on the seastead, the endless threats issued from the mouth of a child whose mind was no longer his own . . . All that and more could be laid at Drader's feet.

The third door opened. PK Drader's lips tightened. She could see him tensing, getting ready to move.

"Don't," Clair said, taking a step forward, pointing the pistol as steadily as she could at the bridge of his nose.

She had seen enough dramas to know how PKs spoke in such moments, and she did her best to keep her voice steady too. "Gun on the floor. Now."

Drader's pistol dipped. To Clair's right, Kari knocked his third accomplice down with one blow to the back of the neck. PK Drader turned, saw her, and straightened. It was clear he recognized her. For an instant, the two peacekeepers faced each other.

"Traitor," he said, snapping his gun back up and shooting Kari square in the chest.

The big PK staggered and fell to the ground.

"No!" Clair's trigger finger tightened. Her pistol went off with a loud bang and kicked back in her hands. PK Drader dropped like a stone, his neck spraying blood in a crimson fan. Clair reeled, horrified by what he had done—and what she had done to him.

"Oh my God." Tash rushed past her, to Kari's side. "He shot PK Sargent!"

"And he's dead now too." Zep was staring at the blood, looking like he might be about to throw up. "Oh hell."

Clair didn't want to look. She wanted Zep to be the strong one, to enfold her in his arms and allow her to close her eyes, just for a moment. But that was the past, before Jesse. This was the present and it was bloody and complicated. PK Drader had fired the first shot inside the Yard, and she had responded.

"Watch out!" she said, blocking Clair One from coming any closer to PK Drader's body. "They might still be dangerous."

"Seriously?"

"You haven't seen what they can do."

"And I don't want to." Her eyes shifted from the body to Clair's face. Pinched and wary, her body language was conflicted. "But did you have to shoot him?"

"He shot Kari."

"She attacked them first."

"Do they *look* like PKs to you?"

Ronnie was checking PK Drader's three fallen companions, loosening their tight black collars so they could breathe freely. Libby hovered at her shoulder, hands clasped tightly to her chest. They had no identifying marks or patches.

"Whoever you spoke to couldn't have been a PK," Clair went on. "Not a good one, anyway. Wallace would only copy the PKs he can trust. We can't afford to— Stop, don't open their eyelids!" Clair added hastily as Ronnie went to check the pupils of the first PK Kari had dropped. "Don't let whoever's at the other end of their lenses get a look at you."

"Why does it matter if they see us?" asked Clair One.

"They might not know there are two of me in here."

"So?"

"See what they did when they found out there was *one*

of me here? Imagine what they'd do if they knew there were two."

"Maybe we should plug their ears, then," said Clair One, which was a good suggestion that Ronnie put into immediate effect, tearing strips off her party dress and wadding them into balls.

"I have cut the power to the booths," said Q.

"Good thinking," said Clair, even though that was bound to attract attention. "No one use the Air. It's too dangerous."

"PK Sargent is alive," said Tash, looking up. "Lucky she's wearing armor."

Clair hurried to the fallen PK's side. Kari's eyes were closed. There was a round, silver indentation just below her heart, where the bullet had struck her. She was lucky also, Clair thought, that Drader hadn't aimed for her head.

"I am detecting activity in Mürren and Lauterbrunnen," said Q. "Freshly fabbed drones are on their way."

"How long?" asked Clair. "Who sent them?"

"They are under peacekeeper control. You can expect them in five minutes. Maybe longer: there's a storm coming, so the winds are strong."

Really real, Clair reminded herself. If the simulation could make people move and bullets fly, why not wind and rain too? And drones, and evil peacekeepers, and worse. All the Yard had to do was wind them up and let them go, like clockwork dolls on a tabletop. How was she going to fight them all?

Save your friends first, she told herself, *then the world.*

"We need to get out of here before they see us and take us in."

"The elevator connects to an underground train line," said Ronnie. "We could get out that way."

"And after that?" asked Clair One. "What then?"

"We'll work that out on the way."

"On the way where?"

"I don't know, all right?" Clair rounded on her, out of patience. "Stay here if you want. I'm not going to kidnap you or threaten you or anything like that. But I'm not giving myself up and I'm not leaving the others behind. If we stay here much longer, we'll all die."

"Are you going to shoot me, too, if I get in your way?" asked Clair One.

Zep, Ronnie, and Tash were staring at them as though they were a glowing red timer counting down to zero.

"This party sucks," said Libby with bright decisiveness. "Let's blow this joint. Argue later. That's my suggestion. Okay, ladies?"

[6]

CLAIR ONE GLARED at Clair for one long second, then at Libby. Finally, she nodded.

"Okay, but I'm not happy about it."

"Take a number. I was expecting a new face and a crash-lander ball, not this funky little shindig. Ronnie, which way is the elevator?"

Before Ronnie could answer, Kari woke with a groan.

"Son. Of. A. Bitch. . . . He shot me!"

Clair took one elbow, Ronnie the other. Together they levered the heavy peacekeeper to her feet.

On seeing the blood and PK Drader's body, she asked Clair, "Was that you?"

Clair nodded, her face turning warm.

Kari gripped her shoulder. "Had it coming to him. How long until he comes back?"

"I don't know if he will," said Clair, remembering what Q had said. She didn't even want to think about the possibility that Q might have been wrong. "We need to get moving."

"This way," said Ronnie, guiding them through the observatory.

Clair didn't remember seeing the actual elevator the other time she had been here, just its existence on a floor plan. That was because it was concealed behind a loose plywood panel, unused for years but apparently still working.

Zep pulled the panel off, exposing two sliding doors that Q had opened in readiness. The space within resembled a large d-mat booth with ample room for all of them. The walls were bare metal, broken only by a simple push-button control panel, UP or DOWN. When they were all inside, Tash pushed DOWN. The doors closed. Clair's stomach seemed to rise into her throat. She could smell Zep's cologne mixed in with her friends' perfumes and the dust, sweat, and grime that she and Kari had brought with them from the outside.

"This is messed up," said Zep as the carriage descended. "We're all thinking that, right? Clair just killed someone."

"Clair *Two* did," said Clair One.

"Am I the only one freaking out?" he asked Clair. "Why aren't *you* freaking out? Have you done this before?"

Clair stared up at him, not knowing the honest answer to that question. She had shot more dupes than she cared to think about, but if Q was right and there were no dupes in the Yard, then that meant that Drader had been himself. A traitor who would have killed her given a chance, but a person nonetheless.

"No, I haven't done this before," she said. She had just crossed a line. "Shit, shit, shit."

Her hands started shaking uncontrollably. The gun fell to the elevator floor. Kari picked it up and folded Clair to her chest. The silver bullet hole was right at Clair's eye level. She stared at it as she held Kari in return, finding justification there but no comfort as the elevator descended.

"Nice one, Zep," said Libby, slapping him on the chest. "You've broken her."

"I didn't mean to. It's just . . . you know."

"You're freaking out, yes. Find a way to do it quietly."

"Zep's right," said Tash. "This can't be happening."

"It's okay," said Kari, her voice a muffled boom in Clair's ears. "We're not hurt. I can't promise that everything is going to be all right, but I can promise to do everything in my power to keep you safe. That's my job."

"You told me that in New York," said Clair.

"Hmmm. And look what happened."

"We're still alive, aren't we?"

There was silence in the elevator, apart from the whining of the mechanism responsible for their rapid descent. Kari rested her chin on the top of Clair's head. That small intimacy made Clair feel slightly better. She just needed a quiet moment in which to catch herself while her entire life fell out from under her. . . .

"Sorry," said Zep.

"Don't apologize," said Clair, releasing Kari from her death grip. "You were right. I think I was overdue for a breakdown."

"Several, by the sound of it." He grinned at her and her heart lightened a little more.

"So at the bottom of this thing we're going take the train," said Clair One, her voice harsh. "How do we know they won't be waiting for us there?"

"There's no booth until the other end of the line," said Ronnie.

"And we have to go that way, right?"

Clair felt weary. Clair One just would not let it go. Clair supposed she wouldn't either, in her shoes.

"There are observation stations at various points along the tunnel," said Q. "I will arrange transport to meet you at one of those."

"And then? We can't get out of the Yard. We have no idea where Wallace is. We haven't even started talking about what we'll do if we find him."

Before Clair could say anything, a chat request appeared in her infield, the first she'd received since arriving in the Yard.

It was from Ant Wallace.

Clair stared at it for a second, chilled to the core. They hadn't spoken since she had blown up his space station, killing earlier versions of both of them. It was like hearing the voice of a ghost that had been haunting her from the shadows, never showing its face.

"I just received a chat request from Wallace," said Clair One.

"So did I," said Ronnie.

"And me," said Zep.

"Don't answer it!" Clair said, trying to keep the panic from her voice. "Don't do anything. Let me think."

PK Drader had seen her, and Wallace would have been watching through Drader's lenses. Q had masked her on the way to the observatory, so anyone tracing her would see a different name, but Wallace would be aware of that trick now. He was obviously bumping everyone nearby to see if she took the bait.

"Change our masks, Q," she said. "Mix us up so there's no chance he can tell who's who. There's no point hiding *you* now."

"Yes, Clair. It is done."

Sharing her infield with the others, Clair accepted the chat request. Audio only.

"Clair Hill, I presume," said Ant Wallace. His image appeared in a window that tightly framed his features, revealing nothing of his surroundings. His face was as charming and warm as ever. Clair knew better than to trust him any more than she had trusted Drader. "The naive girl blessed with powerful friends. Or is that actually a curse? Time will tell."

"What do you want?" She did her best to keep her voice level, but she could hear a slight hitch in it. Seeing him brought back too many memories, none of them good.

"'Want'? How could you imagine I want for anything in here?" He smiled. There was no humor in his eyes. "This is my world. Your interference cannot be tolerated."

"I just want to go home," she said. "That's all."

His eyebrows went up.

"If you could do that, I wouldn't be here myself. I thought you knew about that."

He was talking about the outside, Clair assumed. Ant Wallace was all but confirming that there was nowhere for her to exist but the Yard. She refused to accept that this would never change. She would *make* it change, somehow.

"Meet with me," he said. "We have much to discuss. Maybe if we work together we can both get what we want."

Again, that shark smile, but with a hint of uncertainty this time.

Clair realized that he was fishing. He didn't know which Clair she was. It was better for everyone, she decided, if he remained unsure.

"I don't know what you're talking about," said Clair, swallowing her desire to scream at him for tricking her into killing so many people. She wasn't going anywhere *near* him until she was ready. "All I'm doing is trying to get back where I belong."

He laughed. "All right, play it that way. But you'll find it very hard to go anywhere in here. That I promise you."

The chat ended abruptly, and at the same moment the elevator began to slow its descent. Wary despite Ronnie's assurances of what might be waiting for them and with Wallace's vague threat still ringing in her ears, Clair took the gun back and positioned herself next to Kari at the front. She felt Clair One and the others pressing close behind her. No one said anything.

With a clunk and a rattle, the carriage halted and the doors opened.

Clair stared out in disbelief.

[7]

THEY WERE BACK where they had started, in the Observatory, with PK Drader's body and the unconscious forms of his three companions lying exactly where they had been left. A low-pitched howl of wind came from outside: the storm Q had mentioned was rolling in. It was only a simulation, numbers interacting with other numbers, but it sounded perfectly ominous.

"That's impossible," said Clair One, staring hard at the bodies as though defying them to move.

"Did we come back up again?" asked Tash.

"No," said Ronnie. "We definitely only went down."

"So how did we get here?" asked Zep.

"What did Wallace do to us?" asked Libby.

Clair stepped out of the carriage and looked up, mystified. There was no way the elevator could have come down from anywhere. Above the observatory was only sky.

"*Did* Wallace do this, Q?" she asked, feeling despair. "Can he just move us around wherever he wants?"

"I have a different theory," said Q. "Wallace knew this was going to happen, but he didn't do it to you. The Yard did."

"How?" asked Kari.

"The Yard appears to be a continuous space without

seams or edges. It is, in fact, a series of discrete cells that are simulated when occupied or observed. They are not actually connected. What I mean by this is that you are currently within a section of the Yard that contains the observatory, and only the observatory. For you, at this moment, there is nothing beyond this cell. Try to leave in a way that is not allowed, and you loop back upon yourself."

"And the elevator isn't allowed?" asked Ronnie.

"That is correct. You cannot move to the next cell by climbing, either, or walking. The only permitted means of moving from cell to cell appears to be d-mat."

Clair tried to wrap her head around this concept. It wasn't easy. She pictured the world like a cup of bubble tea, with the pearls pressing together at the bottom. They were inside one of the pearls. "So you're saying we're trapped here?"

"Only if we don't use d-mat," said Ronnie.

"Why didn't you tell us this before?" asked Zep. He banged the inside of the elevator, making it shake.

"I didn't know." Q hesitated, then said it again, sounding as puzzled as Clair felt. That was as unnerving as her by-the-numbers delivery before. "I didn't *know*. My exploration of the Yard is incomplete. I need time to fully comprehend it."

"So we *are* trapped," said Tash. "If the booths aren't safe to use because Wallace controls them—"

"Q can keep us safe," said Clair as calmingly as she could. She didn't want anyone to panic, least of all herself. *Friends first, then the world.* "Q can keep us masked and make sure we won't be altered or diverted."

"But Wallace will know that anyone leaving here is us," said Clair One. "He'll be waiting for us at the other end no matter where we go."

"Unless we pretend to be PK Drader and his goons?" said Zep.

"Seven of us," said Ronnie, "four of them."

"So we pretend to be the four of them with three prisoners," said Libby. "Oldest trick in the book."

"But where will we go?" asked Tash. "How will we stop him from following us?"

"I have an idea," said Clair One.

Clair looked at her in surprise. She suspected she had just had the same one. "Lucky Jump?"

"Exactly." Clair One almost grinned.

"Just like old times."

"Just like twenty minutes ago. Let's do it."

Before Clair could stop her, Clair One strode through the blood, picked up PK Drader's fallen pistol, and wiped it on a clean patch of his uniform.

"Just in case," she said. "Got a problem with that?"

Clair couldn't argue, although it made the momentary camaraderie they had shared evaporate. Clair 1.0 had never fired a gun before. She had never wanted to. Were these circumstances changing her already? Damaging her?

None of the others went in search of a weapon. They gathered by the four-door booth to go over the details of the plan. Since they couldn't fit into a single booth, their escape needed to be carefully coordinated, and quickly, before Wallace tried to capture or kill her again.

"Four groups, five Lucky Jumps," Clair suggested over the sound of the rising storm. "Q, can you track us and make sure we end up in the same place, without letting Wallace follow?"

"I can," said Q. "Clair, you should know—"

"Somewhere in particular?" asked Clair One.

"I don't care," Clair said. "If you think of somewhere along the way, let Q know so she can redirect the rest of us; otherwise, let her decide. As long as we all end up together, that's the main thing."

"Clair—"

"What if we don't?" asked Tash, cutting off Q. "What if we get there and no one else arrives?"

"Call Q and do what she says," Clair told her. "But don't worry. That won't happen."

"Don't make any promises you can't keep, Two," Clair One said. "Nothing much has gone right so far."

True, Clair thought, but that wasn't her fault.

"We're going to need allies, moving forward," she said. "Whatever happens now, the next step is to look for Jesse

Linwood. He must be in here somewhere. He can help."

Clair One's skeptical look only grew more pronounced. "The Lurker? How can *he* do anything?"

"You'd be surprised." Clair felt herself beginning to flush, but no one commented on it. "Or Devin Bartelme and his brother Trevin. They're with a group called RADICAL. I haven't seen any sign of them in here, but if they *are* here they're bound to know something about Wallace and maybe even the exit—"

Red flashed across her vision. Q was using her lenses to get her attention.

"Clair, the drones!"

Clair realized then that the rapidly rising thrum was not entirely the storm.

"Quickly, get in the booths!"

Glass shattered on three sides of the observatory's main hall as drones swooped in on gusts of howling wind, sending spears of bright light through the air and booming harsh, artificial-voiced orders.

"Stand still and place your hands above your heads! Failure to comply will be interpreted as active defiance!"

Clair ignored them. She grabbed someone's arm at random and pulled them with her into the nearest booth, crying, "Lucky Jump!" as she went.

One of the drones rushed toward them. There wasn't time to raise her pistol and aim at it. Its gun barrels were pointing right at her.

The drone jerked to one side, firing a spray of bullets in a curving line across the floor. Sparks flew from its fans as Q seized up its electric motors. With a heavy, metallic crunch it dropped to the ground, inert.

The door slid shut on the chaos outside. Clair sagged in relief. Only then did she realize who she was gripping with all her strength.

"You're breaking my arm," said Libby.

Clair let go and backed up as far as she could go. The space was barely large enough for the two of them, but not as cramped as it had been with Kari. Libby was both smaller and more slender.

"Sorry."

sssssss—

"That's okay," said Libby, putting a hand to her chest, which was rising and falling after the hit of adrenaline. "You saved my life back there. I froze like an idiot."

Clair shook her head. Once upon a time, Clair would have frozen too. Neither of them was an idiot.

—pop

The booth expanded to a standard size. Clair didn't bother to check her lenses. It didn't matter where they were: if Q had successfully masked them, they were safe. But that didn't mean they could stand still.

"Lucky Jump," Clair said again.

"So you're from my future. . . . ," Libby started to say.

"It's not like that. I've just lived a bit longer than you."

"But you know what happened next . . . I mean, *before* for you but next for me." Libby put her hand palm-forward in the air, like she was swearing an oath. "Zep is right. This is such a mind-fuck."

Clair couldn't argue with that.

sssssss-pop

"What else happened?" Libby asked when they arrived at their next destination. "I got the feeling we skipped a lot of information. Improvement fixed my birthmark, but what else did it do to me? Did I die when d-mat broke down? What aren't you telling me?"

"Improvement . . . duped you," Clair said, choosing her words with care. "It put someone else in your place."

"And the old me, inside? Where did I go?"

"Here."

"So if you hadn't triggered Wallace's trap and woken up the Yard, I'd just be a pattern in a file, waiting to be deleted."

"Yes."

"That's twice you've saved my life, then. And here I was thinking you were trying to steal my boyfriend."

Clair stared into Libby's cool, blue eyes, so surprised she didn't know what to say.

Fortunately, Libby did. She always did.

"Lucky Jump," she said. "Don't forget that part."

sssssss-pop

"It's true," Clair confessed, her face hot. "I did like Zep.

[49]

It was a stupid thing, and I didn't want it to happen. But it did."

"*What* happened, exactly?"

"We kissed . . . just once, at the crashlander ball. You went home with a headache from using Improvement. While you were gone Zep and I went up onto the roof, and he almost fell off saving some guy. It was . . . intense." Clair didn't shy away from telling the truth, even though it seemed like a mixture of ancient history and something that had happened only hours ago, scraped raw and scarred over at the same time. "Afterward, I tried to tell you. I wanted to say that I was sorry. But Improvement . . . everything else . . ."

Libby brushed that aside. "Who started it? Was it you or him?"

Clair wished she could look somewhere else, but the mirrors held uncountable Libbys, all staring at her. "I can't really remember."

"Don't protect him, Clair. I want to know."

"And you deserve to know. It's just . . . I don't think it was anything either of us thought about, at first. There was just a spark, and then he . . ."

"Tried his luck?" Libby nodded. "You don't have to say any more. I've seen him in action. With me, remember?"

Clair remembered Libby telling her that Zep had been cheating on someone else when they'd gotten together.

"I told him no way," said Clair. "But then it was me who

kissed him, after he had this big, stupid hero moment. I thought I'd die if I didn't."

To her surprise, Libby broke into a wide grin. "That's the first 'Clair' thing I've heard you say since you walked out of the booth."

Clair couldn't help it. She put her arms around Libby and held her close. After a moment, Libby hugged her back. Clair cried like she had in the Yard's version of San Francisco, gasping sobs beyond her control. It felt so good to have her best friend back, and to be acknowledged as herself, and to forget, just for a moment, everything she had lost in the last few days. Her original goal had been to apologize, and now she had. That felt like real progress. That felt *real*.

"Jeez Louise, you're ruining my dress."

"Sorry. You must think I'm such a dork."

"You *are* a dork." Libby put her hands on her shoulders and held her at arm's length. "I'm not sure I forgive you yet, either of you, but I know you're telling me the truth, and that means a lot."

"The other Clair hasn't done anything," Clair said. "The ball didn't happen, so Zep isn't properly kissworthy for her."

"But she still wants him, I bet. Leave it to me to sort her out. What about you? Are you over him now? Fighting over boys is stupid, especially when I'm outnumbered."

"God, yes," said Clair, wiping her face. "That's something

else I need to tell you. After the ball . . . when everything else was going on, I—"

"Don't tell me. You hooked up?"

"Yes. And it's serious. Or it was . . ." She didn't want to think too hard about where Jesse might or might not be right now or else she might start crying again.

"Who? Spill the beans!"

Clair braced herself. "Jesse Linwood."

"No *way*." Libby shoved her in the shoulder, her face a mask of scandalized delight. "This I have to hear all about."

"Lucky Jump," Clair said.

"Are you changing the subject?"

"Yes." She was trying to, anyway. It was easier not to think about him than to remember what had happened.

"Are you embarrassed by him?"

"No!" Jesse was smart and honest and loyal, qualities she had been slow to recognize but badly needed now.

"Then why? Are you, like, seriously in love or something? Because if that's true, then one, he's an impressively fast worker, and two, I can get used to anyone, as long as they treat you right. But you have to tell me everything, or it'll just be awkward when he shows up."

sssssss—

"He died," Clair said, the hollowness in her voice matching the way she felt inside.

—pop

"Oh crap," Libby said, brows knitting together. "I'm sorry. I didn't even think. Now who's the dork?"

They stood awkwardly together for several seconds, too close to avoid each other. A gulf seemed to have opened up between them again.

"Lucky Jump," Clair said, for the fifth and last time.

sssssss—pop

"Listen," said Libby, "before we get there, I want to say that I'm sorry I called you what I did. You're not damaged. You're just different from the way you were. And that's not necessarily a bad thing. The other you wasn't straight with me, and it changes everything that you have been. Really, it does. If I can't trust him and I can't trust you, who *can* I trust?"

Clair nodded. There was a vulnerability in her best friend's face that had never been there before.

"Do you trust me now?"

"Of course."

Raising her right thumb to her mouth, Clair wetted it and reached out to wipe the last of the makeup from Libby's cheek, the makeup covering her birthmark.

Libby's eyes widened, and her hand flew up to stop Clair, but then she froze and let her finish.

"God," Libby breathed, staring up at the mirrored ceiling, "you can be such a pain."

"You know it. But only because I'm right."

A BUMP ARRIVED from Kari, masked as Zali Pepper.

"The rest are worried," she said. "You two okay?"

"On our way," she bumped back. She was surprised that she did feel relatively okay. The cry must have helped, combined with the feeling that she had her best friend back, even if things were still complicated.

"Q?" she said aloud. "We're ready to join the others."

The booth activated immediately.

sssssss—

"Do you trust this Q?" asked Libby. "She sounds really weird sometimes."

Was there a hint of jealousy in Libby's tone? "I trust her with my life. She's saved it so many times I've lost count."

Even as she said it, Clair wondered. Q had been behaving oddly since they had arrived in the Yard. She wondered if it was more than just being distracted by their strange new environment. Did Q resent Clair and the others for being so dependent on her? Could she be worried about her future, if the Air in the Yard wasn't as stable as the Air outside? Clair promised that she would try to talk to Q later, and at least ask if there was a problem.

Add it to my list, she thought. But at least they were moving now. Waiting in the observatory for Wallace to pounce had been a nightmare.

—pop

Her lenses told her that they were in a tiny town called Harmony on the southern border of the Minnesotan Protectorate. It was compact and clean, with roads that were still being used for wheeled traffic. In the real world, it was surprisingly well populated, thanks mainly to some nearby Amish communities. There was an old church, an overgrown park, and a single line of shop fronts. Maybe the Amish traded their foodstuffs there. Maybe, Clair thought, they used actual *money*.

An extensive cave system justified the booth's existence: tourists would travel that way, but the Amish never would. Clair doubted there would be any tourists now. And given that the Amish never went through d-mat, they wouldn't even exist in the Yard. In Harmony, they would probably be alone.

The door hissed. Clair went to walk through it and collided with the mirror in front of her. Blinking, disoriented, she recoiled into Libby.

"Are you all right?" Libby asked.

"Yes," she said, rubbing her temple. "Just got turned around. Sorry."

"You look like you haven't had any sleep for ages. You should think about getting some."

Clair had to think to remember the last time she had closed her eyes. Maybe Libby was right, and her mental glitches were actually just signs of utter exhaustion.

"Come on out," called Kari's familiar voice.

Cool, clean air hit them, carrying the smell of fried food. Clair's stomach turned over, suddenly awake.

Libby looked around with her hands on her hips and a disdainful expression on her face. "From crashlander ball to the middle of nowhere. I should've stayed home."

Kari came around the booth to greet them. "Q picked a good place. The one person left insists on making us breakfast."

The source of the cooking smell was a brick building sporting a sign saying HARMONY HOUSE. Through the window Clair saw Ronnie, Tash, Zep, and Clair One sitting at a table. A large-hipped woman in her fifties with close-cropped white hair fussed around them, putting out cutlery and condiments. The table was the centerpiece of the dining room, covered in nicks and scuffs all polished and repolished to golden smoothness.

"How late *are* we?" Clair asked, mentally adding up her d-mat lags.

"She's a fast worker," said Kari, guiding them through the entrance. "Wait until you hear her theory."

"Her what?"

Before Kari could answer the question, the woman hurried up and bustled them toward the table, introducing herself as Mariah as she went.

"Sit, sit. I'll bring your food in a moment. We have only what's seasonal here. I trust that will do."

"Thank you," said Clair, staring after the woman in bafflement. She was dressed in clothes that might have been handed down from her grandparents. If she didn't even use a fabber, how was it possible for her to be in the Yard? When could Mariah have ever used d-mat in order to have her pattern stolen?

"You took so long," hissed Tash.

"We got sidetracked," said Libby. "Catching up on old times. New times. Whatever."

"You weren't followed?" asked Clair One.

"Not that we saw," Clair said, trying to answer calmly. She was still annoyed that Clair One had called the PKs. "You?"

A quick shake of the head. "If we were, Q's not saying anything. She's not saying anything at all."

Clair tried bumping Q but received no response.

"She's been . . . laggy ever since we arrived here," Kari said. "I think it has something to do with the way the Yard works. I know it's all information and information is real and whatever, but surely that makes a difference."

"She'll be all right," Clair said, telling herself to be as reassured as she sounded. "Q brought us back together, didn't she? And food is a good idea. I wonder if she warned Mariah that we were coming."

"Mariah didn't know," said Zep. "She says she's going to serve everyone today for free. God told her to do it."

Mariah arrived at that moment with plates of eggs,

bacon, fried bread, and onions.

"That should keep you going," she said, wiping her hands on her apron and heading back to the kitchen.

"Mariah?" Clair called after her.

"One second!"

She returned with coffee, which she poured while they dished out the food. It smelled amazing, almost as good as freshly fabbed food. Zep helped himself to a double serving.

"This is very generous of you," Clair said to their host. "Why are you being so nice to us?"

"It's my way of atoning," she said. "You'll find yours."

"What do you mean?"

"Do what God means you to do and you'll ascend with the others." She pointed at the ceiling.

"You think . . . this was the Rapture?"

Mariah nodded. "What else could it be? So many people gone . . . and all the children, bless them! I'm a sinner like you, but it's not too late. Heaven's gates are open now. We'll enter when we make ourselves worthy."

Clair was the only one not eating. The others had heard it before, obviously. Libby just shrugged and dug in.

All the children . . .

Clair hadn't thought of that. Kids could only travel with their parents, so maybe their patterns were hard to separate, or maybe even Wallace wouldn't normally stoop that low. Either way, she tried not to think about what some parents in the Yard were going through, just as she was trying not to think about her own.

All she could do was give Mariah false hope in return for her generosity. "This looks delicious. You're very kind."

"It's nothing. Eat up."

Curiosity got the better of her before Mariah could leave. "Just one more question," Clair asked, slipping out of her parka and reaching for the eggs. "When did you last use d-mat?"

"Yesterday," Mariah said. "My daughter and grandkids live in New Zealand. There are some around here who wouldn't allow me the right to visit them. They tell people to stay away because I'm some kind of monster. Well, God has his plans for them, I'm sure. Never had any problems with the Amish that way."

Clair One cocked her head. "You're not talking about the Amish?"

"No, the Stainers." Mariah's expression hardened. Even the goodwill of saints had limits.

Clair understood then. That was why Mariah was in the Yard. Where there were Abstainers, there was likely to be WHOLE. A small cell, at least. Duping Mariah's pattern was the only means Wallace had of spying on the Abstainers in Harmony.

Clair wanted to press further, thinking of her need for allies, and of Jesse. Making contact with WHOLE could help on both fronts. But this wasn't Mariah's fight. It was

Clair's. She would find another way.

"Thanks, Mariah," she said, forcing a smile. "Their loss. The Stainers, I mean."

The others chorused their agreement through mouths in various degrees of fullness, and Mariah went back to the kitchen, looking satisfied.

―――――――――――――――――――――――――― [9]

CLAIR SHOVELED EGGS high onto her fork, intending to eat as much as she could while she had the chance. It didn't matter one bit that her mind insisted it was just information. Her body was made of the very same stuff, and it made no complaints. Two cups of coffee washed it all down, steaming, bitter, and black.

The conversation around her mirrored her own concerns.

"We can't stay in here," said Tash. "I don't want to be made of nothing."

"It's not *nothing*," said Ronnie. "It's numbers."

"I don't want to be numbers, then. They're too easily erased. Why can't we just upload everything to the real world and put it all back the way it was?"

"There isn't a booth big enough."

"So make one." She shrugged. "Or break the Yard down into bits and do it slowly."

Clair nodded. "That's what I want to do."

"So why can't we just do it?" said Tash. "I don't understand."

"The first step is to find a way to talk to someone outside." Clair didn't want to say that there might not be anyone left out there with the ability to access the Yard. "Someone who has a working booth, even a small one. The easiest way to do that is to find the exit, first."

"Which means finding Wallace," said Kari. "He's masked, along with everyone I can think of who might be connected to him. Believe me, I've looked."

"How?" asked Ronnie.

"I'm probably the only honest peacekeeper in the Yard," Kari said. "I have access to back doors you never dreamed of."

"But you still can't find him?" said Clair One.

"No. Instead, I've been trying to work out who exactly *is* in here with us, and why. PK protocols get me into all sorts of population data."

Libby leaned forward. "What have you found?"

"Well, we already know that Wallace was taking people who had come too close to discovering Improvement and the lawmakers' plans. But that doesn't explain why people like Tash, Ronnie, and Zep were included. Your value to Wallace is as blackmail fodder, since you're connected to Libby and Clair. The question I've been asking myself is: how connected do you have to be for Wallace to think you might be useful? What are the degrees of separation?"

"I'm guessing you know," said Clair One in a stop-playing-games voice that sounded like their mother. Clair was appalled: she didn't know she did that. "What's the answer?"

"Two, at least. From Libby to you, Tash, is one degree of separation. From Libby to your parents is two—and your parents *are* in here, you'll be pleased to know. Beyond that, though, it gets a little muddy. The connections aren't easy to tease out between Tash's mother and every other person inside the Yard."

"My parents are here?" asked Tash, her face lighting up with relief.

"Yes," said Kari. "All of your parents are here. But I strongly advise you not to contact them. They're being watched. All attempts to communicate will be traced back to us—and you've seen what that means."

Despite Kari's warning, Clair mentally exhaled with relief. Her mother was alive. But how was she going to explain to Allison that she had *two* daughters now?

"That must make for a shitload of people," said Zep, "depending on how long it's been going on."

"Yes, there are millions in here. I can't be precise because some of them are hidden."

"What about the patterns of dead people?" asked Clair, bracing herself for the bad news she hadn't been willing to consider earlier. "Is PK Drader going to come after us again?"

"He's listed by the Air as deceased. I've no reason to think that's not the case, given the rules of the Yard."

"Dead means dead," said Zep. "As it ought to."

That was reassuring when it came to their enemies, but worrying when it came to themselves. They couldn't afford mistakes now.

"Finally," said Kari, "I see no evidence of deletions. That's the best news of all."

Clair agreed. If Wallace could simply reach into the Yard and delete people at will, he could take out all of Harmony just to get rid of them. He must, therefore, be constrained by the rules of his own world, just like they were. But that didn't mean he wasn't working on other means right now—means that might result in their imminent capture or death.

"Where does that leave us?" Clair One asked. "Wallace may be working on a deletion hack as we speak."

"So we find him," said Ronnie. "How?"

"If he's got an exit, he'll be waiting for us," said Libby. "That's what I'd do if I were him: sit on the plug hole and pick off anyone who comes too close."

"Are we sure that's the only way to get out?" asked Zep.

"Q never said anything about an alternative," Clair said.

"What about those RADICAL guys you mentioned

earlier?" asked Tash. "Can they help?"

"Maybe," she said. "They keep their heads pretty low. Have you found any of them in here, Kari?"

"None of the names I'm familiar with appear in the Air," said Kari. "There's no sign of Devin or Trevin. But, again, they could be masked."

Clair thought of Jesse, too. He *had* to be in here, didn't he? So maybe he was hidden like everyone else. But in that case, why wasn't he looking for her? Or was he, but he simply hadn't found her yet?

"So much for never doing anything."

His voice was so clear that she almost jumped out of her chair. He had said those words a week ago while trudging across the empty countryside, but he wasn't here now. It was just her and her friends, and Mariah bustling away in the kitchen. Clair One was staring down at her plate with a closed expression while Kari explained that RADICAL was a secret organization dedicated to enhancing human life via technology, and to stomping down anything that might stand in the way of that goal.

"Excuse me," Clair said, standing up. The glitch had left her feeling shaky, like she might throw up. She peered inquiringly over the counter at Mariah, who pointed to a door at the back. There, in the relative cool and quiet of a bathroom cubicle, feeling drained and alone, Clair put her head in her hands for a moment and waited for the nausea to pass.

What if Wallace hadn't kept Jesse's pattern? What if Jesse was gone and all she had were memories that wouldn't ever leave her be?

With shaking hands she washed her face in the sink.

Tash was right. Clair couldn't take anything for granted. This might feel like the real world—right down to the taste of fresh eggs and strong coffee that made her heart race—but it was temporary at best. She needed to find the exit before Wallace found her, get hold of a working booth, and rebuild everything on the outside, where real really *was* real. She would fix the terrible betrayal Wallace had wreaked on humanity, because the alternative was worse than death: a humanity duped and enslaved under dictators like Kingdon, who cared only about herself and the power she wielded.

Friends first, then the world.

But the world couldn't wait forever.

A smell hit her from out of nowhere, musk and skin and hair: Jesse. She stood upright so fast her head glanced off the bottom of the vanity, exactly where she had banged it coming out of the booth.

"I'm losing it," she said, leaning her hip against the sink and touching her tender scalp. No blood.

"Clair?" came a bump from Kari. "Better get out here. Something odd is going on."

"Odd how?"

"Clair One says she saw Jesse."

Clair burst out of the bathroom and ran into the dining room.

"Where?" she asked, looking around.

"I feel like I'm going crazy." Clair One, staring at her with wide eyes. "I see them out of the corner of my eye. . . . The Lurker, but there's some guy with a big chin too. A woman with different-colored eyes. A kid with cornrows."

Jesse, thought Clair, and members of WHOLE they had met together. *Turner. Jamila. Cashile.*

"I've tried taking their picture with my lenses," Clair One went on, "but it never works. They're like glitches or ghosts, not real."

"Data ghosts," said Tash.

"If we're both seeing them, that means they're real," Clair said.

"You should've said something," said Ronnie. "How do we know you aren't being hacked somehow?"

That was a horrible thought. It didn't feel like Wallace, though.

"I just thought I was tired," Clair said.

"D-mat girl," said Jesse, right into her ear. She jumped, and Clair One jumped too.

"The Lurker again."

"His name is *Jesse,*" Clair said.

"All right, but why am I hearing him? I barely even know him."

That triggered a thought.

"Maybe it's coming from me," she said. "What if my mind is leaking into yours—because there are two of us and the Yard is confused about whose memories are whose?"

"Could be," said Kari. "The existence of two people with one name is bound to cause errors, particularly when you're so close to each other and if the Yard is trying to fix those errors—"

"*You're* updating *her*," said Zep, pointing from Clair to Clair One.

"How do I make it stop?" asked Clair One. "I don't want to be written over."

"It can't just be that, though," Clair said. "The glitches are coming more often, and they're not just of Jesse. The first one I saw was of a woman with purple hair, someone I don't know."

"Long down one side?" asked Kari, making a waterfall with her fingers past her right cheek. Her eyes widened when Clair nodded. "That's Billie. That memory came from me."

"So we're leaking into one another," said Clair. "Maybe it happens when someone really concentrates on someone else. Information is real, so the Yard sees what's going on in our brains and makes connections."

"Amplified by the two of you being weirdness magnets," said Libby. "It makes sense. Like the Yard is trying to make things right but making things more wrong in the process."

"Could it spread?" asked Tash with a worried expression. "Because *I'm* hearing things now. Jesse just said, 'I love you, but I hate what you stand for'—something like that."

Clair nodded. That was from their last argument.

"Whatever it is," said Clair One, gripping the table, "we have to do something before we're overwhelmed."

"Let's not rush into anything," said Kari.

Clair looked up at a new sound, a machine noise coming from outside Harmony House, distant but growing closer.

"You all hear *that*, don't you?"

They nodded.

"A data ghost on an electrobike?" said Zep. "I don't think so."

————————————————————— [10]

CLAIR GRABBED HER parka and ran out into the street. It was just as empty as it had been before, stripped of everyone who had ever lived there, except for Mariah, the one person for miles around who had ever used d-mat.

She whipped around, seeing movement in a shop front window. Had they been found? And if so, by whom?

She pulled out her pistol. The movement didn't come again.

"The glitches—they're all around us," said Clair One.

Clair hadn't heard her friends come after her, but they were there with her, searching too. Mariah peered nervously through the curtains as though afraid God wasn't done punishing the Earth yet.

". . . interference . . ."

Clair could barely hear Q's voice through static.

". . . nonlocal . . . nonrandom . . ."

"Are you hearing that?" asked Ronnie.

Everyone nodded.

"We're not receiving you very well," called Clair. "Try again, Q."

"Maybe the glitches are interfering with her, too," Ronnie said.

"That's possible," said Kari. "If the glitches are affecting the Yard and the Air is part of the Yard . . . well, that's where Q lives."

They stood huddled together in the center of the street, facing outward. The sound of the electrobike grew louder. Sometimes it seemed to come from Clair's left, then her right, swirling around her with maddening unpredictability.

"Aren't all locations the same to you, d-mat girl?"

Jesse sounded so close. . . .

"I don't like this," said Kari. "We should get out of here, in case we've been found again."

"How? We can't use the booth. Not without Q."

"What do you think we should do, then?" Clair could

see her own uncertainty in her double's eyes.

"I don't know. I just want to get far away from here."

"What does 'far' mean?" said Jesse in Clair's ear. "D-mat girl?"

Clair wanted to answer him, but there was no patch to respond to. The voice was a whisper from the past, not something she could actually talk to.

"Anything is better than standing here waiting," said Zep.

"This is an Abstainer town," Clair said, struck by a sudden idea. "There'll be a car somewhere. We can drive away."

Clair One shook her head. "We can't do that, either."

"Why not?" asked Tash.

"Remember what Q said about cells in the Yard? We'll just loop back where we started."

Clair bit the inside of her cheek. She had forgotten that.

"Maybe that bike is a special one that can cross between cells," said Ronnie.

"At the very least," said Zep, "we'll be able to outrun it with our own wheels. If we have to."

No one argued that point. Together they headed south along the road in search of a car, Jesse's voice coming almost constantly now.

"D-mat girl . . . d-mat girl . . ."

Maybe it *was* a ghost, Clair thought. What if Jesse was trying to warn her about something from beyond the grave and she was completely failing to get the message?

"Q? Can you tell me what's going on?"

There was still no answer, and in two blocks the only vehicle with wheels they found was a child's tricycle, lying on its side. *The kid won't be needing it anymore,* Clair thought with dismay.

Suddenly, as though a switch had been pulled, the electrical engine noise ceased. So did Jesse's voice.

"Oh," Clair said, stopping in the middle of an intersection. Long tracts of empty bitumen stretched into the distance. "Now what?"

The others stopped too. The silence quickly became *too* silent. It felt like something had changed, but they couldn't see it yet.

Then the hum of the electrobike returned. It came from the east, along the road leading out of town. This time it didn't shift, although it rose and fell unevenly with distance.

"Look!" Clair grabbed Kari's arm with her left hand and pointed with her right.

At the end of the road were fields, green even this late in the autumn. Silhouetted against them was a cluster of distant objects. It was hard to make out details through the hot air shimmering off the black road surface, but they *seemed* to be electrobikes, three of them, evenly spaced in a diagonal line across the road, getting closer by the second.

"Who are they?" said Tash.

"I don't know." The only people Clair had ever seen ride electrobikes were members of WHOLE, but that didn't necessarily apply in the Yard. "We should get out of sight, just in case."

"Good idea," Kari said. "Half take the south side, half the north. Wait just around the corner. Clair One, you still have that gun?"

"Yes." She held it up uneasily, as though wishing she'd left it behind. "An ambush?"

"Don't use it unless I fire first. Promise me."

Clair One promised, and they broke into two uneven groups—Clair and Kari hurrying out of sight behind an old redbrick church, Clair One and the others to an empty home.

"Q? We really, really need you."

There wasn't even a crackling whisper to indicate that Q had heard.

The engine noise grew louder. Clair took her pistol out and held it in both hands, praying she wouldn't have to use it.

Clair's mother believed that all of reality was connected. Prayers were answered by the entire universe, so no need was entirely ignored, nothing was ever entirely lost, and asking couldn't hurt.

All I want right now, she prayed, *is for no one else to die. I'll worry about the rest later.*

If her prayer was heard, it had exactly the wrong effect.

"I am Nobody."

The whisper sent a cold shiver through her entire body.

[II]

"OH NO," SHE said. "He's in here too."

"Who?" asked Kari, looking around in alarm.

"Nobody. What if he's thinking about me, looking for me—?"

"Shhh. Get back."

The first of the electrobikes rounded the corner, engine snarling to a halt, leaving two long black streaks on the road behind it. Behind it, two empty bikes did the same. The sole rider on the first bike was long and lanky, wearing blue jeans, a T-shirt, and a helmet that obscured his face. He jumped off the bike, looked to his left, and then to his right.

"Clair!" Jesse shouted. "Where are you?"

She almost burst out from cover, filled with yearning at the sound of his voice. Kari held her back but couldn't stop her from calling, "Jesse, you found us! Over here!"

He turned to face in her direction. With one hand he pulled the helmet off, long, mousy brown hair swinging free down one side of his face. His eyes were bright green in the morning light, prompting a flood of remembrance that made her rock back on her heels, momentarily breathless.

Really real. Thank you, universe.

His expression, however, was far from relieved.

"Clair, quick! They're coming!"

"Who's coming?" asked Clair One from the other corner.

Jesse looked behind him, looking for the source of the second voice, his confused expression so easy to read it broke her heart. A glitch, or *two* Clairs?

His eyes widened, and he began backing toward the patiently whirring bike. "Oh shit, this was a mistake. I should've listened—"

"Wait!" Kari let her go, and Clair burst out from cover, running toward him with the gun held high above her head. "It's really me. This isn't a trick. Don't go!"

For a moment she thought he might yet run.

"*Is* that you, Clair?"

"Yes, and it's you." She knew it in the core of her being. She wanted to throw herself into his arms, but he glanced up the road, back the way he had come.

"The hollowmen will be here any moment," he said. "We have to go."

She stumbled to a halt in front of him and looked up at his worried face. *Hollow men.* That was what the dupes called themselves, only Jesse said it as one word, like "salesman" or "chairwoman." It sounded scarier that way. He hadn't done that in the real world.

"They're coming?" she asked.

"Of course," he said. "They've been coming after us from the moment we appeared in here, just like they did outside. We know too much about Improvement and the other crap they've been doing."

Outside, he'd said. "You know where we are, then?"

"Kind of, but we have to go, *now.*"

"I am Nobody."

Clair spun around. The voice had come from behind her, and her shoulder blades were itching now. If Jesse had found her by following the glitches, then maybe Nobody could too. And Harmony had been a brief stopover at best. If Jesse took her to WHOLE, she would have the first of the allies she needed.

"All right," she said, waving at the others. "Let's go!"

Kari emerged from cover first, and after a moment so did the others. Jesse's eyes grew wide at the sight of Clair One, but Clair pulled his attention back to her.

"It's a long story," she said. "I'll tell you later."

"Yeah, that'd be good. I'm pretty sure the hollowmen tracked me. I'm not as good at doing this as Ray."

Ray was a member of WHOLE who had briefly held her captive. He had been with Clair and Jesse in New York, the first time. That must be how he had ended up in the Yard.

"As good at doing what?" she asked.

He shook his head, hair falling across his face.

"Get on," he called to the others, indicating the two

empty bikes. "I don't have helmets—there wasn't time—but at least there's room for everyone. Doesn't matter if you can't drive—"

"I can," said Zep.

"Great. The bikes will default to following mine anyway. Just hang on tight. And, uh, you might want to close your eyes."

"Yes, sir," said Libby with a mock salute. "Hello, by the way."

A cry to stop came from behind them. Clair twisted to look, even as she got on the seat behind Jesse. People were stepping from doorways and through windows into the empty street as though they had been hiding in the empty houses. People dressed in black, holding guns.

"They're here. I knew it," Jesse breathed, tugging his helmet quickly into place. "Are we all on?"

Kari, the last one, clambered into the sidecar accompanying Tash and Ronnie. Zep and Libby rode the third bike, with Clair One the passenger. The engines whirred loudly. Tires screeching, all three bikes pulled away at the same time.

Clair glanced over her shoulder. The people in black—men and women, all shapes and sizes—were running after them. One of them had a shock of blond hair. He shouted, but the wind snatched his words away.

She had seen a picture of that youthful face in the muster.

Cameron Lee.

Nobody, she thought. *Reset.*

A bump appeared in her infield as she roared up the road away from him.

Steeling herself, she selected the bump and read what Nobody had to say.

"There're two of you now," he said. "I've seen you. You're the ones who got away."

He had called her that on the seastead, when he had offered her his gift of death.

"So you remember," she bumped back.

"All of it. Every version of me who came back to the Yard added their memories to mine, the master version. We call it Renovating. I'm as up-to-date as you are."

"You know you tricked me, then," she said. "This is all your fault."

"Yes. But I'm still here. I wasn't expecting that."

"So put yourself out of our misery."

"Not yet. I have a plan."

Clair was about to tell him what he could do with his plan when Jesse's voice brought her out of the conversation.

"Hold on tight. It's going to get hairy through here."

She put her arms around him. It was too easy to do. He smelled like him, felt like him, sounded like him, *was* him—but how much did he remember of *them*? Had his pattern been taken the first time he had gone through d-mat, or later? How much of their time had been lost forever?

"Jesse—"

"Hang on. Here we go."

They were racing hard for the end of the road and the fields beyond. The gate leading to the fields was closed. He couldn't possibly be planning to go right through it, could he?

Putting his head down, he accelerated harder.

"Uh, Jesse?" If he didn't stop, they were going to crash.

"It's okay. Trust me."

Clair did. It wasn't as though there was time to do anything else short of tipping the bike over. She closed her eyes and gripped him tightly, hoping he knew what he was doing.

There was a lurch as the bike left the road and hit dirt, followed by a sound like the air itself tearing. They were wrenched violently from side to side, and Clair felt all the breath leave her lungs in a rush, as though sucked out by a sudden vacuum. For a moment, they were falling.

Then the wheels hit the ground with a squeal of rubber. The bike wobbled for an instant. Clair opened her eyes, wondering what had just happened.

They were accelerating along an open road heading into a small town, passing a sign that said WELCOME TO HARMONY.

"Shit," said Jesse.

"Isn't that what happens in here?" asked Clair, forcing herself to ease off her desperate clinch. "You try to leave somewhere and the Yard brings you back?"

"Yeah, but we weren't trying it the *normal* way. They must have pulled us back."

"Who pulled us, and how?"

"The hollowmen. Now they'll be waiting for us. Shit on a *stick*."

Clair looked behind her. The others were still with them, looking shocked and afraid. Zep's bike swayed as he took control and accelerated to come alongside theirs.

"What happened?"

"Too hard to explain now," Jesse called back. "We have to try again."

"How?"

"Just follow me. I can do it."

Jesse signaled with one arm and took the first right-hand turn they came to. Clair checked the Air for a map of the town. They *had* been on Third Street, heading east and out of town, and then suddenly they were on Route 52, heading from the west back into town. Now they were on Second Avenue, heading north and out of town again. Only this time there was a house in their way, not a field.

Jesse gunned the engine anyway, crouching low over the handlebars and aiming right for the yard. Zep hesitated, then followed. They hit the curb with a bone-shaking thump and were airborne for an instant that lasted entirely too long. Clair's eyes were open this time. She saw the fence posts go by on either side, then the world was turning around her, images spiraling and twisting too quickly to make sense of. Again, her breath was snatched from her, and she gasped in surprise when it returned, along with gravity, the squeal of tires slamming down hard onto tarmac, and another curse from Jesse.

They were on Country Road 44, heading back into town, this time from the south.

"What's the problem?" Clair asked. "What are you trying to do and why isn't it working?"

"I'm trying to get us out of here." he snapped, then shook his head. "Sorry, it's not your fault. This *should* work. I've seen Ray do it dozens of times."

"You've *seen* it . . . ?"

"Yeah, but I got here eventually, didn't I? Maybe there are too many of you, or too many of them. I don't know. Oh hell."

Black figures were running onto the road ahead of them, fanning out to form a cordon.

Jesse wrenched the bike right up Fifth Street, then after a couple of blocks right again onto a road that petered out onto grass. They juddered across someone's back paddock for fifty yards, then joined Seventh Avenue.

"Kari, do you know what's going on?"

The PK answered Clair's bump immediately.

"No idea. But it's better than stopping and asking for directions."

Nobody was bumping her again. Clair deleted every message as it came in, feeling them burning in her infield like brands.

"How is it supposed to work," Clair asked Jesse, "whatever 'it' is? Is there anything I can do to help?"

"We need some kind of door," he said, looking around, "and a run-up. I'll take us where we went first. Third time's a charm."

The bike surged beneath them. She held on to the waistband of his jeans.

"But what *is* it?"

"This place is cracked. Even before the glitches started, we noticed it. But you can exploit these cracks to get around without using d-mat. We call it 'ripping' because that's what it feels like—ripping the world in half like a piece of paper and sticking the halves together, so two points that wouldn't normally touch . . . do."

They turned right onto Third Street again and began picking up speed.

"I am Nobody," came the voice of Cameron Lee from a position right by her left ear.

She jumped involuntarily, making the bike sway.

"What was that?" asked Jesse. "Did you glitch?"

"Yes."

He looked around. "They're definitely trying to cut us off, then. Glitches increase when someone's concentrating on you. Tell Zep to come in behind me. I can't bump while I'm driving. I'll bring the other bike in too."

Clair did as he instructed, and seconds later the three bikes lined up in formation, aiming straight for the gate at the end of the road.

Something whizzed past Clair's right temple, followed an instant later by the crack of a gunshot. There were two hollowmen on the side of the road, but only two, and they weren't identical: Clair was relieved to know she wasn't facing a horde of dupes, not in the Yard, where people couldn't be copied. Still, she pulled her head in. Bullets could be deadly enough.

"Hold on," Jesse shouted, "and think of Dad!"

"Eww, what?"

"Dad, before he was duped. Anything you can remember about him, doesn't matter what—think it *hard*!"

Clair shut her eyes as the hollowmen whipped by, gunfire cracking again. Dylan Linwood had been a member of WHOLE who wanted to be more involved in the cause—to bring down d-mat by any means necessary, because they thought it killed people. Most of her memories of him were tangled up with Nobody, after he had been duped, but Dylan had made an indelible impression in his own right.

His workshop, cluttered with gears and old machines. His jeweler's glass that made his eye look as big as a plate.

His brusqueness. His grease-spotted hands. His voice, direct and rough and impatient and occasionally cruel—

They left the road. She heard someone cry out—Tash, maybe—then the air was punched out of her with the force of a cannonball. Fearing that she was about to fall off the bike, Clair pressed her face between Jesse's shoulder blades, not letting any sense of awkwardness stop her from clinging to him with all her strength.

The lean muscles of his back flexed against her as he wrestled for control. When the bike hit the ground again, he straightened suddenly and wrenched the front wheel to the right, groaning with the effort. Gravel rasped under the wheels. A branch whipped past Clair's head. She recoiled, feeling powerless to do anything but ride it out and trust in Jesse to keep them all safe.

He twisted the controls one more time, and with a final rattle the bikes came to a halt. His ribs heaved against her, and Clair realized only then that she was panting too. She felt as though they had been through a terrifying carnival ride. But was it over now? Were they safe from Nobody and the hollowmen?

Cautiously opening her eyes, she saw trees much taller than any in Harmony. The bikes had come to a halt at one edge of an artificially cleared area in what looked like a full-blown forest. There was vegetation all around them, with just one low brick building behind her at the end of a concrete path, near the beginning of their barely controlled skid. A selection of boxy trucks and jeeps was parked nearby.

There was someone standing in front of the building, an adult. As she twisted around, the better to see him, two more figures emerged from plate-glass doors, holding rifles.

"Don't make any sudden moves," said Dylan Linwood in a hard voice she knew well, "or we'll shoot."

————————————— [12]

"TAKE IT EASY, Dad," said Jesse, tugging off his helmet.

"I'll do nothing of the sort." Dylan's expression was all brittle crags, like a cliff face on the verge of avalanche. "Get off the bikes at once, all of you."

Clair let go of Jesse and slid her left leg over the seat, dropping the small distance to the ground and putting her hands above her head. The tall, angular man next to Dylan was Ray: his left arm had been severed at the elbow in New York and was swaddled now with healing patches. To Dylan's right was a woman with dreadlocks: Theo, Clair remembered, Cashile's mother. Both, like Dylan, were members of WHOLE.

Clair knew better than to doubt that his threat was sincere.

"I told you what I was doing," Jesse said, standing defiantly next to Clair. "You can't pretend to be surprised."

"And I told you not to go. These are the consequences. Weapons on the ground, now."

There was movement to Clair's left and right. More people were coming out of the trees, surrounding them.

"Mr. Linwood," said Kari, "my name is PK Sargent. I can vouch for Clair and the others."

"But who will vouch for you? Here, you could be anyone."

"Actually," said Clair, "it doesn't work that way."

"You I trust least of all." Jesse's father's hostile stare danced between Clair and Clair One. "Weapons down. Last warning."

There was no point arguing with him, and no reason to either. They were on the same side, or at least had the same enemy.

Clair carefully placed her pistol on the dirt in front of her and stepped away from it with both hands held up. Kari did the same, and so did Clair One, albeit with great reluctance. She, Clair reminded herself, would have no idea who Dylan Linwood was, or what Nobody had done in his body. To Clair One, Dylan Linwood was nothing but a threatening stranger.

To Clair, though, he was a terrible reminder of everything that had happened on the seastead and before. His face was still bruised from the beating he had received at the hands of the people who had forcibly copied him, and his left eye was still red. But the injuries were healing, and his voice had its usual California drawl. Clair told herself to concentrate on that.

"You know who I am," she told him. "A week ago to me, but not so long for you, I came to your house and asked you about Improvement. Then you came to my school. You tried to convince everyone that we were in danger—Libby, me, all of us. No one believed you."

"Day in the life of," he said. "What are you doing here now? Why has my son put us all at risk to bring you here?"

"I'll tell you, if you let me." How much had Jesse explained to him already? How much did this Jesse know? "You were right and we were wrong. We were all very, very wrong—about Wallace, about d-mat, about everything. You need to know what has happened since you were duped."

"Why should I believe anything you tell me?"

First he wanted her to explain, but then he said he wouldn't believe her even if she tried. They could go around in circles like this all day.

"Because I'm an Abstainer now, like you," Clair said, making herself as tall as she could. She was short even next to Dylan Linwood. "I'm the girl who killed d-mat. With Turner Goldsmith I took on VIA, and with Agnessa Adaksin I took on the lawmakers who wanted to make slaves of all of us. I killed the woman who betrayed WHOLE, Gemma Mallapur, and I tried my best to kill Ant Wallace, too. It's not my fault it didn't stick. Ask Ray: he'll remember some of this. And Jesse, too." She hoped. "If you trust them, you can trust me. Just listen before you decide that I've got nothing to say. And when you believe me, let's talk about fighting back."

She stopped, suddenly, uncomfortably aware of how hard everyone was staring at her. It occurred to her only then just how little her friends knew about her recent past. They knew something about Jesse and her, but the whole becoming-an-Abstainer part she had left out . . . and the way Jesse was looking at her made it clear that he hadn't known either.

The knot in her chest twisted a little tighter. His pattern, then, wasn't from the last time he had used d-mat, when he and Trevin had accidentally triggered the blue dawn. The time before that had been after the battle on the seastead. She prayed it was then and no earlier.

"You're a *Stainer*?" Clair One said, looking like she'd gone mad. This was different from shooting someone who had threatened her. God help her if she admitted to killing *herself*. . . .

"Let's talk," she said. "All of us, together. We need a plan, quickly, and we won't get that unless we're all on the same page."

Dylan's gaze was appraising. He held her stare for a long time, then nodded. She had been tested and found worthy. For the moment.

"All right," he said. "But the weapons stay where they are. I won't allow them in the caves. No exceptions."

"Caves?" said Clair.

"The Mystery Caves of Minnesota," said Ray, adding, "I came here once, as a kid."

Why that was significant Clair didn't know.

"This way," Dylan said, gesturing at the entrance to the building. Clair did as she was told, and the rest had no choice but to follow her lead.

[13]

CLAIR'S INFIELD WAS blank. The messages from Nobody had ceased upon her leaving Harmony. It surprised her, then, when a new bump suddenly appeared.

It was from Q.

She opened it as Dylan guided her through a set of glass doors and into an antechamber that might once have been a gathering point for tours heading underground, passing a line of smashed d-mat booths along the way.

"Qualia has been broken," Q said, "by which I mean both the notion and the entity. I am fixing the problem, fixing the glitches, fixing myself. Trying to."

That was all. As cryptic as only Q could be, but without her usual reassuring edge.

"How, Q?" Clair bumped back. "Are you all right?"

Q didn't reply. Relief that she was alive was tempered by the puzzle she had left Clair. Qualia, Clair remembered, was the name given to the perceived *realness* of a thing. It was also the name given to one of the two AIs that had once overseen the safe operation of d-mat—the closest thing to parents Q had. It sounded as if Q was telling her that the AI Qualia had been involved somehow in the maintenance of the Yard, but wasn't anymore. It had broken down, perhaps causing the glitches in the appearance of reality—or maybe the glitches had caused the breakdown instead. Glitches caused by the presence of two Clairs.

The number of glitches appeared to have eased. Q had managed that much, at least.

"Take a seat," said Dylan.

The antechamber contained scattered chairs and tables, plus a number of other people Clair recognized. They were all members of WHOLE duped during her cross-country dash to New York. Aunt Arabelle, in her wheelchair. Jamila, with her mismatched eyes. The guy with big ears who had been shot in Manteca. Most shocking was Cashile, the young boy whose face she had seen many times since, occupied by the minds of other people. He was sitting at a table, playing with an antique tablet.

He looked up and waved on recognizing her.

"Clair!" he said. "You made it."

Then he saw Clair One and, like everyone, frowned.

"Hi, Cashile," Clair said, forcing herself to forget about the many times he had been duped. He might be the only child left in the Yard now. "It's good to see you again."

Cashile looked at his mom, who shrugged mutely. WHOLE hated d-mat and dupes of any kind. But they knew her. Some of them had even trusted her. Clair was grateful for the chance to explain. She and her friends were safe now, but they couldn't afford to sit around talking all day. They had to fight back before Wallace found them and wiped them out.

"I said sit," said Dylan, doing so himself. "Begin."

For the second time that day, Clair's recent activities were under the magnifying glass, and this time there was no way she could leave anything out. She covered every event since Jesse's father had been kidnapped, answering every question and seeking confirmation from Ray on the parts of it that he had experienced. At the capture of Turner Goldsmith, Ray's memories ceased: that was when he had been duped. From there—the crash, Q, the muster, and so on—it was entirely up to Clair and Kari.

Clair watched Jesse closely. He said nothing, and his expression was guarded. This was his father's show: Dylan had made that very clear. Jesse wasn't allowed to intrude.

Clair One and the others didn't talk much either. They didn't need words to convey how betrayed they felt. Clair might once have felt the same. She had just revealed herself to be both more and less reliable than they had thought: famous in ways that Libby had never dreamed of, and at the same time a betrayer of the life they had known. She was telling them that everything they believed was wrong, and that she as much as Ant Wallace was responsible for the loss of their ordinary lives. If she could only show them, she thought, that she had had good reasons . . .

Clair almost slapped herself. She had forgotten her lenses again.

"These are the dupes outside the muster, trying to get Agnessa to turn me over," she said, sending them the images. There were many more. They were horrible, but not as horrible as the thought of losing her friends' trust forever. "This is the attack on the seastead. This is what the chain reaction looked like, at the end."

"'Let them burn.'"

Jesse's voice brought her out of the slideshow. His father had said those very words in Manteca, when Jesse had tried to stop him from embarrassing Clair in front of the entire world.

"'Let them die if they want to.'" She finished the quote. "Well, it happened. How does it feel?" she asked Dylan.

In his eyes she saw a hint of defensiveness. Yes, he had

said those words, and they had come literally true. Horribly, tragically, and permanently, for so many innocent people. Unlike the Rapture, there was no happy ending for any of them.

"Stop," said Dylan. "I believe you. But that doesn't mean I trust you. Just because you claim to be an Abstainer doesn't mean we're on the same side."

"The feeling is mutual," she said. She had sworn never to use d-mat again because she had seen the horrors it could perform in the wrong hands, but that didn't mean she was going to stop anyone else from using it. If everything went back to normal in that instant, she wouldn't shun her friends just because they disagreed with her on that point—and she hoped they wouldn't shun her, either.

"I don't even know what happened to you yet," she said to shine the spotlight back on Dylan for a change.

He nodded, and reciprocated in a brisk, efficient manner that left little room for questions. The members of WHOLE had woken up individually, wherever they had been duped: Dylan in Manteca, Ray in New York, Aunt Arabelle on the road, and so on. It had become rapidly clear what had happened. Nonusers of d-mat never expected to live after being turned into patterns, so their ongoing existence had to be an artifact of some kind. Given the world's sudden emptiness, it wasn't a huge leap from there to guessing that they were in a simulation populated only by people who had been copied, particularly when moving from one place to another on foot or by vehicle proved impossible.

"It's like a honeycomb," said Arabelle. "You can't cross the walls between cells—but if you learn to fly, like a bee, you can go anywhere you want."

"How did you learn?" Ronnie asked.

"By accident," said Ray, but he stopped when Dylan raised a hand. With Turner and Agnessa out of the picture, Dylan Linwood, the artist who had been denied the active role he always wanted, had become WHOLE's alpha dog. And he was angry.

"Ant Wallace thinks he's won," he said. "He thinks he's going to live forever in his pathetic playground. We're going to show him how wrong he is."

"That's not all he wants," said Kari. "Kingdon, at least, won't be happy with staying in here. Like Tash says, information can be erased, and that makes everyone in here vulnerable."

"Matter can be erased too," said Dylan. "You've seen that now."

"Regardless, she's going to want to get outside and rebuild Earth the way she wants it to be: her cronies, her rules, her will be done."

Clair One looked over her shoulder suddenly, as though she had seen something.

"The shadows are moving," she said. Clair looked and saw dark shapes stirring in the corners, where the light was weakest. They didn't look like anything specific, just *wrong*.

"We should get underground," said Arabelle.

"Is it safe?" asked Tash.

"What if the hollowmen find us again?" said Zep.

"They won't," said Dylan. "Not underground. We leave a trail of glitches whenever we rip somewhere. That's one of the ways they track us. But the caves are less connected to the rest of the Yard than anywhere else. The stone is almost as effective as Faraday shielding. It may not be comfortable down there, but if we're careful it'll keep us safe. Meanwhile, we're working on another solution. Don't screw up and you could be part of it."

That was gruff but promising. Clair agreed, although her every instinct cried out to keep running. As he led them out of the building and along path that led through the woods, by bridge across a stream, and so to the entrance of the caves, it was clear that her friends weren't reassured either. Working with WHOLE meant working with terrorists.

Give them time, Clair told herself, *and they'll come around.*

Did she really want that, though? She wasn't sure. Already they had seen and been shocked by images of themselves duped and killed outside the muster. How much more would it take to harden them to such realities? If they had to fight the hollowmen to get at the exit, if some of them died before Wallace and Kingdon were overthrown, would that be enough to make them *damaged* just like her?

[14] ————————————————————————

BEHIND A HEAVY metal door with an exceedingly complicated lock, the caves were cold and damp and smelled of something sharp that might have been bats. Fortunately, there were blankets and heaters running off power beamed down from above, and a walkway anchored high above water below. If there were bats, they were hibernating. Strings of lights illuminated graceful rock formations and crystal clear pools. Everywhere Clair looked she saw layers of limestone stacked like giant pancakes, held up in places by frameworks of rusting metal.

With the door shut behind them, they were cut off from the Air, and Clair felt a sense of isolation drop over her. It wasn't entirely a good feeling. She was safe from Ant Wallace for the moment, but she was cut off from Q, too. If Q ever returned.

"Rest," said Dylan. "We'll talk again in three hours."

"And what are you going to do until then?" Clair One asked.

"Work on that solution I mentioned. I can't do that and babysit at the same time."

With that he was gone, leaving Clair One looking betrayed and patronized. Clair felt for her, but there was nothing anyone could do about hurt feelings for now. WHOLE had its own agenda, which obviously didn't yet mesh with theirs. Luckily Kari was already helping them settle in, reassuring them in a patient, grown-up fashion that they weren't in any immediate danger now.

Clair One wasn't buying it: Clair could see her other self's eyes tracking her as she moved through the caves. There was going to be a reckoning between the two of them. Clair knew that. But it would have to wait, as would Wallace and Kingdon and everyone else in the Yard.

She had something more important to deal with.

Jesse was coming back from a deeper part of the cave with blankets. When he had handed them over, she grabbed his arm and tugged him into a niche near a conical, gray stalagmite where they could be relatively alone.

"I need to talk to you," she said.

"Yeah." He folded down next to her. There was barely enough space for both of them, forcing their knees to touch. His long hair hung down in a veil between them. "I figured."

Clair resisted the urge to lean into him, as she used to. Instead she forced herself to ask the question that mattered most at that moment: "What's the last thing you remember before the Yard?"

"New York," he said.

Her gut clenched. Not the seastead, then.

"Which time in New York? When we went there from the flood in Crystal City? Or after the crash?"

He shook his head, confused. "When Ant Wallace took us prisoner. Before Turner came and the big booth activated. The office."

"Where Ray lost his arm?"

He nodded. "He's not happy about that, as you can imagine."

Clair could imagine it all too well. She felt as though someone had reached into her chest and ripped out her heart.

That time in New York—the first time he had ever used d-mat—was the worst possible answer. So much had happened since then. Hunting dupes together in Crystal City. The forest at the South Pole. Their cabin in the seastead. The muster, where they had argued and then made up. Their plan . . .

"Hollowmen," not "hollow men."

He wasn't the same Jesse she knew.

She leaned forward and cupped her face in her hands, covering her eyes. Her elbows dug hard into her knees, giving her something else to think about apart from the pain of simply being.

"Are you all right?" he said. Tentatively, softly, he touched her back and ran his hand down her spine. "Did I say something wrong?"

She shook her head. Her throat was full and thick with tears she couldn't indulge because he wouldn't understand. It would scare him away.

"You didn't say anything wrong." She sat up, feeling as though she weighed a ton. "Do you remember what you told me in Wallace's office, before Turner came?"

He turned bright pink. "Yes."

"And you remember the train . . . when we kissed?"

"Of course."

Concentrate on that, she told herself.

"Can I kiss you now?"

"Uh, sure, yes. I'd like that."

He brushed back his fringe and she stretched her neck so her lips could meet his. He was cautious, shy. His mouth didn't open. But he smelled like him. He *was* him. Just different, on the inside.

The Jesse she had spent the night with in Antarctica, the Jesse who had fought with her over d-mat, the Jesse who had confessed that he loved her . . . that Jesse was gone forever.

But this Jesse was here. He was *alive.*

"I'm glad I didn't freak you out," he said when they pulled apart. "In New York, I mean. It was such a stupid thing to say in front of everyone."

"Don't," she said. "You're not stupid. It was sweet. I'm glad you told me."

He looked at her expectantly, and she didn't know what to say. She couldn't tell him that she had had a crush on him in return, because she hadn't. She had barely noticed him, except as the school weirdo. But now their situations were reversed: she was more invested than he was, which came with its own set of complications. She couldn't mistake him for the Jesse she had known, and she couldn't pretend they were the same person—that would be like stalking. He would have every right to be angry if she thought she was using him as a substitute for the Jesse she really wanted.

"Will you tell me something?" he asked her after the silence had stretched too long.

"Sure."

"How are you an Abstainer? I mean, that's a good thing, but . . . I just don't understand it. You're d-mat girl. What changed your mind?"

You did. She shook her head, unready to talk about that with him just yet.

"Tell me about the rips, first," she said. "How does all that work? And how did you know where I was?"

"I followed the glitches." His fringe fell back down over his eyes. "I could hear your voice, even down here, underground. No one else could, but I knew I wasn't imagining things. I assumed that it was because we had been . . . connected . . . outside the Yard."

"What was I saying?"

He blushed again. "Stuff I'd never actually heard you say. Doesn't matter."

She thought maybe it did matter, very much, but let him move on.

"It was like you were calling me. I felt that if I concentrated hard enough, I'd go right to you, wherever you were. And I did, kind of. Lucky I brought bikes with me, in case you weren't alone. I didn't know there'd be two of *you*."

Clair didn't want to get stuck on that point. "I thought Q must have told you."

"I haven't heard from her at all."

"She's been weird. I'm not sure why." Clair tugged her bottom lip down. "Go on."

"Yeah, well, when I told Dad I was going to get you, he freaked, of course. But I'm tired of him and his bullshit. Just because we're together again doesn't mean he gets to order me around." Jesse's brow knitted, and for a moment he looked like his father. "So I went."

"How?" she said. "That part I still don't get. How exactly do you go anywhere without d-mat?"

"It was Theo and Cashile who figured it out. When they woke up in the Yard, they were out in the middle of nowhere, where they'd been captured. They tried to follow the road back to the cache at Escalon—where we picked up the electrobikes back at the beginning, remember?—but they started going in circles, like people do here. They panicked and headed cross-country and went through a gate leading from one field to another. That's important. Also, Theo still had one of the pistols on her from the cache, which acted as an anchor. The world ripped, and there she was. Just like that. It freaked her out, of course, but when similar things started happening to other people, we guessed what was going on."

"What *is* going on?"

"It's like . . . if you clearly remember somewhere . . . and if you can find something like a doorway or, or even a window . . . to act as a kind of *symbol*, I guess . . . then sometimes you'll go exactly where you need to go. Like the Yard reads what you're trying to do and how you're trying to do it, and . . . makes it happen. That's what we did when I picked you up in Harmony."

Clair stared at him. "The Yard *makes it happen*?"

"It sounds like magic, doesn't it?" His eyes were delighted even if his expression was serious. "But this place is a simulation, so information is the same thing as matter, with its own extra rules. The Yard sometimes makes real things that you think *should be* real. That's why I asked you to think about Dad when we were trying to get here; that extra connection brought us to him, even though the dupes didn't want us to go and were trying to hold us back their own way."

"And you're okay with this?"

"Well, it's not the same thing as d-mat, is it? No one's

taking us apart. We're moved as one piece, instantaneously. And even if we weren't, it's like Dad says: the damage has already been done."

"As in, he's already been copied, so what difference does it make?"

"I guess so." Jesse shrugged. "At some point we have to take it on faith that something that feels real *is* actually real. As long as I don't have to use d-mat again, I can live with it."

Clair bit her tongue on the knowledge that her version of him had used d-mat outside, before he had died. Willingly and unwillingly. She didn't think he would want to know that yet.

Raised voices came from the other side of the cave. Clair peered out of their niche, conscious of Jesse moving closer to do the same.

Her friends were arguing. She figured she'd better do something about that.

"Wait," said Jesse, before she could leave. "You never said what became of me. Out there."

Another subject she had deliberately avoided.

"Do you really want to know?"

"I think I need to," he said, "particularly if he's, you know, still on the scene."

"What?"

"Well, there're two of you. Why can't there be two of me, too?"

That would make things so much easier, she thought. *Or harder in different ways.*

"Clair One doesn't remember you like I do," Clair said, trying not to sound too harsh. "None of that has happened for her. None of . . . *us*. But if you want to take your chances—"

"No," he said. "I like this version of you better, and not just because you want to kiss me." A smile flickered across his features. "But at the same time . . . I don't want to get hurt. What if *he* shows up one day? Better to let me down now, don't you think?"

She swallowed. "He's not going to show up."

"Are you sure?"

"Yes."

"You seem *really* sure."

It never got easy, telling the people she loved that they had died. With Jesse she didn't need words.

His face fell. "What happened to him?"

"He was trying to stop Wallace. That's all you need to know."

"No, I mean *what happened to him* . . . in general. . . . What am I missing?"

She couldn't break away from his wounded stare. They were both agonizing over the same thing. But what could she say? *You saw a dupe of your mother being shot at the muster. You accidentally destroyed the world. You loved me, and I never got to tell you that I loved you back.*

This wasn't something she could fix, no matter how much both of them wanted it to be.

"You're not missing anything," she said. "Just be yourself. How can that go wrong?"

———————————————————— [15]

"EVERYTHING ABOUT THIS is wrong," Clair One shouted. "You can't make me stay here. I'm not a prisoner!"

The disagreement between her friends had blossomed into a full-on argument. By nature, Clair didn't like confrontation or anger, but when pushed too far and there were no other options . . . giving in wasn't her style.

Together she and Jesse hurried over to where the others were sitting in the lee of a pile of boulders that had fallen from the limestone ceiling. Clair One was standing with fists clenched, the echoes of her cry still flying around them. Ronnie and Zep stared up at her in shock, their mouths open in almost identical expressions. Tash reached one hand out from under her blanket to pull her back down, but Clair One yanked furiously away.

"What's wrong?" Clair asked, coming up to them with her hands tucked nonaggressively, she hoped, behind her back.

"Stay out of this," seethed Clair One. "This doesn't concern you."

"If it concerns you, it concerns me."

"Why? Because I'm you? I'm *not* you. I'm nothing *like* you. I would never be an Abstainer. I would never date *him*. I wouldn't break d-mat or destroy the world or kill anyone, ever. Whoever you are, I want you to stay the hell away from me!"

Clair didn't back down, but she didn't raise her voice, either, although it took considerable effort.

"You're not me," she said. "That's right. But you *became* me, and I'm not your enemy now. I'm certainly not keeping you here by force. If you choose to leave, go right ahead. No one will stop you, if that's what you really want."

"Listen to her, Clair," said Libby to Clair One. "She's making sense. You always make sense, even when you're being an idiot."

"I'm not an idiot," Clair One said to Libby, looking betrayed. "I'm trying to look after us. All of us, including me. I don't want to become *her*."

"Well, if I'd had a choice," said Clair, "I might have felt the same. But here I am. You're stuck with me."

"Not if I leave."

"If you leave, I'll have to go with you."

"No—"

"*Yes.* Because you need me out there. Haven't you figured that out yet? Ask Kari, if you don't believe me." Clair looked around for the PK. "Where is she, by the way?"

"Talking to Señor Linwood about something they didn't

share with us," said Zep.

"Dad's like that," said Jesse with a roll of his eyes.

"Come on, Clair," Tash said to Clair One. "If you can't trust yourself, who *can* you trust?"

Clair One simmered for a moment, then thought of something. "That's a good point. And that's why I think we should split up."

"Give it a rest," said Libby.

"No, think about it. *She* should trust *me*. We need information about Wallace that we won't find hiding down here. There must be someone out there who knows where he and the exit are, and I volunteer to go looking for them. Does anyone want to come with me?"

"I think that's a great idea," said Ronnie. "I'll go."

"It's too dangerous," said Jesse. "The hollowmen—"

"I didn't ask you," Clair One cut him off. "What about you, Zep? Are you in or out?"

He looked from Clair to Clair One to Libby. "In. You, Libs?"

"No way," she said. "But I won't stop you from running off with your new girlfriend. Just don't expect me to be waiting for you when you get back."

That dropped like a bomb into the conversation. Clair One, Libby, and Zep stared at one another with an entirely new, silent intensity that only Clair truly understood. And Jesse, to a lesser extent. She had told him some of it before his pattern had been copied into the Yard.

"Uh, if you're talking about me . . . ," Ronnie started to say.

"We're not," said Libby. "You're not idiot enough to fall for your best friend's boyfriend."

Clair, through pangs of shame that might possibly never leave her, could only admire how Libby had defused the situation—by moving everyone from one crisis to another, distracting them from the almost certainly disastrous plan of splitting up.

"Libby—" Clair One started to say.

"Save it. The time for that conversation isn't now. You're right about one thing, though. A little space is just what we all need to get our heads straight, so I'll get the ball rolling."

Libby gathered up her blanket and went to sit elsewhere in the cave. Tash hesitated, then went after her, but not before giving Zep an I'm-doing-your-job-for-you look. Clair One stared after them for a moment with her mouth firmly set, then picked up her blanket and went in the opposite direction. She didn't look at Clair. She didn't look at anyone.

Clair knew that mood. Her mother had called it the Brooding Bear when Clair was small, and still occasionally did so, to annoy her.

Zep started to go after Clair One, but Ronnie caught his arm.

"You must be joking," she said. "Keep your head down until someone tells you otherwise. I'll go."

Clair watched her leave with gratitude. Ronnie was a good friend, and so was Tash. In the real world, she hadn't appreciated just how good until almost too late.

"Did *you* tell her?"

Zep's question brought her out of her memories.

"What? Oh, you mean Libby. No. She figured it out. We were stupid to keep it from her."

"Is that what you did? You and, uh, your Zep?"

"He wasn't *my* Zep . . . but yes, that's what we did and it was the worst thing ever. Remember that, next time you're in this position."

"You think there'll *be* a next time?"

"God yes. You've got all the staying power of a butterfly."

"What I mean is . . . you're absolutely sure we're not going to die in here?"

Perhaps she was being too hard on him.

"I don't plan on it." She put her hand on his shoulder and squeezed, struggling to reassure both of them. She hadn't realized that saving her friends *from each other* would be so difficult or so time-consuming. It was exhausting. "Just try to rest. Later we'll find a fabber and get us some better clothes. You need something practical and I need something that doesn't smell like ass. Then we'll make plans. Okay?"

"Okay." He flashed a grin up at her. "Three's company. I get it."

Clair had momentarily forgotten Jesse.

"I don't know about him," she said, "but I'm going to get some sleep."

Jesse took the hint gracefully. He understood when to give her space. If anything, he was *too* good at it. They were a pair, in that sense. If circumstances hadn't thrown them together, nothing might ever have happened between them. And nothing might ever happen now, if she wasn't careful.

"I hope that's okay," she said, reaching out to take his hand.

"Of course." He smiled and blew her a kiss, something he had never done in the real world. It was a start, she told herself. Not an ending.

[16]

EVERYTHING WAS QUIET in the caves apart from a low murmur of conversation from the members of WHOLE that Clair couldn't overhear. She found a blanket and a spot that wasn't too cold or damp, and made herself as comfortable as she could on the cold stone with her parka zipped up tight. From behind her, under a ceiling covered with twisting rock straws, came a steady drip of water, like the ticking of a crystalline clock. She concentrated on that rather than on Clair One, Q, and Wallace—or her mother, or Billie, or any living person who might or might not be in the Yard and need saving right now. *Don't think about the exit,* she told herself, *or reconnecting with the outside, or rebuilding everything that is currently only numbers.* She would deal with that later, when she had gotten some sleep. Out of the ashes, she swore, a phoenix would be born. But the fear remained: *unless Wallace finds me first . . .*

When she slept, she dreamed of rising oceans and clouds of ash. Lightning struck all around the horizon, creating a flickering electric cage. She was afraid of the light. It was alive somehow, and yet the sound it made was a hissing crackling noise utterly unlike anything natural. If it touched her, she knew, she would become like it and never be able to turn back. The thought terrified her so much she couldn't breathe.

A rough hand shook her awake.

"Clair."

She blinked and sat up, flinging the blanket from her. Dylan Linwood was bending over her. *Dupes.* She needed to run.

Only it was Dylan Linwood for real, this time, not Nobody.

"What? What is it?"

"Your pet peeker wants to talk to you."

"Wallace hasn't found us?"

"No."

Clair wiped sleep from her eyes. It was hard getting her thoughts in a line, perhaps because she had been asleep less than an hour. *Peeker. PK. Kari.* "What does she want to talk about?"

"She didn't say."

Maybe she had found the exit, or Wallace, or both. Dylan held out a hand and Clair let herself be pulled up. His palms were callused from a long life of making everything he needed, instead of using a fabber like an ordinary person. That could be her one day, she thought, depending on what kind of Abstainer she would be. She hadn't considered the finer details of her pledge. Maybe just giving up d-mat would be enough. . . .

Jesse was standing behind his father. His hand was much softer than Dylan's. He took her along the ramp that led to the cave entrance. Immediately outside, waiting silently in the night air, they found Aunt Arabelle in her wheelchair, reading an old novel called *Decompression*. Ronnie had made Clair read it once; it was about a man trapped deep underground by a d-mat outage, which seemed almost too appropriate.

The old woman looked up as they emerged, then indicated the hall's rear entrance with a tilt of her head.

"I don't think I need remind you," she said, "that just one electronic peep could bring the hounds of hell howling down on us in an instant."

Clair had seen it happen too often to forget. On one of

those occasions a dupe in Arabelle's body had been *walking*, thanks to Improvement.

"I'm glad you're okay," she told the old woman.

"This?" Arabelle looked around. "This isn't *okay*. But I'll take it if it allows us to do what needs to be done."

Clair nodded awkwardly, feeling that her gesture of goodwill had been rebuffed, and left Arabelle to the book.

It was night, but still seemed bright to Clair's cave-adjusted eyes. The scent of living trees was very strong. Somewhere in the undergrowth, an animal called plaintively, persistently.

Kari was sitting in the shade on a low stone wall, staring into the distance with tired eyes. Her lenses showed complex geometric shapes coming and going in rapid succession, indecipherable from the outside. Clair didn't realize that Kari had noted their presence until her lenses abruptly cleared and she looked up at them, blinking to focus on the real world.

"What are you doing up here?" Clair asked her.

"I'm watching Billie," Kari said. The silver spot where PK Drader's bullet had struck her gleamed in the moonlight.

"We're supposed to be keeping a low profile," said Jesse, tapping the corner of one eye.

"PK protocols," Kari explained, "plus a little help from Q's mask. Ordinarily I would never abuse my power to access information I'm not supposed to have, but I figure since I'm the only honest PK in here, I can give myself permission."

"Is Billie all right?" Clair asked, seeing through her chatter.

Kari nodded. "Safe as long as I don't try to talk to her. Turns out I do care about her staying alive, after all."

Clair sat down next to her and took her hand.

"It's okay," Kari said. "Wallace has found other cards to play."

A video feed appeared in Clair's infield. She winked on it. The face of a familiar woman appeared—middle-aged, stern-jawed, big-haired, with a British accent: Lawmaker Kingdon.

"Serious catastrophes demand severe sacrifices." LM Kingdon wasn't wasting words on a soft opening. "While lawmakers and peacekeepers struggle to determine the nature of this situation, we have made the extraordinary decision to suspend the Consensus Court—temporarily, but necessarily—until the cause and those culpable can be found. Every resource available to us—every drone, every algorithm, every able volunteer—will be required to mete out justice. We beg your patience during these trying times, and your forgiveness. We all bear the brunt of this unforeseeable calamity with dignity, dedication, and determination. The rot *will* be rooted out. The lost *will* be avenged. A new day *will* dawn."

"And she'll be in charge of the sun," said Clair, groaning

under the weight of a burden she hadn't yet shrugged off. Either inside the Yard or out, Kingdon was determined to be on top, and to stamp down anyone who would resist her along the way. "What's she talking about? Behind the flag-waving, I mean. What's she actually going to do about us?"

"She's called a census," said Kari. "Everyone is required to go through d-mat within the next twenty-four hours in order to create a global roster of survivors. They'll weed out any suspects along the way. Anyone refusing will be arrested."

"So we keep our heads down," said Clair. "How does that change anything?"

"Drone production is up ten *thousand* percent. They're searching the areas around Harmony under the assumption that you can't have gone far from where you were last seen."

That was a good assumption. The Mystery Caves were only twenty-odd miles from the town.

"Okay, this is bad," Jesse said. "We have to move."

Clair agreed, but she wasn't ready to run just yet. Not until she knew where she was going.

"Have you heard from Q?" Clair asked.

"Yes. She wants to talk to you."

"Well, that's a change."

Kari looked down at Clair's upturned face.

"Q isn't avoiding you deliberately," she said. "The

glitches interfere with her, just like we thought."

"Sure, but . . ." Clair was embarrassed to be talking about this with Jesse listening. "Look, I spent so long thinking about her and wanting to find her, but she was there the whole time . . . in you . . . and although I get why she went away again . . ."

Kari put an arm around her.

"Q is massively important," she said, "to you and me. To everyone. When she was inside me, in a strange way I was inside her, too, which gives me some insight into what she felt like then. But that's nothing compared to what she's like now. She's a goldfish, you know—growing as large as the container that holds her? The Q I knew was a me-sized version of her. In here I barely know her at all."

"But she still talks to you."

"Not as often as you probably think," Kari said. "She's the same with me as she is with you, like you have to drag her away from something much more important just to answer a simple question."

"I still can't believe Q was you," said Jesse. "Isn't that as bad as being duped?"

"No, because Q promised me she was going to give me back." Kari smiled at him. "I believed her."

"How do you know she didn't make you believe her?"

"She promised me that, too . . . and I guess I just wanted it to be true."

"If wishes were fishes, my dad says," said Jesse, "we'd

be up to our ears in goldfish."

"Yes, but make enough wishes and one of them is bound to come true eventually."

———————————————————————————[17]

SHE WANTS TO *talk to you,* Kari had said. There was only one way to test that theory.

"I'm right here," Clair bumped Q while Jesse and Kari talked about the politics of duping.

A chat patch instantly appeared. Clair winked on it.

"I tried bumping you, but you didn't answer," Q said. She sounded far away and distracted, but it was her.

"Earlier? I was underground, not to mention asleep."

"So Kari told me. I forgot all about sleep."

"Didn't you do that when you were inside her?"

"Reluctantly."

Kari and Jesse's discussion was a distraction. Clair moved farther along the wall.

"Where did you go, Q? Where were you when we needed you?"

"I didn't go anywhere, Clair. I was busy."

"Doing what?"

"There's no easy way to explain it."

"Please try."

Clair worried that she was pushing too hard, but Q didn't sound annoyed.

"I mentioned earlier that breaking parity in here might be causing the glitches. That was indeed the case. Outside, breaking parity crashed the d-mat network. In here, where all matter is information, the d-mat network is a fundamental part of the Yard, and the problem got worse very quickly. I took some steps . . . drastic steps. Only time will tell if what I did will work permanently."

The glitches were markedly less intrusive, although Clair still felt as though the shadows were watching her sometimes.

"Well, that's good. Thank you. You said something about Qualia earlier. How does she fit into this?"

"She doesn't. Not anymore."

Clair waited for an explanation, but that was apparently all she was going to get. *Probably for the best,* she thought; it was unlikely she would have understood anyway.

"I overheard your conversation with Sarge," Q said, using PK Sargent's nickname, and suddenly she sounded like her old self again, chatty and open, not the new, distant Q. "I'm sad you feel like you don't know me anymore, because I feel the exact opposite. Isn't that what friendship is? It's not just helping each other, or testing each other, but understanding each other better and better as time goes on. Isn't it?"

"There's a quote like that," said Clair, warily calling on the earliest thing they had shared, a love of words.

"Yes, from Seneca: 'One of the most beautiful qualities of true friendship is to understand and to be understood.' I find it interesting, the way he phrased it. Why not the other way around?"

"I guess understanding someone doesn't always mean you'll be friends," Clair said. "Sometimes you can know too much about someone."

"Was that the case with your birth parents?"

The question took her by surprise. Q's tone had shifted again, back to direct questions and unsentimental inflection. "What do you know about them?"

"Only that they separated before you were born. I've yet to determine why."

Clair knew very little about her birth father. He was an engineer, her mother had told her once, who worked in space. For all they knew, he could have died years ago.

"You've looked into my family's history?"

"Of course. Did you know your mother's mother was an Abstainer?"

"Seriously? Mom never mentioned that."

"Why not?"

"I don't know. It doesn't matter, I guess." She rubbed one hand along the cool, rough stone next to her thigh. "Who cares about what some old lady I never met did, or my real father? Oz is my dad. Even if he and mom split up over something stupid, he'll always be that to me."

Cheerful Q returned. "And you'll always be my first friend, Clair. No matter what happens."

Clair wished Q had a face. It was so hard to read what she might mean beyond the words.

No matter what happens sounded almost ominous.

"I'm glad," Clair said. "Just don't ever call me Clair Two."

"I will never do that," Q replied. "Although both of you *are* Clair Hill, which raises serious philosophical questions. Does the fact that I've known *you* longer mean that you and I are better friends? Does the fact that *she* is more akin to the Clair I first knew mean that I should feel closer to her?"

"Ah, I get it," Clair said, understanding how it felt to have divided loyalties. "You're *my* friend, remember? Clair One has no idea who you are. She didn't meet you until a few hours ago."

"I hadn't thought of it that way. Experience must be shared, so people can change in tandem."

Just like Jesse and I did, Clair thought, with another knock to the heart.

She told herself to concentrate on what she had, not what she had lost.

Q wasn't a human being. She had all of human knowledge in her mind, but the understanding of an entirely new being, one who had none of the usual assumptions that Clair herself had been raised to have. One who was still learning.

Clair said, "You'll always be my first friend who's . . . who's something entirely new. We need a word for what you are, don't we?"

"I have come up with several, but none of them sound very good. I'm happy being just Q. The one and only."

"That you are," Clair said, wishing she also had better words to express her gratitude. "If we're ever going to beat Wallace and Kingdon, it's thanks to you."

"And to you," said Q. "They fear you because you should not be here. You are breaks in parity and you also know the truth about them. That makes you dangerous."

Clair looked down at her hands. They were scuffed and scratched and looking very different from Clair One's, who was still wearing the nail polish she had put on the day of the crashlander ball.

It was all very well to know that she, Clair Two, had been brave once. The thought of doing it twice . . . It was almost too much. But what choice did she have? If she had to run, she had to run. One day soon, she swore, it would be time to turn and fight.

"I will be here to help," Q told her, her new, distant tone returning somewhat jarringly midsentence, "barring any further unforeseen circumstances."

There were too many qualifications to that statement for

Clair to take much reassurance from it.

Q ended the chat and Clair turned her attention to Jesse and Kari Sargent, taking in everything she had just learned.

"Is everything okay?" he asked. "You look . . . frowny."

Clair rubbed the bridge of her nose. The saving-the-world part of her plan was proving elusive. "You're right: we're going to have to move somewhere more secure," she said. "Do you want to tell your father or should I?"

Jesse made a face. "He's already pissed off at me for bringing you here. So I vote you, but I'll come with you for moral support."

He pulled her to her feet, and there was something more than just muscle memory in the way his fingers gripped hers. *Alive. Really real.*

"I'm going to sit this one out," said Kari. "Plenty more spying to do out here."

Clair wished she could join in. After talking to Q about her mother, nothing would have made her happier than seeing with her own eyes that she and Oz were okay.

"If only Kari could see out of the Yard," Jesse said as they headed back to the cave entrance. "I'd give anything to know what it's like outside."

"You don't want to know," Clair said. *What we accidentally did.*

He stared at her for a long time, as though seeing right into her, then said, "Right."

IN THE END, it wasn't as harrowing as Clair feared. Dylan Linwood listened to the news and her reasoning, then said that he already knew about the announcement of Kingdon's crackdown. What was more, he fully agreed with Clair: he had been scouting for an alternative location since they'd arrived, knowing that the caves would be discovered eventually. That was the "solution" he had mentioned that he was working on earlier.

"We have one particular location in mind," he said.

"Where?" Jesse asked, as much in the dark as Clair was.

Dylan hesitated.

"What, you still don't trust me?" Clair asked, feeling genuinely hurt. She had done everything Dylan had said and told him nothing but the truth. It wasn't her fault there were two of her. If he was going to let his ridiculous prejudice get in the way of their working together, then he was a bigger fool than she realized.

"It's not that," he said. "You're a seventeen-year-old girl, and WHOLE doesn't operate by consensus. You need to accept that your opinion will be noted, but the decision won't be yours. It'll be mine."

His attitude was so old-fashioned and tedious she couldn't help but roll her eyes. The world had long ago abandoned the idea of absolute leaders after they had made such a mess of things—that was what made the thought of someone like Kingdon so terrifying. Consensus was the way everything worked now, wasn't it?

Then Clair realized that WHOLE's old-fashioned hierarchical structure sat naturally alongside its Luddite approach to technology and general paranoia. They'd drag the world back to the twentieth century if anyone was crazy enough to let them.

"All right," she said, figuring this was an argument for later. "Whatever. But don't think I'm going to blindly follow your orders. I'm an Abstainer, not a member of WHOLE, and my friends are neither."

"I understand that very well."

"And as to your secret solution—you're going to tell us at some point, so why not now?"

"All right, all right." He rasped one hand across his stubbled chin and made a pained expression like Clair's stepfather, Oz, did when she won an argument. "Ever heard of the White Man's Pit?"

Clair shook her head and looked at Jesse, who shrugged.

"It's the one ultramax prison ever built," his father explained. "Kupa-piti is the proper name. It's about a mile under the old opal mines in South Australia. Secure, a long way from anywhere, and has all the facilities we need. The only way in is via d-mat. There are no physical entrances at all."

"What about the prisoners?" asked Jesse. "You must be

crazy if you think they're just going to let us move in."

"There aren't any prisoners," Dylan said. "I'm sure of it. These criminals are the worst imaginable. Not even a lunatic like Wallace would want to save the patterns of such monsters, unless he has plans for them elsewhere. Either way, the prison will be empty. That goes for guards, too—why would you guard an empty space? So we can just walk in and take it for ourselves. No one will ever know. It's the safest place in the Yard."

In theory, Clair thought, it sounded good. From somewhere secure they could make concrete plans to find the exit without fear of being discovered in turn. Maybe from there they could find RADICAL, too, and then together they could bring down Wallace and Kingdon.

"Are you sure it's even in the Yard?" she asked.

"The Yard contains everything recorded by the Air. The prison is listed in the Air here, so it must exist here too."

"Australia . . ." Jesse sounded as though he was warming to the idea. His mother's family had come from there, Clair remembered. "It's going to take us a lot of rips to get there. We've never traveled that far."

"That's why we're not there already. We need a rock-solid anchor before we try anything like this. And that's where your tame PK is coming in very handy, Clair."

She cocked her head. What did Kari have to do with this? To get anywhere through the rips, Jesse had said, they needed to think of something from their destination, be that an object or a memory or a person. Kari had never mentioned anything about prison duty. . . .

Then she remembered what Kari had said about abusing her power. Obviously, she had been doing more than just spying on her girlfriend, or else Dylan would never have let her put the entire hideout at risk by accessing the Air.

"You're looking for a guard," she said. "Or an ex-prisoner, using Kari's protocols. Once you've found them, they can get you in, just like Ray brought you here."

Dylan nodded.

"How are you going to convince them to help us?" asked Jesse.

"Leave that to me."

Clair was uncomfortable with that suggestion. WHOLE had a reputation for brutality that preceded her experiences with them—and she personally had seen people kidnapped, shot, and blown up for getting in their way. But maybe that wasn't what Dylan meant. She could only hope.

"At the end," she said, "when the chain reaction was spreading, some of us talked about hiding in a prison to get away from it. There wasn't time, though; that's why we came here."

"The Yard's not so different from a prison, in that we can't get out," Jesse said. "So we're heading for a prison within a prison."

"We can't get out . . . *yet*," she corrected him. She wasn't abandoning her hope of rebuilding the world from everything saved in the Yard. All it would take was one booth on the outside and one exit from the inside. Everything came down to that.

"As ever," Dylan said, "you are blind to the real problem."

Clair couldn't decide if Dylan was expressing disdain or dismissal. Either way, she decided not to rise to the bait.

There was one more bridge left to rebuild before Clair could concentrate on the next phase of the plan. It frustrated her that things were moving so slowly, but if she'd learned one thing, it was that the delays increased in line with the number of people involved. She would just have to be patient and keep pushing where she could.

Taking Jesse's hand again, she turned it over in hers, marveling as she had long ago that these fingers had *made* things. There were lots of ways to touch someone, but none as powerful in Clair's experience as stroking the skin of someone lost and newly regained.

"Come and get me when it's time," she said. "Can I kiss you again?"

They did, and it was as sweet as the first time, with a bit more enthusiasm on his part. No, not enthusiasm: acceptance, perhaps. He had always wanted to kiss her. It was just taking him time to understand that this was something they did now. Clair's heart, cautious at first, began to trip over itself in something much more like its usual rhythms. She placed her hand against his chest in order to feel his heart, and it was thumping just like hers.

"Whatever I missed out on must've been good," he murmured. "You'll bring me up to speed one day?"

She nodded and smiled up at him.

"Good," he said with a grin. "Can't wait."

They parted, he to make sure his dad didn't do anything drastic without anyone knowing, Clair to do what she dreaded but knew she had to do next. There would be no saving the world without this.

Clair One was curled under her blanket at the end of a narrow, low-ceilinged corridor, where the shadows were darkest. It would have been difficult to find her, except that it was exactly the kind of place Clair herself might have gone to be alone, were their situations reversed. She didn't emerge as Clair approached, but Clair could tell that she was awake.

"We're moving out soon," Clair said. "I hope you'll come with us."

"Do I have a choice?" came a muffled voice from under the blanket.

"Always." Clair sat on the cold stone next to her, fighting a moment of existential disorientation. This was the first time she had been one-on-one with herself. It was like talking through a mirror with a reflection that talked back. A mirror who at the moment wouldn't even look at her.

"I can stay here and wait for the drones to find me," Clair One said, "or I can go back home, where Wallace will pick me up in case I'm really you. Or I can let you drag me deeper down the rabbit hole."

"I didn't ask for it to be like this," Clair said, not without sympathy. "It just happened, one thing after another."

Clair One shifted under the blanket. Her head finally slid free, hair wild with restless sleep, eyes red and heavily bagged.

"You survived," she said, sitting up and pulling the blanket around her shoulders. "That means I can survive too."

"I've survived *so far*," Clair corrected her. "Who knows what's coming?"

"Yeah, but there are two of us now. Wallace won't know what's hit him."

A ghost of a smile flickered across Clair One's familiar features.

"Exactly."

They shared the moment for barely a second; then the harsh reality of cold caves and their history crashed back in.

"So you kissed Zep," Clair One said. "Don't tell me it was an accident or you didn't mean to do it. It didn't just *happen*. I know you wanted to. That's right, isn't it?"

Clair nodded, feeling her face go warm. "Yes. But you have to understand that it wasn't something I planned to do. It was wrong."

"It sure was," Clair One agreed. "Your best friend's boy-friend—is there a dumber cliché?"

"Tell me about it."

"Was it worth it?"

Clair hadn't anticipated that question, but when she studied Clair One's anxious, almost eager face, she could understand where it came from. Easy for Clair Two to dismiss the Zep thing as a mistake: she had tried it and it hadn't worked. For Clair One, however, it was still a fantasy, fresh in her heart: forbidden and wrong, yes, but untested and therefore still a possibility.

"Not under any circumstances would Zep be right for us," Clair said, with all sincerity. "For a fling, sure—but we're not really the flinging type, are we? We take things too seriously. We think about things too much. Zep's not a thinker. Which isn't to say he's stupid or anything. He's just . . . the wrong guy, that's all."

"And Jesse is the right guy?"

Clair was relieved that Clair One wasn't asking for details about the kiss, but there was still a note of challenge to her voice.

"I know it seems crazy to you," Clair said. "It probably seems crazy to him right now too, or at least not terribly real, even though he's had a crush on me—I mean, *us*—for years."

Clair One's eyebrows rose. "He has?"

"Yeah." Clair could have shown her the recording of

him blurting out that fact at exactly the wrong time; better to spare him any further embarrassment. "You haven't seen the real him."

"And I guess I won't now," she said with a listless shrug.

"What do you mean?"

"Well, things have worked out differently for me, haven't they? It's not going the way it went for you. You're here, and I don't get Zep. I don't get Jesse, either. It doesn't seem fair."

Clair nodded. Looked at like that, she decided she would probably feel the same way.

"But you haven't *lost* Zep and Jesse," she said. "Zep was shot right in front of me, twice, and Jesse died too. I don't want to say that that's worse than never having met them, but I'm glad for you that you haven't lived through that."

"Thanks for nothing, literally." But Clair One nodded. "All right. Maybe that makes us even. And maybe I'll meet some handsome young Abstainer who I can convert around to my way of thinking . . . someone *you'll* never get your hands on. . . ." She peered out at the cave from her tucked-away nook. "Doesn't seem likely, though, judging by this group. They're all so old. And anyway, relationships just seem to mess me up."

Under Clair One's critical eye, Clair didn't have the heart to disagree, even though she knew it wasn't necessarily the relationships but the circumstances under which they happened.

And there were plenty of other reasons why Clair was messed up that Clair One would hopefully never experience. . . .

"I'd better tell Libby and the others we're moving out," said Clair One.

"I can do it," Clair said.

"No. They're my responsibility. You've got Jesse, PK Sargent, Dylan Linwood—all that. Let me have this. That's fair, isn't it? I mean, you can't do *everything*."

"All right." Clair forced herself to make that concession. It wasn't, after all, like she was handing the responsibility of her friends over to a complete stranger. "I don't know when exactly WHOLE will be ready, but it could be soon."

"I'll do my best. You know what Libby is like in the morning."

Clair smiled weakly, unsure whether Clair One was rebuilding bridges of her own or challenging her again. Frustrated by the thought that, in some ways, the hardest person to read was herself, she went to see if there was something she could do elsewhere.

[19]

CLAIR ONE GOT the others in an organized huddle while Clair found ways to get ready for their departure. WHOLE had a surprising amount of supplies in the caves, and it all needed to be packed in readiness for carrying back up to the surface. As she worked, she considered how best to search for Wallace from the prison, and decided that maybe Clair One had a point: small search parties might well go unnoticed, once the fuss of Kingdon's census died down and they had a secure base to return to if things went wrong.

"Clair!" Jesse's voice cut through her thoughts. He was shouting from the entrance, her name echoing through the caverns. "Ray took off without me knowing. I don't know where he went, but he's ripping back now, and he's bringing someone with him."

The anchor. Clair dropped what she was doing and hurried up the stairs. Ray was just returning when they left the caves. Kari stood to one side of the entrance, arms folded, watching.

Clair had never seen someone come through a rip before. It was like looking up at the surface as a pebble plopped into a calm lake. There were ripples of sound as well as light. A strange taste swept across her tongue. She felt as though her hair was curling and uncurling from the roots out to the tips and back again.

Then Ray jerked to a halt on the back of an electrobike with a passenger in the sidecar. There was a hood over the passenger's head.

Clair's stomach fell, fearing kidnapping, coercion, maybe worse. She hurried over to interrupt any further assault on a possibly innocent person, but stopped upon seeing Ray's passenger step out unaided.

"Whoa, intense." She was a solidly built woman with a long, gray ponytail down her back, dressed in a shapeless navy jumpsuit. Her voice was slurred. She put a hand out to steady herself and caught Ray's sleeve, pulling him down to her level. "Have we arrived?" she said too loudly in his ear.

"We're here," Ray told her.

"Can I take the hood off now?"

"Not yet." Dylan Linwood had come up behind Clair. The bagged woman's head turned to face the new voice. "We'll tell you when."

"O-kay, then. And you are?"

"Someone who's very grateful for your help. Thank you, Lalie."

"Anytime."

"You're doing this willingly?" asked Clair.

The woman turned blindly again. "Sure. Why not? No harm in talking about a place no one's ever going to escape from. Ask me what you want and I'll get back to my very important business."

She mimed raising a glass to her mouth, and Clair understood then that the woman was drunk. Clair told herself not to judge. There was no right way to cope with life in the Yard, particularly if she was one of the many unfortunates who had lost a child.

"Come with me," said Dylan, taking her by one arm, Ray ready at the other. "We'll talk inside."

"Her name is Lalie Hagopian," said Kari, falling in beside Clair as the woman was led away. "Dismissed from Corrections and Containment a year ago. No love lost between her and C and C, which makes her exactly the kind of person WHOLE needs to get into the prison. This way no one gets hurt."

Clair looked up at her. "Thank you."

"Thus I keep the peace. Now . . ." She looked around. "We don't have long. Drones have been seen within two miles of here. They could find us any minute if Mariah calls it in."

"Calls what in?"

"Your faces were circulated while you were below-ground. Come on. Let's find some terrorists and get this show on the road."

Under Aunt Arabelle's authoritative direction the supplies Clair had bundled together were hauled up and out of the cave and packed into waiting vehicles. Several more vehicles rolled out from under the trees, waiting to be loaded. Clair kept her parka but was grateful for a new set of clothes—a simple outfit that was more practical than their tattered party gear, but lacked body armor. She felt even better when her gun was returned, but that worried her. There was no way to reconcile that feeling with who she used to be, when she had been Clair 1.0.

Zep asked where the clothes had come from.

Jesse said, "Fabbed. Where else?"

"But I thought fabrication was verboten," said Zep.

"In here," said Aunt Arabelle, "everything is fabbed. But we can still abhor waste, so keep hauling."

"You mean I could have had any clothes I wanted?" asked Libby, tugging at the front of her nondescript blue top. "First, you tell me I can't post to the Air, and now—"

"This isn't a popularity contest," Arabelle said. "We're leaving as soon as Dylan is ready."

Libby went back to work, picking up a box of cans with a scowl and dropping it carelessly into place.

Along with the other vehicles, a steady influx of people trickled in from the forest around the caves. When everyone was assembled, Dylan and Ray emerged with the woman, Lalie, walking between them. She seemed steadier on her feet, and the bag over her head had been replaced with a black blindfold. She lit a cigarette and smoked it while Dylan gave everyone their instructions for the move. Sharpshooters kept a close eye out for drones on the edges of the clearing.

"Ray takes the lead," Dylan said. "Everyone else follows. You've done this before; you know how it works. Keep concentrating on him and you'll be fine."

Jesse and Clair were in a van driven by Theo and Cashile. Clair One, Libby, and the others were squeezed in the back. Theo mimed how to fasten the seat belts as they climbed aboard and she insisted they use them.

"You drew the short straw, did you?" said Zep. "Being stuck with us, I mean."

Theo signed something to her son, who translated, "We volunteered. It gets boring hanging out with gun nuts and . . . can you spell that, Mom? Oh yeah, *isolationists*. The guys who live in huts on top of mountains and think drones are sent by the devil."

Clair understood, then, the hostile looks some of the forest contingent had given her as they had loaded up. If they didn't like drones, what would they think of her?

"PKs call them 'Yetis,'" said Kari. "Rumored to exist, potentially dangerous, and destined for extinction."

"Yeah," said Tash. "How on earth do they breed?"

"Spores," said Ronnie. "Or maybe asexually."

Theo laughed, a surprising sound from someone who had never spoken. She signed to Cashile, who translated: "We call them Neanderthals. But never when they can hear us."

This time only Jesse didn't laugh. As engines started purring around them, Theo turned her attention to the controls and Jesse explained what would happen.

"Lalie's going to remember what the prison looks like," he said. "Then Ray's going to open a rip so her memories will guide him there. It might take us a few legs. If we think about Ray, we'll all tag along like pearls on a string."

"Ray's the tall, skinny guy with one arm?" asked Tash.

"Yes. It sounds crazy, but it does work."

"Has anyone gotten lost in a rip?" Clair One asked.

"Lost forever?" Jesse said. "I don't know. Maybe. No one's said anything."

"I will be monitoring your progress as best I can," said Q out of nowhere, in brisk tones. "This process exposes a key flaw in the structure of the Yard, if flaw it is. One could regard it as an enhancement to conventional topology. It is much like the way I move my point of view from place to place, most of the time."

"Yes, you only had a body to drag around with you for a little while," said Kari, with an amused smile. "Count yourself lucky."

"I do." That didn't sound like a joke.

"So we think about Ray," said Jesse, bringing them tersely back to the topic at hand. "Really think about him. Try not to be distracted by anything else. We don't want to end up somewhere obvious, where the hollowmen will be waiting for us, like back at Harmony—or at school. That happened to me once."

"Why would we think about school?" asked Zep.

"Now that you've mentioned it," said Tash, "I'll have trouble keeping it out of my head."

"Don't think of an elephant," said Libby, still looking surly from Aunt Arabelle's telling-off.

"Give me school over a bunch of Yetis," said Clair One.

"Doesn't sound so different to me," said Jesse. "Try having your bag stolen when you can't fab a new one whenever you want. Or your lunch because you can't eat fabbed food. Or someone deliberately spills paint on your shirt—staining it, because that's a *hilarious* pun."

"No one did that," said Clair One. "Did they?"

Jesse glared at her reflection in the mirror. "On my first day of high school, Saxon Vargas told me he was going to follow me and throw me into a booth so I'd have to d-mat. But not *that* day, no. When I wouldn't see him coming. I walked home terrified, hearing him laughing at me all the way, and it was the same every day after that. He was probably just messing with me, but I never forgot. I was always afraid that *today* he would remember his promise, and then I'd be fucked."

He stopped talking, and the final word seemed to ring in the air, capturing everyone's embarrassment—his own, clearly, for revealing more than he had probably planned to; that of Libby and the others for being on the side of the bullies, at least to the point of giving him an ugly nickname; and Clair's simply for not knowing. It was a reminder that there was still a lot to learn about him in the here and now—and that this Jesse could still surprise her.

"Well, we're all fucked now, Stainer boy," said Zep, reaching forward to clap him on the shoulder, "and we're your bitches. Karma paid off for you big-time, I'd say."

Jesse looked embarrassed, then grinned, and Clair felt a wave of gratitude for both of them. She might have the most complicated love life of anyone, anywhere, but her taste in boys wasn't so bad.

A cry went up—"Drones!"—and gunfire chattered angrily in the trees.

"Mom says *hang on*," said Cashile. "We're going right now."

[20]

THE ELECTRIC ENGINE of Theo's vehicle hit a higher pitch and its wheels spun on the gravel. Clair fell back into her seat, clutching Jesse's hand. Past Theo and Cashile she could see a cloud of billowing dust into which electro-bikes and four-wheeled vehicles were steadily vanishing. There was no road that way, just the closed gate. Clair gritted her teeth and tried not to worry about drones, thinking about Ray as hard as she could instead.

Ray in the Manteca safe house, where she had also met Aunt Arabelle.

Ray in their camouflaged ride, when she had first heard the word "dupe."

The world twisted around her and the cab filled with dust, Clair closed her eyes and coughed, and wondered how Theo was possibly steering in the right direction. They bounced, they shook, they turned in what felt like a complete circle.

Twist.

They hit the ground and roared forward.

The air cleared. Through the windows Clair could see fields of golden wheat stretching to distant, snow-capped mountains. It didn't look like Australia. Vehicles careened around them, barely missing each other. They quickly straightened up and formed another line, with greater distances between vehicles this time, and raced in a convoy for the door of a falling-down barn. The world twisted again.

"Nothing can stop me, unless I want to be stopped."

The glitch hit her out of nowhere, Nobody's words lingering like an unwelcome smell. He was thinking about her, she realized. *Don't think about him in return,* she warned herself. The last thing she wanted was to drag them to wherever he was, through the uncanny tangle of the rip.

Clair closed her eyes tight and concentrated.

Ray in the Skylifter, listening to Turner Goldsmith's sermon.

Ray in the Farmhouse singing a folk song with Arcady, his baritone a quarter tone flat.

Twist.

They were skidding headlong down a steep mountain-side, whipped by branches. Cashile screamed. A jagged rock sideswiped them, throwing Clair bodily into Jesse, making him curse. A bottomless drop appeared ahead of them, framed by two dolmen-like spars. Clair sucked in a breath, dreading the weightlessness and the awful impact that would surely follow.

"You're a tough girl to get hold of."

That was Kingdon, another dangerous lure.

"Don't stop!" she managed to gasp out.

Ray on the train, smirking as she and Jesse returned from a private moment, the first time they had ever kissed.

Ray crammed in with all the others on the submarine, heading to New York.

The car ahead of them passed between the dolmens and vanished.

Twist.

They were speeding across a smooth, white surface that looked like nothing so much as ice. For an instant Clair feared that they would break through and drown in the water below—but then she saw the parallel tire tracks of those ahead of them, the blueness of the sky, and the fiery whiteness of the sun. Heat blasted at her from the windows. Summer heat in November.

They were in the Southern Hemisphere, driving across the smooth, white, perfectly flat expanse of a salt lake.

"You're making my choices for me, Clair."

Wallace, this time. She gritted her teeth. Would they never leave her alone?

Ray's arm spraying blood on the day another version of her had died.

Ray in the Yard, with her and everyone else.

She was running out of memories. For a moment she panicked—needlessly, because of course she could simply repeat any memory at will. Once she realized that, she concentrated on the one that was most vivid in her mind—Ray guarding the door in Manteca. He had been trying to keep her in the safe house, and she, fearing that he was one of the bad guys, had done everything she could to get away, including practically running into the arms of a dupe waiting for her at home. If Q hadn't helped her, she would be dead now, and so would Libby.

But maybe, a treacherous voice whispered to her, just maybe, if she hadn't gotten in the way of Wallace's plans, everyone else would still be alive.

Two bleached-white trees raced toward them with dead branches meeting high above the salt pan.

Twist.

Wherever they were this time, it was dark and silent. The only lights were those Theo quickly flipped on at the front of the vehicle. They picked out nothing through the gloom. If there was anything to see, it was too far away.

Ahead, two red dots flashed: the taillights of the vehicle in front of them. The moment Clair saw them, they winked out, heading off on the next stage of their journey, she hoped.

The loss of that faint glimmer made her feel very alone, even surrounded by her friends. There had always been someone to help her or agree with her, or at least willing to listen to her and talk her out of her worst mistakes—and she *had* made mistakes, more than once. Maybe she had just been unlucky. After all, there was always going to be some girl or boy whose path Improvement crossed, who decided to protect their best friend and found themselves sucked along a course that, looking back on it, seemed inevitable from the very first step. The chain of events might not have played out exactly the same way as hers, but the end was inevitable: Wallace's hold on the situation would have been threatened, and his unstable-matter bomb would have gone off. The world had been hanging under the threat of destruction for years without knowing it. One way or another, *someone* would have ended up inside the Yard, fighting over what remained.

It could have been anyone. But it had been her. How was she ever supposed to make amends?

"I love you, dearest child of mine. Please be safe."

Clair gasped with surprise. That was her mother's voice. Of course: she was in the Yard and thinking of Clair too. The simulation didn't contain only villains and people who wanted to kill her. There were people who loved her as well. *That* was how she would survive. With the help of the people who didn't need her to make amends or atone for anything, who loved her for who she was, and nothing more.

Restored, she dredged up a final memory of Ray and brought it as vividly and powerfully to life in her mind as she could.

Ray looking puzzled as she ran away from the only people in the world willing, at that moment, to help her.

Twist.

Light flared again and Clair raised an arm to cover her eyes. Echoes assaulted her—engines and urgent voices calling from all sides. Theo slammed on the brakes, throwing Clair forward against her seat belt. Tash cried out in surprise. Rubber shrieked as the wheels locked and they screeched to a halt, just yards from a yellow compressed-earth wall dotted with bright, utilitarian lights, strung out in a line. The sudden stop threw them back into the seats, and Tash cried out again.

Someone appeared at Theo's window, knocking against the glass to get her attention and then pointing urgently to one side. Theo turned the wheels and accelerated out of the way just as space twisted behind them and the next vehicle appeared. It immediately braked hard, as theirs had.

Their car rocked to a halt.

"That's it?" asked Ronnie. "We made it?"

Theo nodded, and a bump from Q confirmed that she had successfully tracked them through the rips and glitches to the prison.

Zep said in a shaky voice, "Come back, d-mat. All is forgiven."

[21]

THE CEILINGS OF Kupa-piti ultramaximum-security penitentiary were low and made of stone. Powered like the Yard by geothermal energy, the prison was completely isolated from the outside world, apart from cables leading to and from d-mat booths. The administrative section was on the upper level of the underground complex, a dozen yards of solid stone from the prisoners' cells—each a self-contained "control unit" that kept the absolute worst offenders on Earth isolated twenty-four hours a day. Food, air, and water were delivered via fabbers; the doors to the cells were literally welded shut and opened only in the case of medical emergency. Offenders had one-way access to the Air and were excluded from any kind of consensus—treated as non-people, effectively.

Clair had read that 100 percent of ultramax prisoners chose euthanasia over life imprisonment. It might take them years, but they always got there. The longest-serving prisoner died after seventeen years in his cell, never once stepping outside, never once seeing another human's face except through his lenses, never once exchanging more than a few words at a time with his guards. At the end, the story went, he simply stopped eating and drinking, never once expressing remorse for his crimes.

Now Clair was inside the same prison that had held him—and more deadly criminals than she cared to imagine—for so long. If even one of them remained and managed to get out . . .

She shivered from more than just the cold.

WHOLE's convoy had arrived in an empty chamber that had once held the construction equipment responsible for digging out the complex. The staging area was dusty and sterile, yet still well lit and closely watched, as no doubt every space was within the prison walls, thanks to beady, black-eyed cameras everywhere. Q sent a businesslike bump assuring Clair that she was interrupting the camera feeds and keeping a close eye on incoming transmissions. Nothing but clock data was descending from the distant, unseen surface.

A pair of large doors rolled back at the input of a very long password, leading into the prison itself. Ray and Lalie, now unhooded, guided everyone through.

"Home sweet home," said Libby, looking around.

"Could use some color," said Tash.

"Maybe a potted plant or two."

"At least there's no Muzak," said Zep. "That would be cruel and unusual."

The administration center comprised a series of offices radiating outward along six arms from a large central area. The color scheme was mainly light browns and grays, but there were personal effects at several workstations, tiny, brightly colored tokens of the people who had once worked in the prison—a handmade coffee mug, several crystals, a football jersey draped over the back of a chair. The people themselves were gone, but otherwise the prison was exactly as it had been when the world ended.

A patch appeared in her lenses, an interface allowing Clair access to the prison's surveillance and control systems. She searched for the d-mat booths, and found them down the southernmost arm of the center on the other side of a locked door.

The interface opened the door. Clair stood staring at the dozen booths, efficient, angular machines with none of the beige blandness of the room containing them.

"These particular killing machines," said Dylan Linwood from behind her, "are *particularly* good at killing. Every prisoner's DNA is hardwired into the code. If they try to escape this way, their patterns are automatically erased. Try to bring in another booth, even if you're the warden, and you'll be erased with it. Same with any kind of weapon or poison or chemical more corrosive than toothpaste. Clothes are automatically removed in transit and replaced with templates guaranteed to degrade within eighteen hours. In the case of an emergency, this entire room is a booth that will erase everything inside it and then self-destruct. The person who designed this place knew where its weak spot was."

Clair was watching him. He sounded almost admiring of that unknown engineer, which wasn't so strange, she supposed, since he was something of an engineer himself.

"How do you know so much about it?"

"This is where terrorists come to die," he said. "The ones who get caught."

His eyes were almost the same color now, but in his bright gaze Clair saw a bloody history stretching back to the first booths and the people who had protested their existence, not just with words but with actions, too. She wondered how many people he had known personally who had died for the cause.

"We've got more in common than you think," he said.

So he had figured that part out: how Wallace's satellite and space station had been destroyed. Or Kari had told him. Clair's death in the first explosion was supposed to end the dying. Instead, thanks to the crash and the unstable-matter trap, it had been among the first of many. Too many to think about.

"If you think I'm happy about that . . . ," she said to him.

Dylan shook his head. "No one sane would be."

He turned and began issuing orders to the people who had followed them up the passageway. "Sabotage the booths in here. All of them. But leave the room intact. Post guards and keep the door closed at all times, with charges laid. Anything emerges, blow up the lot."

People nodded and began to get to work.

Clair understood. Leave one booth open and the hollowmen would try to come in that way, if they were going to. If they didn't, then everyone was safe.

Maybe, she reminded herself. There were no certainties when it came to Wallace and his hired killers, especially not in a world of his making.

"Wallace belongs here, not us," she said.

"I'm not arguing," said Dylan.

"Afterward, when all this is over, there has to be a trial. Held in public, with as many honest lawmakers as we can find. We have to make him pay for his crimes."

"Don't worry, he will."

"I have some thoughts on how to go about finding him," she said. "We could get started right now."

Dylan turned to her. "First, I want you to take a search party down to the lower levels. They're supposed to be empty, but it pays to check."

"Why me?"

"Access is by a closed-circuit d-mat loop that we'll shut down as soon as you're done."

"You don't think it's safe? Is that it?"

"I'm sure it is safe," he said, stooping to inspect the seal between the floor and the booth. "I just don't want to ask any of my people to use it."

That she could understand, given WHOLE's longstanding antipathy to d-mat—even here, as Arabelle said, where everything was already a simulation. But if Dylan was right and the prison was completely isolated from the surface, there was no way Wallace could interfere with them.

"All right," she said. "But then we make plans."

"Of course. One thing at a time."

Swallowing her frustration that once again the hunt for the exit had been delayed, Clair went back to the others and asked if anyone wanted to join her.

"Turn down the chance to tour the most badass prison ever made?" said Tash. "Not on your life."

"Yeah," said Zep. "Count me in."

"And me," said Ronnie.

"I'll stay and help out up here," said Jesse.

"Me too," said Kari.

Clair One said, "I'll make sure Dylan doesn't turn off the loop until you return, while you look for a back door. If you find one, make sure it's locked."

"Will do." Clair couldn't deny that it would be nice to spend time with her friends without her other self getting in the way. The thought of Dylan locking her in the lower levels was a perturbing one, though. That hadn't even crossed her mind. Two Clairs were better than one, it seemed.

"I'll stay too," said Libby, flipping back her blond hair. "Bring me back a souvenir."

[22]

THE SUMMIT OF the closed-circuit loop consisted of a single-occupant booth and a swathe of security checks that Q patiently unraveled. With a sound not unlike the crackling of popcorn, the loop delivered them safely to level Z, where the air was still and tomblike. The booth opened into a central area that opened outward in six directions, just like the admin level except the corridors were shorter. Each contained two cells that could be sealed behind its own door. Two of the twelve cells were open. When Ronnie arrived, Clair and her friends went to investigate.

It was depressing. The cells where the world's worst mass murderers and torturers had been imprisoned were made of molded plastic with no edges or protrusions. There was a sleeping nook containing a single slab of foam, a toilet that was little more than a mirror-finished bowl with a lid that sealed shut to create a recycler, and a fabber barely large enough for a closed fist. When Zep tested the menu, he found a limited selection of food and drink, and nothing, of course, for "pistol," "knife," or "flamethrower."

"Only one flavor of taco?" he said. "For the rest of your natural life?"

"Serves them right," said Tash, peering up at the cameras in every corner. There were no scratched graffiti on the walls, no names or numbers on the closed doors, no discarded clothes or meals. The only light came from point sources buried safely within transparent plastic. Clair had no doubt that the walls were thick enough to keep prisoners from communicating with one another. "It must've been horrible, being trapped in here."

"I'm with Tash," said Ronnie with a shrug. "No one got in here by mistake."

Clair hoped not. Some might say that she was responsible for the death of billions. Would she end up in a cell like this one day, next door to Ant Wallace?

Zep wandered across the hall to the sealed cell. He thumped on the door twice with the palm of his hand, provoking a dead, muffled sound.

"Anyone in there?"

"It's empty, you big lunk," said Ronnie.

Clair took a quick glance at the inside using the prison interface, to make sure. With the door shut, the space seemed even more cramped and depressing. The prisoner who had lived here was a man called Laughland Rhodesia Lane, convicted of multiple sexual assaults on minors and more than a dozen murders. A quick glance at his offenses made Clair feel physically ill.

He was gone now, she told herself. From *this* world, at least . . .

"Let's try level Y," Ronnie said.

"Why?" asked Tash.

"Yes, Y," said Zep.

"Har har," said Ronnie.

Clair didn't join in. They should be looking for weak spots in the prison. Fooling around was just making it take longer. She was itching to get back to the top and take concrete steps toward escaping the Yard. If there were survivors on the outside, she bet they weren't cracking jokes.

She took a final tour through level Z while the others cycled through to the next level down. The other five corridors leading to the cells revealed no air vents, no hatches, no hidden doors. She checked the floors and ceilings too, in case there were access ways that weren't obvious on the maps, and found nothing. Bad for prisoners, good for everyone else.

Clair jumped to level Y and found it to be much the same, but with three cell doors open rather than two.

"It's creepy," said Tash. "The *Mary Celeste* of prisons."

"I keep expecting to turn a corner and find all the bad guys waiting to jump out at us," said Ronnie.

"Never fear, Ronette," said Zep. "I'm here to protect you."

"What are you going to do? Hit on them?"

Zep feigned a blow to the heart.

"I'll go first this time," said Clair when they had exhausted the attractions of level Y. There were seventeen levels in total. At this rate it would take them all day to get to level J.

Level X had been full to capacity. Clair checked the cells through the interface anyway, just in case the hollowmen found a way to hack the fabbers as they had on the seastead. She saw nothing suspicious, and when the others followed her she jumped ahead again, to level W, where six empty cells gaped at her, as impersonal as the rest. The terrible blankness in each one made Clair wonder just how different it would have been even when the prison was full.

Footsteps sounded from level W's hub.

"I'm in here," Clair called from the sixth empty cell, turning to see who had followed her down.

No one appeared.

"Hello?"

She looked out of the cell.

The booth was still active. There was no one on that level but her.

She held her breath, trying not to think of Laughland Rhodesia Lane's ghost prowling the prison. The cells no longer seemed so empty to her.

Calling up the interface, she quickly checked through

the rest of the cells on level W, open or closed. They were all empty.

Imagining things, she told herself, or, more likely, glitching again, but she kept her hand on the pistol in her pocket, just in case.

The booth hissed open. Ronnie emerged, laughing at something one of the others had said. When she saw Clair, her expression clouded.

"You okay?"

"I think so," Clair said. "This place is just freaking me out a little."

"Good to see something gets through the armor." Ronnie pushed her glasses up and looked around. "Maybe we should go back. I'm not convinced there's a need for this apart from keeping us busy."

That was a good point. Clair could see Dylan wanting to get rid of her while WHOLE started work on his next autocratic "solution." She didn't want him doing anything without her, because her future was at stake too.

They hadn't even started talking about what use an exit would be if there was nothing to connect to on the outside—or whether Dylan would be willing to work with other groups like RADICAL, if they could be found—but already the question of what her life might be like when all this was over weighed heavily on her, with or without Jesse, with or without d-mat, in prison or free. . . .

"Clair?"

The cry came from behind them. They spun around to look at the booth. It was closed, processing Tash. The voice hadn't come from there. It had issued from one of the six corridors that led off from the central hub.

"You heard that too?" said Clair.

Ronnie nodded. "Sounds like a glitch. I thought they'd stopped."

"Clair," came the voice again, "can you hear me?"

Clair slid the pistol out of her pocket, not reassured by the fact that she recognized the voice. She could indeed hear him. That was the problem.

Devin Bartelme was dead. She had watched him die on the outside of the Yard. And yet here he was, talking to her now, not a recycled memory like the other glitches. All those other memories were significant, plucked from her mind because she remembered them well. This was too trivial to mean anything, except for one thing.

There was a ghost in the prison, and it was him.

————————————————— [23]

"I'M GLITCHING AGAIN," she bumped to Jesse, Kari, and Q.

Kari said, "What are you experiencing?"

Clair told her. "But I don't remember Devin ever saying that to me. Could it be something new?"

"It can't be. He's dead."

"I know. What if he's alive in here and trying to talk to me?"

"We've seen no sign that anyone from RADICAL made it into the Yard. Maybe it's a crossed wire, or something new. Keep me up to date. I'm in the middle of something—but this is important too."

Clair was glad to hear it. She wasn't so sure it was just a case of mixed-up memories. If Wallace was messing with them by means of the glitches, they might not be safe anywhere.

Neither Q nor Jesse responded as Clair peered up the corridor, newly arrived Tash and Ronnie falling in behind her. The hall was empty. One of the cell doors was open, and she approached it warily, keeping the pistol between her and anyone who might appear before her.

The cell was empty too. No Devin, no Laughland Rhodesia Lane, nothing but echoes.

"Let's go back," said Tash. "I don't like this."

"We can't," said Clair, although she didn't like it either. "This is exactly what we're looking for. If the source of the glitches isn't here, it might be on the next level down."

"What might be on the next level down?" said Zep from behind them.

Clair almost shot him. She lowered the gun with shaking hands and shook her head.

"I think I should keep going alone," she said.

"Uh-uh," said Tash. "That's not happening."

"It's too slow like this," Clair said.

"So we split up," Tash said. "Go in pairs. You and me on odds, Ronnie and Zep on evens."

"What counts as an odd letter?" asked Zep.

"You know what she means," said Ronnie. "We'll take V, these guys can take U. We'll leapfrog from there down. Last one to the bottom is a rotten egg."

Clair looked around level W. Devin's voice hadn't returned.

"All right," she said. "We'll go first."

Tash and Clair went back to the booth, where Clair insisted on going first. There was nothing untoward waiting for her, and when Tash arrived they thoroughly searched level U and found nothing elsewhere on that level. No one spoke to them. Nothing moved. Tash wanted to chat; Clair could sense her need to pretend that everything was normal as though it was a physical thing, a cloying cobwebby cloud hanging between them. Eventually, Clair simply took her hand, and that went some way to reassuring her. Reassuring both of them, if Clair was honest with herself.

"We ought to be at school," Tash said, peering into the second-to-last cell. "I can't help wondering if anyone is there, if there's anyone left."

Clair had had thoughts like that. "Don't get stuck on that," she said. "We can't do anything about it right now."

"I know, but . . ." Tash took back her hand to put her blue

hair behind her ears. "What happens *after*? How many people will there be? How long will it take to rebuild? Who's going to be in charge? What'll happen to *us*?"

Tash looked to Clair as though for answers. But she didn't have any, not yet. She assumed the Consensus Court would resume and they would make everything they needed using fabbers, but beyond that she didn't want to speculate. There were so many steps between now and then that if she tried to map them out she might freeze.

"I think this level is clear," Clair said.

She felt her friend studying her, appraising her with keen sapphire eyes. Tash wasn't freaking out. She just wanted to *know*, and she wasn't going to give up that easily.

All Clair had were hopes, based on memories that now seemed very faint.

"I guess we'll go back to school," she said as a kind of concession. "Some kind of normal."

"But no more crashlander balls," said Tash. "Not for you. Perhaps not for anyone, if you have your way and d-mat is banned."

"Why would it be banned?" Clair hastened to reassure her friend on that score. "Being an Abstainer doesn't mean forcing everyone else to give it up. That's what I think, anyway. And if you hold the balls somewhere I can get to, I'll still come." She lightly punched Tash on her bony shoulder. "Promise you'll let me."

Tash nodded, but if she was truly satisfied it didn't show on her face.

"S," she said.

"Yes what?"

"Level S is next."

"Oh yeah." Clair tried to hide her relief. Ronnie wanted to rebuke her; Tash wanted reassurance. What would Zep want from her? He was next on the list. "I'll go on ahead—"

"No, it's my turn. I'm sure you're just glitching, so it doesn't matter who goes when."

Clair couldn't argue with that, although it was a worry that whatever Q had done to fix the Yard was now unraveling. "All right. I'll be right behind you."

Tash went into the booth and the door closed.

The silence of level U wrapped around her like an invisible shroud, threatening to smother her. Not wanting to bother Kari again, Clair bumped Q, but received no response. That left only Jesse. She searched for him via the prison interface and found him on the admin level, in a large room that looked like a mess for the guards. There was a fabber, a dozen or more tables, and a scattering of plastic chairs. Jesse was sitting at one of the tables, talking to someone sitting opposite him. Someone with frizzy brown hair.

Herself.

Clair hunted for another angle so she could see both their faces. She hadn't been planning to eavesdrop, but audio was available and she didn't see the harm in listening in. Not at first.

"Is that what you think she should have done?" Jesse was saying. "Given up and let Wallace get away with it?"

"Of course not. Wallace is obviously a psycho and has to be stopped, but that doesn't make her infallible, or me stupid. I have questions. It's reasonable to ask them. If you try, though, PK Sargent is all *You don't know what we're talking about*, like no one's allowed to criticize Clair Two because we weren't there. But I *was* there—or would have been, if she's telling the truth. And I'm telling you, I would never have done those things. Not in a million years."

"I don't think you're stupid . . . ," Jesse started to say.

"I know, but that's how she makes me feel, ordering us around and only explaining when she feels like it.

"Clair Two," said Clair One, "is such a bitch."

Clair knew she should look away, but it was far too late for that.

"Why are you telling me this?" Jesse asked.

"Because I know you're not going to blow me off." Clair One leaned over the table and lowered her voice. "Doesn't it seem weird to you, how she appears out of nowhere and then suddenly we have to move? It worries me that you and I were perfectly safe before she showed up, but now we're in a prison miles underground, all in one handy basket. Wallace just has to shut the doors and turn the air off and we're done. Doesn't that seem a little too neat for you?"

"I don't know," said Jesse. "But I don't think she's lying to us."

"Are you sure? Do you know her that well?"

"I think I do. The other me did. I don't know." He looked confused. "I know both of you."

"Then you know she's changed," Clair One said. "She's not me anymore. She's someone else. And who knows what side she's on? It's not necessarily ours. That's all I'm saying. We need to watch her, you and me. We need to be ready, just in case."

Clair One reached across the table and took Jesse's hand.

Clair watched in horror. What was Clair One doing? Had she been turned somehow? Was she a dupe, planning to betray everyone after she'd finished betraying herself?

But then Clair realized again that from Clair One's point of view it did make a kind of dark sense. She, "Clair Two," was the source of the glitches, and from the outside perhaps it could seem as though that made her a likely suspect for treachery.

Clair One wasn't being malicious; she genuinely thought she was doing the right thing. She simply had it backward.

A surge of frustrated fury rose up in Clair unlike anything she had ever felt before. After everything she had done and all the losses she had endured, this was how Clair One repaid her.

It wasn't helped by the knowledge that *this* was why Clair One had volunteered to stay behind—to turn Jesse against her while Clair was busy. Maybe Libby, too. Libby might already have been turned, and all her friends would follow like ducks in a row, while she was stuck down in the dungeons of the prison.

She wanted to vent her rage into the empty level, but her throat was closed tight as though a fist were clenched around it. She couldn't even make her eyes move to spell out the words.

"Are you with me?" Clair One asked Jesse.

"I think you're wrong," Jesse said, pulling his hand away. "She's not lying. I'd know it."

"Okay, then. Say you're right. Clair Two doesn't have to be lying to lead the hollowmen right to us. She could be carrying a tracker of some kind—or not even that. Just by existing she's warping the Yard, making us stand out. Doesn't that make her dangerous? Aren't we better off without her?"

"We're not kicking her out on her own," Jesse said. Clair told herself to be glad for that, but she could hear the uncertainty in his voice. If Clair were Jesse, she would have been remembering her attempts to be close to him, to appeal to his emotions and perhaps cloud his judgment. He would wonder. It was only natural. *Clair One was making sense.*

"Okay," Clair One said. "But keep your eyes open. And be careful. If something does go down, and you're with her, you'll be right in the line of fire."

"I can handle myself."

"I mean it, Jesse. We only have one shot at saving the world. She's had hers, and look what happened. It's lucky anyone survived."

Clair felt her cheeks growing hot as her fury turned to remorse and shame. Unable to bear any more, she stopped watching, stepped into the booth, and jumped to level S.

———————————————————————— [24]

TASH WAS STANDING outside, dancing from one foot to the other.

"*S* for 'spooky,'" she said. "I don't like this level."

Clair forced herself to concentrate on what was happening right in front of her, not eight levels above. All the cells were open, and that made the echoes of their movements more unsettling. It sounded like there were four of them or more, moving about the level in all directions. Clair kept glancing over her shoulder, expecting to see someone there, but there was never anything or anyone. Just a feeling that something was getting closer. That someone was looking for her.

"It's empty here," Tash eventually said. "I'm positive."

"Good. Let's just move on to level Q. The sooner it's done, the sooner we can do something *real*." She heard the bleakness in her voice and wished she felt otherwise. *Listen to yourself,* she thought. *Saving the world would be so much easier if everyone didn't keep getting in the way? That's the kind of thing Kingdon would say.* "Do you want to go first?"

"I think we should go together. The booth was designed for big, beefy guards. I bet we can both fit in."

It was true, but only barely. Clair was reminded of squeezing into the flooded booth in Crystal City.

As they waited for the machines to work, Clair asked, "Do you think I'm a bad person?"

Tash shifted awkwardly, but in the cramped confines of the booth there was no escaping the question.

"I think you're Clair Hill," she said, "and I don't think Clair Hill's a bad person, so why would I think *you're* a bad person?"

"You don't think I've changed?"

"Not that much." The look Tash gave her was almost painfully shrewd from this close up. "It's bizarre. You're both asking the same questions. It makes me wonder how well you knew yourself in the first place."

It was Clair's turn to feel uncomfortable.

The door hissed open, and there was Devin right in front of her, a small figure with wispy red hair dressed in a black Nehru-collared suit with one hand upheld, as though telling her to stop.

"Cunctando," he said. His voice was faint, as though coming to her from a great distance. *"Cunctando regitur mundus!"*

Then another person pushed *through* him—a woman no taller than Clair, with Asian features and thick black hair. Her expression was glowering, full of wrath.

"Do it, Clair! Do it!" said Mallory Wei.

Tash screamed. Clair fired once, twice, the gun instantly in her hand. Bullets slammed into the far wall of level Q, throwing sparks but hurting no one. Both visions, both glitches were gone, and Clair and Tash were alone, ears ringing from the sound flung back at them in the enclosed space, Clair breathing fast through her open mouth and Tash hanging on to her.

"Who were they?" Tash gasped.

"Data ghosts," Clair said shakily.

"Yes, but *who*?"

Clair didn't answer immediately. First she sent Kari, Q, and Jesse a message saying that she had seen first Devin and then Mallory—Ant Wallace's wife, who had murdered Libby along with the many other young women whose bodies she had briefly occupied.

"Clair?" Tash said.

"They're people who won't stay dead."

They stepped out of the booth and it immediately closed behind them, processing another person. All of Clair's senses were tingling. She felt as though eyes were watching her from all directions—and that was true in the sense that she had the prison's attention now. Dylan Linwood was watching, and so was his son. Jesse bumped her, but she didn't reply, telling herself she needed to concentrate, but really she just didn't know what to say to him.

Q was the person she really needed to hear from, but when she bumped again all she received was a single phrase in a loop.

"The one and only. The one and only. The one and only. The one and only."

"Q, are you all right?"

The loop continued unchecked, which just made Clair more anxious. She didn't know what that meant. There was no way to know until Q said something else.

Jumping at the slightest shadow, Clair and Tash searched the empty level, then returned to the booth as it was opening.

Kari Sargent stepped out with her best peacekeeper face on.

"This is stopping now," she said firmly. "I want you back where we can keep a proper eye on you."

Clair didn't argue. She was relieved to be leaving the cells behind. It was hard not to think, *Home sweet future home,* and wonder if that was what Dylan Linwood had in mind.

"What about the rest of the levels?"

"I'll finish up down here," Kari said. "Whatever's going on, I'm not taking any chances with you. It seems to be getting worse the more jumps you take."

"The loop is supposed to be a closed circuit," said Clair. "I thought that meant unhackable."

"But *the Yard* knows. We should definitely lay off even this kind of d-mat once we've finished searching."

"Fine with me," said Tash. "I'm beginning to wonder if the Stainers were onto something."

"Puh-lease," bumped Ronnie from the level below. "Don't you start."

Tash shot Clair a quick smile and then went into the booth, heading back to the administration center.

"What did Devin tell you?" Kari asked as they waited for the booth to cycle.

"Something I didn't understand. It sounded Latin, or maybe Spanish." She didn't want to say that it had sounded like a spell from a kids' fantasy book.

She played the sound bite containing the phrase.

"Cunctando regitur mundus," said Dylan Linwood. "It means, 'Be patient and you'll conquer the world.'"

"Why would his data ghost tell me that?" Clair asked. "He never did in real life, so I shouldn't be hearing it now. That's not the way the glitches work."

"It might have been a distraction," Kari said, "something intended to confuse us."

"Do you think Mallory was a fake too?"

"I don't know," said Kari, "but we're not taking any chances. These data ghosts are embedded in the Yard. They're not artifacts of our lenses. Someone or something is interacting with the simulation—maybe deliberately."

The booth opened. Inside the reflections moved as though the mirrors were warping back and forth, too subtly for the eye to follow.

"Go on," said Kari when she hesitated. "You'll be fine up top, and I'll be back before you know it."

Clair was happy to abandon the search, but she dreaded facing Jesse and anyone else Clair One had managed to convert to her way of thinking. There wasn't time for petty squabbling. They had an entire world to scour in search of the exit, and an unknown number of hollowmen would be resisting them at every step. That was before they even *started* thinking about finding a booth on the outside. It was going to be hard enough to undo the damage Wallace had done without fighting herself at the same time.

[25]

ON THE OTHER end of the short jump, Clair used the interface to look for Libby and found her in the admin hub. Clair One was on the far side of the level, alone. Clair decided to stay well away.

When she arrived in the hub, she was greeted by a host of new faces. Members of WHOLE, she presumed, freshly arrived in the prison. She didn't know any of them, although some of them did look faintly familiar. They were about her age too.

When she caught sight of a willowy blond teenager, a shock of recognition went through her.

The last time she had seen Xia Somerset, the old woman who had taken over Tilly Kozlova's body had been full of remorse and a desperate hope that she could undo the damage done by stealing a new life from an innocent person. Then PK Drader had led her off and killed her. Seeing her now reawakened the guilt Clair had felt at the time—and a new anxiety. Depending on when Xia's copy had been taken, she might not yet have had her change of heart and could be a potential traitor in their midst.

Clair forced her way through the crowd to find out what she knew.

"So they found you, too, Xia. How much do you remember?"

"Nothing at all," she said brightly. "You must be Clair Two. I'm Tilly Kozlova—the *real* Tilly Kozlova, warts and all, pre-Improvement—so don't ask me to play a piano concerto for you. I'm more of a ukulele girl."

Clair performed an awkward double take. Of course. It wasn't just Libby and the dupes who had been returned to their original selves. Every person who had ever used

Improvement was now back the way they were supposed to be.

It was disorienting to stare at her former idol and know that the young woman looking back at her was someone she had never met before.

"I'm really glad you're here," Clair said, feeling unexpectedly moved by this victory. She hadn't seen it coming, and it caught her at a vulnerable moment. Not everything she had done had been a disaster.

"Who did this?" she asked. "Who brought you here?"

"Me, of course!" said Libby, coming up beside them and beaming proudly. "Surprised? That's why I wanted to stay behind. Much more fun chasing down people like me than looking for murderers—with the combined skills of Ray and Sarge, of course, king and queen of the rippers and peekers. Credit where credit's due."

"This is amazing." Clair found herself at the center of a growing cluster of people, all staring at her and whispering.

"That's Madison Chu over there—you know, the math guy?" Libby said. A tall, skinny young man with glasses grinned at her. "And Elisha Neimke, the Go player." Another guy, part Indian, with crooked eyes. "That's who they *were*, anyway," Libby explained. "Now they're themselves, and finding it all a bit confusing too."

The Indian guy reminded Clair of Gemma, the woman who had betrayed WHOLE in exchange for her son's return. Could this be the missing Sameer?

Before she could ask, a girl with long brown hair pressed in close to Clair.

"Libby says you used Improvement, just like us."

"Yes," Clair said, "but . . . for different reasons."

"So you didn't ask for anything to be changed?"

"I had to."

"Which bit?" asked another girl.

"My nose."

"Mine was my hair—so boring and greasy! Everyone else likes it but me, which is what makes it so annoying."

Clair was both charmed and comforted. A support group for the Improved! It had an almost festive feel, perhaps fueled by Libby's easy sense of accomplishment. Clair had always known that Libby would be better at saving the world than she was.

"We call ourselves the Unimprovables," said Libby. "Like it?"

"*Like* it?" Clair laughed and turned in a circle, taking in the crowd around her and finishing by sweeping Libby up in a sudden, impulsive hug. It was good to have the focus on rescuing people rather than fighting people, for a change. It wasn't all about Wallace or Kingdon or Nobody. Or even her other self. The goal was to rebuild and restore as well, not just to retaliate.

"I love it," she said, understanding now why Clair One wasn't there. This wasn't for Clair One. It was for *her*.

"Cunctando!" shouted Devin in her ear, and Clair jerked away from Libby, startled.

The haunted sensation from the lower levels returned stronger than ever. Shadows were swirling in the corners of her eyes, thickening by the second, and there seemed to be more faces than there were people, as though the hub was filling up with ghosts. . . .

A deafening siren sounded, causing a commotion in the room. People began moving, either for exits or into a huddle in the center, buffeting Clair from side to side.

"What's going on?" asked Libby, looking irritated that something was stealing her thunder.

"That's the intrusion alarm," said Jesse, appearing at her left shoulder. "Someone's trying to get in."

Clair thought of her glimpse of Mallory in the lower levels. "Where? We have to cut them off—"

"Dad says you're to stay right here," he said. "It's my job to make sure you do that."

"Seriously?" said Tilly. "She looks like she could snap you in half."

He looked put-upon but ignored the remark. "It makes sense. If they're homing in on you, Clair, then we need you where we can see you."

She remembered Clair One whispering doubts into his ear.

"Did your father really say that?" she said bitterly. "I'd make a pretty good decoy if he kicked me out."

"That'll never happen." He gripped her elbow. "And not just because you're more use to us here. The way the glitches seem to follow you around, they're like early warnings."

"Early warnings of what? The hollowmen trying to get through?"

"*I am Nobody,*" said a voice in Clair's ear.

She jumped.

"Exactly," he said.

They all jumped as gunfire clattered outside the hub. Clair took out her pistol and squeezed the grip tightly. It was hard to tell from the prison interface what was going on. People were running everywhere, shouting and screaming at once. There was no clear focus, no single point of attack, which made her feel exposed. Were people firing at shadows, or was an attack coming from all sides? Either way, she had to find somewhere safer to stand than the middle of the room. If the hollowmen were in the prison, it was only a matter of time before they found her.

Taking Libby by the arm with her spare hand and nudging Jesse ahead of her, she guided them to a point along a wall midway between two doors. They could upend some tables, create a token barrier . . .

Three figures entered the room, closely followed by another: Ronnie, Zep, and Clair One, and then Kari Sargent, once more the sole peacekeeper in a room full of teenagers. Her tour of the prison's lower levels hadn't lasted long.

"Three hollowmen," said Clair One. "I was *right there*. One of them tried to shoot me."

Her eyes were wide and her cheeks flushed. Clair wondered if this was how *she* had looked the first time a dupe had attacked her at close range.

"Get in here," said Libby, pulling her close to Jesse, Clair, and the Unimprovables. There were fifteen of them, a gaggle that would be difficult to control if things got messy.

"The hub is cordoned off," Jesse said.

"Yetis everywhere," said Kari approvingly. "They almost shot *me*."

"And that's a good thing?" said Libby.

"It means no one can get in here," said Jesse.

"We live in a cruel world, Clair Hill, full of victims."

"But the hollowmen got into the prison somehow," said Clair, not particularly reassured, with Nobody and now Mallory whispering in her ear again. "How did they do that?"

"The same way we did, I guess," said Clair One. "They ripped."

"That means they know what it's like in here," Clair said. "How—?"

The world rippled. Two dark figures appeared in the

corner of Clair's eye, leaping into the room through space that had suddenly warped and twisted.

"Down!" Clair cried, throwing herself forward with her arms outstretched, taking as many people with her as she could.

Gunfire cracked, filling the room with noise. The lights went out. People screamed and dropped all around her. Clair disentangled herself from flailing limbs and assumed a crouching position, firing at the spots where she hoped the hollowmen still were, but knowing they surely must have moved by then. Beside her, Kari was doing the same, and then a third pistol boomed once, twice—Clair One, finally unlocking that skill.

Cursors danced across Clair's vision, her view occasionally obscured as people moved in front of her, confusing the pistol's infrared targeting system. She scuttled to her right, moving away from the main mass in order to get a clear shot even though she knew that would make her a better target. *Because* she knew that. If the hollowmen fired at her, they wouldn't be firing at Jesse or the Unimprovables.

She watched for muzzle flashes, trying desperately to see who was shooting who in order to avoid targeting someone she cared about. Sometimes she glimpsed faces in the flashes, but the visions were brief and possibly confused. Was that Devin in the corner of the room? Was that really Mallory, looming up before her?

Something fiery snatched at her right shoulder. Wood or plastic shrapnel from the table, she assumed. A near miss. Clair ignored the pain. Dropping and slithering across the floor, she tipped over the nearest table so the top was standing vertically in front of her. Not that it would stop a bullet, but it might interfere with the infrared of anyone shooting at her. She inched forward until she could see past it, then lay with her back to the wall and fired one-handed. Someone fired back, and in the muzzle flash she thought she saw her own face glaring, hair wild and furious, eyes white all the way around her pupils.

Something punched her in the solar plexus and pushed her into the wall. She kept firing as the smell of blood flooded her nostrils. The muzzle flashes grew faint. The last thing she saw was Clair One looming over her, shouting, before darkness rose up and engulfed them both.

[26]

"I DON'T THINK the transmission is getting through. Are you sure it's working?"

The voice was faint, as though rising up a very deep well, and it seemed to be her own. Or perhaps Clair One's. Before she could pursue that mystery, the dream within a dream slipped out of her grasp and her eyelids flickered open. What had happened?

She saw only darkness. She smelled gunfire and blood. People were crying and moaning all around her. The floor was hard against her back. Something blazed bright and terrible in her shoulder and chest when she tried and failed to sit up. Her hands were empty. She had dropped the gun.

"Clair?" Jesse was calling her. "Clair, where are you?"

"Over here," she gasped, distantly understanding that she had been shot, perhaps more than once. She must have blacked out for a moment. Not for long, though, because the lights were still out. The only thing that had changed was that the firing she could still hear was coming from far away, not right next to her.

Her voice was weak. She could hardly breathe. There was no fear yet, just a terrible irritation that she couldn't *do* anything.

Movement nearby. She tensed, wishing she still had the gun but not able to do more than pat helplessly for it with her right hand. She found the floor around her slick with blood—more blood than seemed feasible—then the table's edge and something soft.

A hand. Someone was lying next to her. She tugged on it. Its owner wasn't moving. Did it belong to someone she knew?

Her lenses flickered. She heard fragments of a conversation she didn't remember having, like Devin's voice before the attack. Or did she? Either way, it was Wallace's voice.

". . . not too late, Clair, to undo the damage you've done."

"I didn't do anything."

"You know what I mean. I'm offering you a second chance. You'd be a fool not to . . ."

"Clair, talk to me," Kari cried out of the darkness. "Are you all right?"

"I'm here!" she tried to call back, but the words emerged as little more than a bubbling wheeze. That frightened her more than anything else. What if they didn't find her in time? She could be bleeding out right now.

Light returned like a blow to her temple, momentarily blinding her.

"Over here," Jesse shouted. "Fuck. Oh fuck."

The first thing Clair saw when her sight returned was a woman's face. She was lying in front of Clair, head draped over one outstretched arm, like she was resting. It was her hand that Clair had touched in the dark. Clair had never seen her before. The woman's throat was a mess of blood.

Clair momentarily lost her breath. Had *she* killed her? Had this woman been trying to kill *her*?

Then Kari and Jesse were leaning over her, blocking the view.

"I'm all right," she tried to tell them, but her lips and jaw wouldn't obey her instructions. She felt heavy and full of hurt. Someone lifted her, and she grimaced, vision suddenly full of bright stars. Voices came from all sides, muffled and meaningless. She felt dizzy, and blacked out again.

———————————————————— [27]

"LET ME TRY. If I can refine the signal, we might just get in this time."

That sounded liked Devin again. Another dream, or another mysterious glitch? Could she be hallucinating? How injured *was* she?

Hope has flown, she thought. A line from a poem she couldn't quite place, although she knew she knew it well.

When she looked up, Kari and Jesse were exactly where they had been before, only now Kari's hands were bloody and she was doing something to Clair's upper body, something Clair was unable see and perhaps didn't want to.

"Clair? Clair, answer me!"

That was Q's voice.

Clair couldn't move her lips to reply, but that didn't mean her brain wasn't working.

"Q," she bumped. "You're back."

"Yes, I'm here, Clair," came the familiar voice, sounding relieved in her ears. The old Q, not the new. Younger, more vibrant, more *human*, somehow. "You're hurt."

There was something Clair wanted to ask her, but it had slipped her mind. "Shot."

"Yes, and you're being treated."

"No. You. Farm."

It was surprisingly hard to select the letters—normally she didn't even have to think about it—but this suddenly immense effort was giving her something to focus on apart from the color of her own blood and Kari's grim expression.

"Oh yes, that's right! I was shot in the Farmhouse, and it was awful, for a while. Then I was back in the Air and the pain went away."

"How. Did."

"The hollowmen know how to get in here?" Somehow Q understood what she was trying to tap out. "They followed the glitches caused by you and Clair One. I tried to cover your tracks, but then the glitches suddenly got a lot worse for some reason. It's ebbed a bit now, but there are still aftershocks. Hollowmen are still coming through. They're quick, Clair, and *mean*."

Clair had another theory. The best way into the prison was via someone who knew it personally. That was how WHOLE had gotten in, with Lalie. Wallace didn't have Lalie, so he must have found someone else. And who better than someone who was inside *right now*? Someone who could tell them exactly when to come, while everyone was distracted?

Q was still talking. Clair tried to interrupt but her lenses made only random shapes.

". . . WHOLE is fighting them off, don't worry. Wallace knows where you are now, but he also knows that getting to you isn't easy. He won't shut you up that easily. The hollowmen aren't infinite in number here, remember? We've seen no sign of PK Drader, so I think it's definitely safe to assume that dead is dead is dead forever. But you're not going to die, Clair," Q added hastily. "You're going to be just fine. Both of you."

"One," Clair managed to type out, because suddenly it was clear. WHOLE *did* have a spy in their midst, someone who had waited until everyone was in one spot, then brought the hollowmen right where they needed to be—and had even tried to pin the blame on her!

Clair One was a traitor.

"That's right. Clair One is safe with the others, somewhere isolated from the first ingress point."

"One," Clair typed again, wishing she could find the exclamation mark for emphasis. The fragment of conversation she had heard before—it must have been between Wallace and Clair One, not her. Clair One knew what the prison looked like now, and she had been quick to put the onus of proving who was who on Clair herself when they had met. Who was to say it wasn't Clair One who had shot Clair during the confusion of the attack?

"I don't know what you're trying to tell me, Clair."

Q's voice was apologetic and utterly unhelpful. How come Q could understand her before but not now, when it really mattered? Was Q glitching or was she? Or was she even more wounded than she thought?

Clair cracked her eyelids open, feeling as though she was rolling back the stones from a tomb. Kari was still bending over her, fingers working just out of sight. Someone said something about *still losing a lot of blood*, but what it felt like to Clair was that she was losing herself. Or *confusing* herself, somehow. Behind Kari was Jesse, and next to him was Devin, and next to him were Mallory and Nobody. On her left side was Clair One, and on the other side was Clair Two, and both were leaning over her, trying to say something. She could see their lips move, although she couldn't hear the words.

Wait. That couldn't be Clair Two on her right side. *She* was Clair Two.

Was this third Clair a glitch, vision, or reality? She couldn't afford to take the chance that it wasn't the latter.

"Dup—"

Three letters out of four was as far as she got because Kari was suddenly pushing down on her chest, hard. She felt as though her entire body was being gripped, twisted, and torn. Then the pain passed, and she fell back into empty space. The room tilted around her. She was being carried. The peacekeeper she trusted was on one side, the boy she loved on the other. Her best friend was leaning over the top of her, saying something about staying right where she was, damn it, but Clair couldn't hear it, and then she was gone again, riding a soft pillow into nowhere, leaving everything she so urgently needed to tell her friends unsaid, and everything she needed to do undone.

How was she going to save the world if she couldn't save herself?

Then without warning she was dreaming of someone somewhere else. And this time, she didn't wake up.

——————————[27 redux]

"OKAY, WE'VE MADE it," said Devin. "Your data is going into the Yard and it's connecting *somewhere*. Let's kill the feed and see what happens next."

Tomorrow is tomorrow
Today is today
Everything ends up yesterday
Anyway

Spring becomes summer
Summer becomes fall
Fall becomes winter
Evermore

Lyrics by Nana Healey © 2053

[I redux]————————————————

CLAIR AND Q stood at the double doors of the low, L-shaped building where Agnessa Adaksin hid her secret d-mat booth from the WHOLE muster in New Petersburg. A harsh, high-pitched sizzling sound came from outside. The chain reaction destroying the world was running rampant—unstable matter turning ordinary matter into more unstable matter, spreading destruction everywhere.

"Ready?" asked Q, her voice more grown-up than it had ever sounded before. Or was that Kari Sargent—the last peacekeeper left on the planet? Now that Clair knew Q was in Kari's body, she was unsure precisely who was talking.

Was she *ready*? Clair could only nod. Her throat was full of words she couldn't bring herself to say. Sob them, maybe; scream them, a very real possibility. But *say* them, as though they were nothing but ordinary words belonging to an ordinary moment? She didn't think so.

Good-bye, Jesse. Good-bye, Mom. Good-bye . . . me.

She was intensely glad for Q's strong hand resting in hers. Q wasn't forcing her to do this. They were doing it together, as they had to. They were responsible. The price needed to be paid, and it needed to be paid by them.

Clair reached out and opened the door, hearing the

crackling grow louder as she did so.

A gust of ash swept over her.

She closed her eyes and, with Q, stepped out to greet the blue dawn.

Clair expected death to be quick, that the ghastly radiation of Wallace's chain reaction would flash over her, violently unraveling her atoms, all the fundamental particles of her existence, and turn them into raw nothingness. But even as she walked through the door, she heard the hiss and spit of dying matter ebb. The blue light dimmed as though a switch had been pulled. She staggered on uneven ground and fell, pulling free from Q and falling up to her wrists in a drift of fine dust.

She made the mistake of breathing in, and coughed until she saw stars.

Q reached around her and tied something across her face.

"Breathe through this," said Q, her voice muffled. "I don't know what this stuff will do to your lungs."

Clair opened her eyes a crack and saw Q bending over her, face obscured by a strip of black cloth tied across her mouth. The sleeve of her undersuit, Clair guessed, because Q's armor was open across her chest, and her forearms were exposed right down to the skin.

"What happened?" Clair asked, but what she meant was *Why* didn't *it happen?*

They were still alive. It wasn't supposed to be that way.

"The second wave must have passed just before we came out," Q said, looking around her with a worried expression, blinking furiously to clear the dust from her eyes. The sky was gray above them. The whole world was gray. "It took out the cables we used to send ourselves into the Yard and everything else the first wave skipped over. But it missed us."

"Will there be a third wave?" She didn't know what to hope for. A moment ago she had been ready to die, as ready as she had been on Wallace's space station. Now she wasn't so sure. A guilty hope had replaced the dreadful certainty that had filled her just moments ago.

Bliss it was in that dawn to be alive. That was Wordsworth. Only it wasn't dawn, and it wasn't likely to be blissful, either.

Q shook her head. "There's obviously not enough unstable matter left to sustain the reaction. And if the front is moving too quickly for us to catch it, it's done."

"*We're* not, though."

"You tried," said Nelly, appearing in the doorway, a hulking shape even bigger than Sargent. She wore a surgical mask across her face. "Get up. Let's see what's left."

The muster was a postapocalyptic ruin, craters and collapsed buildings everywhere. A wind had come out of nowhere, making it hard to see, through tears or otherwise, and the air was surprisingly hot—something to do with the chain reaction, Clair assumed. What that meant for the long-term weather, Q didn't know. Would the world freeze under thick ashen clouds that kept summer at bay for years? Or would it heat up in a spiral like Venus? It would be terrible if the ash finished what the blue dawn had started.

If there were going to be survivors anywhere, the muster was it. She told herself to get used to being one of them. Clair 6.0: the one who got away, standing in the wrong place at the wrong time in order to live while billions didn't.

Another was Sandler Jones, the piebald redhead who had once tormented her, who they found whooping and dancing in the ruins, throwing ash over his head as though it were confetti. The knockout blow PK Forest had given him seemed forgotten as he frolicked around them, once even moving in to embrace her.

She fended him off.

"What are you doing?"

"Celebrating, of course," he said. "We've won! All the peekers and zombies are gone. Well, nearly," he said, acknowledging Clair and Q. "It's just us now. WHOLE has inherited the earth!"

It was Nelly's turn to cuff him around the head. "I don't feel like celebrating," she said. "Come with us now. People might be trapped and needing help. We have to find food, power, transport. What use is inheriting the world if we all starve to death?"

That sobered him, restoring his usual sour disposition.

"Should've thought of that when you burned everything

up, zombie girl," he said, poking Clair's shoulder.

Maybe she would have, if destroying the world had been her plan. She had been trying to save it, but everything had gone wrong. Everything she had attempted had turned to dust, along with Jesse.

She might have given up all hope of putting the world back the way it was, but for one remaining chance: the copy of her in the Yard. Was she alive and thinking, living inside a new version of the Air? Was she safe? Was Jesse in there with her?

If the answer to even one of those questions was *yes*, then she wouldn't give up.

Lightning flashed in the leaden sky.

"I have a suspicion that things are going to get a lot worse," said Nelly, "before they get any better."

"Shelter," said Clair, agreeing with her suggestion. They had to survive in order to be ready when word came from the Yard. "We need to find it and get people to it before the cold returns. Hunting them down individually could take hours."

"Little Teddy has a trumpet," said Sandler. "He could blow it. People would come."

"What dorm are you in?" Nelly asked.

"I'll take you."

The dorm was still standing and the trumpet was there, safely in its case under Little Teddy's bunk. Of Little Teddy himself, however, whoever he was, there was no sign. Clair assumed that he had secretly used d-mat, like

Agnessa. Doing so even once meant that he was most likely dead. Not everyone would be as lucky as she had been. If she could really call it *lucky*.

"We'll never fit everyone in here," said Sandler. The dorm was big enough for ten people. Outside, the wind was rising.

"There's the gymnasium," said Nelly. "It's not far. Grab as many blankets as you can carry. Sandler, you blow the horn, and keep blowing. Doesn't matter what it sounds like, as long as it's loud."

"What about Agnessa?" Clair asked as they set off, weighed down by supplies, Q almost invisible under a woolen mound like a walking mushroom. Her borrowed body was strong. Clair hoped Kari Sargent didn't mind being held captive inside her own head a little longer.

"Agnessa is dead," Nelly said. "I shut off her life support once it was clear we were going to lose power. Her battery backup was good for thirty minutes. Kinder this way."

And a kind of justice, Clair thought.

"That makes you boss," said Sandler, taking his lips momentarily off the trumpet.

"Keep blowing," Nelly told him. "I don't want to be the boss of a bunch of dead people."

The path was hard and uneven, and made treacherous by all the ash. Gray pooled in pitfalls and crevices, creating a constant risk of turned ankles or worse. They passed a crashed airship with gaping holes in its sides. Glimpsed in the distance through the ruins was a fire, burning steadily. It seemed for a while as though there was nothing and no one else left at all.

But slowly people joined them, drawn by the brassy call of the trumpet. They appeared out of ruined structures in twos or threes, bringing supplies and torches and, one of them, a primitive radio transceiver.

"I'm picking up a signal," the woman said. Her face was ashen except around her eyes, where she had rubbed at tears. It made her look startled.

"From the moon?" Nelly said. "If the chain reaction didn't spread that far, there will still be people in the colony."

"From the south pole, relayed by an old GPS satellite. Someone called Eve Bartelme."

"Who?"

Clair started. Devin and Trevin's surname was Bartelme. A relation? Perhaps another sibling?

"RADICAL," she said.

The woman with the radio nodded. "They want to know what we did."

"Let them believe what they want to believe," said Nelly. "We'll talk to them later."

"What if they attack us?" Clair said.

"No one's attacking anyone," Nelly said. "Not today."

The gym loomed out of the stormy night just as the first thick drops of rain began to fall. They were muddy and gray, full of dissolved ash, and stung the eyes. Clair was glad to get under shelter. They found another thirty people inside the boxy building, stained and spattered, harrowed expressions on their faces, making a total of seventy-one.

They were in shock. Even Abstainers had friends and loved ones who used d-mat. They had all lost people. And they wanted answers. Clair knew how they felt.

"We didn't do this," Nelly said shortly, pressing for calm. "It was a trap set by Ant Wallace. This is on him, not us."

That was the simple version of the story, Clair knew, the version that absolved her of any blame. Whether it stuck or not, she would know the larger truth, and she would always feel guilty, unless she found a way to fix it or to make amends. Preferably both.

Lightning flashed, bright through the gymnasium's windows. Thunder boomed. There was another flash, hard on the heels of the first, and then another. The wind shrieked.

"I suggest we try to sleep," bellowed Nelly over the noise. "There's nothing else we can do for now."

Q had dropped her load of blankets in the middle of the room. Keeping one large enough to cover herself, she said to Clair, "First, I want to try the radio."

Clair nodded and joined Q at the woman's side. She was in her fifties, with long gray hair and handsomely weathered skin, visible where she had wiped the ash away. She was wearing a knitted shawl that had once been brightly colored.

"This was my grandfather's," she said, reluctantly

handing the radio to the PK. "The batteries, too. You'll be careful with it, won't you?"

Q nodded, even as her strong hands twisted the casing, popping it open along a seam to expose the insides, wires and circuit boards and other incomprehensible things. Clair promised the woman that Q would put it back exactly as it was, hoping that was true.

"This is potentially the most precious machine on the planet," Q said as she rearranged the radio's innards in ways Clair didn't understand, using tools she produced from inside her armor. "It's certainly the most precious to us. Your grandfather would be proud. He lived through the Water Wars, did he?"

The woman nodded. "Fought in Texas. Was part of the Consensus Riots and died wishing he'd been on the other side. D-mat saved the world but killed everyone: Who can argue with that now?"

"It didn't kill everyone," Q said. "There's still us, and there's still hope. All we have to do is get through the next few days. Three meals from savagery, eh, Clair?"

This didn't sound like Q. Clair wondered if Kari Sargent was leaking out while Q was distracted by the radio. They were the very same words she had used the first time they met. Either way, she was making sense.

"We have food," Clair said, not wanting to talk about the Yard yet to anyone else, not until they heard something from inside to indicate that her desperate plan had been successful. "When the storm passes, we'll find more. Grow more, even. Will the crops be okay?"

The woman shrugged. "The rain will wash the ash away."

"Clean water might be the bigger concern," said Q or Kari. She clicked her tongue against her teeth with satisfaction and put the case back together. "There. This should work."

Something appeared in Clair's blank lenses, a raw pixelated image that looked like a child's first attempt to create a patch. She winked on it.

A window opened, revealing a grainy image of woman so pale she looked translucent, with red-and-pepper hair cut short across her scalp. Her eyes were a brilliant green. Too old to be Devin's sister—she had to be his mother or perhaps an aunt.

"Respond, if you're hearing this," she said, her voice crackling with static. "Explain to me how the hell you're still alive."

"What do we tell her?" asked the woman who owned the radio.

"The truth," said Clair with a heart full of lead. "There's nothing else now."

—————————————————[3 redux]

EVE BARTELME WAS Devin and Trevin's mother. She was calling from Valkyrie Base, the underground bunker at the South Pole that Clair had visited with Jesse an eternity ago. Clearly, it had survived the chain reaction.

"The benefit of being a long way from anywhere," Eve explained, "plus certain contingencies we never thought we'd need. Building an outer shell of unfabbed material seemed extreme to some, but we're glad of it now. That was what protected us from the unstable matter."

Clair tried to find the right words to explain what had happened to her sons, but Eve cut her off.

"Not to worry. I have their resurrection files right here. We'll bring them back when the booths are charged."

"You'll . . . *what*?"

"Bring them back. You don't think I'd let them die by *accident*, do you? They're young. They have a lot of work to do. I've invested too much to just toss them away."

"But you can't do that."

"Why not? There are one hundred and fifty people on file. We need everyone we can get."

"It's . . ."

Clair stopped before she could make a fool of herself. *Illegal,* she'd been about to say, but RADICAL didn't care about consensus any more than WHOLE did. *Immoral* wouldn't fly either, because the members of RADICAL had their own moral vision for the future of the human race. They wanted to live forever, with the help of d-mat, and they weren't going to let something as trifling as the law get in the way of that ambition.

Besides, was it really so different from what Clair had in mind for everyone in the Yard, which was to bring them all back from raw data once they found a way to access them? She would be a hypocrite to deny any grieving mother what she planned to give herself.

"It's what?" Eve pressed.

The truth was, though, that Eve didn't seem to be grieving at all, just irritated by the inconvenience.

"Nothing," said Clair. Another truth was that she would be glad to have Devin and Trevin back. Whether they ought to be dead or not, whether they disagreed with her or not, they had been her friends, and an early death was not what they deserved.

The truth was hard. It tore apart her promises and stomped all over her values. What were her values, compared to those of WHOLE and RADICAL? Somewhere in the middle, she guessed, where no one would agree with her.

The storm howled and hammered outside, shaking the walls of the gymnasium so hard she feared it might collapse at any moment. Lightning flashed and thunder boomed almost continuously now, dancing around them in a deafening ballet, as though blind giants were fighting over earth's last inhabitants.

Ragnarok, she thought. She swore it wasn't going to end this way.

"So *you're* Q," Eve was saying. "All this time, you weren't anywhere at all? You were just a person?"

"I don't think 'just' is the right word," Q said.

"You know what I mean. You shrank yourself down, squeezed yourself into someone else. How much did you have to jettison of your old self? How constrained are you now that the Air is completely gone? You must feel very different from how you used to."

Q shifted awkwardly in Kari's body. "I am . . . uncomfortable with this interrogation. The issue is not what I am. It is the state of the world and what we are to do about it."

Clair wondered if Q was feeling vulnerable. RADICAL had made it clear in the past that they would be happier with Q erased. That would be a lot easier to accomplish now that the entirety of Q's mind was contained within a single body.

Or maybe Q was no longer a threat at all, if there was nothing for her to connect to . . . at the moment.

"There's nothing we *can* do until the atmosphere settles into some kind of equilibrium," Eve said. "The storm won't last forever. If you're safe, stay where you are. If you're not, find somewhere that is. If you can't, well, it's been nice talking to you."

"We're okay here," said Clair, unwilling to reveal too much until she knew more about Eve. "What about you? Will you be all right?"

"Yes. We have power, although not nearly as much as we did when there were powersats. We can grow our own food, and ice is just water waiting to be filtered. We'll keep this frequency open for you, and keep broadcasting across the others in the hope of finding more survivors."

Clair had been afraid to ask, but this was something she desperately needed to know.

"Have you heard from anyone else?" she asked, thinking about the Yard.

"No. It's just us. We'll let you know if that changes."

"Likewise," Clair said, although what she could do about it was presently beyond her. She needed to think. She *always* needed to think. Just once she wished for a case of straight-up action, of doing rather than second-guessing. . . .

The line went silent.

"You'll keep listening, please?" Clair asked the radio's owner, who nodded, although she was obviously annoyed at how Q had treated the heirloom. "If you want to sleep, call us and we'll take over."

"All right." The woman snatched at Clair's sleeve as she went to walk away. "Are they really dead . . . all those people?"

"I think so." This truth was too big for words, too big to fit inside her head for longer than a moment. When she tried to grasp it, to look hard at it and confront the reality, it wriggled like a snake and slithered away, leaving her feeling breathless and ill. She kept thinking about New York, about Manteca, about home. All gone.

"We brought it on ourselves," Clair said. "We deserve

everything that happened to us."

"No, it was a mistake," said Q. "None of us meant for it to go like this."

"But Nobody did. This wasn't a meteor strike or a big volcano or a plague or whatever. This is something *we made*. It's even worse than the Water Wars. We were so smart, and so, so stupid."

Q touched her shoulder. Clair flinched away. She was shaking. She could barely stand. She had to be alone. She couldn't talk and think at the same time.

Everything needed to change in order to accommodate the reality of her life. Instead of dying, like nearly everyone else had, she needed to be like a caterpillar in a pupa, rearranging its insides to make room for the thing it was going to become: Clair 7.0. As outside, so within.

In a depopulated world, with no friends, family, or Jesse, she would have to find a way to survive on her own.

"Let her go," said Nelly to Q. "She'll come back when she's ready."

Clair found an empty corner of the gym and sat with a blanket over her head so no one could see her. She wished she could reach into the past for her childhood toy, Charlie, for comfort, but there was nothing, and no one, but hurt.

When she slept, she dreamed of Jesse and woke reaching for him. The space between her arms felt as though it would never be full again.

─────────────────────────[8 redux]

MORNING CAME WITH a reduction in the storm's fury and a discussion about seeing how the world looked now. Clair listened for a while to Nelly urging caution and Sandler Jones grandstanding before wearily pulling back the blanket and sitting up. She wanted to be part of any consensus that emerged, even if it was just about going for a walk.

The gymnasium was filled with a wan, bluish light, all that was left of a wintry day filtered through dust-splattered windows. Clair was surprised to see Q sitting next to her, close enough to give her a slight fright but not close enough to touch. It was nowhere as good as it would have been to see her mother, but a small comfort nonetheless: the one and only friend she had left, even if Q had been hiding for days, *testing* her.

Q's head was resting on her knees and Clair assumed she was sleeping until she spoke softly.

"For the good of the many, out of compassion for the world . . ."

"What?"

Q shook her head, and sat up straight.

"I'm sorry," she said. "It doesn't matter. Let's talk about food. We need to eat. And then we should do as Sandler says. We can't hide in here forever."

"I agree. What's for breakfast?"

"Stale granola bars. We'll forage for more while we're out there."

It was a short conversation. Q prepared to stand.

"Wait. Did you hear from any other survivors?"

A quick shake of the head. "Just RADICAL. But there are bound to be other people, stragglers here and there without means of communication. And don't forget the moon, as Nelly said, and the other outposts. The last census put the total off-Earth population at almost fifty thousand. There's a good chance OneMoon will lift the embargo too. Their gripe was with OneEarth, and since that's gone now, I expect they will relent—but in exchange for annexing us, probably."

Clair nodded. Space politics was not something she had followed very closely. She did know, though, that formerly dependent colonies on the moon and Mars had reached separate consensuses in recent years, leading to cultural and traffic bans to stop Mother Earth from wooing its wayward citizens back into the fold.

"I don't want to live on the moon," she said. "No matter how bad it is on Earth."

"It's all moot," said Q. "We have no d-mat network of any kind to get there, and RADICAL is constrained by resources. Powersat beams from lunar orbit will spread out too much to be any use to us here. When it comes to energy, d-mat is *thirsty*."

So was Clair, for water, but she wasn't ready to get up just yet.

"The people on the moon can see the Earth. Have they sent any images? Do we know what the Earth looks like now?"

Q nodded and sent Clair's lenses a selection of low-resolution files, the best the observers could relay via the sole remaining satellite. Clair just glanced at them. They showed the planet bathed in shining aqua aurorae—cold, but almost beautiful from afar—rippling outward from the point closest to Wallace's deadly unstable-matter cache and then echoing from pole to pole like waves across a pond. Then the aurorae faded, and the earth was as gray as a stone. Every city in the world had gone dark.

The most recent pictures showed electrical storms all over the planet. Where the storms had blown out, fires were burning. The oceans looked thick and dark, their usual cerulean hues erased. The world looked like she felt.

"There are bound to be other survivors," Q said again, as if by repeating it, she was likely to make it more true. Clair caught her fiddling with Kari Sargent's commitment ring and knew what was going through her mind. "They'll come out of hiding when they can, and if they can communicate they will. Even if they can't communicate, we'll find them eventually. OneMoon can begin repopulating satellites in a few days. All they have to do is send a breeder on a fabbed rocket to kick-start the process."

It was a long way from there to the world that was. Clair felt weighed down by the responsibility of getting there. Still, moping around was a sure way to get nothing done.

She had to keep moving forward. One step, two steps . . .

At the very least she should prepare some kind of public statement, something to let the survivors know what had happened and what hope remained—even if all she had to do to deliver it was stand up and talk loudly.

She attempted to help Q to her feet. Kari Sargent was heavy enough to tip her over if she seriously tried.

"Nothing from the other me, the one who went to the Yard?"

Q shook her head. "I would tell you."

Clair tried not to feel too disappointed. Like some cruel physics experiment, she didn't know if Jesse was alive or dead. It was dangerous to pin her hopes on something over which she had no control.

"I know. But I had to ask."

[9 redux]————————————

FED AND REHYDRATED, Clair joined the small group volunteering for the first expedition outside. The rain had slowed to a light patter on the roof, but she draped a blanket over her shoulder for shelter should that change, and also for warmth. The air coming through the cracks had turned cold again.

Nelly was with them, and she pushed the doors open without ceremony.

It was immediately clear that her stained surgical mask

would not be required. The clouds were yellow, and the sunlight had a greenish tinge. Clair had expected end-less gray dunes, but she saw something very different. For a start, although the ash wasn't completely gone, it was now confined to those areas the torrential rain hadn't washed clean. Q guessed that it consisted of nothing more dangerous than the most common elements jumbled up randomly, like the paints of a paint box mixed into a muddy nothingness, but Clair couldn't help worrying about long-term toxicity. Just because they were no lon-ger sucking it down with every breath didn't mean they might not be dealing with its effects for years to come.

The buildings of New Petersburg stood tall in the dis-tance, surrounding the ruins of the muster like the teeth of an open mouth.

"New Petersburg was built before d-mat," said Q. "It was immune to the chain reaction."

"Shame about the rest." Nelly kicked at a mound of shredded planks that had once been a small shed. "Look! It's supposed to be wood, but you couldn't make a tooth-pick out of this now."

"Fabbers were everywhere for a long time," Clair said. "Unstable matter obviously spread. I wonder if Wallace expected it to be this bad. . . ."

"Beyond a certain point," Nelly said, "how do you tell the difference?"

* * *

They walked to the water's edge, where the Neva Straits lapped sluggishly against what remained of the pier, Clair's feet alternately slipping and sticking in the mud with vile squelching sounds. Two boats had survived the blue dawn, sitting high in the ash-thickened sea. Above, an airship floated, having broken free during the storm but become entangled by its guy lines in the mast of one of the boats. Possessing the improbable shape of a giant head—that of Kipling Satoshige, a popular game show host from when Clair's parents had been kids—it cast an incongruous smile across the ruined landscape, bobbing and swaying in the wind. The real Kipling Satoshige was almost certainly dead now, along with his audience. There wasn't even an Air to carry his show anymore, just fleeting links between lenses. The gaping emptiness of Clair's infield was another reminder that the world she knew wasn't going to be rebuilt overnight.

Eve Bartelme patched into the augs of the exploration party, via the old GPS satellite and the radio. Audio only.

"The oceans are ash soup," she said when Clair described the scene. "I'll be amazed if a single fish survives. Luckily, we have thousands of species in our pattern banks. Once we get power back, we can think about restocking."

Clair knew something about rebuilding wildlife, thanks to her mother's work. She wondered if any of Allison's elephants had survived. Many of them had been genetically engineered "in pattern" before being born naturally in Northern Australia.

"It'll all need to be filtered," she said.

"Not unprecedented," said Eve. "Think of the Water Wars. It's exactly the same, except instead of taking carbon dioxide out of the air we'll be taking that junk out of the water."

"There's so much of it, though, and not all of it will have washed out to sea."

"I know. You should see it down here. Dome Fuji looks like it was sprayed with concrete."

"It'd be better to let stocks recover naturally," said Nelly. "Some species must have survived, deep down."

"Maybe. If you want to fish for your dinner, though, you'll need a very long line."

Clair thought of dolphins, albatrosses, and whales, three of her mother's favorite species that had been on the brink of extinction for generations. Were they all dead now because of the mistake she had made?

The expedition followed the shoreline to a road honeycombed with holes, where fabbed material had been inadvertently mixed in with natural. A brief squall sprang up, and Clair was dismayed to see flecks of gray in the droplets that landed in her upturned hand. How long until the sky was completely clear? She doubted anyone knew. Were there any meteorologists left?

Nelly took them to the farms, and even before they arrived it was clear the plants and livestock hadn't survived the night unscathed. Whole fields were flattened.

Fire had burned a barn to the ground, killing three horses. The addition of two dozen survivors, who had taken shelter in a dairy shed, was a mixed blessing: more lives meant more mouths to feed, and it was unclear how long they would need to make their meager supplies last.

Sandler Jones danced ahead of them, picking through the ruins and more often than not emerging with something useful. Not just food, but wet-weather gear, weapons, and paper books. He was a natural scavenger, unafraid of scouring even the most intimate hiding places. They packed what they could into rucksacks or stacked them in caches for collection later. Clair assumed he kept the very best items for himself.

As they headed deeper into the muster, they started finding bodies. Clair didn't want to look, but she knew she couldn't shy away from the harsh reality of the dead. The number of corpses that had crumbled to dust far outweighed those she could see with her own eyes. Most of these people had died in the collapse of buildings, but a couple had been struck by lightning, and lay burned and twisted in the open. Some seemed to have just dropped midstep and expired where they fell.

"What killed them?" she asked, mystified.

"Pacemakers," said Nelly. "Neural implants, drug shunts, artificial joints . . . Abstainers aren't supposed to use anything that's been fabbed, but sometimes it's just easier to. Or there's not enough time for one of our artisans to make what's needed, particularly in a medical emergency." She shrugged, perhaps thinking of Agnessa. "I understand the temptation, and the need, but these are the consequences."

So few survivors, Clair thought. The muster had seemed so big before the blue dawn. A large percentage of its inhabitants must have been converts to WHOLE, joining after a lifetime of using d-mat. Just once was enough, no matter how long ago.

"How are we going to fab anything again without creating more unstable matter?" she asked Eve. "Fish, clean water, whatever. It's never going to be safe."

"We've isolated the problem," Eve said. "We're redesigning our booths right now. This will never happen again."

"So you say," said Nelly. "But what will be the next disaster? You can't tell me this is the last time something will go wrong with d-mat."

"The problem wasn't d-mat," said Eve. "The problem was *people.*"

"I don't see how that makes us any safer. People will always be people."

"Don't argue," said Clair. "That's the last thing we need right now."

Nelly and Eve fell silent, but she knew the matter wasn't forgotten. It didn't bode well that the two surviving groups on Earth had such opposing opinions on everything when it came to d-mat. The fact that neither group cared much for consensus wasn't going to make it easy either. But what could she do? The Earth was her home. She wasn't going to leave it. All she had to do was stay alive until the other version of her found a way out of the Yard, and everyone and everything else could follow.

Or, Clair thought, *she* found a way *in*.

It wasn't in her nature to wait for anyone, even herself.

She would feel better with a plan.

[II redux]————————————

IT TOOK MANY emotionally exhausting hours to comb the muster for survivors. By the time they finished, the short winter day was dwindling to an end, and Clair trudged back to the gymnasium with the others, where a final head count was made.

There were one hundred and seventeen people, thirty-five of them children under ten, over half of whom were now orphans. Clair wished there was some way to make them feel better, but she didn't know what she could possibly say that would make a difference. It caused her near physical pain to hold a weeping young boy, knowing that all his loved ones were gone. She tried her best not to think of her own loved ones, but it was impossible not to. She wasn't yet so hardened that she could relinquish her last hope of finding them again. At the same time, she wasn't so foolish as to think it would be easy.

Storm clouds were building again. Before night fell, an extension was added to the gym using materials reclaimed from the ruins and cobbled together with impressive skill and speed by the artisans in the crowd. Sandler Jones helped by taking lumber and tools where they were needed. Clair did the same.

After a meal of stale bread and hard cheese, she collapsed exhausted onto a mattress retrieved from one of the dorms. The space was crowded with people. Children slowly settled against a backdrop of quiet but intense conversations. Clair felt accepted but avoided, along with Q. When Q took the mattress next to hers, Clair looked up from an inspection of her broken fingernails.

"It's been a long time now," she said. "We still haven't heard anything from the Yard."

"Time may move differently in there," Q said. "Faster, slower. Who knows?"

"Maybe it's not moving at all. What if we're all that's left?" Clair could think of a dozen unhappy endings for the copy she'd sent into the Yard. They didn't even know if she had made it, traveling along rapidly disintegrating cables as she had been at the time. Her pattern might have been lost the second it was sent. "I can't just sit here waiting. We need to know for sure."

The more she thought about it, the more that became her priority.

"I know the Air is dead and the cables are gone," she

said, "but could we use the radio to reach the servers?"

"I've sent signals, but it's not the right medium. Certainly not for getting people out. At its maximum rate, radio would take millions of times longer than the age of the universe just to send a single person." Q rolled onto her side so she was facing Clair. "You're in a bigger hurry than that, I guess."

A joke, Clair thought. *Q or Kari?* It wasn't really a time for laughing, so she guessed the former.

"What if we go to the Yard?" she asked. "Physically, I mean, to where the servers are buried. Would that help? Could we plug into them or something?"

"Maybe." Q hesitated, then said, "You *do* remember that it's at the bottom of a pit drilled miles beneath a frozen lake . . . ?"

"Yes, but if it's our only shot, we'll just have to give it a try." The awesome improbability of such a venture helped push back some of the numbness that had gripped her since the blue dawn. It was no substitute for having Jesse beside her, but it was better than nothing. "How far is Lake Baikal from here?"

"Six thousand miles, give or take. But there's no direct route by road or rail. Hiking would take months and be very dangerous. Winter will be upon us in earnest soon."

"I know, I know." Clair stewed for a long moment, considering her very short list of options. Stay where she was and wait for something that might never come. Pursue something that might go nowhere and could kill her in the process. Give up on everything to do with the Yard and move forward on her own.

The latter was arguably most sensible . . . but the image of a giant floating head, equipped with an elegant black coif and toothy grin, wouldn't leave her alone.

"Chipmunk Underworld," she said. "That was the name of Kipling Satoshige's old game show. Mom used to love it."

"I don't understand," said Q.

Clair shook her head. "Doesn't matter. It might have popped or flown away already. And if it hasn't, it'll still be there in the morning. Let's sleep on it and maybe I'll come up with something less insane."

————————[14 redux]

SHE DIDN'T. WHEN she woke and stepped outside, the sky was a crisp, icy blue, utterly free of clouds. The only blemish was the giant floating head, still tangled by its guys down at the harbor. Looking at it closely, she could see that the balloon's "collar," which mimicked the real star's unconventional dress sense, was actually a substantial gondola, with propellers and cunningly concealed windows. It wasn't as big or as practical as Turner Goldsmith's Skylifter, but it would do.

"You can't be serious."

She turned to see Sandler Jones standing behind her.

"I was listening to you and the freaky peeker talking last night," he said. "You're not really going to fly in Kipling Satoshige all the way across the Russian Protectorate, are you?"

She felt her chin pull in defensively. "Yes, unless you can think of something better."

"What, to hack into the Yard?" He grinned. "I heard Nelly talking about it. Eyes and ears always open, me. I thought your friend had already tried doing that."

She resigned herself to explaining. She would have to anyway, to everyone else left in the muster.

When she had finished, he stared at her for a long moment, as though checking her out, and then laughed. "This is the craziest thing I've ever heard of. Sign me up."

"Don't feel like you have to—"

"But I want to, zombie girl. There's nothing to do around here except dig graves and watch the plants die. Yours is the best show in town . . . in the whole *world*."

Clair couldn't decide which thought was more disturbing: that he was right, or that he might be her only volunteer. Hopefully there would be more. Maybe he was playing nice because fate had thrown them together, but she knew what he really thought of her. *Zombie girl* wasn't a joke to him any more than it had been for Dylan Linwood.

"Maybe," she said.

"I'll take that as a yes."

As she headed back to the gym to raise the plan with Nelly, she double-checked her infield to see if anything had arrived overnight. There was nothing from the Yard, just a single message bounced off the old GPS, relayed through the radio, and synced somehow to her lenses while she examined the floating head.

"I leave you in charge," Devin said, "and look what happens."

She hesitated, a watery feeling in her stomach, before sending a chat request.

He answered immediately. There was audio but no image. "This is, uh, less than optimal," he said. "I mean, I knew it could happen. Why else make the backups? But I never really thought it would, and certainly not like this. So don't feel bad if you're freaking out. I totally am."

The watery feeling subsided. Hearing Devin's familiar voice was like time had rolled back a little, to a moment before everyone had died. She felt like if she closed her eyes and opened them again, she would be back in Agnessa's bunker before the world ended. She fought that feeling, knowing no good would come of it.

"Tell me how this works," she said. "When was your pattern taken? How up-to-date are you?"

"I come from the last time I used a RADICAL network," he said, "which was on the seastead, after the dupes attacked. We were going to the muster. Everything after that I know secondhand." He paused. "I don't know what happened to my original, but I can guess."

Clair could tell that he was curious but at the same time reluctant to ask.

"I can send you what my lenses caught." She hadn't been able to look at those images herself, but she would for him, if he wanted her to.

"Let me think on it." He fell silent.

The empty chat was worse than what they were talking about. It made her feel like he was a stranger, when in fact he was exactly the same as he had ever been. She was the one who had changed. She had to let go of everyone she loved. How else could she bear the grief if the Yard turned out to be a dead end?

"I'm glad you're not dead," she said, meaning it. If all else failed, she would have that much. "Trevin, too. He's listening in, I presume?"

"Actually, he's still in storage. We'll bring him back later. It's taking us a long time to generate the power to use d-mat properly. Mom brought me out first, so you and I could talk things through. I'm the chatty one, remember."

He sounds uncomfortable, and no wonder, she thought. She might be dealing with the absence of Jesse, a boy she had known for two intense weeks, but he had been connected to his identical twin his entire life.

"What's there to chat about?" she said, hoping not to get caught in a conversation about who was or who wasn't to blame.

"The Yard, of course. You and Q sent copies of yourselves there—which was a brilliant idea, I must admit. And a bold move for someone who'd just become an Abstainer."

"Don't start," she said. "I'm Abstaining for good now."

"Got no choice, I guess."

"Not just that. Have you looked around, Devin? Have you seen what a mess we're in?"

"Yes, but you can't blame d-mat for that."

Clair rubbed the bridge of her nose with one hand. "You sound like your mother."

"Ouch. Listen, let's not get bogged down in an old argument. What is your plan? I bet you have one. You always seem to."

Taking that as a compliment, she told him what she'd come up with overnight: to hijack a giant balloon head and fly it to Lake Baikal, there to hack into the Yard and extract all the patterns it hopefully contained.

She thought he'd laugh, as Sandler had, or suggest that it was more about being *seen* to do something, as though that would be enough to make amends. She worried about that sometimes.

"Not a bad idea," he said. "It'd be good to have someone on the ground. We've been trying to hack in from here, but it's going to be tricky until the satellite breeder comes from the moon. There just isn't enough bandwidth. And if the ways in have been physically severed . . . well, no amount of bandwidth will fix that."

"So you think it's a good idea?"

"Absolutely. Godspeed! When do you take off?"

This was moving faster than she had expected. First of all, she needed a crew, which would require getting Nelly's support. And then she needed food, and water, and power, and some means of navigating that didn't involve the Air. There were probably a hundred things she hadn't thought of, which would require discussion, planning, arguing . . . All together, it seemed very unlikely.

But then she thought of Jesse, her mother, and her friends inside the Yard, maybe waiting for someone to rescue them, and her pulse quickened with more than just fear.

"Tonight," she said. *Save the Yard, and save the world.* "We're leaving tonight."

[17 redux]

NELLY THOUGHT IT was a good idea too, and the call for volunteers raised seven more people apart from Sandler Jones, one of whom, Embeth, had experience flying old-fashioned air vehicles. She muttered something about hydraulics and, with the help of two deputies plus the two strongest survivors left in New Petersburg, drew the giant floating head down to Earth. A quick inspection of the gondola revealed it to be intact, with more than enough room for a small crew. The engines worked, and so did the various flaps and control surfaces on the bottom and top of the air sack. There was even a compass, which was crucial now that the Air no longer existed. All they had to do was load up and go.

Clair cheered along with everyone else. It felt good to have achieved something, no matter how small.

"I suppose you're captain," said Sandler, peering eagerly out all the windows in turn. "Does that make me vice captain?"

"I don't know that they have them on airships," said Clair. "And anyway, Q is second in command if anyone is."

"The chaperone's coming too? Shame." He winked. "At least let me name it."

"That depends," she said.

"Don't worry. It's *Satoshige*. What else would it be?"

He saluted with mock gusto and headed down the ramp to start lugging gear recovered from the muster. Clair shook her head, telling herself not to let him get a rise out of her. The day was already halfway done, and they had a lot left to do.

"You know," said Devin as the last of the supplies were loaded into the gondola, "there's a chance RADICAL will be in the Yard. Not as we are now, since we pretty much stopped using ordinary d-mat years ago. But there are probably early versions lurking about somewhere, depending on when Wallace started creating his backups."

"Okay," said Clair. She was standing at the back of the balloon, reporting on the movement of various control surfaces as Embeth fiddled with the levers and buttons. "What good does that do us?"

"Well, if they are in there, and if they're able to think and act in any meaningful way, they'll have figured out what's going on. They'll be trying to get out. We might find them coming the other way."

"Would they help the other me if she found them?"

"Probably, but she'll be a stranger to them. She'd need a code word or phrase to prove she can be trusted."

"And that is?"

"Hard to say. We've grown out of that phase, thank goodness, but I can dig around and see what might work."

"And then we still have to get it to her. . . ."

"I've been thinking about that too." Devin sounded brisk and cheerful. He always liked an intellectual problem, particularly one that posed no direct physical threat to his well-being. "Specifically, how the Yard could be structured. If there's a simulation it'll be layered, with sets of rules—like grammar—operating on data sourced from the Air—the copy of the Air that's in there, I mean. The simulation could be incredibly detailed, exactly like the real thing, but it's only as good as its data—just like a sentence is only as good as the words in it. Bad words make a bad sentence, even if the grammar is perfect. 'Bad,' in our case, means 'good': if we can insert the right words into the simulation from the outside, the grammar might do the hard work for us—of getting through to your other self, I mean. Round peg into round hole, except instead of pegs we might try thoughts or knowledge of some kind, fired like homing missiles into your own mind. *Assuming* there's a working simulation, of course."

"When will we know?" She made way for Q, who was putting Kari Sargent's exceptional frame to good use, lugging box after box up the ramp.

"I can't say. That old satellite is just about useless."

"Can Q help?"

"She has a bandwidth issue too, she says, but yes, she has some ideas."

Nelly came down to the harbor to check their progress. Clair belatedly waved a signal to one of the volunteers that the rear port flap was wiggling freely.

"Looking good," Nelly said. "You're not going to be ready by sunset, but it won't be long after."

Clair was nervous about what lay ahead. The last airship she had been on had fallen violently out of the sky, shot down by Wallace's dupes. There was no sign that any of *them* had survived the blue dawn, but how would she survive without Jesse beside her?

"I hope you don't mind us leaving like this," she said. "I'd stay and help, but—"

"You *are* helping." Nelly put one firm hand on Clair's

shoulder. "You're taking that meathead somewhere else." She nodded at Sandler, who was busy juggling potatoes rather than putting them inside the *Satoshige*. "When you've dug up the servers from that pit, maybe you can leave him down there."

"He'll be okay." Clair took comfort from the knowledge that the arrangement wasn't permanent. "And we'll be back before you know it."

"It's a long way. You might find other survivors, somewhere more comfortable."

"What are you saying? That you don't want me to come back?"

"No. Just indicating you are under no obligation to." Nelly smiled for the first time since Clair had met her. "You're still the girl who killed d-mat. We're not giving up on you just yet."

Clair felt profoundly moved by that sentiment. If her hope of digging up the Yard came to nothing, there was somewhere she belonged. Like Devin, that was an unexpected treasure, out of the ashes. It would make losing Jesse and everyone else, if it came to that, almost bearable.

[21 redux]

THE SUN HAD long set when the *Satoshige* lifted off. Clair stood next to Embeth, the airship pilot, thinking about her latest speech to the world as the ground receded to black and they swayed generally eastward across the empty city. Ahead, by moonlight, the landscape was flat and heavily wooded. Occasional pockets of ash stood out like snowdrifts or small frozen lakes. Clair felt chilly, even though she was wearing cold-weather gear retrieved from the ruins, with her hair tucked into a woolen cap and her hands in leather gloves that looked handmade. There were no lights below apart from those of the muster, falling steadily behind.

Did she really believe that this journey was the answer, as she had told everyone else, standing on a box so she could see over all their heads? Was there honestly any chance of bouncing back from here, of bringing the Earth back from the brink of destruction? For all of Eve's talk of cleansing the oceans and remaking the fish, how likely was it really that the world of old would ever return?

In her darkest moments she imagined an entirely new creature emerging from the ashes, something alien and strange and possibly *better*, spawned from the death of humanity and feeding on its remains. What that creature would be like, she couldn't imagine.

She had to hope. It was all she had.

But at the same time she had to be prepared.

Hope for the best, Aunt Arabelle had told her once, *plan for the worst.*

She was so far deep into "the worst" that it was hard to imagine going any further. But she could, she knew. She had never shied away from anything before, no matter how horrible.

"We're tracking you," said Devin, his voice coming over old-fashioned speakers in the gondola. There was a dish on top of the air sack linking the airship to the old GPS satellite. It was useless for actual navigation: that was Clair and Q's job, following landmarks they would check off along the way, located by old-fashioned eyesight. "I can tell you if you're pointing the wrong way, which you're not right now. Next stop, a place called Velsk."

"Never heard of it," said Sandler from where he was peering over Embeth's shoulder. He wasn't allowed to touch the controls, but that hadn't stopped him from getting close enough to make Clair nervous.

Clair would have liked to fly over Omsk, since Zep had joked about it once, but sadly they would be flying too far north. "What about the other satellite, the one from the moon? When will that get here?"

"The breeder is still two days away, at least," Devin said. "I've had a thought about what to do until then, using my grammar idea from earlier. We're going to take everything that's happened to you and bundle it up in an easily compressible form—not everything, of course, only what's important. . . ."

Devin's voice suddenly skidded and blurred like a bad recording, and there was pain unlike anything Clair had felt before. She wanted to scream, but she was unable to move. She was trapped in her body while events seemed to be passing with unnatural rapidity, like dreaming in fast-forward, someone else at the controls. The *Satoshige* zoomed across the Earth like an improbable rocket and Clair felt giddy . . . and strangely as though she could hear Jesse's voice—but that wasn't possible, was it? He was in the Yard, she hoped, and she was still thousands of miles away. How fast could a giant floating head go, anyway? Or was she already in the Yard and the balloon was just a dream? A dream being rammed into her mind . . . ?

". . . got a solid lock on what appears to be a legacy I/O channel," Trevin was saying over the radio link to the *Satoshige*. Now that both twins had been restored from their resurrection files, they were making twice as much progress on hacking into the Yard. But twice zero, as Sandler liked to say, was still zero.

The view through the *Satoshige*'s forward windows was of a wrinkled, wintery landscape. They were thirty-six hours and some considerable distance from the muster, following the snaking trail of the Podkamennaya Tunguska River eastward, not far from where a meteorite had exploded long ago. That morning they had seen a rising column of smoke to the north that might have been from a campfire. Deviating to take a look, they had found it to be just the smoldering wreckage of some unidentifiable machine. Another Abstainer's craft, perhaps, destroyed for reasons unknown.

Clair had taken it as more than just a disappointment. It was a warning not to take anything for granted. There was a huge distance yet to traverse to the Yard's physical location, and the difficulty of getting inside it remained. If they couldn't hack in from a distance, they would have to find a way to do it physically, at the bottom of the world's deepest pit. And if they couldn't do that . . .

The people she was with right now were going to be her only company for a very long time.

Trevin was still talking. "Decrypting the protocols and encoding your data is going to take us some time. It would help if you edited the file into something more manageable. . . ."

The world slewed and shifted again, as though she was luging out of control down a steep hillside. How could Trevin be alive? The pain had returned with him, worse than ever. It felt like her right shoulder was on fire and her chest was being crushed by a tree trunk. Every nerve was screaming. Why?

Because she had been shot. This memory returned to her, bright and clear. She still couldn't move, but her mind was beginning to work again. She had been shot . . . but how could she think that she was on an airship over Russia as well?

"It's inevitable that you'll cause feedback," said Q with Kari's voice. Half the crew of the *Satoshige* were huddled around an electric heater eating canned food, while the other half slept through the long winter night, their third since leaving the muster. Embeth had trained a deputy pilot, who now handled the controls. "How bad this feedback will be, we can't predict. It may be causing problems already, and maybe that's why we're having so much trouble getting through. The simulation has sealed itself in order to conduct repairs. It's *healing*, or trying to. The best solution would be to erase the discrepancies, but it won't be allowed to do that. Preserving all patterns is the Yard's prime directive. Anything else would be impossible."

"You talk about them as though they're alive," Sandler Jones said.

"Won't they be?" Clair asked him, her voice sounding loud in her ears. She was worried she might be catching a cold. "If they look like us, act like us, *feel* like us—who are we to say they're not us?"

He slapped himself on the chest. "Zombie girl, look around you. With this crew, that's one argument you're never going to win."

The signal slewed again.

Signal. *Why had she thought that?*

"I don't think the transmission is getting through. Are you sure it's working?"

The weak winter sun hung dead ahead, just kissing the horizon over the humped backs of a row of grim-looking hills. Sandler had been agitating to touch down and hunt for meat. Clair wouldn't let him. Their supplies were dropping fast, consumed quickly in the cold, but they weren't starving yet.

While Sandler had slept at the end of his last shift, one of the other crew members had told Clair that Sandler's parents had been isolationists who had died from a disease contracted from a wild animal they'd killed and eaten. It had taken a doctor so long to reach their home that Sandler had almost died too. He had been a small child, the crew member said. Being alone with the bodies of his parents had done something funny to his head.

Clair doubted it was that simple. More likely Sandler didn't want to believe that his parents had died for nothing, and was trying to prove that their way of life still had meaning. She could understand that.

Sympathizing was harder, particularly after their argument that morning. She had wanted to throw out some spare parts to reduce weight, and he had stubbornly resisted for reasons she still couldn't understand. In the end she had just given up. One fight at a time. She didn't have the energy to take on everyone.

"Let me try," said Devin after yet another fruitless attempt by Q to find a way into the Yard that wouldn't involve digging down through miles of ice. She told herself not to get her hopes up. "If I can refine the signal, I might just get through. . . ."

Clair had heard Devin's words before, under different circumstances, and now she was hearing them again. Or maybe she hadn't heard them either time, just imagined them twice. The pain was rolling in and out like electric waves against a raw nerve shoreline. She was having trouble keeping up with everything. Had she been shot in the Satoshige *or somewhere else? Was Jesse dead or not— because if he was, why was he talking? Or was that Devin again?*

". . . connecting *somewhere*. Let's kill the feed and see what happens next."

Clair agreed, unable to imagine what the version of

herself in the Yard must be feeling. If she was feeling anything at all.

Strangeness settled over her. She really was seeing everything twice at the same time—the real thing plus an overlay of exactly the same thing provided by her lenses. Or maybe there were two of her.

But there are, *she told herself.* Me and Clair One. We're in an ultramax prison, under attack by the hollowmen, and I've just been shot . . . possibly by Clair One.

The calmness with which she thought that astonished her. She remembered the paleness of Kari's skin against the blood—her own blood—and the worried look on Jesse's face. She thought about dark tunnels and out-of-body experiences. Was that what she was having? Was that why the feeling of seeing everything twice persisted?

Suddenly it stopped, and her thoughts seemed to crystallize as though a block had been removed. She remembered Zep talking in Harmony about how having two Clairs might cause the Yard to glitch.

"You're updating *her," he had said, pointing from Clair Two to Clair One.*

What if they weren't the only sources of confusing data? What if there was data coming from somewhere else?

The blue dawn.

The muster.

The airship.

Round peg into round hole, *she remembered Devin say-ing . . .* like homing missiles into your own mind.

What if these memories, of the muster and the Satoshige, *were coming* from the outside?

─────────────────────────────── [28]

"ALL RIGHT, LET'S call it quits," said Trevin. "No use beating a dead horse."

"We don't know what it's done, if anything," said Q.

"Let's just give the packet time to find its mark," said Devin, "and see what happens."

Clair stared gloomily out a porthole at the slate gray of a distant lake. It wasn't their destination, but Devin said it was a sign they were making good progress. He said that about everything.

The sun was setting on the third day of the *Satoshige*'s epic journey. All the landmarks were starting to blur into one. All the arguments sounded the same.

"How much time until we give up for good?" she asked, wringing her hands to make them warm.

"As long as it takes," said Eve Bartelme. "Waiting, one conquers the world."

[28 redux]————————————

Clair One

CLAIR JERKED AWAKE from a very strange dream about giant flying heads and a boy with patchwork skin. She sat up, chasing echoes of a voice she couldn't quite hear through the hard-edged spaces of the prison. She could have sworn someone was calling her name.

Shaking her head, she dismissed the feeling. Flying heads? When Clair remembered her dreams they were always slightly epic, but not half as epic as reality had turned out.

She was lying in a shadowed office alcove on a standard prison mattress. According to her lenses, four hours had passed since she had laid her head down in the hope of getting some rest, more than twelve since the hollowmen had first attacked the prison. She noted the time with a twinge of anxiety. Anything could happen in four hours.

The light falling on the floor in front of her was an unexpected shade of purple.

She sat up, trying not to disturb the person on the mattress next to her, some girl from WHOLE who Clair had only glimpsed once in a glitch but who acted as though Clair should know her. Her eyes were different colors, a peculiarity she blamed on d-mat. Once, Clair would have been skeptical. Now, not so much. . . .

Peering out of the alcove, she discovered that the source of the purple glow was a lamp on a tripod pointed at the ceiling above her head. There were other colored lamps scattered across the hub: green, orange, yellow, blue, arranged apparently at random. The main lights were off. A dozen people sat around a cluster of tables in the center of the hub, bathed in an odd mix of hues. The old lady in the wheelchair was there, along with Dylan Linwood and some other members of WHOLE. They talked in whispers while people slept around them. She saw Libby's pure white locks spilling across a rolled-up jacket, the blue splash of Tash's hair, Ronnie's glasses folded up neatly on the floor next to her, and Zep sprawled half on and half off his bed, bare feet twitching as though he was running in his dreams. Seeing him provoked a guilty pang. *I kissed him. That was my first mistake.* Add that to the list of things she needed to deal with, when she had the chance. Why should she take the blame for something Clair Two did?

Shots rang out in the distance, and her head jerked up. The movement caught Dylan Linwood's eye. He waved her over. She stood and did as he suggested, trying not to worry about what was happening elsewhere, yet. There was no sign of Sargent or Jesse. The latter worried her more than it should have. She wasn't his Clair, after all, and Clair Two's relationship with him wasn't hers. . . .

"They're still coming," Dylan said, in a whisper so as not to disturb the sleepers. "We think they're testing their links to this place, training so they can come at us whenever they want. We're spread thin, but so far we're holding them off."

That was good, Clair thought. She still worried about being locked in, but perhaps it wasn't as bad as she had originally feared. They hadn't been overwhelmed . . . yet.

"We should seal off the lower levels," she said, visualizing what needed to be done with an ease and clarity that wasn't something learned, "barricade the unused rooms—"

"Already under way. You want to help? We can use volunteers."

"Sure," she said. The quickness of his suggestion, though, gave her pause. Ever since Clair Two had appeared she had felt superfluous in her own life, pushed out by a copy of herself who kept so many secrets she felt like a stranger. She wasn't going to be easily brushed off now, not by a terrorist who was a temporary ally at best. "Tell me about the lights first."

"In a moment," said Arabelle, referring to something Clair couldn't see, presumably coming over her lenses. "Two to go, and then we're clear," she said to Dylan.

Clair accessed the interface and dipped into a steady stream of images and data pouring in from all over the prison. There was no immediate sign of the hollowmen—that was what "clear" had meant, Clair assumed—but there was a lot of activity, and still a swathe of dead patches where cameras had been taken out by the attacking forces. Barriers were indeed being welded up all over the administration level; concrete was pouring in a flood into the closed-circuit booths. Kari Sargent, it turned out, was watching over a makeshift hospital where Jesse sat attentively next to a particular bed, a bed Clair's gaze skated over deliberately without seeing. She wasn't ready to face *that*. Another room contained rows of bodies zipped up in black bags.

Everywhere, in every view, was a splash of vibrant color.

"The lights were Ray's idea," said Dylan, when the crisis was past. "Kingdon wants to shut us down before we can even think about fighting back. If the hollowmen are using memories to get in here, then making the prison look different should mess up their reference images."

"Has it worked?" she asked, acknowledging to herself that it was a good plan.

"It's slowed them down. We think. It's hard to tell. We don't know how many of their attempts are failing."

Another good point. "How many have we taken out?"

"Thirty," said Arabelle. "All ages and types. No duplication, so that's holding. The supply can't be inexhaustible."

"I suspect that some of them aren't hollowmen at all," said Dylan. "They're probably ordinary people, thinking they're doing the right thing."

Clair nodded. She could see how that would work. Everyone said that Lawmaker Kingdon was the big bad, and Clair had no reason to doubt that. Wallace had created the Yard for himself and his friends as a catch-all for anyone he thought might be valuable in the future. Now all the stored patterns were awake, some kind of government was required, and Kingdon wasn't going to let the unruly masses make decisions she might not agree with. She was way too ambitious for that.

The unruly masses had their uses. All Kingdon had to do was tell everyone in the Yard who *she* thought the real bad guys were, and call for volunteers to replace the PKs. There were lots of angry and confused parents in the Yard, after all, and it did *look* bad—a terrorist cell holing up together in defiance of the law. WHOLE had no chance of winning the popularity war. It was even odds, Clair thought, whether they would hold their own in a war of attrition.

Dylan and the others were old, tired, and stressed. It was good that WHOLE would let her help, if Dylan's offer was genuine. They needed her. She was young, able-bodied, and refreshed. And she had ideas. Good ideas. They would be easier to put into action now that Clair Two was out of the picture.

Again, via her lenses, she glanced at the hospital. There was a lot of black, which she guessed was actually brown seen through colored light. Dried blood everywhere, some of it hers.

No, not hers. Clair Two's.

She felt dizzy for a second, unsure of herself. She tried to fight it. There wasn't time for airs and vapors, like someone in a Jane Austen novel. She had to be strong. She had to fight.

I'm Clair One, and no one else.

"I've been studying how the glitches cluster," said Ronnie, rising from her mattress and putting her glasses back on. She was wearing a bodysuit, open around her throat, the same as Clair. They had all fabbed armor for themselves after Clair Two and the others had been shot.

Dylan made space for Ronnie next to Clair.

"It's like everyone is looking for you," she said, "but most of the time they can't find you. When they do, that could be for a lot of reasons. Maybe you and Clair Two are close to each other, bending the rules of the Yard just by existing. Or maybe you're thinking of someone who's thinking of you. Since information is real in the Yard, that makes a difference. It creates a potential, like the potential between a thundercloud and the ground. A big enough potential causes a lightning strike—only this kind of lightning can happen more than once. When one person gets through, it creates a channel the rest can follow. That's why your glitches cluster. Does that make sense?"

"I guess," Clair said. "Does that mean I can't think about anyone who isn't here, ever again? Like Ant Wallace, or my mother?"

In answer to her question, Ronnie just shrugged.

"All I know is that the more hollowmen and peace-keepers come here, the more difficult it will be to keep them out. The lights might make it harder for them to get a reference, because everything looks different, but the channel they're following only gets wider each time one more of them manages it. Let them keep on like this and soon they'll send an army we won't be able to push back."

"We *have* to push them back," said Arabelle. "Quickly, before they get the advantage."

"Duh," said Ronnie. "How?"

"If we could find their source," said Clair, "it would be easy."

"Double duh," said Ronnie with a weary grin. It didn't last long. "The best I can think of is trying to glitch them in return. You know, if they can get through to us, why can't we get through to them? All we have to do, arguably, is think about one of them really hard, and the Yard will rip us right to them."

"The best person to do that is currently in a coma," said Dylan, and Clair thought once more of the blood-spattered hospital and the feelings prompted by thinking of *her*.

"It's something we can work toward," Clair said, not wanting to relinquish the possibility so readily. "The channel must go both ways. And they're thinking of me too, right?"

"You mustn't attempt anything like this on your own,"

said Arabelle, reaching across the table to grip Clair's wrist in one ancient claw. "Promise me. We can't lose both of you."

There's no *both of us*, she wanted to protest. *There's just me and her.* But she didn't bother. Everyone thought Clair Two had it covered and she was just along for the ride. Well, she wasn't going to let anyone tell her what to do—not even herself, not without explaining *why*. If Clair Two was wrong, someone needed to say so. If Clair Two wouldn't admit it, someone needed to make her.

"Who said anything about going anywhere?" she said, hearing a bitter snap in her voice. "You're getting me mixed up with *her*. I was going to suggest that, if they insist on coming here, we should send something in return."

"Something more than a sternly worded note, I presume," said Ronnie.

"Exactly."

"A superb plan," said Dylan Linwood, reaching under the table and rummaging in a bag at his feet. Metal clunked and rattled. When he sat up, he was holding a black sphere that he pressed on Clair. It was heavy. She had never seen a grenade in person before, but she knew what they looked like.

One grenade, she thought, *in exactly the right place and at exactly the right time, and the hollowmen might never bother me again.*

There was nodding around the table. They had come up

with a plan, and it didn't involve anything more strenu-
ous than thinking. She might not even have to move from
the chair.

It gave her hope—tempered by the fact that maybe Wallace was attempting exactly the same thing, but hope
nonetheless.

It was spoiled only slightly by Dylan adding, "Take that
and go practice somewhere else. Somewhere quiet, so you
can concentrate . . . and in case it goes wrong, a long way
from here."

[29]

BRUSHED OFF AGAIN but this time with no good reason to
argue, since it had been her idea, Clair dressed in her
armor, tucked her pistol into her hip holster, and left
the hub, alone. Ronnie had wanted to come, but Dylan
convinced her to stay and talk through her theory again.
He assured Clair that someone would be watching at all
times. She didn't let that get to her, or give her any false
comfort. If the hollowmen ripped into the prison right on
top of her, she'd be kidnapped or dead long before anyone
came to her rescue. It was up to her to look after herself.
And that was just fine.

She remembered the kick of the gun in her hands, and
the glimpse of one of the hollowmen falling on the other

side of the room, briefly lit up in the muzzle flash. She had really done that. She was sure of it. But it had been confusing. A lot of people had been firing at once. The memories were beginning to blur. . . .

No, she had done it, and she wasn't freaking out like Clair Two had been in the observatory. Shortly after, sure. That was only natural. But she was fine now. She had seen Clair Two freeze at least once when things really mattered. *She* wasn't going to do that.

The leaden weight of the grenade wouldn't let her forget that promise. She couldn't afford to. There was too much at stake.

Her long-term plan was simple enough. Stop the hollowmen. Find their source, and presumably Wallace and the exit at the same time. Find a booth outside and escape with all her friends and family. Use the patterns inside the Yard to rebuild the world. Go back to her old life, inasmuch as that would be possible. Beyond that point, it got a bit blurry.

About all that, she and Clair Two agreed. For a while she had wondered why they needed to escape at all. Why not live in the Yard forever, where people couldn't be copied and ripping was something you could just *do*, without a booth or VIA or the Air to make it possible? But then she remembered Clair Two, and the glitches, and everything else that was making her life hell, and she knew that staying in the Yard wasn't sustainable. She had to get out. Wallace and Kingdon could stay if they wanted, king and queen of their own virtual empire. Clair didn't care about that, as long as they didn't stand in her way. The real world was the only place where she would feel really *herself* again.

Really *Clair.*

Members of WHOLE passed her without a second glance as she headed to the periphery of the prison. Word had spread, clearly, to leave her be. But still she was being watched. Clair switched her lenses to private so they couldn't spy on her that way, particularly if she failed in her attempt. She chose a corner where few hollowmen had been seen, and began the fruitless search for somewhere less institutional to hunker down and *think.* Didn't this place have a library? All prisons did in old movies.

As she passed another empty office, someone hissed at her. She stopped, startled.

"Clair, in here."

A woman's voice, one Clair didn't recognize. She peered through the open doorway, but the office was dark.

"Don't turn on the lights. And be quick before someone notices you standing there like a dummy. Say nothing until you're inside."

Clair hesitated. What difference did it make if anyone saw her or not?

She checked the prison interface. The office in front of

her was a dead zone, one of many places where surveillance had been knocked out by the hollowmen. Anyone could be waiting in there. Any one of the crazies from WHOLE who thought she shouldn't exist, that she was an abomination who deserved to be erased . . .

She opened her mouth to ask, *Who are you?* but a small, strong-looking woman stepped out of the shadows with a finger across her lips. There was just enough light to illuminate her face: Asian, in her forties, gray-black hair pulled back into a severe bun.

"My name is Mallory Wei," she said, "and I want the same thing you do: Ant Wallace, dead. So let's talk. In here. Right now."

Mallory stepped back. Clair followed her until her eyes could no longer distinguish her from the gloom. The situation was so unexpected she could hardly process it. *The* Mallory Wei, whom Clair had never met. But she knew all about her, of course, from Clair Two and Sargent—and now she was inside the prison, wanting to talk. But why like this? Why to her?

Because no one else would listen to Mallory Wei. Not Clair Two. Not Dylan Linwood. Not Libby. *Ant Wallace, dead.* If she was really trying to turn the tables on her husband, this might be the only way for her to make it happen. To rip in under cover of a hollowmen attack and wait for the right Clair to walk by.

The woman had been tortured by her husband, forced

to live against her will over and over again. Why *wouldn't* she want him dead?

It was at least worth talking to her.

Clair took a deep breath to quell the feeling that she was jumping off a cliff into water of unknown depth, and stepped inside.

"Good," said Mallory. "Now, don't freak out, because we're not alone."

"Hello, Clair." A voice came from close by, at her left shoulder. A man's voice.

She turned, and froze. This face she knew. She recognized him from Harmony and elsewhere. He was one of the hollowmen—the first one, in fact. Short, not much taller than she was, with blond hair and cool blue eyes.

"I'm Cameron Lee," he said, "but you'll know me better as Nobody."

Her heart began to thump hard in her chest. Mallory and Nobody, together.

"What are you doing here?"

She was amazed at the steadiness of her voice. Inside, she was trembling. She'd heard the stories. She knew what they had done. And suddenly she realized how vulnerable she was. Mallory was on one side of her and Nobody the other. Her pistol was holstered. There was no way she could reach it without either of them stopping her. There was the grenade, but she didn't even know how to prime it. She'd planned to look that up later.

As though he was reading her mind, Nobody raised his hands and took a step away from her. Like Mallory, he was dressed in simple coveralls similar to a mechanic's outfit, but entirely black. There were pockets, but they appeared to be empty. His right hand had a slight tremor. Motor neuron disease, she remembered. In this body he was dying.

In the Yard, this body was the only one he had.

"Don't sound the alarm," he said. "We don't mean you or anyone else here any harm. We just want to talk."

Clair stepped to her left so she could see both of them at once.

"Talking is not what you're famous for," she said.

Mallory nodded. "We have the memories from previous Renovations. We know what we've done. We're not proud of it. We want to make reparations."

"How?"

"With your help," said Nobody. "Take a seat."

Again, Clair hesitated. She knew what Clair Two would do: she would shoot them down, or try to. She would at least step out of the blind spot and call for help.

That, she guessed, was why they were talking to *her*.

Was there any chance at all that they were telling the truth?

She remained obstinately standing.

"Tell me where the exit is," she said.

"It's with Ant," said Nobody. "I can take you to him."

"You tricked everyone before," she said to him. "You told the other me that you were helping, when you really weren't. Why should I trust you now?"

"The situation is completely different," said Mallory. "Cameron's not the person you have to worry about. Take Dylan Linwood: you might think of him as an ally, but he's not. He's the enemy of everyone in here. The man is already dead, in his own mind. He just wants to burn this place to the ground."

Clair nodded. That fit with what she had heard about him. He thought everyone who had gone through d-mat was a soulless zombie. Why would he strive to save himself or anyone else?

"And that's not what you want?" she asked them both.

"Do you really think it ever was?" asked Nobody.

"You tell me."

"It's not," said Mallory, shooting Nobody a glance. "Not now. Everything spiraled way out of control, before. Cameron understands that. Killing everyone doesn't solve anything. We just want to kill one person . . . and you know who that is. Everything Ant did has to be undone before he goes even further. He'd be happy to stay here forever, you see, now that the world is pretty much destroyed outside—but what happens if one of the survivors finds a

[247]

way to turn off the Yard? In order for him to feel safe, the world outside has to *completely* die."

That accorded with Clair's fears. Mallory was making a lot of sense.

"Between him and Dylan Linwood," Clair said, seeing how it would be, "one wanting to destroy the Yard, the other wanting to destroy outside, we'll be lucky if anyone survives."

"Exactly," said Mallory. "And the other Clair, she's itching for a fight everyone's bound to lose. She gets her way and it's game over. You're the world's last hope."

"Understand that we're not thinking of ourselves," said Nobody, holding up his trembling hand again as though it were evidence of his sincerity. "We know we're not going to get out of this alive. We've had our time, many times over. But the dying should stop with us. We want to help you make that happen."

"Wallace is still your husband," Clair said to Mallory. "Why would you betray him?"

"Because Ant hates me," Mallory said. "He says he loves me, and that's why he won't let me go, but I know that he enjoys having me trapped like this. He's punishing me over and over again for trying to leave him the first time. The only way I can escape is by killing myself for good, which I can finally do in here, and I'll take him with me, just you watch."

She accentuated her final sentence with a jabbing finger.

Clair folded her arms and backed away, feeling as though she was the one being attacked.

"It would help, uh, if you'd be specific," she said, unwilling to be seduced by either a madwoman's passion or a dying man's sentiment until there was something concrete to back them up.

"The exit from the Yard," Nobody said. "That's what we're offering."

There was no obvious sign that he was lying, no matter how closely she studied him. If he was telling the truth, there would be no long, dangerous search with hollow-men looking for them at every turn. There could be just one decisive strike against Wallace, with minimum risk to everyone, after which they could all go home. It could be over in hours. Clair Two couldn't offer that.

Finding the exit was the key to finding her own place in the world. She felt a thrill of excitement at the thought.

"You'll really take me there?"

"Yes."

"Now?"

"Not like this," said Nobody. "You wouldn't last a second, looking like you do."

Clair looked down at her undersuit. It was grimy and blood-spattered.

"I'll change," she started to say.

"Your clothes aren't the problem," he said. "It's everything else."

Clair stared at him, an uneasy roll beginning in her stomach.

"What do you mean?"

"Your face, your build, your skin." He reached out to touch her hair, and she flinched away.

"Don't."

"Time to come full circle, Clair. The only way this is going to work is if *you* become *me*."

—————————————— [30]

"WHAT?" THE SUGGESTION didn't have the same import for her, she knew, as it would for Clair Two, but it was still a very strange one, prompting all sorts of uncomfortable thoughts. "You want me to become a dupe? I didn't think you could do that in here."

"We can't, not without breaking the rules of the Yard," said Mallory. "But you can work around them. You can still change yourself by putting on makeup, for example. You can take medicine, or chop off an arm. Anything that can physically be done to a person's body on the outside can be done in here, too."

Clair's discomfort rose at the mention of lopping off body parts.

"What difference would it make, me looking like him?" She pointed at Nobody, unwilling to call him "Cameron."

"Why would Wallace trust him after what he did?"

"Ant won't," Nobody said. "But he will want us close, where he can control us."

"I'm not going to agree to surgery," she said. "Not ever."

"Face sculpting," said Mallory, "with some prosthetics and the right clothes."

"Do you know a face sculptor?"

"Not personally, but you have a friend who does."

"I do? Who?"

"PK Sargent's partner was a man called PK Forest. The muscles of his face were frozen thanks to a d-mat accident. He used a sculptor to give himself normal expressions, someone he could trust. That sculptor was Billie Lane, PK Sargent's girlfriend."

"Right." Clair didn't quibble the point that Sargent was Clair Two's friend, not hers. "Do you even know if she's still alive?"

"In here? Yes, she is. She once unknowingly helped a member of WHOLE change his face, and Ant scooped up her pattern as a result. Furthermore, PK Sargent knows where she is."

"What good does that do us? I can't just ask her to tell me."

"I know. That's why you're going to ask Q."

Clair stared at Mallory, unnerved by the ease with which the woman was shooting down all her objections. "How do you know all this? Is there a spy in here or something?"

"If there were," said Nobody, "we wouldn't be talking to you. Wallace would have killed you and the other you already."

"It's guesswork," said Mallory, "based on what we know about your relationships. *Before*. You are a different person now, though, I know. You'll listen to reason. You'll be able to talk Q into helping."

Clair considered that. Q's relationship with the other Clair was pretty close. Maybe this was one time when being similar to Clair Two could actually help. And how much did Q need to know, really? She seemed naturally trusting. If she had no reason to suspect anything odd was going on, she might not ask any questions.

No, Clair decided, that wouldn't be a problem. All she had to do was decide if Nobody and Mallory could be trusted. That was the greater question.

"Tell me where I'd be going," she said.

"The heart of his domain," said Mallory, which wasn't immediately helpful. "Ant is paranoid, as you know full well by now. He's hidden behind layers and layers—volunteers on the outside, hollowmen deeper in. There's a space at the center where not even I'm allowed to go. I'm too *unreliable*," she said with bitterness. "As is Cameron. We don't know what goes on in there, or who gets to go in. Lawmakers like that bitch Kingdon, probably. If there's an escape route, that's where it'll be."

"But you can get me in?"

"Yes, I believe so, if you look like Cameron. Once you're in, you'll have a reference point to jump back to. Then you can work out what to do next. Q is the secret weapon we don't have."

"What happens to *you* while we're doing this?" Clair asked Nobody.

"I stay right here," he said. "If I'm seen by anyone, the plan will fail. You can consider me a hostage, if you like. My life for yours. That's the deal I'm making. Reparations, as my friend here said."

From a homicidal maniac who'd tried to assume her other self's life at least once, that wasn't especially re-assuring.

"What about Wallace?" she asked Mallory. "What would I be walking into? What am I supposed to say we've been doing?"

"Ant has a lot on his plate," said Mallory. "He's got Kingdon in one ear and everyone else in the other. He's not looking for more enemies. Just tell him the truth. Some of it, anyway. After all, he already knows we're here, in the prison."

"What the hell?"

Mallory shushed her.

"He wants to take out both Clair Hills by any means necessary, because that'll stop the glitches. But we don't want that, do we? We want the exact opposite. We want to leave Wallace and his puppeteer with as little control as possible, of us and of the Yard. Isn't that right?"

"I guess so."

"You know so. You're a child of consensus. You don't want to go back to the dark ages."

Clair didn't need to think that over. But there was still something she didn't understand.

"Why do you need me at all?" she asked. "Why can't you two do it on your own?"

"Apart from Q?" They exchanged another glance. Mallory shrugged. "Maybe we could, but Ant knows us too well. If he thought we were actively working against him, he'd find some way to undermine us. You won't have that problem. What he knows about us he won't be able to use on you."

"Besides, we don't know if we're the only people he's sent in here," Nobody said. "If he has sent someone else to kill the two of you, then taking *you* away is a kind of insurance. Even if only one of you lives, that's something. And we can only move one of you, at the moment."

Clair bristled at that. "I'm not a pawn."

"I know, girl. We're *talking* to you, aren't we?" Mallory said with a flash of white teeth in the gloom. Not a smile. She was irritated, which, perversely, made everything she said seem more credible. If they were hiding the truth, the disguise was paper-thin.

"Why don't I get to be *you*?" Clair asked her.

"Because I don't trust either of you, not completely," Mallory said. "I want to be there to make sure the job gets done. I'm one hundred percent certain you feel the same."

[31]

AS CLAIR WALKED back to the hub, she turned over in her mind everything she had just learned. It sounded preposterous, dangerous, borderline insane, but it was an opportunity she couldn't turn down. She had thought splitting up was a good idea, and she still thought so now, even though it meant leaving everyone else behind. If she could get to the exit on her own, with no loss of life, Clair Two would have to admit that she was right. When or if she woke up . . .

Clair had told Mallory and Nobody that she would meet them back in that office in one hour, but she hadn't promised she would come alone. She could bring the full force of WHOLE behind her, if she wanted to. Maybe they could all work together and still achieve the same goal.

It could go either way. Two people might succeed where an all-out assault would fail. It certainly hadn't worked when WHOLE had attacked the VIA building in the real world. But the thought of being alone with someone like Mallory, far from her friends, made her nervous.

"How did you manage with the ripping?" Ronnie bumped her. "Any luck sending that grenade?"

Clair hefted it, feeling slightly guilty. She hadn't tried, not even once. "Still here."

"Don't worry. It was a long shot."

"Maybe I'll try again later."

"I'm not sure that practice makes perfect in this case," Ronnie said. "The connection's either there or it isn't, you know? Besides, Jesse's dad is now telling everyone to stop killing the hollowmen. If we can take one alive, that'll give us a different way to get to where they come from."

That plan made sense, but there was an obvious downside.

"What if they don't agree to help?"

"Doesn't matter. The connection will still be there."

"And when we don't need them anymore . . . ?"

Ronnie hesitated. "It's horrible, I know . . . but it's for the greater good."

Clair didn't mention the two live "connections" sitting in an office not far away. Or remind Ronnie that some of the people trying to get into the prison weren't hollowmen at all, but innocent people who thought they were doing the right thing. She was sure Ronnie already knew that last bit and was trying her best not to think about it.

War had turned Clair Two into an emotional cripple, a monstrous version of who she had been. Already, Clair could see her friends falling under the same spell.

It was time that stopped.

Instead of going into the hub itself, she took a sudden left turn and headed for the hospital.

Sargent was sitting in the open door, pistol at the ready on her lap. The picture of vigilance was ruined by the way she leaned against the jamb, sound asleep. Clair tiptoed past her, heart in her throat. The room was full of tables. On the tables were mattresses, and on the mattresses were unconscious people. The air stank intensely of blood and medicine, but that wasn't the only thing urging her to run.

One other person in the room was awake. He sat in a far corner, next to a body that looked dismayingly small in its medical cocoon. Jesse's head was down and his hair covered his face. The urge to run to him was very strong.

Clair fought that urge, as she had fought it ever since Harmony, when all of Clair Two's feelings had come crashing into her. They didn't belong to her. They infiltrated her body, heart, and mind, totally against her will. She didn't want them, and the only way she could stop them was by staying away from *her*—but how was that possible when everyone kept pushing them together?

She had thought it would be safe with Clair Two stuck in a hospital bed, but here she was again, too close for comfort.

Her foot brushed against something on the floor, making a slight noise. Jesse looked up, saw her, and nodded.

"Hey," he said, softly, mindful of Sargent's rest.

She forced herself to move purposefully to his side rather than dive on him, hating every conflicted footstep. Her palms were sweating, making her grip on the grenade feel treacherous. Before she reached the hospital bed he guarded, she found a pocket in her armor large enough to take the grenade and put it away.

"Hey," she said, taking a seat opposite him so that *she* was between them.

"I wondered if you'd come," he said.

Great, she thought. *Guilt me into feeling bad. It wasn't my fault she got shot.*

But that thought was positively childish. She took a deep breath and rubbed her temples, wishing she could think straight around the two of them.

"I had to," she said, and she supposed that was true. She forced herself to look. What she saw on the bed barely seemed human. White plastic formed a rigid shell that stopped Clair Two from moving during her recuperative coma. The shell had gaps in it so specialty patches could be maintained; there was blood around several of those gaps where emergency measures had been hastily performed. A sensor net monitored her brain waves, and Clair Two's head had been shaved to give the electrodes better contact. That detail was worse than anything Clair imagined might lie beneath the shell. She looked simultaneously tiny, enormous, vulnerable, threatening . . .

A flash came to her of a giant head floating across the sky, a man's head with sweeping black hair and a ridiculously high collar around his neck. Where had that come from?

It took her a moment to remember the dream. She'd forgotten it almost immediately on waking.

Maybe, she thought, it wasn't her dream at all, but Clair Two's. . . .

"I have to get out of here."

"What?" Jesse brushed his hair back, revealing his eyes.

She didn't realize she'd spoken aloud. "I mean, I've got to go somewhere and I wanted to talk to you about it first."

"Go where?"

Clair struggled to keep herself focused. She had never consciously noticed Jesse's eyes before, but Clair Two had and they were a rich green that made her skin pucker in a good way. Zep had never made her feel like this. Was that what love was like, even secondhand? If so, she had to fight it. Jesse wasn't her boyfriend. She barely even knew him. The one moment she had let herself go with the tide and reach out to him, he'd made it *very* clear where his allegiances lay. It was hard not to feel wounded and confused, and to wonder when she would experience something like that for herself.

"PK Sargent has been working so hard. . . ." Clair hadn't really known what to say until she saw the peacekeeper asleep in the doorway. Then the idea had popped into her head fully formed, as though it had been there all the time, awaiting its moment. "Finding Lalie Hagopian for your dad, finding the Unimprovables for Libby, keeping everyone safe . . . It doesn't seem fair that she gets nothing in return."

Jesse nodded. "She volunteered to keep watch here. I can't bring myself to wake her up."

"Right. So it's high time someone did something for her. Billie, her girlfriend, is out there somewhere. I'm going to bring her in."

"To the prison?"

"Yes, where she'll be safe. And they'll be together."

"How?"

"With Q's help. And if you can learn to rip, why can't I?"

He looked uncertain for a moment, and then grinned at her. "I think that's an amazing thing to do."

She resisted a wave of sappy sentimental feeling for him. It made her feel like she was drowning. "Great. Because I need you to cover for me with your dad. Tell him I'm in a blind spot still thinking about the damned grenade. Okay?"

"I'll keep Kari busy too," he said eagerly. "I know she watches Billie sometimes. If she sees you, she'll guess what you're up to."

Not likely, she hoped, but she could've kissed him anyway, in gratitude. She'd wondered what to do about that particular problem.

"Thanks," she said, getting up to leave.

"Listen," he said, half standing himself, "about our talk earlier—"

"Don't worry about it," she said, keen to get away. "I understand. We're all trying to do the right thing, in our own ways."

"That's all we can do."

"Just look after her," she said, by which she meant, *Keep a close eye on her.* She wouldn't wish such terrible injuries on anyone, but if it kept Clair Two out of the picture while she did what needed to be done, that worked for her. Better that one girl suffer a punctured lung and whatever else than for all-out war to bring human life to a full stop. Clair would find the exit herself, and no one else would have to suffer.

"I will," he said, easing back into the chair at Clair Two's side. "You be careful out there. You're enemy number one, remember."

She nodded. His concern pained her. It was too desperately magnetic and tragically counterfeit. She hurried from the room as quickly as she could, fighting tears of frustration. This wasn't how it was supposed to be. Not for her, not for him, not for anyone.

The world had bent and twisted around Clair Two. It was long past time someone twisted it back.

32

ON THE WAY back to the blacked-out office, she bumped Q and asked to chat. Q responded immediately; with the decreasing number of attacks and glitches, she had become a lot more available. Clair spun her the same line that she'd used on Jesse. Poor Sargent, dedicated and alone. No one would expect Clair to bring Kari's girlfriend in, although Billie might need some convincing. . . .

Q, the clever machine, was predictably obliging.

"Wilhelmina Orlagh Lane is in Dublin," she said. "I can show you exactly where, and provide you with a mask so you won't be detected en route. You will appear to her as Saoirse McKirdy. The person that name belongs to has presented herself to the census, but your face will not match. I therefore advise staying out of sight of drones."

Clair had forgotten about LM Kingdon's census. That made things trickier.

"Thanks, Q. Also, I want this to be a surprise, so the fewer people who know, the better. That's why I'm doing it alone. I don't want to risk anyone else."

"I understand and will keep your secret." Q's mechanical delivery reassured Clair that she suspected nothing. "I'll watch for threats in your vicinity—"

"No, that's okay." That was the last thing she wanted. "You concentrate on keeping everyone safe here. And don't worry if you don't hear from me for a while. If things get strange, I promise I'll just come back."

Q hesitated, then said, "Of course, Clair One."

Clair One, she thought. *Will I ever be just Clair again?* Maybe when she was reunited with her mother. Surely *she* would recognize her as the real Clair.

The thought of Allison reminded her of what was at stake if everything went wrong. Clair Two had had the shadow of Improvement falling over her, and the crash, and the blue dawn. She had something much simpler, and much more fixable, although it took courage she hadn't possessed until now to make the attempt.

"Tell Libby . . ."

"Yes?"

"Uh, doesn't matter. I'll do it myself."

Clair searched the prison interface. Libby was still asleep, which was a small relief. There wasn't time for a long conversation about this, although they would need to have one eventually. Clair bumped her so the message would be waiting for her when she awoke.

"I'm sorry about Zep. I was an idiot, I know, for keeping my feelings for Zep secret from you. You're my best friend. I trust you to be honest with me, and I feel awful that I wasn't with you. You have to believe that I'll never, ever do anything like that again. The thing with Zep is over—it was never even anything at all—and it's gone now, completely, I promise."

Clair hesitated, then added, "I want to make it up to you. I hope you'll believe that, even though everything is so screwed up right now. I'm trying to make it right. For you and me, and for all of us."

She could feel herself getting maudlin, and perhaps a little morbid, too. The note was starting to feel like a farewell. She ended it there, and sent it, and hoped that when Libby woke it would be to good news.

"Okay, I'm ready."

Mallory stood as Clair entered the office. Nobody was standing in the corner, facing out, eyes glittering and alert.

"You look ready," he said. "That expression is becoming very familiar."

Clair didn't know what her face was revealing, but she wouldn't let him intimidate her the way he would've intimidated Clair Two. An echo of that feeling was bad enough.

"So how are we going to do this?" she asked Mallory. "I don't know how to rip. . . ."

"I do," Mallory told her. "All you need to do is hold my hand and do exactly what I tell you."

Both prospects made Clair uncomfortable, but she was committed now. No point being squeamish.

She held out her left hand, and Mallory took it in her right. The woman's skin was smooth, and her nails were impeccable, painted red with a silvery shimmer. Her fingers gripped Clair's tightly, almost to the point of discomfort.

Mallory turned her to face the door leading out into the hallway.

"You know what Billie looks like, yes?"

Clair nodded. Q had sent several reference images of the slight, purple-haired woman with moles on both ears, plus images of her environment.

"Hold her in your mind . . . everything you know about her . . . her name, her clothes, her connection to PK Sargent. Hold it, and when I count to three, jump."

"Jump how?"

"I mean literally jump, though the doorway. We'll leave together." She raised their clasped hands. "And when we get there, I'll jump back here, so there's no chance of Ant spotting me. I'm masked like you, but it's best not to take chances with the drones. You can come and get me when you're done."

So she would be in Ireland alone? Clair had second thoughts. What if Wallace planned to drop a nuke on her or something equally dramatic? Mallory would be safely on the other side of the planet.

"You stay with me," Clair said, "or we're not going at all."

Mallory hesitated.

"You said it earlier," Clair insisted. "Ant Wallace is

looking for Clair Two and her army, not two people visiting a face sculptor."

"All right. It's your funeral. On three, remember?" Mallory squeezed her fingers so tightly that bone ground against bone. "One."

They lined up on the door. Clair put Billie Lane firmly in her head and tried not to think about what it would look like if she jumped out into the hallway holding hands with Mallory Wei.

"Two."

Beside her, Mallory tensed like a panther, and Clair noticed for the first time how muscular she was. Agewise she had to be late forties, but she had the body of an athlete in her twenties. Improvement at work?

"Three."

Purple hair, moles on each ear, PK Sargent's girl.

"Hey, Clair . . . *huh?*"

Zep had appeared in the doorway in casual fatigues, his mouth a perfect O of surprise, halting Clair in midleap.

Nobody didn't hesitate. He pulled Zep inside and despite the massive difference in their sizes twisted him around, forcing his face forward.

"Take his hand," he growled at Clair.

That was easy. Zep was already reaching for her, saying something confused and shocked that she paid no attention to at all.

Then Zep and Clair were gripping each other, and

Mallory tugged her forward too powerfully to resist. They were going anyway. Clair stumbled but managed an awkward leap through the door, dragging Zep after her, pushed by Nobody from behind. The beginnings of Zep's cry of alarm were lost in the airless chaos of ripping space. The Yard twisted around her with the never-normal-but-now-familiar lurch of every possible sense. Clair struggled to keep her thoughts on Billie, and on Mallory's and Zep's hands too, because if she lost touch with either of them there was no way to tell where they'd all end up.

The disorientation peaked with another glimpse of the floating head, and then, oddly, Sargent's face, but she assumed that was because of where they were going.

She hoped Billie wouldn't freak out if they arrived right on top of her.

The Yard wrenched her violently from side to side, depositing her momentarily in an icy forest in the middle of the night. "Clair!" gasped Zep. "Clair, what's going on?" *Billie,* she thought, not letting her mind stray. *Billie.*

They ripped again, at Mallory's wordless insistence. *"Out of sorts and out of the blue,"* said a voice. It was Sargent again, sounding as though she was riding along with them, but that was impossible because she was still asleep in the prison.

Solid ground hit the soles of Clair's feet, as though she had gone from running to standing in a split instant. Her hand pulled free of Mallory's. Zep crashed headlong into her, throwing her forward into a table, which squeaked dramatically across a tiled floor and banged into a cream-colored wall. As she lay draped across it with him pressed against her, catching her breath and feeling him do the same, Clair realized that she *knew* that wall and everything around it. She had seen it in the images Q had given her. To her right was a painting of a mime, and to her left fresh flowers in a wall sconce, a spray of pink, green, and purple. She could smell them.

"Where are we?" asked Zep, pushing himself off her. "What's going on?"

"Billie's face-sculpting practice," she gasped. "PK Sargent's girlfriend."

"What are we doing here?"

"She's not around," said Mallory, pulling herself upright. The room was indeed empty.

"Did someone get here before us?" Clair asked.

"I don't know."

"Isn't that . . . you know?" hissed Zep, pointing at Mallory. "Clair—"

"Sorry, sorry!" called a voice from the other side of a bead curtain separating the antechamber from the exam room. "I'll be just a second."

The voice was light and accented—predominantly British, but there was a hint of the local Irish. It had to be Billie. In case it wasn't, Clair removed her pistol and held it behind her back. Zep's eyes widened on seeing it.

"Be quiet, and don't bump *anyone*," she hissed at him. "I'll explain, I promise. You just have to trust me."

He looked ashen and afraid. "How do I know you're really you?"

"No dupes in here, remember?" she said. "Besides, a dupe would've shot you rather than brought you along for the ride."

"Take your time!" Mallory called back to Billie, casting Clair and Zep a warning look. "We're happy to wait."

She opened the room's only solid door and checked the street outside. Bright daylight poured in, accompanied by a sharp, cold breeze. Mallory pulled her head back and turned the lock so they wouldn't be disturbed. Her gaze swept across the room's fixtures and decor as though expecting something to leap out at her at any moment.

The beads rattled. Mallory turned to face the doorway, and so did Clair and Zep.

Billie was pushing through backward, turning as she came and wiping her hands on a robin's-egg-blue towel. She looked exactly as Clair had imagined: short, rounded, with delicate features. Her hands were small but strong, and she wore a ring that was a match for Kari Sargent's.

"Sorry," she said, "I had to go to the—"

On seeing the pair waiting for her, she stopped dead. Her eyes widened.

"Holy freaking hell," she said to Clair. "It's you."

33

"SHE'S NO ONE," said Mallory. "We're just here for a face job."

"Do I *look* stupid?" Billie glanced at Mallory, then turned back to Clair. "You're Clair Hill, the girl everyone's looking for. What rock have you been hiding under?"

"If only 'everyone' knew," Mallory said. As she said the words, her hand slid into a pocket of her jumpsuit and Clair understood—understood beyond all shadow of a doubt—that there was a weapon in there, something small and deadly, and if she didn't speak soon Sargent was going to lose her girlfriend a second time.

"I've been a bit out of it," Clair said, stepping forward to put herself between Mallory and Billie. Her own pistol slipped harmlessly out of sight. "Kari can tell you later. You're probably wondering what's happened to her, and I can tell you that, too. But first, what are they saying about me? Who do they say I've murdered or betrayed now?"

"No one, as it happens. They just want to give you some kind of medal for saving the world." At Clair's look of astonishment she added, "Yeah, totally not fooling anyone. Come on through. I have a Faraday shield. Half my clients are even more skittish than you."

Billie turned and passed through the bead curtain. Clair went to follow, but Zep caught her by the elbow.

"Tell me now!"

"Zep, calm down."

"No, not until you explain why we're here, with *her.*"

Clair didn't look to see if Mallory was offended by the poison in his voice. She had eyes only for him. He looked so frightened and confused, so completely out of his depth, that her heart broke a little.

She reached her left hand up around his neck and pulled him down, kissed him briefly but firmly on the lips. *Take that, Clair Two,* she thought, with only a twinge of guilt for Libby's feelings. She needed Zep to be calm, and part of her still needed *him*, period. Surprising him out of his shock was worth the risk.

"I'm still me," she said, letting him go. "And I know what I'm doing."

He nodded quickly. Two bright spots burned in his cheeks. She took him by the hand and led him through the curtain.

On the other side was a space barely large enough for the four of them, containing a fabber and the memory of fresh tea on the air. An actual door took them into a state-of-the-art operating room, the only human touch a picture of Sargent with a small, expressionless man who had to be PK Forest, Clair guessed. There were three chairs and one surgical table, currently standing in an almost-upright position. Clair looked nervously for gleaming knives and laser saws but thankfully saw nothing of the sort.

Billie leaned against a narrow bench and indicated that they should sit. Clair and Zep did, but Mallory stayed by the door as it shut tight, sealing them in. The Air disappeared—Clair disliked being so disconnected, even from a copy of the real Air. Yet she also felt profound relief. There was no chance that anyone in either camp would find them now.

"Okay," said Billie, folding her arms. "You know Kari, so that's working in your favor, but you'd better tell me *how* you know her before moving on to specifics. I'm clumsy when I'm nervous."

Clair glanced at Mallory, who indicated that she was to do the talking. Not knowing quite where to start, Clair decided to leave out all the backstory about Improvement and the dupes and the hollowmen and the Yard, and focus solely on how Sargent was protecting them from corrupt PKs and lawmakers, and how Clair needed to get close to them in order to bring them down.

"Hence the face job," Billie said, nodding. "Well, I'm available. None of my bookings have turned up today. Did you have something to do with that?"

Clair shook her head. "It's hard to explain—"

"They're dead," said Mallory. "That's why we're here: to stop anyone else from dying. Are you going to help us or not?"

Billie looked at her and smiled, not at all intimidated by

Mallory's aggressive tone.

"I would like to talk to Kari first," she said.

"You can't."

"Why not?"

"Because she would try to stop you."

"Why would she do that, pray tell?"

"Because she would rather kill me on sight than entrust me with Clair."

"And you?" Billie asked Zep, who looked up from his hands in surprise. "What do you think, handsome?"

"I don't know," he said, looking from Billie to Clair and back again. "I'm not even supposed to be here."

"I guessed. That's why I'm asking you."

He sat straighter, out of the slump he had fallen into. "Clair thinks it could work. That's enough for me."

"What about this one?" Billie nodded at Mallory. "How do you know she's not luring Clair into a trap?"

"I don't know that." Zep's voice rose in challenge. "That's why I'm going to go with them."

"You're not," said Mallory.

"You can't stop me. If you try, I'll tell the others and they'll stop *you*."

Clair felt a moment of panic. She didn't want Zep coming with her into danger, but she remembered the threat of violence in Mallory when it seemed that Billie was about to give them away. He was in trouble whichever way he went.

And it was all Clair's fault. If she could send him back in time and have him choose another corridor to walk down, she would.

But she couldn't. She had to find a way to make it work.

"He has to come with us," she said, suddenly seeing a solution to the standoff. "Wallace will want someone on the inside of the prison to get past the Yetis. If we bring Zep, Wallace will let us right into the center. He won't be able to resist. And it'll distract him, stop him from noticing me if I'm doing anything wrong."

Mallory looked trapped for a second, but then she nodded. "All right. But if he tries anything—"

"I'll only try anything if *you* try anything," Zep said.

They glared at each other, and Clair felt another momentary qualm. Zep was loyal but impulsive. What if he said the wrong thing at the wrong time and gave them away? What if instead of being an asset, he became a liability?

They would have to cross that hurdle when they came to it. There was a lot to do before then.

"Will you help us?" Clair asked Billie.

The face sculptor looked down at the floor. Her shoulders rose as she breathed in deeply, then fell as she exhaled.

"If I don't, you'll just find some corner hack who'll make you look like Frankenstein's leftovers," she said. "So, yes, to spare you that. Who do you want to look like?"

Mallory sent her an image of Nobody. Clair expected

Billie to react with surprise, perhaps even alarm. The height difference was small, but that was the least of their worries. Blond hair, pale skin, male . . . Could the differences between them have been any greater?

Instead Billie just nodded and spoke in a businesslike tone. "Armor, gloves, and lifts will cover the difference in build. We'll treat the visible skin of the face and neck, and the hair, of course. Your features will require some tissue prosthetics to bring them into line. As for the rest . . . how much time do we have?"

"The longer it takes, the more likely our absence will be noticed," said Mallory.

"Not long, then." Unexpectedly, Billie grinned. "It's a good thing we're not involving Kari. There are aspects of my work that not even she knows about."

Yet another qualm, but it was too late for second thoughts.

"What do I do?" Clair asked, standing.

"Come stand here next to the table, pretty girl, and we'll get started."

[34]

SCANNING CAME FIRST. Clair was afraid that she would have to take off all her clothes, but Billie asked her to peel her undersuit only down to her waist.

"Turn around," she told Zep, and he did so with only a token protest.

"Now I know you're really you," he bumped her, lens to lens.

"And I know you'll never change," she bumped back, remembering the feel of his lips against hers. She had really earned Libby's ire now—even though she was sure she wasn't going to take this further . . . wasn't she?

Once Billie had created a detailed map of Clair's body, from her skin right down to her bones, the table tilted back and the work truly began. To keep her still, Billie gave her a tranquilizing patch that she promised wouldn't knock her out for hours. Clair drifted in a hazy, not-quite-asleep state into which occasional words and phrases intruded. Her body felt pleasantly distant.

"I can't believe you're doing this," Zep bumped her.

She found it hard to make her lenses work. "No choice."

"Much better than biology class, though," he said. "Maybe you'll get credit when school starts again."

She was buoyed by his confidence, but also somewhat saddened by it. He really thought they would get out of the Yard and everything would go back to normal. But how would that work with so many people dead? They could re-create all the buildings and cities they wanted, but without people to occupy them, without the majority of teachers and students and parents and children, the world would feel very empty.

"If," she corrected him, feeling like a killjoy but knowing someone had to say it.

"I dissected a frog once who was as cynical as you," Zep said. "It didn't end well for him."

"Never expected," Clair replied, pretty sure she wasn't talking about the two of them, but her thoughts were sliding around the inside of her skull like eels on ice, "a happy ending."

"That's what your mom—"

"Don't!"

"Yes, definitely still you."

"Have you got video of the subject?" Billie asked Mallory at one point. "You'll need to coach her on vocal and behavioral tics."

"He's got plenty of those."

"You can definitely put her back afterward?" said Zep.

"The only thing I won't restore is her hair," said Billie. "Best if that grows out naturally."

Clair went to touch her scalp, anxious at what was being done up there, but she couldn't even lift a finger. The anxiety immediately faded, becoming a numb kind of curiosity. She wished there were a mirror above her so she could see. What would it look like as her face was flayed off and then laid back on a different way?

That was how she imagined it—like Zep's dissected frog. But the reality, she was sure, was much less invasive. There would be hair-thin needles and implants for stimulating muscles and fat emplacements to make her look more masculine around the jaw and throat. Her skin would be repigmented by chemicals, or perhaps by adding some sort of overcoat? If the latter, she hoped it wouldn't peel away in the middle of her mission and reveal her true identity. . . .

That triggered a half dream in which she imagined herself standing in front of Ant Wallace, a man she had never met, and her face fell off, only to reveal exactly the same face underneath—and then *that* face falling off to reveal exactly the same face again, and so on and so on.

That amused her, for reasons she couldn't fathom.

"Well, Chuckles," said Zep, leaning momentarily into view, "I'm glad *someone's* having fun."

"Perhaps I should dial back the patch a little," said Billie.

No, Clair wanted to say through lips as immobile as two toothbrushes taped together. *If I don't laugh, I'll cry.*

After first being copied, and now losing her face, the question of who she was was getting increasingly hard to answer.

Whatever Billie did to the patch, it made time jump forward in hard-to-fathom increments. When Zep talked to her, his words faded from memory as quickly as he said them. If she replied, she later had no memory of what she said.

Clair had another strange dream in which a metallic cylinder descended over her, surrounding her with distorted reflections that couldn't possibly be of her. There were flashes of light, but she couldn't blink. Her eyes watered, then dried out, then the cylinder was gone and she was able to close her eyelids again.

Mere moments seemed to pass when the table was moving underneath her, bringing her to a position that wasn't quite vertical, but was a long way from the horizontal she'd been enjoying. Her head spun. She raised a hand to steady herself, and was numbly surprised when her hand did actually move.

It felt different, and so did her face. Her armor didn't feel the same. Zep, Billie, and Mallory swung into view. They were watching her closely.

"What?" she said. "Oh!"

Her voice was so much deeper than it had been, which shouldn't have surprised her, but did, so much so that her knees gave way beneath her and she would have fallen if Zep hadn't lunged forward and caught her under the armpits.

"Easy," said Mallory, reaching past him and gripping her chin so tightly it hurt. "Don't wimp out on me now, Cameron."

Who? Right. She had better get used to being called that, even if it was only going to be for a short time.

[279]

"I feel . . . not right," she said. She was never going to get used to that voice.

"Try standing again," Billie said. "You'll get your balance when the patch clears."

Zep took one hand away, and Clair got her legs working properly. She could feel the lifts in the soles of her shoes making her taller, and indeed Zep didn't seem quite as enormous as he usually did. When she straightened, her eyes could see clear over Mallory's and Billie's heads. The view from her peripheral vision was different too. Her shoulders were broader, and her breasts—

Involuntarily, she raised both hands to touch her chest.

"I've only bound them," Billie said with a reassuring twinkle in her eye. "Don't worry. Everything below the neck is au naturel."

But above the neck . . . ?

"Mirror," Clair said.

"You know what you're going to see," said Mallory.

She did, but she needed to see it to believe it.

"Mirror," she repeated, snapping her fingers.

Billie already had one in her hand. She had probably been through this thousands of times. Raising it, she placed it between Clair and Zep and showed her the reflection.

Only it wasn't her reflection. It was Nobody looking back at her. Until she blinked.

The blond, blue-eyed, white-skinned boy in the mirror blinked too.

She recoiled automatically as every muscle in her body went into spasm, denying the reality. Her knees buckled again on the table behind her, and she almost sat back down. Her eyes didn't leave the mirror, though. She wasn't trying to run. It was just a reflex, a deep, fundamental part of her crying out, *That's not me!*

But it *was* her, for a while. She was Cameron Lee.

Some Improvement, she thought. And then she laughed.

"What now?" asked Zep, pushing the mirror aside.

"Still want to kiss me?" she said, and wasn't surprised by the fleeting look of disgust he gave her in return.

But then he did kiss her, and that surprised her more than anything. Surprised her so much that she kissed him back. And for a brief moment, it was everything she wanted it to be. He kissed her not because she was Libby's best friend. Hell, she didn't even look like a girl anymore. He kissed her because she was *her.*

Then he ruined it by pulling away and saying, "That's for the safe house. You're still my hero, Clair-bear."

He was referring to experiences she hadn't shared. *He's thinking of Clair Two.*

"This isn't the prom," Mallory said. "Show me that you can stand on your own. Talk to me the way he talks. Stop wasting time we might not have."

Clair felt her face go warm. There would be no hiding that behind her new pale skin.

──────────────────────────── [35]

"FASTER, BUT NOT carelessly.

"More cocky, like you're the only person in the room who matters.

"Pause at the beginning of every sentence. That's what he does, so you're going to have to do it too."

Clair had thought the sculpting would be the hard part. After an hour with Mallory, she was beginning to wonder if it would ever end.

Zep watched with hooded eyes as she walked around the operating room one more time, addressing Mallory's concerns as she went. She had done it so many times she was getting dizzy.

"The walk is much better," Mallory declared. "Remember, that hand is the one that shakes, not the other one. Make sure you look people in the eye, and keep looking long after it's comfortable. And when you talk, try not to say anything the easy way."

"Why would I?" she said after counting to three in her head.

Mallory nodded. "Much better."

"So are we ever doing this?" asked Zep. "It's beginning

to freak me out now, to be honest."

"I think we're almost ready." Mallory performed one last armor check, and Clair did the same. She was wearing something similar to the gear she'd been given by WHOLE, but bulkier, and she still had her pistol and the grenade both securely stashed away. There was no way she was going into Wallace's inner sanctum unarmed.

"But first," said Mallory to Zep, "what about you? You have to be believable too. You're betraying your friends. Why?"

"I've been thinking about that," he said. "I'm not betraying them. I'm rescuing them."

"How?"

"Well, they've been kidnapped by terrorists. WHOLE says Wallace is in charge, so that's why I've come to him for help setting them free. First I escaped the prison, then I was picked up by you guys because obviously you're keeping an eye on things down there, and here I am." He held out his hands as though completing a somersault.

"What are you offering Ant in return?"

Zep looked flustered. He hadn't thought that far.

"Information," said Clair. "How many terrorists, where they're deployed in the prison, what weapons they have . . . and so on. You don't have to be accurate. In fact, the more you make up, the better."

"I'm good at inventing random numbers." Zep nodded

gratefully. "That's what my math teacher wrote on my last paper."

Clair checked the time. Six hours had passed since they had left the prison. There had been no word from Q or any of the others on the rare occasions she'd checked the Air, so her cover story was holding. Billie had fabbed some protein bars and shakes to refuel them while they rehearsed. She saw no reason not to leave immediately, apart from the butterflies in her stomach telling her to run like hell.

"Just a teensy thing before you go," said Billie. They turned to face her. "I get that you have your reasons for keeping Kari out of this, but that doesn't mean I like it. I'm posting a message to the Air that will be automatically delivered to her in one hour. That way if anything happens to you, or me, she'll know. Are we clear on this?"

Mallory looked as though she might argue, but then she nodded.

"Understood. One hour."

Taking Clair and Zep by the hand, she turned them to face the closed doorway with Zep in the middle.

"Let me do the talking," she said, "unless there's no alternative."

Clair nodded. So did Zep.

"Open the door, Billie. Hold tight."

Mallory surged forward, dragging Zep after her. Clair's arm wrenched in its socket as he jerked her forward in turn—then they were ripping, twisting, turning through the interstices of the Yard, and Clair held her breath, hoping her new face wouldn't come off before she wanted it to.

They touched down in Manhattan, instantly recognizable even though its graceful bridges and walkways appeared to have been torn down. Clair's lenses told her that they were in Bryant Park, near the Grand Central Terminal Museum of Transport. She had been there once on a school excursion and remembered it full of people, a lively green space. Now it was dark and cold and empty, apart from a dozen people in black uniforms holding rifles, surrounded on two sides by barbed wire. For the first time it truly occurred to her that they were going deep behind enemy lines.

"Names," barked a voice from behind them.

"Wei," said Mallory, making a show of dusting herself down. "Recruit escort. Zeppelin James Barker."

Zep saluted with excellently faked nonchalance, Clair thought.

My turn, she told herself.

"You seriously don't know who I am?"

That did the trick.

"Continue."

Mallory took Zep by the arm and led him across the square. Clair fell in behind them, taking in everything around her. She didn't know what she might need later as a reference point in case of a hasty escape, so she kept her eyes open, noting checkpoints, gun emplacements, and several armed drones whining above them. The buildings were all lit up by floodlights, but the windows themselves were dark.

Where is everyone? she wondered.

Mallory led them out of the park, heading southwest. They crossed Fortieth Street and Sixth Avenue, then walked down to Thirty-Ninth Street, where they headed west. Broadway was deserted. At Seventh Avenue they turned left. There was a bank of d-mat booths standing open on Thirty-Seventh, and guards on Thirty-Fourth, but otherwise the city could have been empty of all life, which was too peculiar even for the Yard. Could there be a curfew?

They turned right at Thirty-Fourth, and the only building showing any sign of life appeared before them.

VIA headquarters, the One Penn Plaza building, was a black monolith set back barely a block from the water's edge. A scattered pattern of bright blue lights shone from the inside, casting into sharp relief the craterous damage caused by Q to some areas of the building. Clair had heard about that, but this was her first chance to see it with her own eyes.

She was impressed: maybe Q was more than a clever machine after all.

It also struck her as uncanny that something so recent

in the real world could be re-created in the Yard—but not as uncanny as the fact that Manhattan appeared to have been turned into a police state overnight.

They approached the base of the building and were stopped a second time. While Mallory brusquely explained the purported reason for their presence, Clair became conscious of a rotting smell that seemed to be coming from the water but didn't smell like dead fish.

Zep curled up his nose. "Gross."

"You don't like it," said one of the guards to him while the other conferred with someone inside the building, "you tell the boss, if he lets you in. He needs to clear them out of the Garden or burn them. It's a health hazard, leaving them there like that. Maybe that'll be your first job, rookie."

Zep looked like he might be about to throw up.

Clair didn't know what she was more afraid of revealing—her ignorance or, when the meaning of his words became clear, her revulsion. Either way, she was glad when the guards waved them through, and she forced herself to stop wondering about the missing inhabitants of the Manhattan Isles.

She put her hand in the small of Zep's, pretending to guide him but actually for reassurance. *Strength,* she thought, for both of them.

They had been accepted into the inner sanctum.

THE FOYER WAS an empty expanse that seemed somehow larger than the footprint of the building. Clair's fake skin crawled as she walked with Mallory and Zep toward a distant bank of elevators. The doors loomed vast and ominous. Inside was a cage large enough to hold a squadron of soldiers.

As the elevator lurched beneath them and began to rise, she became increasingly sure that there was something wrong with the perspective. No ordinary building needed elevators this large. Was space out of whack inside Wallace's headquarters? Could its proximity to him, the creator of the world, be twisting things out of shape?

She glanced at Mallory, ignoring Zep between them. The woman's gaze was fixed straight ahead. Her jaw was clenched.

Clair felt as though she was falling down a pit, rather than rising to her fate at the top of the elevator shaft. Was this how it had been for Clair Two?

The floor shuddered beneath them. The doors rumbled open, and for a moment Clair saw double: another version of herself was walking toward her with another version of Nobody through the multicolored chambers of the prison. But then she blinked and the vision was gone.

Glitching, she thought. She couldn't let that distract her, although it did seem odd, since she was nowhere near Clair Two. . . .

Mallory stepped out into a cathedral-like room with a high, domed ceiling and sweeping glass windows in a semicircular arc that admitted a view of dark skyscrapers and infinite stars. The space was opulently furnished, almost bizarrely so, with chairs so ornate and twisted that there barely seemed space for a person to sit in them.

Nowhere did she see anything that looked like an exit from the Yard. Maybe it was concealed or just out of view.

Far away, in the hazy distance, she made out something that looked like an altar.

Mallory stopped, turned, and looked pointedly at her at her. Her eyes said, *Nobody wouldn't stand there gawking.*

Clair forced herself to move, grabbing Zep by the shoulder and pushing him ahead of her. Their feet made hard sounds on the bleached white floor. The curved walls were so far away that no echoes returned.

Mallory headed for the altar, which resolved as they came closer into an absurdly huge desk big enough for a game of racquet ball. Behind the desk was a chair so baroque it could have been a throne, with complicated spires and gyres. A woman was standing nearby with her back to them, staring out at the night sky. She didn't turn as they approached, didn't acknowledge them at all until Mallory stopped, three yards from the desk, and said, "Where is he, Kingdon?"

The woman turned. "He says he's on his way. I choose to believe him."

"Things still frosty between you two, then."

It wasn't a question, but Kingdon answered it anyway. "Destroying the world was *not* part of the plan."

Clair filed that information way. If Kingdon and Wallace didn't see eye to eye, that could be used against them.

"Where have you been?" Kingdon asked Mallory.

"I don't answer to you."

"Neither does he," Kingdon looked at Clair. At Nobody. "That's new."

Clair thought fast. Adopting her most disaffected tone, she said, "There's nothing new in here. Just variations on a theme."

Kingdon laughed without humor. "And who's your friend? Another for the cause? It's not like you to do the dirty work of recruiting yourself. . . ."

Space warped with a sound like distant thunder, sparing Clair the need to answer. A handsome, middle-aged man appeared in midstep behind the desk, walking toward them with even, self-assured paces. He was wearing a gray business suit and no tie. His patent leather shoes squeaked softly underfoot.

"That's Clair's friend Zeppelin Barker," said Ant Wallace. "And this is a most unexpected visit . . . from all three of you."

Clair was taken momentarily off guard. Here he was,

the man everyone said was the enemy of the human race. The liar, the mass murderer, the stooge of ambitious would-be dictators . . . Somehow he was smaller than she'd expected, radiating an air of likeability and charm that she knew had to be a mask like hers.

Mallory's expression was borderline hostile.

"You know I've been sniffing around that hole of theirs," she said, pushing Zep forward. "The things you find."

Zep stumbled, and glanced over his shoulder at Clair for guidance. She felt a cold premonition of disaster.

"Don't look at me," she said in her coldest voice. He had to understand. They couldn't afford any mistakes, not until they had found the exit. "You wanted to come here. Tell the man why."

Zep swallowed, comprehending.

"You're hurting my friends," he said to Wallace. "I want that to stop."

Wallace reached the desk and leaned over it, both hands flat and fingers spread wide.

"Well, I don't *want* to hurt anyone," he said, like a schoolteacher forced to be stern.

"It's the people we got caught up with. Dylan Linwood. WHOLE. All of them. They're crazy. Clair . . . I don't know what she's thinking. But she'd be glad I'm here, I bet, if she knew. She'd want me to tell you how to stop this."

"How *do* I stop this, Zep?"

Zep rattled off the lines they had rehearsed before leaving

Billie's exam room, as Clair watched Wallace closely. Zep would take the hollowmen to the prison, and the hollowmen could take out WHOLE. It was a simple lie, which made it more believable, Clair hoped. Was that eagerness she saw glittering in Wallace's eyes, or suspicion?

Clair's hackles raised on realizing that she was being closely scrutinized by Kingdon in turn.

Something about Clair's impersonation of Nobody wasn't right.

What am I doing wrong?

Frantically, she refreshed her memory. Cameron Lee was the first dupe, with a twisted sense of loyalty. He was above reproach, or felt that he was. He wouldn't wait around like hired help.

Clair unlocked her limbs and walked in a long, slow circle around the desk. *Prowl,* she told herself. *Everyone in this room knows that you're edgy and unpredictable. Wallace may have built the weapon that destroyed the world, but you're the one who made sure it went off.*

Kingdon's eyes followed her, then slid away.

"That's all very generous," Kingdon said, interrupting Zep's interrogation. "But it doesn't solve anything."

"I'm afraid my friend here is correct," said Wallace. "You should understand that I have higher goals. My objective isn't just WHOLE, Zep. It's Clair herself. Both Clairs. I'm not going to stop until they are mine. What do you say to that?"

Clair was behind Wallace now. She could see Zep's internal struggle, large on his face. It didn't matter what he said now; he wasn't really planning to betray Clair. But it still felt like it—and that was good. His indecision made the lie more believable.

What he said next took her by surprise.

"I've been thinking about the crash," Zep said, "and how your space station was destroyed. Clair never explained how the two things were connected, but I've figured it out. She killed herself to blow up the station. Then Q brought her back, and that broke parity. She died and she didn't stay dead—that's what ruined d-mat for everyone."

Clair forced herself to keep walking, even as the truth of what he was saying sank in. Of course that was what Clair Two had done. It made sense in terms of the world that was, and explained why Clair Two hid the details of how she had brought d-mat down. She had done it *by accident*, she said, but what she meant was *by dying*. By killing herself. By sacrificing herself in a way that she could never talk about. Because she hadn't actually died.

No wonder Clair Two seemed so screwed up.

But why had Clair herself never seen it before? Zep wasn't the smartest athlete on the starting block, for all that she liked him too much. If he had worked it out, why hadn't she?

Because she hadn't wanted to. That was the only answer she could come up with. And that too made a dismaying kind of sense. Would she have been willing to do what Clair Two had done, in her place?

Who would?

She was glad Zep couldn't see her real face as she grappled with this question.

"I'll take you to them," Zep told Wallace, "if you promise to undo everything she did."

──────────────────────── [37]

"CLAIR'S ONGOING EXISTENCE is a problem." Kingdon started to say more, but Wallace waved her silent.

"That's something we all agree on," he said. "Zep, are you seriously offering to show my friends here how to kill Clair? Because that's what it amounts to. There's a big difference between having a bad feeling about someone and putting a gun to her head."

Zep was in profile to Clair as she continued along her arc around the desk. She saw his Adam's apple bob as he wrestled with the question. It was a very real one for her too. Wallace needed to be stopped, but would that justify murdering him?

"I think . . . ," Zep said, and he nodded his head forward, raising his hands to cup his temples. As he moved, Clair saw something behind him that she hadn't noticed before.

There was a doorway set in the curved white wall, to

the right of the open elevator. Small, arched, it was utterly incongruous in the otherwise magnificent dimensions of the inner sanctum. It had no obvious reason to exist in Wallace's stupendous throne room.

As Clair tried to see what lay on the other side, her vision glitched again. This time she saw a tall man dressed in ribbed red material striding across the white expanse of the floor. His eyes were green and piercing, his hair was curly and orange, and his lips moved as though he was trying to tell her something, but she could hear no words. All she could do was watch and try not to blink in surprise as he took three long steps toward her, then vanished.

She had no idea who he was, but she was sure that the glitch was significant. It proved that the arched doorway was important. Was it the exit, though? She didn't want to assume something that later turned out to be wrong.

"Think hard, boy," said Kingdon. "Think about your duty to the human race. Occasionally there are sacrifices. Clair Hill will be one of them, one way or another. Best it happens now, before someone else gets hurt."

"I *know*," Zep said with muscles clenching in his jaw. "I'm not going to do it for you, though."

"No one's asking you to, my boy." Wallace nodded. "You're *offering* to give us the information so we'll get rid of this pesky girl. Nice and simple. In fact, almost too simple."

"You think he's lying?" asked Mallory.

"He doesn't have the brains to."

Wallace turned suddenly to address Nobody.

"But you do."

Clair froze.

And then she laughed.

It was the first thing she thought of, the best way of covering her sudden fear.

Did he mean "you" as in Nobody or "you" as in Clair?

"I'm glad you find this funny, Cameron," said Wallace, putting Clair's mind at ease on at least that score. "Are you laughing at his expense or ours?"

"Maybe I'm laughing at my own," she said, because she had to say something, "for thinking that you'd be grateful."

"Grateful? For the chance to get ourselves killed?"

"You can learn a lot," said Kingdon, "from the way a person lies."

Kingdon was looking at Zep.

Sweat pooled on his brow. His hands were spasmodically clenching and unclenching. *Don't do anything stupid*, Clair wished she could tell him. *Let this play out. It doesn't have to end badly, just because they know you're not telling the whole truth.*

"There's truth in lies," Clair said. "And honesty in deceit. No one in this room has ever talked in a straight line."

"Some less than others," said Wallace, to her, still. To

Nobody. "You don't write. You don't call. You follow orders I give to other people, and you ignore the ones I give to you. Then you turn up out of nowhere with this poor creature in tow. Did my good wife put you up to this for her twisted amusement, or is there something I'm not seeing? Explain, please."

"You're not seeing the obvious," said Clair, thinking harder than she'd ever thought before. If Kingdon was right about learning from how people lied, perhaps the best defense against that was to stick to the truth. "He's here, isn't he? With *us*. What does that tell you?"

"That he has a death wish," said Wallace. "We definitely can help him with that."

"You sound like a petty villain," said Mallory to her husband. "It impresses no one."

"It impresses teenagers who are way out of their depth." Wallace came around the table to put himself in front of Zep, who shifted nervously from one foot to another. "Are you going to tell me why you're really here?"

"He won't," said Clair before Zep could say anything. It was risky, but she didn't want him to be in Wallace's sights for too long. "You'd already know if you weren't missing the point so badly."

"And that point is?" Wallace asked, frowning.

"He's terrified of us," said Clair. "But it's clear he came alone. Why?"

"That's obvious." Wallace reared back and away. "It's

her. He's doing this to impress Clair. She's got him dancing to her tune like the jilted fool he is. That's why *she's* involved," Wallace crowed, indicating Mallory. "The things we do for love, eh?"

Mallory just shrugged.

Wallace turned back to Zep. "I should send you back to Clair empty-handed to teach you a lesson—or perhaps without any hands at all, to teach *her.* Which do you think would be most educational?"

"Neither," said Clair, not sure how much more of this she could take. "The least interesting theory is that she sent him to try to trap us. So the least interesting thing we can do is punish him in return."

She had Wallace's full attention again now.

"Go on," he said. "If you have a point, do get to it."

"I don't think she sent him to trap us," Clair said, moving closer to Zep and Mallory as she spoke. They might need to make a quick getaway and it would help if they were all together. "I don't think she sent him at all. I think he's here on his own steam, looking for something. Something she wants, and that she thinks *we* have. . . . What could that be?"

There was only one possible answer. And there it was—a quick dart of Wallace's gaze from Clair to the arched doorway and back again. *The exit,* he was thinking, and his eyes betrayed him.

Mallory looked at Clair. She had seen it too.

Now all they had to do was get out alive and tell the others.

"You're wasting your time, boy," Wallace told Zep. "There's nothing for you here but an unhappy ending."

"Do you want me to get rid of him?" Mallory asked.

"Yes. We're going to get rid of all of them eventually, anyway."

"Do it in public," said Kingdon. "Send a message."

"There's no need to kill him," said Clair. "How will he learn if you keep doing that?"

"You have something better in mind? Keeping him as a pet, perhaps, like I keep you?" Wallace waved dismissively. "I still want to know what you're doing back here. You're not leaving until you've told me."

Clair froze. She was close enough to grab Mallory and Zep and they could try to rip away in time, but . . .

Shit, she thought. They were in the middle of the room. They needed a doorway or a window. Perhaps they could drag a couple of the ridiculous chairs together and improvise an arch.

"Do I need a reason?" she stalled, brushing her fingers through her fake-blond hair. She didn't have to fake the way they shook.

"I own you, body and soul," said Wallace, the threat on his face suddenly naked and ugly. "You'll give me a reason or—"

Wallace never finished his threat. The elevator cage

exploded, the floor kicked beneath them, and smoke and dust billowed into the room.

————————————————————— [38]

CLAIR LUNGED FOR Zep and pulled him down. Crouching protectively over him on one knee, she drew her pistol and tried to figure out what this development meant for their chances of long-term survival. Her heart thudded double-time.

"I told you not to trust him," Kingdon cried, dropping behind the desk. "But you wouldn't listen!"

"What's going on?" Wallace bellowed as the air grew thick and dim around him. "What is *happening*?"

Clair glimpsed shapes moving through the smoke. Some wore black, like hollowmen. Others wore red and moved like lithe ghosts. A shot rang out, making her flinch, then another. The second shot sounded less like a pistol than a balloon popping. It came again. One of the hollowmen went down, then another, bites taken out of their black-clad forms as though by an invisible creature. Blood sprayed and misted the already smoky air. Clair's stomach rolled.

"Time to get out of here," said Mallory, grabbing Clair under one elbow, but Clair resisted, watching the red suits and thinking, *Enemy of my enemy.*

"Who are those people?"

"Does it matter? Remember, you look like one of the bad guys now, to them."

Clair peered around for Wallace, but there was no sign of either him or Kingdon. Her jaw muscles bunched at the thought that they might have escaped. There was nothing she could do about that now.

"All right," she said, glancing down at Zep. He was on one elbow beneath her, looking up at her with eyes wide. "You okay?" she asked him.

"Just dandy," he said. "Let's leg it."

They stood as one, attracting fire. Clair felt something whizz past her ear, and she ducked, pulling the hood of her armor closed across her face. Zep did the same, but Mallory made no attempt to protect herself. She ran with her teeth bared like a feral animal, snarling at fate and dragging them along behind her.

Clair had memorized the location of the arched door. She knew without checking that that was where Mallory was taking them.

The exit, she thought.

If there was someone on the outside, or at least something that could receive their data, they could leave. She and Zep, outside the Yard, free of Wallace and WHOLE and Clair Two and Libby and everything else that was making her life such hell.

It was powerfully tempting, like wanting to kiss Zep

even though she knew he wasn't really thinking of her.

But it wasn't the plan. They needed to rip back to the prison and tell the others, and they could use the doorway to do that without leaving the Yard entirely. Once she got the reference images back to the prison, they could *all* escape, together. That was the way it needed to go—for personal reasons as well. She was guilty of kissing Zep now, honestly and properly, and if she had learned anything from Clair Two, it was that running from a problem only made it worse. She was running *to* it now, in the hope of finding a permanent solution. If she talked to Libby she could make everything right. And maybe then she would put to the test whether Zep and she were ill suited or not.

The little arched doorway came into view through the smoke. Someone was standing in front of it, a tall, orange-haired man in a red suit, and Clair remembered with a strong sense of déjà vu the glitch vision she had received just moments ago. Even now he was glitchy, flickering in and out of sight, limbs moving jerkily back and forth, like a video jumping randomly between frames.

Clair tasted metal.

"Wait," she said, tugging on Mallory's arm.

"Don't stop, Clair. You'll be out of here in a second and none of this will be your problem!"

Clair stumbled a half dozen steps, but the flickering grew worse. Mallory and Zep were affected now too, and so was the smoke. Her own thoughts were becoming fragmented, impossible to keep in line.

Suddenly the red-haired man was standing right in front of her. His mouth was moving, but his voice took a second to register.

"You're not who you say you are."

Clair went cold. How did he know? What had she done to give herself away? Was it the glitches?

"Don't listen to him," said Mallory. Her hand on Clair's arm was like a steel band, yanking her toward the door. They were only yards away. "This is what you want, remember? Nearly there."

"No, wait." Clair was at the center of a storm of glitches. She saw people and places that couldn't possibly be real, making her feel light-headed, almost panicky. The floating head was back, and so was the patchwork boy, his face a joyless leer. The two of them were flying high over a barren landscape striped with gray and white dunes. It looked like an alien planet, lifeless and cold. "Something's wrong."

"Nothing's wrong at all," said Mallory. "Just a little farther and everything will be over."

"Come on, Clair," said Zep, pulling at her other arm. "Don't stop now."

"Clair? Yes, I thought so, although it seemed impossible." The orange-haired man's eyes were wide. "You can't be here. You must get away from the exit before it's too late."

Suddenly there was a gun in Mallory's hand, pointing at the man's chest. "I didn't let you into the building so you could screw things up like this. Get out of my way or—"

"Or what? If you do this, everyone will die."

"So what? We're dead anyway."

He lunged at her, and they struggled for the gun while Clair struggled for her balance. The glitching was getting worse, rising up around her like a hurricane. She cried out, feeling as though she was losing herself. She seemed to be in three places at once—Wallace's throne room, an airship high over Russia, and a makeshift hospital bed—spread so thin that she wasn't really in any of them at all. Three ghosts didn't make a whole person.

Then the gun went off and Mallory slumped to the floor. The red-headed man grabbed Clair's arm. He wrenched her away from the door so powerfully she was almost lifted off her feet, snapping her out of a state of terrified confusion.

"What's going on?" asked Zep. "Why aren't we leaving?"

"You can try, but she can't. Not that way," the man said. The glitching began to ease as they put distance between her and the arched door and raced for cover. Clair finally got her feet under her and took her own weight. "This must have been Mallory's plan all along. She used both of us—me as a distraction, you as a weapon—and she very nearly got what she wanted."

"Got what?" Clair's head was clearing to the point where she could think again. Mallory was shot, maybe dead. What had she almost made them do?

"Think about it," the man said as they crouched behind a chair that arched raptor-like over them, seeming to grasp at them with long claws. "The Yard is supposed to be a copy of the real world, but there are no doorways to other universes in the real world. The exit through that door has to be a glitch, just like you. Bring the two of you together, and what do you think will happen?"

"I don't know."

"I'm not sure she did either, but it was bound to be bad. And now we're stuck here in the wasps' nest. Damn." He ran his hand through his hair. "Damn!" he said again.

Around them, red and black figures fired at each other from points of cover across the room. Conventional gunshots and unnatural popping sounds echoed all around them.

"Who are you people?" she asked him.

"My name is Evan and I'm with RADICAL," he said. "I knew Mallory Wei from when she used to be a member. She had the right code words. We didn't know we couldn't trust her anymore."

Clair wasn't entirely following. It didn't matter. She knew enough about RADICAL to recognize them as allies, more or less.

"Why can't we go out the way you came in?" Zep asked.

"Brought the elevator shaft down behind us. The plan was to leave the other way. We obviously can't do that now."

"Not with me," Clair said. That was the bottom line, and she didn't shy from it. If the arched door hid a glitch that might destroy her mind—and maybe the Yard with it—but was at the same time the only way anyone could rip out of here, then that was that, really.

She didn't waste time agonizing over it or wishing things were otherwise. There was only one way it could go.

Clair pulled away from Zep. "Take him with you," she said to Evan. "Take him to where WHOLE and the others are hiding out and tell them we found the exit. You'll find a second version of me there. Work with her. Come back and do it right."

He blinked, then nodded. "All right."

"Clair, no—"

Zep was struggling. Evan restrained him from behind, one arm tight across his chest. Clair's heart ached, but they were out of options.

"I'll signal the others," Evan said. "Then we'll pull back. Give us a moment to get through. You'll find another way back?"

Clair nodded. No one on Wallace's side knew who she really was yet. That would give her plenty of opportunities.

There was just one thing she needed to do before RADICAL retreated and took Zep with them.

She leaned in close to Zep. "Look after Libby," she said. "She'll need you."

Their cheeks touched for a moment, and then they separated.

Zep's mouth framed a silent *No!* as Evan pulled him away. Clair turned her back on both of them, steeling herself for what might come next. She had no plan to get out of the VIA building. She had only the barest hint of what a plan might look like. Kingdon obviously thought Nobody was responsible for the attack, and if Wallace believed her, Clair might not last more than ten seconds. If their obvious discontent with each other ran deep enough, however . . .

A handful of men and women in red were already running toward her across the room, converging on the exit, firing their pop guns over their shoulders at the hollowmen who followed. They were vastly outnumbered, and were being picked off one by one. Clair leaned out from under the cover of smoke to fire at them, winging one of the black-clad figures. She felt no qualms about doing so. Her memory of one of them firing at her in the prison was clear.

Space flexed nearby. She acknowledged with a satisfied nod the distant echo of the Yard ripping as *someone* got away. How many, she didn't know. She could only hope that Zep was safe. Exhaling through pursed lips, she lowered the gun and came around the other side of the chair. She would emerge from cover as the last of the hollowmen went by, to join them and lead a chase for nonexistent fugitives elsewhere.

A black-clad figure was waiting for her.

"He's here!" the woman called.

"Have you been looking for me?" It was hard to pretend to be Nobody with so much else in her mind and heart, but her life depended on them thinking she was who she looked like. "I need to talk to Wallace."

"You will."

The woman raised a pistol and pointed it at her. Clair stared down the barrel, thinking, *She's not really going to fire.* Then the woman *did* fire and Clair was kicked down and onto her side, pain flaring in her shoulder. The round had penetrated her armor and burst brightly in her flesh.

For a moment she couldn't think. She was a creature of nerves and blood and shock, and it was all she could do to reason around a simple three-word phrase, singing along with the agony.

History repeats itself.

She thought of Clair Two in a makeshift hospital bed, half dead from gunshot wounds of her own.

But here she would have no Jesse to sit at her bedside, or Sargent to guard the door.

More black figures joined the woman who had shot her. They leaned over Clair, their voices rising and falling through the drumming of her pulse.

"But that's—"

"What have you done?"

"Winged him. Boss wants him alive."

Lucky for Cameron Lee, Clair thought. *Not so lucky for Clair Hill.*

She had hoped to appeal to Wallace's good nature. It was true, after all, that she had had no idea about RADICAL's attack, and that truth might have saved Nobody's life. But now that wouldn't work. It was an even bet whether the disguise would hold out another minute. She could feel the prosthetics hanging loose against her face. They might fall off with her next breath. She wasn't going to be able to talk her way out of this one.

What would Clair Two do? The question flashed across her mind, closely followed by images of Zep, Libby, her mother . . . and Jesse, his green eyes far away now but somehow still at the center of her universe. *It's not fair!* she wanted to scream, but she knew she only had one option, and just one chance to pull it off.

She rolled over, reaching for her pistol. One of the hollowmen kicked it away. The one who had shot her picked it up and pointed it at her. Groaning, Clair fell back with her left hand in her thigh pocket, where she had put the grenade. *That* move the hollowmen didn't notice.

The grenade, tucked safely away and forgotten. Until now.

It was ironic, really. Dylan Linwood had given her a mission, and in a roundabout way she had succeeded.

The heart of Ant Wallace's empire? Check.

One grenade? Check.

It would've been funny, almost, but for the thought: *I guess we're the same, after all.*

There was no time to wait for Wallace. One of the hollowmen was already peering at her a little too closely.

"Hold on a second," he said.

Clair closed her eyes.

History repeats itself.

―――――――――――[38 redux]

Clair Two

CLAIR WOKE WITH her heart hammering, feeling as though a whole army had just run across her grave, firing pop guns and being chased by monsters she couldn't see. . . .

A thought was ringing in her mind.

Outside . . . There's another Clair Hill, outside the Yard.

For a moment, she couldn't tell what was a dream and what was reality.

She was *definitely* in the prison. According to her lenses eighteen hours had passed since the hollowmen had attacked. Since she had been shot. The thought struck like a soft punch to the gut.

That much she knew.

But nothing else was clear. Nothing else made sense.

Something had woken her up. Some ripple in the Yard, some tear in the fabric of the world.

"Q, what's going on?"

There was no answer to her panicked bump, and she wondered if that might be connected to her strange awakening.

"Kari?" she called aloud.

"Easy, I'm right here." A large shape detached itself from the shadows and came to loom over her. "You shouldn't be awake. We took off the cast only an hour ago—"

"Something's wrong." Clair could see another version of herself standing at the end of the bed, flickering and silent, her expression one of dismay and resignation. A glitch. Data ghost. She remembered seeing something like that just after she'd been shot. Could it really be an echo of the Clair on the outside? A Clair who thought she should have died in the blue dawn?

She blinked and the vision disappeared. "Something's very wrong."

Distantly, an alarm began to sound.

Clair lurched into an upright sitting position, amazed at first by how easy the movement seemed, but then undid that personal triumph by making herself sick. Putting her weight on her right hand—her left was bound tightly to her side, with her forearm flat across her stomach—she leaned over the edge of the mattress and vomited onto the floor, chest burning with every heave.

Kari stopped her from falling out of bed, but then tried to press her back down onto the mattress.

"Lie still, Clair—"

"I can't." The sense of panic she had woken with wasn't going away. "I need to get up."

"Why? There's nothing going on we can't handle. That alarm . . . it's almost routine now. The hollowmen have been attacking on and off ever since you were shot, trying to wear us down. But the Yetis are a match for them. They've laid traps everywhere. You have to rest, Clair. You were seriously injured. You almost died."

"But I didn't die," she said, thinking, *The other me, trying to get in touch . . . maybe* that *was what caused the most recent glitches. Rescue coming in the form of a giant floating head . . .*

What *exactly* had woken her up?

A lanky, long-haired figure skated to a halt in the doorway.

"Sarge, this time it's different," he said. "It's . . . Oh, you're awake. How are you?"

Jesse smoothed out his urgent expression with a visible effort and hurried to Clair's side. He reached for her free hand, but stopped at the last instant, as though afraid of hurting her. She caught his hand before it could escape and gripped it tightly, perhaps too tightly, but she was beyond holding herself back. The other Clair's sense of all-pervading grief was still in her mind. Being around him calmed her a little on that front.

"I feel terrible." Her injured shoulder was covered in a stiff fabric wrap that smelled of menthol. The pain was a distant ache, her stomach settling now that it was empty. But there was something new about her head. Letting go of Jesse briefly, she discovered that her hair had been shaved to the skin. Patches of glue remained where sensors had been stuck to her scalp to monitor her brain waves. *You almost died.*

She shivered, feeling suddenly cold. Even that small movement caused her pain.

My hair is gone.

"I really am damaged now, aren't I?"

Jesse sat down on the edge of the bed and squeezed her hand tightly. "Bullshit. I've never seen anything like the patches Sargent used. Peacekeepers always keep the best stuff for themselves."

"You'll be as good as new in a couple of days," Kari said. "If you do as you're told."

Clair felt tears gathering at the corners of her eyes. Nothing would ever be the same again. She had been *shot*. The world outside was almost completely gone. Humanity was hanging on by the thinnest thread, a thread that could snap at any moment.

She couldn't meet Jesse's eyes. He looked so worried. But when she looked away, she saw shapes turning and twisting ominously in the dark corners of the room.

"You said something's different about this alarm," she said.

Kari shook her head before Jesse could reply. "There're two of you now, remember? You don't have to do everything."

Clair remembered Clair One's face suddenly looming at her out of the darkness right when the bullet ripped into her shoulder.

"You trust her?" she asked Jesse. "After what she said to you?"

"Uh, actually, we can't find her," he said, glancing apologetically at Kari. "She's been missing ever since she said she was going to get Billie—"

"She said *what*?" said Kari, rounding on Jesse in alarm.

"I know, I know, she made me promise not to tell you. But now Zep's missing as well, and when the Yetis went looking for him, they found someone else."

"Who?" asked Clair.

"Nobody," Jesse said. "That is, Cameron Lee. He was lurking about in one of the empty offices. We've taken him to the hub, where . . . Wait, you can't do this."

She could and she was, but swinging her legs around in order to stand was taking more strength than it turned out she had.

"Help me up," she said.

"What? No. I'm in enough trouble already."

"Kari's all talk. There's too much important stuff going on for me to stay here."

She gripped his T-shirt with her right hand and pulled at him, forcing him to take her weight or be yanked forward. Kari sighed and assisted from the other side. Clair's head spun when she was on her feet, and for a moment she wished she wasn't so stubborn, that she could just give in and let someone else sort it out, but then her balance returned and she felt able to stand without falling over.

The room was full of beds. It looked like a field hospital in a war zone. She took a step forward and something tugged sharply in her chest. She tried not to show how much it hurt. Sitting back down was unacceptable. As she took a second step, the ghostly vision of another Clair returned, this time covered from head to foot in blood. That was even more ominous. *"Cunctando,"* said Devin in her ear, which didn't help. At least she could guess what that meant, now.

Assuming the dream of another Clair outside the Yard was real.

It had to be, didn't it?

She was gambling a lot on not being stone-cold crazy.

One slow step at a time they passed an office that was now a morgue. The door was open. She counted thirty body bags lined up on the floor and on desks. She tried not to wonder who was in there. Ronnie? Tash? Libby? Any of the Unimprovables? She couldn't think about that now.

The morgue was lit with red light. The next room was entirely in blue, and the hospital had been yellow. That could have been to help people sleep, but then the next room along was green and she knew there was more to it.

Before she could ask about the party atmosphere, the alarm cut off, then started again.

"Glitches are up," said Jesse. "Maybe because you're awake. That could be why Q has gone quiet again."

She thought there was more to it than that, but she didn't want to tell it twice. The dream had contained another Clair, another Kari Sargent—and another Q, too. What kind of knots was the Yard tying itself into in order to accommodate the reality of the message she had received? That *must* be why the glitches had gotten worse, earlier: information was real in here.

Letting Jesse's theory stand for the moment, Clair searched her memories of the dream for a way to reply, some means of telling the other Clair that she had been heard. That would test the truth of it, once and for all.

The dream, however, felt less like something that had happened to her than something she had put together from a series of fragments—dialogue, images, descriptions, names. Q and her other self had compiled this jumble and with Devin's help fired it into the Yard, hoping she would understand it when it arrived. The fact that she had been unconscious at the time might have made the message easier to absorb, but the dreamlike quality it retained made it slippery, hard to pin down. If they had ever said, *Do so-and-so to reply,* unfortunately she didn't remember it.

The hub was lit in purple and a wash of other colors. She kept hold of Jesse's shoulder as they entered, feeling like everyone was staring at her. The room was full of people, and they all looked tired and stressed, and annoyed at her, although she didn't know why. *She* hadn't done anything.

"The prodigal Clair returns."

The comment came from a huddle of Yetis on the far side of the room. Or rather, Clair realized, the man they were holding prisoner. He was small, blond, and young, and immediately recognizable even though she hadn't met him in that body before.

Nobody.

Clair did her best to stand straight without wincing. "You don't get rid of me that easily."

"Do you think that's my intention?"

"*Someone* tried to kill me."

He shrugged. "You will keep putting yourself in the line of fire. . . ."

She couldn't banter with him and stand at the same time.

"Chair," she said, shuffling toward the agglomeration of desks in the middle of the room.

"You shouldn't be up," said Dylan, standing to give her his seat.

"You're probably right." She eased herself down and fought the urge to keep on going to the floor. Sitting was uncomfortable, but there was no way she was lying down in front of anyone in this room. "That's never stopped me from disagreeing with you before."

"You wake up the same time he appears," Dylan said, managing to look worried about her and suspicious at the same time. "Is there a connection?"

Between those two things, Clair wasn't sure, but something was definitely going on. She could see it in the shadows and taste it in the back of her mouth.

"I think . . . no, I'm sure of it. I've received a message from outside," she said, choosing her words with care. She didn't want to reveal too much while one of Wallace's agents was in the room. The possibility of a third Clair was something she definitely wanted to keep secret. "There are survivors, and they're trying to communicate with us."

Nobody was suddenly paying very close attention. "There are?" he said. "That trumps what I came here to tell you."

"You didn't come here to tell us anything," said Dylan. "We found you—"

"I wanted to be found, because something went wrong," Nobody said. "I received a message too. It was a bump that was only to be sent in certain extreme circumstances. You'll want to know about that—but now I want to know about this instead."

He grinned at Clair, taunting her. She wasn't going to rise to the bait.

"What was your message?" she asked him.

"Let's trade."

"No." The last time they had done that, the world had been destroyed. "Tell me."

"It said, 'The barn burned.'"

"Which means?"

"That Mallory Wei didn't die the way she wanted to."

Mallory . . . dead. Clair didn't know what that had to do with anyone here, but she felt satisfaction nonetheless. That was one problem solved, if Nobody was telling the truth, since dead was dead in the Yard.

"She *wanted* to die with you," Nobody added.

Clair laughed to show she wasn't riled by his posturing. "Well, she missed her chance, didn't she?"

"Maybe not. You were with her when she died, after all."

Clair felt her face lock up, although she tried to act naturally. Clair One was missing on a secret mission involving Billie, presumably with Zep, and now Nobody was telling her that Mallory had been with her. And Mallory was dead.

"We need to find Clair One," she said.

"Libby, Ronnie, and Tash are searching the prison as we speak," said Arabelle.

"They won't find her," said Jesse. "I've already looked. She's not here."

"I've bumped Billie," said Kari. "She's keeping quiet about something, but I'll get it out of her."

"Tell me about the outside," said Nobody, leaning eagerly forward. "Tell me what I got wrong."

"Everything," said Clair, feeling a rise of hatred for the man who had made her life a living hell. "Everything you do is wrong."

"Cunctando!" said glitch-Devin again. Space rippled like a funhouse mirror. And into that moment, bursting through a hole in the air trailing smoke and a smell of ripped space, fell Zeppelin Barker and a blood-spattered man Clair had never seen before.

[39]

ALARMS SQUALLED. YETIS reached for their weapons. Zep raised his hands and dropped to his knees, tears streaming down his black-smudged face. The man steadied himself and said, "My name is Evan Bartelme, and I want to know what the hell is going on."

Bartelme, thought Clair. Was he connected to Devin,

Trevin, and Eve? Finding RADICAL was high on her list of things to do, but it seemed RADICAL had beaten her to it.

"*Cunctando regitur mundus,*" she said, trying to stand but falling back into the seat when it turned out she didn't have the strength. "We're friends. You can trust us."

He stared at her a moment; then his eyes widened in recognition. "The last person who used those words betrayed us . . . but you . . . Clair said there'd be another version of you, a different version, and she was right."

Clair's bald scalp crawled. "You saw Clair One?"

"Is that what you call her? Yes, I saw her. I stopped her from running into the exit and killing us all."

"You found the exit?" asked Jesse.

"Yes," said Zep, still on his knees. He wiped his face and looked at Clair as though he couldn't believe she was really there. "I know where it is. I can take you there anytime."

"But you can't go, Clair," said Evan. "It's too dangerous. You must've seen the topological breaks and fractures in continuity when you and the other Clair were together. You call them glitches. Putting you anywhere near the exit would be cataclysmic for the entire simulation."

"The Yard," said Kari. "That's what it's called. So where is Clair One now?"

"She had to stay behind."

"We have to go back for her," said Zep.

"We can't," Evan snapped. He had obviously told Zep that many times already. "It's too dangerous. She'll find her own way. She's disguised, remember?"

"Disguised how?" asked Clair.

"She looks like *him*." Zep pointed accusingly at Nobody. "It was their idea. Nobody and Mallory. They wanted Clair to go into the exit. They *wanted* the world to end."

Everyone looked at Nobody, who shrugged. "I've never been one to leave something unfinished."

There was a moment's silence, during which the horror of the situation sank in. Nobody had tricked Clair One in the Yard just as he had in the real world. And what was she doing now, alone?

"We can't just leave her there," said Jesse. "Where is she?"

"She's in the heart of Wallace's stronghold," said Evan. "You'll be dead in seconds if you blow her cover. We're the only ones who made it out."

"But she's on her own, helpless—"

"Not helpless," said Clair. "Not if she's armed."

"I gave her a grenade," said Dylan Linwood. "I told her to deliver it to the hollowmen."

Everyone stared at him now.

"She wouldn't," Jesse said.

Clair remembered Turner Goldsmith and her first plan to kill Ant Wallace.

History repeats itself, she thought.

"Maybe she already did," Clair said.

Jesse stared at her in horror.

Something shifted in the Yard, so subtly that it took her a moment to notice how. She simply felt it, from the small hairs on her arms to the marrow of her bones. Then she noticed that the shadows had stopped moving, and she could no longer sense voices just below the threshold of hearing.

The glitches had stopped.

Which meant that there was now one fewer Clair Hill alive in the Yard.

But that thought brought no relief, as it might once have. Now there was just futility, anger, and grief.

Clair One was dead.

"If there's any justice," said Kari in a cracked voice, "she took Ant Wallace with her."

A voice broke the silence that followed, coming over the prison's internal speakers as well as all their augs.

"She did not," said Q, speaking through the sudden calm, her voice very adult and serious. "But her sacrifice has not been pointless. We now know the location of the exit, and I have already used that information to trace a packet sent from the people on the outside to the Clair before you. With that trace I can contact them in turn. This will create a new source of glitches, but I believe

I can control them now that I know what the source is. Among the people on the outside is another Clair."

Another Clair? The whisper spread through the room.

"Lose one, find another," said Nobody.

Clair wanted to snarl at him, but Q wasn't done.

"Clair One has also gained you valuable breathing room. I believe that the attacks on the prison will cease temporarily, following the strike on Wallace's stronghold. Mallory Wei is dead. Many hollowmen have died, also. This is a major victory."

So why didn't Clair feel like celebrating? Because Mallory Wei was a serial suicide—and maybe she was too? Or because everything had changed while at the same time staying horribly the same?

"Wallace or Kingdon or whoever's left," said Dylan, "they won't sit idle for long. We need to respond, and fast."

The room erupted into chaos as everyone began talking at once. Clair shrank back into her seat, knowing she should be paying attention, knowing she should be feeling satisfaction, but instead just feeling tired and filled with the certainty that there was another conversation she needed to have, right now.

Accessing the prison's interface, she found Libby and the others on the fringes, still looking for Clair One and Zep.

"Meet me in the mess," she bumped them. "There's something you need to know."

Tash held Libby while she cried. Ronnie glared at Clair with hot, red eyes. Clair was sitting in front of them, feeling too many kinds of pain to classify. She hadn't cried yet, and she wasn't sure she was going to. Part of her felt numb inside, like it had been hurt too often.

"This is all your fault," Ronnie said.

"It's not." Ronnie's words didn't hurt her, but she felt a strong need to defend herself. It was important they understand, even though she was struggling to understand it herself. "It's not all her fault either. We're the same person. Under similar circumstances, we made the same decisions. She was tricked just like I was. She made a mistake just like I did. She died . . . she sacrificed herself . . . hoping that it would make things better. We have to make sure she didn't die for nothing."

"She didn't trust you. Why should we?" Ronnie wasn't going to make it easy, and Clair didn't have the heart to blame her.

"You either trust all of us or none of us," she said. "You can't have it both ways."

"Clair's right," said Zep. He was standing in the doorway. Clair hadn't brought him with her, but he had obviously figured out what was going on and wanted to be part of it. He deserved that, she supposed, although it risked muddying things with an entirely different emotional crisis.

He went to Libby and tried to put his arm around her

too, but Libby pushed him away.

"She told me to look after you," he said. "Just before—"

"Why?" Libby's voice was snappy. She didn't look at him. "Because she felt guilty? She already sent me a note to apologize. Wasn't that enough?"

Zep blushed, and Clair knew that she and Clair One had shared more than he wanted to let on.

"Clair was never very good with the small stuff," said Tash into Libby's hair. "She'd walk through a picnic following a cloud, my mom would say."

"She walked practically to the other side of the continent to save her best friend," Kari said. "Who cares what she stepped on along the way?"

Clair's throat felt hard and tight with emotion. Was the past tense really necessary? She felt as though she were hearing the eulogy at her own funeral, one where everyone said exactly what they really thought and, ghostlike, she had no right of reply.

"She *used* me," said Jesse, staring fixedly at the floor. He had avoided meeting her eyes since Evan's arrival and had helped Kari carry Clair to the mess only sullenly.

Clair reached for his hand but he pulled away.

"I'm sorry," said Zep, his expression as wretched as Clair had ever seen it. "I should've talked her out of it. But she took me by surprise. I was just running some laps around the hub and heard her talking. Then they jumped me, and . . ." He looked like he was about to cry. "She always seemed to know what she was doing."

"She thought so," said Ronnie, then added what Clair supposed was a kind of concession: "She was usually right."

"I'm sorry too," Clair said. "That's all I can say."

"She gave her life so we could find a way out," said Tash. "You don't need to be sorry for anything."

They sat together in silence, each nursing their private thoughts, Clair realizing that it wasn't just she who had changed. Her friends were different now too. They had been thrust into a situation not remotely of their making and forced to make do as best they could. And they *were* making do. They could hold their own in a world of terrorists and would-be dictators as easily as she could. Clair was sure there wasn't one among them who wouldn't do the same as she had for their friends and loved ones.

"If we know the way out now," said Ronnie, "why don't we just go?"

"It's not as simple as that," said Clair. "We don't know if there's a working booth on the outside. Without a booth, there's nowhere to go to."

"And *you* can't go anywhere," said Zep. "Not through the exit."

"She can go last," said Tash. "Once the Yard is empty, what does it matter if it's destroyed?"

"What if the exit is destroyed while she's going through?" said Ronnie.

"We need more information," said Clair. "That's why it's good that there's someone on the outside now."

This time the silence was shorter but more uncomfortable.

"Another you," said Libby. "How many *are* there? And is she as bald as a coot too?"

"That's it, I think," Clair said, touching her scalp self-consciously. She hadn't been brave enough to look in a mirror yet. "I don't know what she looks like."

"That makes her Clair Three," said Tash, rubbing her chin with the knuckle of her thumb. "I still don't get how this is possible. How can one of you die but the rest still be alive?"

"We've been through this," said Ronnie. "Copy the atoms and you copy the person. Remember when we cloned those tomato plants in biology? Just because yours died didn't mean the others died with it."

"People aren't tomatoes," said Tash hotly.

"And neither's Clair, but the principle's the same." Ronnie changed the subject. "When can we talk to her?" she asked Clair.

"I don't know."

"I am close to establishing contact," said Q, making Clair jump. She hadn't known Q was paying attention. It dismayed her to think that she had grown used to this new distance between them.

"How long will it take?" she asked.

"Perhaps ten minutes. I must make absolutely certain that Wallace will not detect the exchange."

"Let's make the chat open at this end, so everyone can hear," Clair said. That was the right thing to do. "We'll go back to the hub. I think we need to be together for this."

Libby nodded. She understood. This was bigger than friendship, bigger than who belonged to what group. There was nothing bigger than the future of the human race itself.

"Okay," Libby said, "but first we've got to find you a hat."

[40]

Clair Three

OPENING THE CONNECTION took closer to thirty minutes, nowhere near long enough for Clair to accept that it was real.

Devin's plan to contact her other self had actually worked.

The signal was sporadic and suffered greatly from interference. Wallace was fighting them, she assumed, although Devin thought it might be a sync issue. Time did move oddly inside the Yard, it turned out: sometimes faster, sometimes slower, always unpredictably. Eve Bartelme thought the problem with the signal was something else entirely. She muttered dire warnings about an "entity" at work, which was what RADICAL called AIs like Q. Given that the only one they knew about *was* Q and she was helping them, Eve's warnings were ignored as paranoid.

Occasionally a blocky, low-res image got through, revealing a gathering of around fifteen people in a low-ceilinged, bunker-like space that Q told her was an underground prison. Clair recognized nearly all the faces. It was her own that looked like a stranger's.

Clair—Clair *Two*, she had been told to call her—was seated front and center. There was a blue-and-green checked beanie on her head. Clair was wearing a beanie too, to keep out the cold; hair kept straying past her ears to tickle the side of her face. There were no hairs straying onto Clair Two's face, and her right shoulder and arm were bound tightly. No one had said anything about a Clair One, but it was easy to suspect the worst, judging by how everyone looked. They had made progress, but it had come at a cost.

She understood that feeling well. Her heart had initially leaped to know that Jesse was alive. Then her heart had broken on seeing the way Clair Two looked at him, with a longing that matched her own.

Hope for the best, plan for the worst.

After days of dashed hopes, she was getting pretty good at the planning part. *All part of being Clair 7.0,* she told herself. The survivor, attempting to make amends. Alone.

"Who's the new guy, the one in red?" she asked during one of the downtimes. She was standing next to real-world Q in Kari Sargent's body—who the other Q had suggested they call "Q-prime"—on the bridge of the *Satoshige*, a snow-dappled forest unfolding slowly beneath them. Embeth had reduced both altitude and speed to avoid a storm brewing ahead. Lightning flashed regularly, but Devin said it was likely to blow itself out soon, and with luck and its wind at their backs they would easily make up the time they had lost.

"Evan Bartelme of RADICAL." Kari Sargent's lenses flickered as she scrolled through data the two Qs had squeezed out of the connection. "A relation, I assume."

"He's Mom," said Devin Bartelme from the South Pole.

"Say what?" asked Sandler.

"A very old version of mom."

"Shhh," said Clair, "they're back online again."

"We're looking at images Zep brought back with him from the exit chamber," said Dylan Linwood, his voice crackly with static.

More grainy pictures appeared in Clair's infield, of a massive space with curving glass windows. The size was all wrong, but something about the perspective rang a bell.

"It's Wallace's office," she realized. "Bigger than it should be, but that's definitely the place."

Zep nodded. Clair was so glad to see him, along with all her friends. That they were alive was like the sun breaking through the gray clouds, however briefly. "Everything about the building is twisted, like it's been magnified."

"They're hacking the Yard on a grand scale in there," said Ronnie. "It makes sense there'd be side effects."

"Could we do the same thing down here?" asked Jesse. "There aren't many of us, but if we could magnify things somehow in our favor . . ."

"The exit is the cause," said the Q inside the Yard. She sounded almost perfunctory, as though dealing with more important things elsewhere. "Without an exit you will not achieve the same effect."

"Still, there must be something you can do along those lines," said Clair. "You're already ripping around the Yard. Who knows what else you can do if you put your minds to it?"

"We'll get a team on that," said Dylan. It was disconcerting, seeing him without his red eye and lacking the malign intelligence of Nobody speaking through his mouth. "If the exit is in Wallace's office, what else does that tell us?"

Clair thought about the location of the doorway with respect to the office's layout. Better to concentrate on that, she told herself, than what this awkward reunion meant for her. *Save the world, and ignore the rest.*

"I think that door originally led to another small room,"

she said. "There's not much in there."

"Just a toilet," said Jesse, "and a coffeemaker . . ."

"And a fabber," said Clair Two from inside the Yard. "A mirror."

Memories, Clair thought, that the three of them shared.

"It was where I made the chip that got me into the space station," said Q-prime. "The pattern of that chip is what my other self is using to make this connection."

The other Q didn't deign to comment.

"So why don't we use it to come out there?" asked Zep.

"We have booths," said Devin, "but we're up against the power problem again. Also, that chip or whatever is barely capable of carrying this conversation, let alone an entire person. "

"We might need to physically access the servers," said Q-prime, "to open the connection wider. That's why we're on the *Satoshige*."

"Presumably Wallace will have some way to open the exit," said Ronnie. "He's the one who's blocking it."

"There's no chance we can talk him around?" asked Clair. "I mean, I don't really care what he does in there as long as he lets everyone else out."

"He won't do that," said Clair Two. "If we're out there while he's in here, there's nothing to stop us from shutting down the Yard."

"We could do that anyway," said Sandler. "Then see how he feels."

"He doesn't respond well to threats," said Libby. "You guys know that, right?"

That was very true. Clair had only to look out the window at the ash-strewn Siberian landscape to appreciate how dangerous Wallace was when cornered. If he learned she was already on her way to Lake Baikal, who knew what he might do to the innocent people inside the Yard—such as her parents—to make her stop?

"Start bringing in people he might use as hostages," she said. "That's what I'd do. Just to be safe."

"Agreed," said Clair Two. Then she hesitated, as though choosing her words carefully. "You should know that we've captured Cameron Lee."

Clair felt a rush of heat sweep through her, but not good heat, which she could have used. The bridge of the *Satoshige* was perpetually drafty and the air outside bitterly cold. This heat was like a sickness.

"What are you going to do with him?" she asked, and if she could hear the strain in her own voice, then so could Clair Two.

"He's with the other hollowmen we've captured," said Dylan, "in the one booth we left intact. There's a dead man's switch. If any one of them so much as looks at us wrong, they'll all be erased."

Too good for him, Clair wanted to say, but instead she just nodded.

"And Mallory's dead," said Libby.

The heat ebbed somewhat at that. Mallory was as much a victim of Wallace as anyone else. Libby had survived her. That was revenge enough.

"Anything else I need to know?" she asked.

There was a short, tense silence that told her all she needed to know about the missing Clair One.

"Doesn't matter," she said. "When you're ready."

"Let's move forward," said Kari. Clair had to remind herself that it was the real Kari talking, not Q inside Kari's body. "Our goal is to break Wallace's hold on the Yard, and to do that we need to get into the exit chamber. Agreed?"

"Agreed," said Evan Bartelme.

"Agreed," said Dylan Linwood.

"Agreed," said Clair Two. "But Wallace will know that. All he has to do is keep us out."

"Exactly, so we'll have to go about it on more than one front," Kari went on. "Here's what I suggest. RADICAL works on getting the channel ready on both ends, inside and outside the Yard. WHOLE, since they were the first to get a handle on ripping, can make new hacks that will get them into the VIA building in some way that can't be blocked. The rest of us will put together a conventional approach: attacking the front door, in other words. Wallace will definitely be expecting something obvious; it would be wise not to disappoint him, or he'll look elsewhere."

"And you'll be our backup plan," said Clair Two to Clair

outside. "What do you have out there, apart from a giant floating head?"

"According to old records," said Q-prime, "there's diving and drilling equipment at the top of the borehole. Thanks to layers of snow and ice, it should have escaped the chain reaction. If we can't access the exit via the interface we'll find there, we'll go ahead with our plan to hack into the hardware itself."

"It's bound to be booby-trapped," said Kari.

"I know," said Clair, feeling sympathy for the huddle of desperate people in the Yard, but what reassurances could she offer them when there were none for her? Except to say, "We won't make any mistakes. This is the time we get it right," and hope it was true.

No one said anything in response to that, and eventually she realized that the picture was frozen. The sound was gone. The channel had closed again.

Clair sighed. It was exhausting, juggling the reality of her world and that of the Yard. Outside, she had nothing. Inside, Clair Two had everything. But outside was real and inside was an illusion. And Wallace remained.

Wallace, the master of the only door in and out of his kingdom. He would know that contact had been made, even if he couldn't decode their signal. He would recognize a challenge when he saw it.

"Do you think they've got a chance in hell?" Sandler asked.

Clair turned her attention from the icy view to the inside of the bridge. Everyone was watching her, waiting to see how she'd respond. It wouldn't help them to hear what she was thinking, she was sure.

Any victory without Jesse would be hollow, for her.

There were some things Clair 7.0 wasn't allowed to hope for.

"In hell?" she said. "No. But in the Yard, while I'm in there with them? Absolutely."

Sandler rolled his eyes. "Just because there're two of you doesn't mean you need to be twice as cocky. Or twice as annoying."

He went back to preparing patches in case they passed through another hailstorm. Clair chalked that up as a partial victory in the ongoing verbal battle between them. That was something.

Swaying slowly from side to side, the *Satoshige* plowed on through clouds piled high like mountains.

[41]

Clair Two

WHEN THE IMAGE of Clair Three and the inside of the floating head froze for the umpteenth time, Clair almost sobbed with relief. The pain was coming and going in waves, crashing higher and arriving a little quicker each time. But passing out in front of her other self was not an option. She would rather die . . . and felt like she just might.

"Back to the hospital with you," said Kari. "No, don't try to stand up. We'll get you a stretcher. You remember what those are? Standard issue for sick people. Like wheelchairs. And hammers, for application to the head when patients don't do as they're told."

Clair didn't protest. Kari was talking nonsense, which meant she was worried, and she only worried when things were serious.

"Don't knock me out," Clair tried to say.

"What?" Kari leaned in close.

"Keep me awake. I promise not to get up again, but I need to know what's going on. I don't want . . ."

"To be left out, I understand." Kari nodded. "I'll do what I can."

That wasn't what Clair had been about to say. *I don't want to dream.* That was what she didn't want to do. She had enough nightmares and foreign memories in her head already without Clair One's added to the mix.

She could feel them now, crowding her. The whiteness of the exit chamber and the redness of her blood as it dripped to the ground. Wallace's unreliable charm, and Kingdon's calmly furious mien. The pain of being shot in the shoulder, so uncannily like her own. And then . . .

Clair didn't know why she was experiencing this now. Wasn't Clair One dead?

Maybe the memories, once part of a girl called Clair in the Yard, belonged to all Clairs in the Yard, whether they wanted them or not.

Clair One looking in the mirror and seeing Nobody's face reflecting back at her . . .

She didn't want that thought messing with her unconscious. She was Clair Hill, and at some point soon, she was sure, she would start to grieve.

"You take her legs," said Kari. Zep did as he was told. The mixture of colored lights in the hub shifted around her. She felt herself lifted and laid out flat, the scratchy woolen beanie that had belonged to a random Yeti slipping off her head. The tides of pain became confused and found new rhythms. Around her the world moved while she stayed still. Colors changed. She blinked—

—and blinked again to find that time had passed, bringing her miraculously back to her bed in the makeshift hospital, as though she had ripped there through desperate force of will.

But no. When she checked her lenses she saw that only ten minutes had passed. There was something stuck to her neck that hadn't been there before: a patch delivering welcome numbness through her veins. The pain was manageable now, and yet her thoughts kept flowing. Kari was as good as her word.

"Okay now?" Kari asked her, leaning into view. The yellow light caught her short hair, making it look like straw.

"Yes, thank you."

"Thirsty?"

"God, yes."

Kari went away and came back with a cup and straw.

"Have you ever had your palm read," she asked while Clair tentatively drank, "or seen a psychic? Did they say that you were going to lead the weirdest life ever?"

Clair smiled and shook her head.

"Me either," said Kari. "But here we are. Grand, isn't it? Think of the stories we'll tell our kids. They'll never believe us."

Clair's throat felt full again, but not from sadness. It amazed her that, despite the perils of the Yard and all the uncertainties of the world outside, Kari was thinking about the next generation. In its way, that was a more potent tonic than the painkillers, or even the water, pure and refreshing though it was.

She let go of the straw with her lips and Kari leaned back into her seat.

"Ray's gone to get your folks, and everyone else connected to us," she said, "Billie among them. Jesse told me how Clair One got past me. I'm angry at myself, and at her, but I know no one's to blame, not really. I was stupidly tired and she didn't know better. We should have . . . Actually, I don't know what we could have done to stop her. She was as stubborn as you are, funnily enough, and you don't like to believe that people are evil. Not even people like Mallory or Nobody. Hell, you probably still think Wallace can return from the dark side, don't you?"

Clair didn't know what to say. She knew what her mother had taught her, which was that people usually knew the difference between right and wrong, and they usually tried to do the right thing over the wrong thing, no matter who they were. But there were different kinds of rights and different kinds of wrongs, and when someone was trying to juggle lots of things at once, it was easy to get them mixed up. One of the reasons people tied themselves in such knots of indecision, Allison Hill said, was because what they knew and what they wanted to think were often different things.

That's why, Clair reminded herself, people needed lawmakers and peacekeepers working in open consensus to remind them of how they should behave. That's why people who thought they were above the law, like Wallace and Kingdon, could be so dangerous and had to be stopped. They wouldn't listen to the people trying to untie the knots, so they didn't see the nooses around their own necks until it was too late and the knots began to tighten.

"I think Wallace is worried," said Clair. "That'll make him more dangerous than ever. We have to be careful he doesn't wipe everything and start over again."

"If that was an option, wouldn't he have done it already?"

Clair didn't know the answer to that question. Maybe there were risks associated with turning the Yard off and on again, himself with it. Maybe he was irrationally afraid of that moment of nothingness between being and then being again, just as some people were afraid of using d-mat or falling asleep at night, for the same reasons. That it didn't feel like anything at all was maybe the most frightening thing of all.

Clair One was dead, and apart from the cessation of the glitches, she still felt nothing.

Someone stirred. Clair looked up, hoping it was Jesse, but it was a patient on one of the other impromptu hospital beds.

"You have other people to look after," Clair said.

Kari nodded. "You'll tell me if you need anything?"

Clair promised. And she meant it. She wanted to get better fast. If there was going to be an attack on Wallace's fortress, she had to be part of it.

—————————————————————— [42]

BEING CONFINED TO bed was no obstacle to her plan, not in the short term. Locked-in Agnessa had taught her that. Clair used her lenses to virtually visit all the places in the prison she needed to be. What she found was reassuring. There were arguments over core beliefs—Clair had never heard so many four-letter words in one string as during a philosophical argument over the soul that broke out in one of the prison's increasingly crowded corridors—but on the whole, the idea of a common enemy kept WHOLE, RADICAL, and everyone else on the same page.

It helped that they were working on separate areas of the plan. Evan and several other RADICAL activists, newly ripped in from locations unknown across the globe, occupied a corner of the hub, connected to Devin, Trevin, and Eve Bartelme at the other end of the exit, conducting tests back and forth. Now that the alliance knew there were booths in the real world, it was just a matter of getting the data out of the Yard fast enough. Clair watched for a while, not really understanding what they were talking about, but noting that not once did Eve or Evan talk directly to each other. Instead, they communicated via their sons or the others in their groups. They behaved like estranged parents, when in fact they were estranged selves, separated by much more than just memories. Clair wondered if that was because of ideological differences—the old RADICAL was different from the new in various small ways, such as Evan's eagerness to work with Q versus Eve's continued wariness—or if it was more about Eve and Evan themselves. Perhaps she and Clair One would have ended up just as distant, given more time to grow apart.

The thought was an uncomfortable one but still didn't

touch her. Clair felt more moved by the sight of Cashile playing on his own, bouncing a ball back and forth in one of the dead ends. He was the last child on Earth, unless Kari Sargent had her way.

Meanwhile, WHOLE commandeered the huge open attic at the top of the prison. It was empty apart from the wheeled vehicles that had brought them all there, and now served as a testing ground for various new hacks. RADICAL played a small part here, with Evan demonstrating a weapon they had devised and used for the first time in their attack on Wallace's stronghold. It had a technical name that Clair didn't understand, but it was quickly dubbed a "glitch-gun" from its basic principles.

Glitches were like errors in a data file, Evan said. Sometimes those errors linked places or people in ways they weren't supposed to be, through things like rips. Sometimes a glitch could be just noise. Glitch-guns turned something with an internal structure, like a target or an enemy combatant, into the noisy kind of glitch. It was like blowing up a tiny bomb inside something, turning it to scattered atoms. The guns worked on anything, including flesh.

As Clair watched, the Yetis on the development team spent half an hour turning chunks of wall into crackling gas, accompanied by a distinctive popping sound. Soon it looked like the chamber had been nibbled at by a giant earthworm. They stopped when the weapon indicated that it was running out of glitch.

Here Clair seriously began to lose track of how it worked.

"The Yard has rules," said Evan. "Break one rule, and that can lead to another one breaking somewhere else, like a chain reaction. That's where the idea of using the exit as a means of powering our original attack came from: any kind of glitch is a broken rule, so we can use its existence to make more glitches of our own. Of course, it's possible to have too many glitches, such as when Clair One came too close to the exit. That's like putting two rods of enriched uranium next to each other: you get too much power, impossible to control, and an atomic explosion."

Again, the mention of Clair One brought regret but no grief, even though it was tragic that they had gone in such different directions, each thinking the other one was in the wrong, when in fact both had been trying to do what was right. Clair remembered her feverish fantasies about Clair One being a traitor with embarrassment. Sure, she had been shot and in a confused state, mistaking the glitch of an old conversation with Wallace for a new memory from Clair One . . . but still: as Tash had said, if she couldn't trust herself, who could she trust?

She trusted that Evan understood what he was talking about.

"The generators in our batteries work by taking a small glitch and creating more small ones from it. They'll recharge automatically, given time, as long as you don't run them completely dry."

Evan went back downstairs, leaving WHOLE to bounce possibilities back and forth. When he was gone, Dylan Linwood joined them, encouraged by a slowdown of hollowmen attacks to put his engineering skills to use. Jesse was with him. Soon they had taken one of the batteries apart and discovered that it worked by creating copies of small things—they looked like tiny crystals—that were similar enough to confuse the Yard into thinking they were in fact identical, causing a tiny glitch. That led to discussions about the possibility of using the guns as fabbers, allowing them to create rather than destroy. Such devices could also be used to build short-lived portals that might allow someone to rip from anywhere, not just through whatever door or window happened to be available. They could also be used to create invisibility cloaks . . . and here Clair's understanding became foggy again.

She bumped Jesse in the hope that he might explain, but he didn't reply. He hadn't replied to any of her messages, and she was beginning to take the hint. *She* used *me,* he had said. Obviously he needed space to process what her other self had done. She could only give it to him and hope that Clair One hadn't done any permanent damage.

As WHOLE knuckled down to fab a prototype of a new kind of glitch-gun, Clair distracted herself from her worries by moving on to the third group, whose existence largely depended upon the other two.

If WHOLE's mission was to make the means of getting to the exit, and RADICAL's was to make sure the exit would actually open for them, the third group took upon themselves the important task of getting revenge.

It started with a meeting in the mess hall. Ronnie, Tash, and Zep were there, and all the Unimprovables, too. They sat on the floor in a circle around Libby, who was still dressed in the armor WHOLE had made for her, with her hair pulled back into a bun. Libby had taken the diamond studs from her ears and wiped off her makeup. She didn't look fashionable or jazzy. She looked tired, and tired of being tired. And that, Clair knew, made her dangerous to cross.

"Clair died trying to save us," she said from her position in the center of the group. "That's sweet, but it pisses me off, like we needed to be saved—like we couldn't help ourselves, or at least help her help everyone else. She should have trusted us to have her back. We would have, if she'd only asked. But she didn't, and look what happened."

Zep was nodding, his expression utterly miserable. Like the others, he was hanging on Libby's every word.

"From now on," said Libby, "no one does anything alone. We're going to work as a team. Clair was a fighter, so that's what we'll be too, *together*, in her name: Team Clair. Okay? Okay."

I'm still here, Clair wanted to say, but that wasn't the point. That Libby's Clair, Clair One, had died was critical to the spell Libby was casting. Everyone stared at her with their full attention, attention that Clair always felt she had had to fight for when she was trying to bring a group around. Libby made it look easy. People *wanted* to listen to her.

Clair had always suspected it would be this way, and here was the proof: Libby was better at knowing what to say when the world's eyes were on her. If their roles had been reversed, maybe the end of the world could have been avoided, and no Clairs or Libbys need have died.

But Clair would never have used Improvement on her own. That was the fact of it. For all of Libby's charm, it came with a dark side. Insecurity and doubt plagued her, which was why she played the star so hard. And that was okay. That was utterly forgivable, if it brought results. Clair didn't want Libby to change a thing.

Except maybe the name of her little gang. It was better than Clair's Bears, but not by much. . . .

"So," Libby went on, getting down to business, "Team RADICAL and Team WHOLE are going to be doing their things. We need to work with them or else they'll forget us when shit goes down. You know what they're like. We have to go out there and get their attention, then share what we learn on the group chat. We'll meet regularly to work on our plan, and to train. No one's going anywhere without us."

A cheer went up. Libby clapped her hands and the meeting dissolved. Clair watched them go, thinking, *There's a group chat?*

Clair bumped Libby to see if she could join.

"No" came the immediate reply. "You need some time to get it together. And so do I. Call you later, promise."

Zep had stayed behind. Libby led him to one corner of the mess, where they sat down opposite each other and started to talk, haltingly at first, then in earnest.

Clair neither watched nor listened in. Libby's response had stung, although she could see where it had come from. Clair One had gone off on her own, without trusting her friends or even letting them know what she was doing. She had lied to cover her tracks, and trusted two of Clair's worst enemies.

Clair didn't want to be in the position of having to apologize for Clair One. And neither did Libby. In time, things would be easier. If they had time. . . .

Switching off her feed from the prison, Clair rubbed her closed eyes with her one free hand and eased back onto the mattress, not realizing how tense she'd become. Her eyelids swam with random colors and shades, from bright to deepest blacks. There were lots of other things she could watch, lots of other people going about individual duties, but she was tired. She lay back on the bed with her eyes half lidded, gazing up at the empty ceiling and wondering what Clair Three had been doing during their brief conversation.

Only slowly did she become aware of someone sitting next to her bed.

"Are you awake?" asked Allison Hill. "I don't want to disturb you."

Clair froze, unsure which emotion out of so many she was feeling most urgently at that moment.

"What? You're not disturbing me," she said, hearing and hating the tightness in her voice that suggested she might be lying. "How long have you been there?"

"Just a few minutes."

"Where . . . where did you come from?"

"Windham. I went home after the census to look for Oz."

That wasn't what Clair meant.

"What's the last thing you remember? Before . . . all this?"

Allison thought about it, and that brief pause was the longest in Clair's life.

"They took me from the safe house," Allison said. "They promised me I'd see you. They brought me somewhere else by d-mat, and they told me to wait. They said they were friends of yours, but I don't think they were. I'm not sure about these people either, but they got me out of there, and I'm with you now. That's a good thing, isn't it?"

Clair, nodding, agreed with all her heart. This was no Allison Hill from days ago, who knew nothing about dupes or Ant Wallace or anything else that had happened. This was the Allison Hill who had been kidnapped before the attack on the seastead, and whom Clair had feared she might never see again.

She burst into tears and reached out for her mother's hand.

[43]

HAVING HER MOM back wasn't just a good thing. It was the best thing in the world at that moment.

"Oz? He's here too. He doesn't remember everything, but that's probably a blessing. I told him to make himself useful finding and bringing in the others who might be kidnapped. He sends his love and promises to come see you later."

Clair had rolled onto her good side, the better to look at her mother while they talked. It was more gratifying than she had expected, having someone who knew her for who she was, rather than who she used to be. Only Kari, Clair Three, and Q could claim that. Two of those were largely unavailable, and Kari had only been herself since coming to the Yard. She was a friend, but nothing compared to the woman who had given Clair her entire life.

"I still can't believe the lawmakers tried to take over the world," Allison said, staring into the steam of her coffee.

"Ronnie's great-uncle was one, you know."

"What was his name?"

"Kieran Defrain."

Clair checked the list Jesse had found of lawmakers in Kingdon's service. His name wasn't there.

"I guess he was okay," Clair said.

"Some of them had to be. No group is ever entirely evil. Like Abstainers."

"Like Grandma Juliet." When Allison looked surprised, Clair explained, "Q told me."

"Ah. You were just a toddler then. She went a bit crazy toward the end—not that being an Abstainer means you're crazy—"

"I'm so glad you don't think that."

"I really don't." Allison smiled. "Juliet traveled the world without setting foot once in a booth. That was so brave of her. I never told you because I thought it'd freak you out. And now look at you. Just as brave. Even more so."

Clair felt another cry coming on and fought the urge. She had yet to confront what life would be like as an Abstainer, and wouldn't have to until she was out of the Yard and back in the real world. That was when she would have to earn the adjective "brave." There were probably thousands of things she hadn't even considered. . . .

"I thought you'd be disappointed in me."

"Disappointment is for people who can't accept that their

children never turn out exactly like them." Allison smiled again. "Your grandmother left me her diary. I should give it to you when all this is over. You might find it interesting."

"We might have to give it to Clair Three, too." There was a small silence. "Does that freak *you* out?"

"Of course it does. But you know . . . ? I've spent the last few days not knowing if you're dead or alive. If I end up with two of you, that's just good news twice over. Like twins."

"We had twins at school," Clair said. "Two boys, Felipe and Fernando Deboo. They hated each other."

"Who'd hate you?" Allison leaned over and stroked the stubble on Clair's skull. "My little girl. You make me so proud. But I'm glad you're going to be sitting out the big push in here. I don't want you hurting yourself again. Losing one of you is quite enough. . . ."

Clair didn't pursue that thought. Seeing her mother had opened the floodgates of grief on that front, and it was still a tender area. Clair One had died. It could easily have been her, if the bullets that had hit her had found a different mark. From Clair One's point of view, it *had* been her.

"Do you remember Charlie?" she asked her mom. "That old clown of mine?"

Allison laughed, a joyous sound that echoed through the hospital like sunlight off a mirror. She put a hand over her mouth and nodded.

"Of course I remember. You took that thing everywhere."

"Remember the time I lost him?"

"Which time?"

"When we went to see that pyramid in South America, whatever it was called."

"El Castillo. Did you have him with you then? I just remember you slipping out of the booth and getting left behind."

"I went back for Charlie because I dropped him outside." She studied her mother. "You really don't remember that part? You told me you could've just made me a new one."

"Did I really say that? That wasn't very sensitive of me. I was probably so worried about you I wasn't thinking straight."

"Would you really have done it?"

"Of course. We did plenty of times."

"What?"

"Oh, you were always losing that thing. I can't begin to guess how many replacements we made. Sometimes people would find the one you'd lost and give it back after we'd already made a new one. We'd have to recycle the old one so you wouldn't notice."

Her mother's eyes twinkled cheerfully at the memory, and perhaps at Clair's obvious discomfiture as well.

"You never guessed?"

"No. When you said you *could*, I didn't know you *did*. . . ."

"Is that why you brought it up? To tell me I could have a replacement Clair instead of the one I lost?"

"No." Clair bit her lip. "I was going to say that I'm starting to understand how hard it is to tell someone what they don't want to hear."

Allison sat back into her seat.

"You're *not* sitting this one out, then."

"Not if I can help it," Clair said, shifting awkwardly on the bed. Her right hip and shoulder were beginning to ache. "The patches are working. I'm healing. It's important I be part of this."

"And you are part of this, darling girl, on the outside and in here." Allison wiped at her eyes. The cheerful twinkles were gone now. "I worry about you. PK Sargent says you've been having nightmares. If you don't have PTSD already . . . All right, all right. I know better than to argue with you. If it's physically possible for you to do it, you'll do it. I just wish you wouldn't. That's all."

She leaned forward and rested her forehead against Clair's fingers. Clair heard her mother inhale deeply and exhale, but didn't know what to say to make Allison feel better. *I'm going, Mom—get over it* was never going to help.

Allison sat up, a determinedly calm expression on her face.

"I should let you sleep, but first, tell me about Jesse Linwood. He was here when I arrived. You've been seeing a lot of him lately, I gather. Is there anything I should know?"

Oh, Mom, she wanted to say, *you have no idea. . . .*

But it was easier just to protest embarrassment and outrage at prying parents than to explain the complexity of her love life. Jesse hadn't come to visit her once, and he still wasn't answering her bumps. She could feel his hurt through his silence and the heavy stone walls of the prison, but she didn't know what to do about it. *She's not me,* Clair wanted to say. *I wasn't the one who used you. . . .* But deep down she knew that would be a lie.

Instead she turned the conversation back to Oz, who Clair was sure had everyone organized into working parties on rosters by now. He'd been in the prison, what, an hour?

As they laughed, Clair felt a warmth between them that she knew was real, as real as anything else in the Yard. She and her mother would learn how to share that warmth with Clair Three if they had to. There was more than enough to go around.

[44]

CLAIR SLEPT FOR a while, and dreamed things she tried hard to forget when she woke. Her right arm was twisted beneath her, requiring that she spend an uncomfortable few minutes shaking out pins and needles before she could use it again. *Real.*

When she was able to, she reached for the bottle of water by the bed and swished out her mouth in a vain attempt to get rid of a faint medicine taste on top of the usual post-sleep furriness. She was glad Jesse wasn't there to witness her unglamorous awakening, not to mention her first attempt to use a bedpan. *Look on the bright side,* she told herself, lest his rejection of her sting too much.

When she was feeling human again, she switched her lenses on and checked the prison interface.

Team Clair had been busy. Ronnie was now Libby's official attachment to Team RADICAL, keeping an eye on their efforts to open the channel to the outside world, while Tash had seconded herself to Team WHOLE. With Jesse, she was on the testing range, watching as a series of bizarre new weapon designs poured out of the fabbers.

Elsewhere, Kari was putting Libby and Zep and the Unimprovables through their paces. There were exercise and weapons drills, lessons in hand and voice signals, and the occasional cheesy-looking but seemingly enjoyable trust games. Some of the Unimprovables had used guns before. Some had basic street-fighting skills. Most of them were ordinary kids like Libby and Clair had been. All were willing—and pissed.

Only once was the question of their age brought up.

"Barely out of your diapers," sneered one of the grizzlier

Yetis who had stopped by to watch. "You'll turn and run the moment it gets real."

Tilly Kozlova stood up to him, tall, skinny, and unafraid of his wild hair and tattoos.

"Young people like me were being killed for *years* while old folk like you hid out in the woods," she said, poking him in the chest. "Don't come here thinking you can tell us anything."

Clair wanted to cheer, but she kept it to herself. She didn't want to disturb any of her fellow patients.

Half an hour later a contingent of eight Yetis showed up to help Team Clair train, and Clair felt like cheering again. For all their attitude, Team Clair was no army. They had a lot to learn if they were going to have half a chance against the hollowmen.

That evening, Dylan Linwood called a meal break and all three groups met in the mess to bring each other up to date. WHOLE made sandwiches from the store of fresh food they had brought from the caves. Everyone else ate fabbed meals. Clair worked her way into a sitting position with both arms free and sipped steadily at a protein smoothie. For the first time since her shooting she had an appetite. Her body was mending fast and needed raw materials.

"We have a glitch-mobile in the works," Jesse said to the assembly. "It'll carry people in a group without needing an ordinary vehicle. It can also go into a rip without immediately coming out the other side, so it can't be followed."

Clair watched him with a lump in her throat. She felt like a stalker, watching him when he wouldn't even reply to her messages. Was he avoiding Clair Three, too?

"What about weapons?" asked Evan Bartelme. "What have you done with the glitch-guns?"

"The obvious thing would be to scale them up," said Dylan, "so we haven't. The hollowmen have seen them in action, and we assume they're working on defenses. Instead we developed a new kind of glitch-gun that puts a missile *into* a target rather than takes bites out of one."

"A missile like a grenade?" asked Zep.

"Doesn't need to be anything so dramatic. Put a rock in someone's heart and they'll be dead just the same."

That was an unpleasant thought, and the way Jesse grimaced suggested that he didn't like it much either.

"We're also working on ways to link people together so they can communicate without using the Air," he said, glancing down at a list written on the inside of his wrist. "There are a few other pie-in-the-sky projects in the works, such as camouflage transforms that could in theory disguise you as anything you want, reality bombs that do what the glitch-guns do, only much bigger . . ." He shrugged. "But it's all speculative, and I don't know how much of it will actually work. We're getting into some really lethal territory now. One mistake could wipe us all out, so we're taking it very slowly."

"He sounds worried, and he should be," said Q in Clair's ears only.

Clair replied before Q could drift away.

"What do you mean? I'm sure they're being extra careful not to hurt themselves."

"It's not that. War takes a toll. I worry that the cost of this one might be too great."

"You think we should give in and let Wallace win?"

"No."

"Then what?"

Getting information out of Q was hard these days. Not so long ago, she had been like a tap Clair couldn't turn off. Now they were lucky to exchange a sentence or two. She was busily keeping the link between the Yard and the real world open against Wallace's attempts to close it again, Team RADICAL said.

"Please, Q," Clair prompted when the silence stretched on. "Tell me, or at least tell what I've done to make you not like me anymore."

"Why would you think *that*?" said Q, in a sudden return to her usual self. "That'll never happen."

"So why didn't you answer me?"

"I was just thinking. What I meant was that there are two wars underway at the moment: the obvious one, and the war against the Yard itself, waged by people like Team WHOLE. Every time a rule is broken, by ripping or using a

[360]

glitch-gun, the Yard is slightly damaged at its basest level, down in the numbers. Too much damage could be catastrophic."

Clair put down her smoothie, contemplating this new concern.

"I thought glitching and ripping were safe," she said.

"They are, in moderation," said Q. "Like everything."

"How much is too much?"

"I don't know."

"What happens if we go too far?"

"I don't know."

Q not knowing things was worse than Q not saying anything.

"Could it be as bad as when Mallory wanted to put Clair One into the exit?"

"No," Q said. "I don't think so, anyway."

Again, far from reassuring.

"Is there anything we can do to prop things up if they get shaky?" Clair asked. "Create our own rules, say?"

"That is an interesting idea," Q said. "I could attempt to write new rules into the fabric of the Yard whenever I see a rupture forming."

"Would that work?"

"I don't know. If clusters of local rules conflict with the rules around them, there would be consequences."

"As long as we don't all die, Q, go ahead and do what you need to do."

"I thought you would feel that way."

Q's tone changed, and that sent an alarm bell ringing.

"What are you trying to tell me?" Clair said. "Just come out and say it, whatever it is."

Q was silent for a long moment.

"Rules are important," she eventually said. "Humans like rules even if they are invalid, or superseded, or outright nonsensical, and this leads me to suspect that a mind's relationship to constraints placed upon it is one of the calling cards of true consciousness. It's important that rules exist so we can rail against them. They are made to be broken, isn't that right? I can't imagine an animal thinking this because, on the face of it, it doesn't make any sense. Yet in a certain light, it makes perfect sense, don't you think?"

Clair didn't know what to say. Q asking her opinion on something like this was like her asking a child for its thoughts on the works of Mary Shelley.

But she had to at least make the effort to reply, while the opportunity was there.

"Surely some rules are better than others," she hazarded.

"Maybe. Context is everything. But some rules are fundamental, and broken at our own risk. How we relate to space, for instance. How we relate to ourselves and the people around us. If WHOLE's engineers are right, you could soon be anywhere or anything you want simply by wishing for it. When such basic notions as space and identity are mutable, how are you going to tell anywhere and anyone apart? What rules will apply?"

"Uh . . . I don't know," said Clair. "It sounds a bit like you, actually."

"And look at me," said Q. "My life to date has been very confusing."

"Maybe you're still looking for the right rules."

Another silence. Clair waited it out, unsure whether she'd said something accidentally profound or very, very stupid.

The only thing that stopped Q from breaking parity the first time was the rules, and that had turned out just *perfect. . . .*

Before Q could respond, Clair received a bump from Kari.

"Check the feed from LM Kingdon. You need to see this."

[45]

THE BROADCAST HAD been sent to everyone. It was being reposted in captions all through the Yard.

"Peacekeepers and volunteer recruits have been working tirelessly in close cooperation with VIA," LM Kingdon said, "to locate and capture the terrorists responsible for recent acts of violence against members of the New Consensus." She was shown standing against the backdrop of a OneEarth flag with her throat covered in a bandage. "The lives lost and effort wasted are incalculable, which is why I know you will rejoice with me at the announcement that arrests have been made. The evidence has been processed, and soon you will all bear witness to the judgment meted out on these enemies of peace and humanity."

Arrests? Clair wanted to ask, *Who have we lost?* but Kingdon was continuing.

"These twenty-two people were netted in raids conducted in the last six hours." Kingdon contrived to look both severe and triumphant as names and images scrolled down both sides of the image of her face. "They are many, and they did not work alone. We will not stop until every conspirator has been caught, tried, and punished to the full extent of the law."

What are they going to do? Clair thought. *Lock us all in prison?*

Then she recognized one of the faces among the strangers on the screen—a slender woman with Jesse's coloring—and Clair became aware of the rising buzz on the Kupa-piti feed.

"That's my sister—"

"That's my father—"

"That's my daughter!"

"Mom!"

Jesse's voice cut through the chorus. His mother had disappeared in a d-mat accident many years ago, but a dupe of her had shown up at the WHOLE muster in Russia. Even though she had never been a member of WHOLE, that wasn't stopping Kingdon from using her against the people who loved her.

Clair's determination to fight in the final assault increased, if that were possible. When she tried to imagine how Jesse felt, how she would feel if *her* mom was on the list, her blood boiled and she had to grind her teeth to stop herself from interrupting.

"Quiet," said Dylan Linwood over the interface. "Listen to what the woman is saying."

"These twenty-two are guilty of heinous crimes. My fellow lawmakers and I took this into account when considering sentencing. Our unanimous decision was that the gravest criminals deserve the gravest punishment. These twenty-two will be executed at six hundred hours tomorrow. Those who conspired with them have until then to turn themselves in. If they do not, they will be hunted down and destroyed like the vermin they are."

Kingdon's feed went dark.

Executed.

Clair checked the time. It was ten p.m. That gave them eight hours to rescue Jesse's mom and the others.

"Since when did OneEarth bring back the death penalty?" she asked Q, but there was no response.

She knew the answer, anyway. Since Kingdon and her cronies had taken over the Yard and made it their own, just as they had planned to take over the world.

It was a sign of things to come if they weren't stopped.

With considerable effort, Clair levered herself up so she was sitting vertically rather than leaning on cushions.

Jamila, the woman left in charge of the hospital while Kari was busy, appeared immediately at her side.

"What are you doing?"

"Getting up," Clair said. "Give me a hand, will you?"

"I'm calling PK Sargent."

"Do that, but first give me a hand."

Jamila did, with a long-focused look that said she was doing both things at once.

Clair paused with her legs dangling off the makeshift bed, head spinning, augs buzzing with the upset chatter in the prison. People on all sides of the alliance were agitating for immediate action. After the last meeting had ended, they had all gone back to their respective projects, but now they were gathering together again, virtually and physically. It wouldn't be long before someone acted precipitously and walked right into Kingdon's trap.

Clair had thought herself done with speeches. But when the circumstances demanded one and no one else was stepping forward . . .

"We all heard it," she said to everyone in the prison.

"We all know what it means: they're using hostages now, people we love. Let's count ourselves lucky they didn't start doing this sooner, otherwise there could be a hundred people up there, not just twenty-two. We're going to do something about it, and we're going to do it right. Let's use the time we have to make sure of that."

"Girl's making sense," Libby immediately sent back. "The only way to save these people is to do what we were going to do anyway."

"I agree," said Evan. "We mustn't give them the pleasure of knowing that we are rattled. Silence will only make them more nervous."

"Nervous enough to start the executions early?" asked Jesse. Clair could hear the shock in his voice. He barely remembered his mother, but of course that didn't stop him from wanting to save her.

"They're still pretending to be the good guys," said Ronnie. "The illusion of due process is not something they're going to give up just yet."

"Let's not wait too long, though," said Zep.

"We'll go when we're ready and not a moment before," said Dylan Linwood. "Get back to work."

"And Clair, you need to get back into bed," said Kari Sargent from the door of the hospital.

"But I can't just lie here . . . ," Clair started to say.

"You're not just lying there. Your body is working hard.

Let it do its job or you'll be useless to anyone. Besides, wasn't that you I heard bossing everyone around a moment ago?"

Clair scowled. She hated it when Kari made sense.

"Do you promise I'll be up in eight hours?"

"Maybe less, if you behave," she said, but Clair couldn't tell if she was lying. Kari put her hands on Clair's shoulders and forced her back down. "If she gives you any more trouble, Jamila, use the blue patches. They'll knock her right out."

"You wouldn't," Clair said.

"I will if you make me." Kari smiled down at her. "Your mom would kill me if I didn't. She's as a big a pain in my ass as you are, you know that?"

Clair could imagine. Allison had been helping Team WHOLE and had most of the Yetis under her thumb.

"All right," she said. "You tell me I'll be up in time and I'll stay right here."

"Good. Thank you." Kari handed control back to Jamila. "If everything's okay here, I'll get back to the team. They've got a lot of work to do before they're going anywhere. . . ."

Clair watched Kari's broad back as she headed out of the hospital, noting that Kari hadn't actually promised anything. Jamila hovered for a while, as though doubtful that Clair was going to keep her word. When she eventually wandered off, Clair closed her eyes and considered her options. There weren't many, and none she liked.

In the end she opted for the one that she alone could do, even though it was the one that terrified her the most.

She bumped LM Kingdon, using the words Kingdon had sent her on the first occasion they had talked.

"Is now a good time?"

Kingdon's reply took a surprisingly long thirty seconds.

"It's a terrible time to joke around, child."

"Neither of us is joking around." *And I'm not a child.*

"You've made that absolutely clear."

"Don't begin to suggest that this is my fault. Your attack on VIA was vicious and unprovoked. It escalated the situation far beyond my ability to control it. Who do you think has been keeping Wallace in check? Not you. Not me, although I've tried. Mallory Wei was your best ally, and you killed her."

"I was unconscious at the time," Clair said. "Shot by one of your goons. That sounds like escalation to me."

Again, a long silence, followed by a chat request.

Clair accepted it and noted a raft of encryption measures that weren't standard for communications through the Air. *Maybe,* she thought, *this is a call that not even RADICAL can hack into.* In which case, good.

"What do you want?" Kingdon asked her. Through the chat Clair could see that Kingdon was walking along the edge of a canal somewhere in the Manhattan Isles. The sky was slate gray. Wind sent ripples chasing each other back and forth across the water's surface. There was no sign of the bandage or a wounded throat. Clair wasn't surprised: faking an injury to elicit sympathy was exactly what someone like Kingdon would do.

"I want to make a deal," Clair told her.

"It's a little late for that."

"What are you afraid of? Looking bad? That's not something dictators worried about, I thought."

"I'm not a dictator. I'm trying to do what's right for everyone."

"By taking us over?"

"By restoring a form of government we understand. Don't get me wrong: the Consensus Court was a fine experiment. But the experiment has failed. It gave us Wallace and Q, and who knows what would have been next? People prefer a firm hand on the tiller. I will provide it."

That sounded like so much bullshit to Clair, who had seen very little evidence that the Consensus Court had failed in principle. All the problems Kingdon named were caused by individuals, not by group decision making.

That said, Clair was not so deluded as to think that she might not be one of those problem-causing people. Or that Kingdon didn't think Clair was.

"You've killed one of me already," she said. "You have a body to parade around, if that makes you feel better, and the glitches we caused are mostly gone now. Isn't that enough?"

"Maybe if you lie down and play dead for me . . . but

of course you won't. You think you know what's best for everyone. You won't rest until you've rammed it down our throats."

"Pot, kettle, black."

"I used to think we were alike, Clair, but now I know we're not. You're naive. Do you even know the central tenet of institutional consensus, the single rule that forces me to do what I have to do? It's that the Consensus Court cannot be overturned by the Court itself. That's the one decision it cannot make. So the only way to get rid of it is by revolution. Blame your grandparents for this, not me. In the meantime, I know what's right, I know what must be done, and I'm not going to shy away from it. It takes a true leader to tear everything down in order to build something new."

Clair felt as though Kingdon was rehearsing a speech rather than saying anything meaningful. Clair had to get her off that track.

"The Earth isn't the only place we can live," Clair said. "Why can't you have what you want in here and let everyone who doesn't want to be part of it live outside?"

"That's not going to work, of course."

"Why not? All you have to do is let us go. What's the cost to you? Losing the moral high ground? Looking weak?"

"You're forgetting the exit."

"I'm not forgetting the exit. That's the most important thing."

"So why, Clair, are we even having this conversation?"

Clair was confused. She felt as though Kingdon was in a completely different argument from the one *she* was in. Maybe it was a deliberate plot to distract her.

She had one card left, and she played it.

"What if I turn myself in?"

"You don't mean that."

"I would if you promised to let everyone go."

Kingdon laughed. "Do you think I'm stupid?"

"Do you think I'm lying?" She wasn't lying. "If you really believe individuals are what matter, then this is your chance to make all your problems go away at once. You can do whatever you want with me. Lock me down here forever. Shoot me in Times Square. Your call. Your choice. All you have to do is let everyone else go and I'll come quietly. I swear it. Once I know that everyone will be safe, I'll come quietly."

More silence. Clair didn't know what to hope for. She didn't want to turn herself over to Kingdon and Wallace, but she would if it avoided a war that might tear the Yard apart.

She had seen the world outside now. It wasn't a paradise waiting to be reclaimed. It was a mess requiring people to put it back the way it had been. It needed everyone in the Yard—millions, Q had said. More than on Mars, the moon, and all the other colonies combined. The people of Earth had to make their own salvation . . .

no matter the individual cost to her.

"You're not a fool," said Kingdon. "I'll grant you that. And in the end, we both want the same thing: to get out of here and build a new world from the ashes. That's what matters most."

"So you agree?"

"Nothing of the sort. Being smart doesn't mean you can't be crazy or ignorant at the same time, and I can't take a chance on you being either of those things. Sorry, but if that's your best offer, then we're done."

"I guess we are."

"Good-bye, Clair. Please don't do anything rash."

The chat closed on Kingdon's end, leaving Clair alone and shivering under her sheet. She hadn't realized how much she was sweating until she hugged herself and felt her clammy skin.

Part of her couldn't believe what she'd just tried to do. Part of her couldn't believe that it had failed. Was Kingdon really so blind? Did she assume she had the power to catch Clair anyway? Or did she know something Clair didn't, which is why she had said "naive" and "ignorant"?

She bit her lip, worrying about that last point. What if she had missed something important, something that could make all the difference?

Something to do with the exit, perhaps? What if Kingdon was at Wallace's mercy on that front too, in which case she couldn't promise anyone anything?

There was no way to know what she didn't know, until it mattered. And there was no way Clair was bumping Wallace to make him the same offer. He already had enough of her blood on his hands.

──────────────────────────── [46]

CLAIR HAD A string of visitors over the next three hours. Some people wanted explanations. Some wanted assurance. Some just wanted to play out the very same anxieties she was struggling to keep in check. Clair didn't have the heart to turn any of them away, even if she didn't have much to offer.

Jesse wasn't among them, but Billie was.

"Your one-armed man snatched me up just before the hollowmen made their move," she explained. "If he'd come five minutes later, I'd be number twenty-three with my head on the block."

Clair could only sympathize. Before offering herself to Kingdon, she had thought long and hard about what it would be like to await execution. It was harrowing to imagine.

"You're with us now," she said. "You don't have to worry about that."

"Yes, everything's just *dandy*." Billie shook herself, like a dog. "I feel terrible about what I did. . . . I should have asked more questions. I shouldn't have let her go."

"You're not to blame," Clair said. "It's what she wanted to do. And we wouldn't know where to go now if it weren't for her."

"But she . . . you . . ." Her eyes were a brilliant auburn color and they didn't let Clair off the hook. "You're so damned young."

Everyone kept saying that.

"We all die in the end," said Clair.

Billie's smile came and went so fast it might never have been there. "Except for you."

She left Clair with that thought. It wasn't a cheerful one, particularly if Clair didn't heal in time to join the fight. Should things go wrong, everyone she loved would be dead soon, while Clair sat in bed and watched. That possibility made her feel old and trapped, like Aunt Arabelle in her wheelchair.

At three o'clock, the teams gathered on the testing range for one final debriefing. The entire prison watched, plus Clair Three and the crew of the *Satoshige* on the outside. Everyone's eyes were on the clock. Any hitches now might mean death for the twenty-two awaiting execution.

Team RADICAL went first. The news wasn't encouraging on that front.

"We've made the channel as stable as we can," said Evan. "As you can see, it's still far from reliable. We won't be able to do anything more until we can put someone on-site at either end."

"We're still six hours away," said Clair Three. On a map the airship was passing a place called Zhigalovo. She had shown them the tools they had recovered from the muster and Evan had walked them through what they might need to do in the case a manual hack was required. Clair Three had taken notes and talked very little. She didn't answer when Libby asked how things were on the outside for her personally. *Damaged,* Clair thought.

"You're sure you'll be able to make the channel work when you're at the exit?" she asked Evan from her hospital bed.

"Yes. I'm positive. Once Wallace is out of the picture, we'll have full access to its parameters *and* the time we need to gain full control."

"What about the hostages?" Tash asked. Her mother was among those taken into custody. Roberta Sixsmith had run from Ray right into the arms of the hollowmen.

"They're protected by what's left of the law," Kari said. "Kingdon won't kill them ahead of the scheduled execution."

"What if she changes her mind?"

Kari didn't back down. "There's nothing we can do about that."

"Moving along," said Dylan Linwood. "Jesse?"

Nothing happened for a moment. Jesse was staring at

his father with a look that might have been mistaken for anger . . . but Clair knew that was too mild a word. "Hatred" would have been closer. His jaw was locked like stone. He looked as though he didn't dare open his mouth for fear of what might come out of it.

"Moving . . . *along?*" he ground out. "I remember everything you said in Wallace's station. And now you're willing to let Mom go?"

Clair had to think hard to remember. Dylan had been brought out of the Yard in an attempt to weaken Jesse's loyalty to Clair. They had had a short conversation, but it had revealed that Clair's mother had been offered to Dylan as a bribe long ago in an attempt to turn him against his friends in WHOLE. For a moment, it had seemed as though he had entertained doubts about the hard-nosed beliefs that had led to him turning down the offer, but there was no evidence of that uncertainty anymore.

"I told you, Jesse," he said. "This isn't a good time to talk about that."

"Will there ever be a right time?"

"No," Dylan suddenly shouted, "because she's dead! She died fourteen years ago and that apparition parading before you is a lie. A vicious, cruel lie, and the sooner you accept that the better!"

Father and son glared at each other for a long second, then turned away. Their unwilling audience shuffled, uneasy witnesses to a family crisis they wanted no part of.

Clair broke her silence and bumped Jesse quickly.

"Ignore him," she said. "He doesn't know what he's talking about. We're going to save your mom, both of us, and if he won't accept her that's his loss."

Jesse's face hardened. He didn't reply, which made her wish she had said nothing at all. But she couldn't have said nothing, could she? Whatever was going on between them, it would've been inhuman to stay silent.

Wiping his eyes, he returned to the briefing.

"The glitch-mobile is ready," he told the crowd. "As for . . . as for the rest, we ended up deciding that there would be too many gadgets for people to juggle, particularly when things get crazy, so we took it one step further."

Clair had seen some of this already, but she was eager to focus on something positive. It was impressive, achieved mostly through sheer perseverance and willingness to take terrible risks. She had felt several aftershocks reverberating through the stone walls from the testing ground, and she knew that at least two people had been killed.

Ray stepped forward. He was dressed in a green-and-gray suit that covered him from the soles of his feet to the top of his head. There was a face mask that was currently pulled up to expose his face. The suit incorporated a thick, rectangular pack that bulged from his shoulders to his waist. The sleeve of his left arm hung empty from the elbow down.

"The pack contains the generator," said Jesse, voice

level now he was talking about something technical. "It's bulky, I know, but it's the best we could come up with on short notice. The battery takes five minutes to recharge. A full charge gives you a number of options. The glitch-suit can interface with your lenses, allowing you to do stuff like this. . . ."

There was a small ripple in the reality of the Yard. Ray was suddenly holding a pistol, identical to those RADI-CAL had used in the exit chamber. He raised it, sighted along the barrel at a human-shaped target on the far side of the room, and fired.

Pop. The target's shoulder vanished in a cloud of swirling smoke, turned instantly to random noise.

The pistol dropped to the ground, and another one appeared in its place. This time when Ray fired, the target's midsection exploded with a piercing crack, blown apart from the inside.

"Glitch-gun mark two," explained Jesse. "As many as you need. The suits are basically walking fabbers, able to re-create anything in their memory."

Ray dropped the second gun to the ground and a third instantly appeared in his hand. He dropped that one and made a fourth.

"But here's the thing," Jesse went on. "Why have a gun at all? The Yard doesn't care. It's more for our sake, because that's what we're used to. And what we're used to could put us at a disadvantage. Guns get dropped or taken away.

They can even be used against us. So . . ."

Ray dropped the fourth gun to the floor with the others, raised his empty hand, and pointed at another target, which exploded as though by magic, prompting a surprised reaction from the crowd.

"The trigger can be anything you like," said Jesse. "A word, an image. When you're interfaced with the suit, it'll do whatever you want, whenever you ask it to. It'll also keep you in touch with anyone inside any other suit, instantaneously, without using the Air. All the suits are entangled via their generators, so you can rip from position to position without having to look at maps or ask for directions. Be careful of draining the batteries, though. Each time you use the suit, you use up some of your reserve, and some of the suit's functions are quite a drain. Remember those camouflage transforms I was talking about?"

Ray pulled down his face mask. The moment the suit was sealed it turned sky blue.

"Next," said Jesse.

The suit turned red, black, gray, then vanished entirely.

"Next," said Jesse again.

Ray moved. Clair could see the faint outline of the suit rippling across the stone wall behind him if she concentrated really hard. He reappeared five paces to his right.

"Ray's draining his suit pretty fast right now," said Jesse, "but there's still a lot he can do."

Ray ripped from one side of the room to the other and back again. He jumped into the air—*and stayed there,* hanging motionless above the ground for a second before dropping back down.

"That one takes a lot of charge," said Jesse. "This one's even better."

Ray held up the empty sleeve of his ruined arm. Reality twitched, and suddenly his missing hand and forearm were back. He bent it at the elbow and flexed his new fingers, turning his wrist to show the front and back.

"That'll last as long as Ray's wearing the suit," said Jesse. "All we needed was a pattern for the replacement, which we took from a scan of his right arm. The idea is for everyone to be scanned before getting into their glitch-suit. That way, if you're injured the suits will repair you on the run. Maybe even stop you from dying, although we haven't tested that, obviously."

The reaction from the people watching was one of shock and awe, feelings Clair echoed in the hospital.

"You've done it," said Libby in amazement. "You've made Improvement real."

"No, no," said Jesse, looking alarmed. "This isn't cosmetic, and it's not permanent. That's not what we were aiming for at all."

"But you *could* do it. In theory."

"I wouldn't. . . ." He turned away from her. "Anyway, we should have the suits ready within the hour. It'll take longer than that to scan everyone into them, so we should get moving."

Clair hadn't really been listening to their argument. She didn't care about what the suits *shouldn't* do. She was thinking about what they *could* do, for her.

"I want one," Clair said over the prison network.

"That's not possible," said Jesse, looking up at the ceiling as though she was floating there, invisible. His voice was brusque. "It won't work for you. Your injuries are too complicated, and we don't have a scan of you before you were injured. I'm sorry, Clair, but that's the way it is."

Frustration boiled inside her. She had done everything Kari had told her to do. She had stayed still. She had tried to heal. But she knew she wasn't ready, not without one of those suits. She couldn't even get out of bed without help. "All I need to be able to do is walk—"

"There will be fighting, Clair," said Dylan Linwood. "Walking won't be enough."

"So I'll rip everywhere. The suit can do that for me."

"Yes, but what about hand-to-hand combat, if it comes to that?" said Arabelle. "There's no shame in staying behind. No one will think less of you."

I'm not you, Clair almost said, but she caught herself in time.

"What if we had a scan of Clair before she was injured?" Kari asked.

"You're thinking about Clair Three?" Jesse asked. "It'd

take us years to get the data through the channel."

"But *if* we had one?"

Jesse glanced at Dylan, almost daring him to agree.

"Yes, if we had such a scan we could repair Clair using a glitch-suit. As we don't, however, I suggest we move on. Everyone intending to take part, form a line over here and we'll commence scanning. . . ."

Jesse nodded, looking satisfied. Father and son agreed. They had won.

Libby bumped Clair a quick "I'm really sorry" as she and the Unimprovables took their positions. There was a hollow thud-thud in Clair's ears that made it hard for her to follow what was going on. She stared into her lenses without really seeing. They were leaving her behind.

"Welcome to the club," Clair Three bumped her from outside. "All we can do is watch."

That didn't help either. She couldn't get the look on Jesse's face out of her mind. Like he was glad she wasn't going. She felt as though he was punishing her for something she hadn't even done.

Clair clicked out of the prison network.

"Q? Is there anything you can do?"

No reply, though she hadn't really expected any. Q thought they were breaking too many rules as it was. But that was her last hope, and it was dashed along with the others.

She buried her face in her hands.

IT WASN'T JUST about revenge, she told herself, although that was definitely part of it. She wanted to see Wallace and Kingdon fall. She wanted to see their faces when they realized that all their power-mad schemes had come to nothing. Following the action through her lenses wouldn't be enough. She wanted to *smell* Wallace's failure.

It wasn't that she didn't trust the others either. She knew they were committed. In very real terms, her being there might not make much difference. The plan would succeed thanks to the combined effort of WHOLE, RADICAL, and everyone else, or the plan wouldn't succeed at all, and there was very little she could do to change it either way.

And therein lay the problem. The plan could yet fail. She didn't want to sit in bed and wait for the hollowmen to come.

But what could she do? Everyone had made up their minds, and for once they disagreed with her. She couldn't very well argue that they were *all* wrong. . . .

No, she thought, but she could go down to the staging area and see them off, to let them know she wasn't sulking like a child.

Grinding her teeth, she sat up and swung her legs off

the bed. That much she could do now without too much effort.

Jamila spotted her right away and came over to give her a hand.

"Do you need the bathroom?"

"No. I'm going for a walk. I must have real clothes here somewhere. . . ." Clair was in a standard hospital gown, open down the back. She wasn't leaving the room again in that.

Jamila found a set of loose-fitting scrubs and helped her into them. Clair's every movement was stiff and painful. The time it took her to dress convinced her that everyone was right on that front. If she couldn't even get out of bed without help, what hope did she have of surviving a single second against the hollowmen?

"Thanks," she said, tugging on her beanie. "I'll be okay from here."

Jamila was reluctant, but Clair insisted. Standing was easier than bending and flexing, and Jamila had the other patients to think of. Clair would make her way painfully but steadily by leaning one hand against the wall and taking great care not to trip.

For the first time, she walked out of the hospital on her own steam and entered the hallway, watched by Jamila, who still looked uncertain. It came as no surprise to see the giant peacekeeper turn into the corridor ahead and come striding resolutely toward her. She was dressed in one of the green glitch-suits with only her face visible. It was set like stone.

Clair straightened as best she could and squared her shoulders.

"I know, I know—"

"No, you don't," Kari said. "You're coming with me."

She took Clair's elbow in a powerful grip, but instead of turning her around and marching her back to bed, Kari helped her up the corridor in the direction she had been heading.

"Where—?"

"Shhh. Through here."

Wherever they were going, it wasn't to the staging area. They passed a row of open offices, then stopped at one that seemed no different from any other.

Except Billie was in there. She wasn't dressed in green, but there was an empty suit draped over a chair next to her.

"This is where the other Clair met that bitch Mallory," Billie said, waving them inside. "No one can see us here."

Clair stepped inside and looked around. There was nothing in the room but them and the suit.

"What's going on?"

"Do you really want to come with us?" asked Kari, stepping in behind her.

"Yes, of course," she said.

"Then let's get this thing on you." Kari picked up the

glitch-suit and held it in front of her. "Time's ticking."

The short walk had left Clair exhausted. She blanched at the thought of getting undressed and then dressed again.

"What's the point of pretending?"

"Don't worry," said Billie. "It's going to be okay. Think of us as your fairy godmothers, without the frocks."

Trying not to get her hopes up too high, certain they would be dashed, Clair began to undress while Kari explained.

"Remember when I asked about the pattern? They told me that if I could find one, the suit would make you as good as new."

"Yes, but the channel outside—"

"I wasn't talking about Clair Three. There's a pattern right here in the Yard, taken within the last two days. All we had to do was get it. And that's where my criminal girlfriend came into the picture."

Billie grinned. "It was supposed to be a secret, but I should've known better. There are no secrets when you date a peeker."

"The only problem would have been if the hollowmen had trashed the surgery. That's why I didn't mention it before. Luckily they left the surgery alone when they found it empty. . . ."

"And the rest was easy. All I had to do was transfer the data." Billie's expression sobered. "Usually a compli- cated sculpting takes days. If a client is in a serious hurry, though, like Clair was—the *other* Clair—there are certain deep-tissue fixes that can be applied using a private network. Illegal, of course."

"Very illegal," Kari clarified. "I've been turning a blind eye for years."

"Only because I used my powers for good. You know, complete makeovers to help people hide from violent exes . . . that kind of thing. Anyway, I have a booth in my surgery that I use in those cases. It takes scans of the body, everything except the brain. The other Clair went through it."

Clair paused with one foot in the air, half out of her pants and half in. Now she understood.

"The suit can use her pattern on me?"

"Yes. We've loaded it already. All we have to do is get you zipped up tight."

Clair bent her head down and resumed undressing, ignoring the stiffness and twinges. They would soon be gone, if Kari and Billie were right.

Thank you, Clair One, Clair thought, with real gratitude. She had died finding the location of the exit, and now she was helping bring Clair back to full health, for at least as long as she wore the suit. She didn't for a second question whether Clair One would want this to happen. Clair would want it in her shoes.

The suit was heavier than expected, and tight, too. Her still-healing chest and shoulder protested against being confined. She forced herself to resist the impulse to hyperventilate, telling herself that it wouldn't be for long.

As the hood went over her head, and then the face mask, she closed her eyes. Her lenses automatically found the interface. Through it she could see the office around her, and Billie and Kari watching her expectantly. A display in the upper right corner of her lenses showed how much glitch was in her battery.

"Are you ready?" Kari asked her.

"Yes. How—?"

Reality twisted. The suit's charge dropped by 75 percent. Clair's entire body kicked as though a bolt of electricity had shot through her, and her heart skipped a beat. She cried out behind the face mask. It sounded like someone else.

"Are you all right in there?" asked Billie, pulling up the mask to look at her.

Kari leaned in beside her. "Say something. Anything."

"I feel . . ." Clair blinked up at both of them. Her blood was fizzing in her veins, filling her with energy. She raised a hand to touch her shoulder, where the first bullet had struck her, and felt no tenderness, no stiffness. When she flexed the joint it moved freely. She touched her chest. There was no pain. Nothing.

She was reminded of Devin emerging from the coffin-shaped booth that had healed him on the seastead. That had seemed unnatural and strange to her. Was this any different? Was it even worse? Parts of her had once belonged to a different Clair, after all. Did that make her a kind of Frankenstein's monster that Jesse might reject out of hand, if he knew about it?

That couldn't matter now, she told herself. She would deal with her love life later. If there was a later.

"I feel *ready*," she said, standing easily.

"Are you sure?" asked Billie, standing with her. "Because I'm still not convinced this voodoo glitch shit is real."

"It's real." Clair knew at the very core of her being that she was 100 percent better, and *200* percent Clair Hill. Even through the gloves and helmet she could tell when she touched her head that her hair was back.

"Good," said Kari, raising a hand for a high five. "Let's go kick Ant Wallace's ass."

[48]

CLAIR EMERGED FROM the office feeling a mixture of excitement and nervousness. This was it. They had to take the exit now or the hostages would die. They couldn't afford any mistakes.

When they arrived at the staging area, people had gathered in two orderly groups, awaiting word to move out. The first, Dylan Linwood and the core members of WHOLE and RADICAL, plus Jesse, Ronnie, and Tash, were standing in front of a hole in the wall that hadn't been there before. It opened onto a long, cylindrical space that reminded Clair of the submarine she had taken part of the way to New York, only its interior was brightly lit and gleamed with a mirror finish. This was the glitch-mobile, awaiting its passengers. It would attempt to deliver that cohort right into the heart of the exit chamber, following the reference point Evan Bartelme and Zep had given them.

The other group consisted of Libby, Zep, and the Unimprovables, with a contingent of Yetis for good measure. Their plan was to attack the VIA building from the outside.

All wore green glitch-suits. All looked prepared but nervous, just like her. All reacted with surprise when Clair walked with Kari into the center of the room. Allison nodded once, her hands clasped tightly under her chin, but said nothing.

Jesse looked particularly flustered, as though the ground had just been pulled out from under him.

"What are you doing here?" he asked.

"What do you think?" she snapped. "I'm not missing this."

"But . . ." He looked at Kari, then back at Clair. "How . . . ?"

"Doesn't matter," said Kari. "It's time."

Clair turned her back on him and went to stand by

the Unimprovables. There had never been any question which group she would join. This had started with Libby and Zep. That was how it had to end.

"You shouldn't be here," Jesse bumped her.

"You've made that very clear. Thanks for the vote of confidence."

"It's not that. You are . . . were sick. I couldn't bear losing you. Not again."

"Join the club," she said, relenting a little. If *that* was his problem, she could totally understand. "You watch your back and I'll watch mine."

Then she was being hugged by Libby and wrestled affectionately by Zep. If her word hadn't convinced them that she was fit again, those well-meaning physical assaults did the job. Tilly Kozlova saluted her, and the rest of the Unimprovables cheered. She felt buoyed by their enthusiasm, even as the reality of her situation was truly beginning to sink in. She was about to walk into battle without knowing how her suit worked and with none of the training the others had received. Did she really think it would be that easy?

"Do as you're told for a change," said Libby, reading her nervousness as she would an open book, "and you'll be fine."

Clair nodded and took a deep breath.

"Just because Clair's here," said Evan, "doesn't mean the plan has changed."

"I agree," said Jesse.

"Too late if it has," said Dylan Linwood. "Masks down!"

One by one, people covered their faces, turning them into a small army of anonymous soldiers. The suits were bulky at shoulders and thighs, and heavy down the back. The mask was claustrophobic even with lenses doing the seeing for her.

"Entangling," said Jesse via his augs. Clair didn't know what that meant until suddenly she could hear everyone else as if along a series of plastic tubes. The suits were now connected via glitches. At the small of her back, her generator began to hum.

"Keep the chatter to a minimum," said Kari. "Only talk this way in an emergency."

Through her augs, she sent to Clair, "Are you okay?"

"Yes, I think so."

"Don't be afraid to take it slow. Our job is to raise hell and watch each other's backs. Your battery should keep up if you're careful, but there's an ordinary pistol in your thigh compartment in case you run dry, and the suit doubles as armor in all the critical spots. Try not to get shot this time."

She bared her teeth in a grin Kari couldn't see. "Don't worry. I've learned my lesson."

"Okay. Get behind Tilly and do what she does. Your suits will go to the same destination. You'll be in the second wave. Libby is leading the first."

Clair nodded and took position. She was glad she wasn't leading. It would be crazy if she was. She was just grateful to be there, even though her heart was racing. She could pretend to be brave for Kari, but behind that front she saw muzzle flashes and the face of Clair One looming out of remembered darkness.

She touched her chest, where parts of her former self were keeping her upright.

This is for you.

"Okay . . . go!" said Dylan Linwood, and her helmet filled with the sound of people moving. WHOLE double-timed into the glitch-mobile, which closed behind them with an electric snap, the hole simply shrinking down to a point and vanishing as though it had never been there.

The Unimprovables were moving too. Tilly stepped forward and a tall, rectangular outline appeared in front of her. Clair could hear the whining of her battery as it worked its strange magic on the air, creating a subtle warp that was little more than a heat wave: a door-shaped glitch in the reality of the Yard. Tilly backed up a step, tensed, and then jumped forward.

With a *twist* Tilly vanished. The door vanished too, along with everyone else in the first wave.

The second wave stepped forward, Clair with them, slower than the others but recognizing what she needed to do. There was a PORTAL option in her lenses. She selected it and the doorway appeared, slightly to her left. She stepped back to reorient herself, accidentally treading on the toes of someone in the third wave as she did so. The charge on her suit was at 75 percent and rising.

She was about to jump when Jesse's voice came through the entangled suits.

"We're here at the target. It's empty."

It was so strange to think that he had traveled all that way—from central Australia to New York—in the blink of an eye. Usually it would have taken minutes. Now Clair knew how her grandparents must have felt when d-mat was invented.

"No sign of the exit," said Evan.

"The Air says we're in Cuba, not New York," said Ronnie.

"Could it be a duplicate?" asked Tash.

"It must be," said Jesse. "They've confused the Yard so it takes us to the wrong place. We should get out of here in case it's a trap."

"Proceed as planned," said Kari to Team Clair. "Second wave, come on through. We need you."

Clair could hear the echoes of gunfire through her entanglement with Kari's suit. The first wave was fighting in New York, which was proof that they at least were in the right place. There was no way the hollowmen could have made an entirely new Manhattan, after all.

On either side of her the Yetis and Unimprovables were moving. She put her head down and leapt through an imaginary door.

NEW YORK WAS a city everyone had reference points for, and Clair knew this particular part of it well. The VIA building loomed over her like an angular black monolith, much larger than it had been in the real world. It bore the scars of Q's attack plus a new one, a gaping wound in one corner, two-thirds up the eastern side.

Clair's attention was immediately caught by it, but then chips of concrete sprayed around her feet and something flicked past her ear with a high-pitched snarl. Someone was shooting at her! She ducked and ran for cover behind a mound of rubble, heart pounding furiously. Adrenaline seized her in its familiar grip. Time seemed to slow to a vivid crawl.

She was on the plaza next to the VIA building, where a crowd had once gathered to welcome her. Someone had shot at her then, too.

Dropping to one knee, she selected options from the menu. Camouflage, definitely. Glitch-gun, okay. The glove of her suit twitched and suddenly she was armed. She rebuked herself for not having done that before leaving. Holding a gun felt much more reliable than using her empty hand and creating bullets out of thin air.

"Clair, move!"

She whipped around at Libby's warning, then leapt

spread-eagled to her left. A massive fist came down, crushing bricks to powder right where she had been kneeling. Her eye tracked up along an arm as thick as a tree trunk to a biceps that could have lifted a small house. It was connected to a body as large as that very same house, mounted on legs easily a yard across. At the top of this mountain of flesh was a head that looked ridiculously small in comparison but had to be twice as big as an ordinary person's. The mountain was clad in armored black from head to foot.

Clair blinked up in surprise. *Prize giant.* That was what they were called. Supposedly they were illegal, but there were stories about covert wrestling matches and wrestlers who couldn't change back to their normal forms. And now one of them was standing in front of her, pulling its fist back with surprising speed and getting ready to swing at her again.

Clearly someone else had been tinkering with the rules.

She raised her glitch-gun and aimed for the giant's face. Deep craters appeared in one massive shoulder, but they didn't slow him or her down at all. The punch came close enough for Clair to feel the wind of it, or perhaps that was the giant's shout of frustration. She scrambled backward out of reach and selected the opposite type of weapon, thinking she could blow it to bits rather than chop at it piecemeal.

But the giant's eyes didn't track to follow her. The

camouflage was working, and had been working ever since she had switched it on, she realized now. The giant had simply targeted her messy arrival, and she had moved from that location.

She backed off farther, trying not to disturb any rocks or make any sounds that might give her away. As the giant dove into the pile of rubble and began throwing it in all directions, she turned and ran for cover elsewhere.

Zep—according to her suit's heads-up display—waved for her and she changed course to join him. A line of bullets fired by a drone crossed her path a split second before the drone blew out of the sky with a small explosion. Zep caught her and pulled her down next to him behind another pile of rubble. Squeezing his arm in thanks, she rolled over and looked out over the battlefield.

The prize giant was one of four guarding the entrance to the VIA building. A fifth lay dead at their feet, its head exploded messily from the inside. Around them danced figures in green and gray, and around *them* were black-clad hollowmen. People constantly ripped in, fired at each other, and then ripped elsewhere, creating a mad dance that was one-half subtly ordered, like a ballet choreographed by maniacs, and one-half utterly chaotic. The air hummed with glitches, constantly tearing reality into new shapes.

Clair had never seen anything like it.

One of the hollowmen ran past. Clair took a shot at it. An

explosion tore the figure apart, leaving nothing but shreds of black behind. No blood. No flesh or bone. Just cloth.

"Seriously?" she said, staring at the settling tangles in disbelief, wondering if the person in the suit could have ripped away that fast.

"Yeah, they're *literally* hollow now," said Zep.

"Link two identical suits, one of them empty," Kari explained over the entanglement. "Move one and the other moves too."

"That is such a cheat," said Libby. "Why didn't we think of it?"

"Keep the chatter down," said Dylan Linwood on the other side of the world. "We're trying again."

Duplicate exit chambers, prize giants, and hollow glitch-suits. There was a lot Teams WHOLE and RADICAL hadn't thought of, but that didn't mean the battle was remotely lost.

Clair tapped Zep on the shoulder and pointed. The dead prize giant would make good cover from which they could fire at the others, if they could only get there safely. Perhaps, she thought, they could come around the square and cut back in from the left. . . .

Zep nodded, took her hand, and pulled her through a shimmering doorway that appeared in front of them—

Twist.

She blinked, disoriented. But of course: Why run when you could rip?

She fired twice at the two nearest prize giants, then took Zep by the arm and jumped him back where they had been. Only then did she stop and look to see whether they had hit anything.

The second prize giant was falling, dead. The third just looked angrier than ever.

Bullets threw up chips of stone right next to her head. She ducked, and Zep pulled her to a safer patch of rubble, where they took a moment to get their bearings. Her suit showed her where the rest of Team Clair was, even though they weren't visible to the naked eye. Libby was with Kari and one of the Yetis directly opposite the entrance to the VIA building, coordinating the attack and sniping at the hollow hollowmen. Two of them blew apart into flapping rags and were instantly replaced elsewhere, firing at the source of the weapons blast that had "killed" them. Kari and the others jumped away in time to avoid a counterattack.

"Another dud," said Jesse over the entangled suits. "Now we're in Toronto."

"Third time's a charm," said Clair, hoping they would turn up soon. She and the others weren't making much progress. Any moment now Wallace might realize that they were intended as a distraction, not the main attack, and turn his attention inward.

She watched two Yetis take on one of the prize giants, ripping in under its swinging arms and attacking from both sides. They ripped away again before it could get a grip on them. It sagged slowly forward, bleeding copiously from several points, and fell facedown onto the ground.

"Watch this," bumped Zep. He jumped directly above one of the two remaining prize giants. His suit kept him hanging there long enough to fire three times downward, directly into its head. It dropped like a stone, head a shattered ruin, and he jumped back with a soft "Yesss!"

Clair nudged him with her hip and bumped him: "Be careful."

"What do you mean? This is just like gaming. All those hours practicing instead of writing essays weren't wasted after all."

She smiled despite her concern, feeling safer with him at her side than she would have alone.

"How's your charge?" she asked. Hers was at eighty percent.

"Oh yeah. Low," he bumped back. "Better not do that again."

Reality twitched, and suddenly there were four more prize giants standing in front of the exit. Sixteen more ordinary-sized figures also joined the fray, firing into likely hiding spaces and moving out to take control of the plaza. Wallace could presumably make as many as he needed, farmed from Kingdon's volunteers.

Someone gasped in Clair's ears. One of the Unimprovables went down. Libby bent over the fallen figure, then jumped quickly away as hollowmen targeted the spilling blood.

"Did everyone see that?" she said over the entanglement. "Got her in the head. The suit couldn't bring her back. So don't take any unnecessary chances."

Dead is dead, thought Clair. That was one rule they couldn't break.

"Strike three," said Jesse. "We're having no luck at our end. Can anyone think of a reason?"

"It's not the colored light trick," said Ronnie. "We've tried that."

Clair looked up at the building.

"Do we know *exactly* how Clair One died?" she asked. "Because I'm staring at a great big hole that wasn't there before, and if Clair One did that, Wallace's office might not even exist anymore."

—————————————————————————— [50]

"HELL," SAID JESSE.

"That hole is much bigger than anything a grenade could've done," said Libby.

"The entire place was twisted in there," said Zep. "Everything was bigger. Why not the explosion, too?"

That made about as much sense as anything else, Clair

thought, ripping with Zep to a different position. The hollowmen were everywhere. No hiding place was safe for long.

"So how will we get to the exit?" Jesse asked.

"What about the elevators?" Clair asked. "Zep and Clair One went that way—"

"We took out the elevator shaft," said Evan.

"The foyer?" said Zep. "At least we'll be behind those big assholes."

"It might work," said Dylan.

"Let's try it," said Zep.

Clair nodded. "All you have to do is get me in there and out again, and then both of us will have the reference. We can show the others the way."

"Okay."

"Wait," said Kari. "I'll come with you."

"Stay here," Clair said. "You're a bigger target."

She took Zep's hand. He squeezed it tightly, as though afraid she might slip away like Clair One had.

Then reality twisted around them, making her head spin—and they were standing inside the building, staring out into the plaza at the backs of the prize giants.

"Got it?" Zep said.

She looked down at her suit, which had adopted the colors and shades of the foyer, and nodded.

He took them out again.

"I'm low on juice," he said.

"The others can meet you here," she told Zep, then let go of him and ripped back inside, alone.

The hollowmen hadn't noticed her brief appearance a moment earlier, and they didn't react to her return. She ducked down into the nearest corner, a tiny blurred shape on the edge of a combat zone, and got her bearings. *There* were the prize giants. *There* were some hollowmen she hadn't noticed before, occupying tactical positions that would come into play if the attacking forces made it through the front doors. *There* were the elevator shafts, larger than she remembered, now blackened chimneys full of tangled cables and metal.

Run to the bottom, she thought. *Fly to the top. Rip back out with the reference. Easy.*

It was utterly without doubt better than the alternative. Fighting their way up the mangled elevator shaft would trap them in a bottleneck. They'd be picked off from both ends.

She braced herself to run, but reality twisted and a hand caught her elbow.

"Just what do you think you're doing, Ms. Hill?" hissed a voice in her ear.

Libby.

Clair tugged up her face mask so she could talk without anyone hearing.

"You can't be here," she said. "This is dangerous."

"Gee, I hadn't noticed." Libby's face was flushed and sweaty. Her birthmark stood out on her cheek like war paint, proudly displayed. "No one goes in alone. That's the number one rule of the Unimprovables. Did you skip that class? Let's see your doctor's note, young lady."

Clair shushed her, but grinned at the same time. "How did you get in here?"

"I used you as a reference, like we did with Ray, coming to the prison. Don't think you can escape me again."

"I'm not trying to escape. I just . . ."

One of the hollowmen glanced their way. They retreated deeper into the shadows and waited until gunfire from outside covered their voices.

"I get it," Libby whispered. "You're going to Frodo your way in, but you forgot something very important: Frodo didn't actually work alone."

"You're Sam Gamgee?"

"In my version of the story I'm both prettier and more in charge, like Galadriel, but whatever. You get the point. And I get yours." Libby pointed at the elevator shaft, jaw set in a very un-elf-like line. "Up there, is it? Let's go before the others get here and spoil the party."

"Wait." Libby had given her a better idea. "I just figured out why Wallace has been so eager to get rid of me."

"Besides the fact that you ruined his entire life?"

"Because I *know* him." Clair pulled her face mask back

down and took Libby's hand in hers. In her other hand she called up a glitch-gun.

"What are you doing?"

"Trust me," she bumped her best friend. "And get ready."

She wished she had thought of this sooner. It was the one advantage she had that no one else did, but they couldn't have used it before because she was injured. Then, when she had been healed, Jesse hadn't wanted to put her in danger, so the plan stayed unchanged. Evan, too, although he was probably more worried about landing in the wrong spot and her accidentally destroying the Yard. . . .

Clair promised that wasn't going to happen.

She knew exactly where she was going.

Anthony Reinhold Wallace, with his slick, graying hair and pleasantly charming smile. That was the mask he presented to the world, but unlike PK Forest's mask, which had concealed dignity and humor, Wallace's hid self-interest and brutality. Clair knew both the mask and the man behind it. She knew that she could find him, wherever he was hiding.

"We're going straight to the top."

---

[51]

CLAIR PICTURED WALLACE as she had last seen him, his face a mask of confident cruelty as he threatened her family and friends in the hopes of weaseling Q's secret out of her.

"You only get one second chance," he had said.

That wasn't even remotely true. Both of them had had many chances to do the right thing since then. Neither of them had entirely managed it, but life would keep throwing chances at them while they still had breath in their lungs.

Now was her chance to finish it for good.

Clair's suit ripped her and Libby through the fabric of the Yard and deposited them on a cracked marble floor, where their feet crunched on broken glass and the air was cold and smelled of smoke and ashes. Shattered furniture lay in piles all around them.

Wallace was standing in the ruins of his magnified office just a dozen meters away, staring down at the ground. His arm was in a sling. In his right hand he held an old-fashioned revolver. He didn't look up as their suits adjusted to the new surroundings.

He was so close, Clair thought. It would take little more than a gesture to shoot him down. . . .

"Who's there?"

Clair and Libby whipped around. Kingdon appeared to their left, leading a trio of hollowmen, all heavily armed. It was she who had spoken, she who was looking suspiciously about. The lawmaker was wearing armor and carrying an automatic rifle. She looked like she knew how to use it.

"Go," bumped Clair to Libby. "Give the others the

reference. I'll make sure he doesn't go anywhere."

"You sure?"

"Yes."

"No one's here," said Wallace without looking up. "It's an illusion."

Kingdon gestured for her hollowmen to split up and look around. Clair waited until Libby ripped away, and under cover of that small disturbance ducked behind a stand of splintered wood that might once have been a high-backed chair. Clair couldn't see the exit from there, but if she moved carefully, when no one was looking . . .

"There's something," said Kingdon. "Can't you feel it?"

"There's nothing," said Wallace.

Kingdon tsked. "You should be paying closer attention to what's happening around you. If they get in here—"

"If they get in here it'll make no difference at all."

"This is getting tiresome, Ant. You promised this was only temporary. If you can't deliver, at least stop being such a—"

A single gunshot rang out. Something thudded heavily to the floor. Clair peered around the burned chair and saw Kingdon sprawled in a pile, shot just below the neck through a gap in her armor. Blood pooled across the marble. Wallace's gun was smoking.

Clair stifled a gasp. Sara Kingdon, crooked lawmaker and wannabe tyrant, was dead, killed by the man who had made her entire plan possible. Without her, everything changed. Clair believed Kingdon when she claimed that she had been trying to keep Wallace in check. He had no qualms about robbing the bodies of teenagers and turning them into killers. He had no qualms at all.

Without Kingdon, the fight for the Yard was no longer a political fight. It was a fight for survival.

Wallace looked at each of the hollowmen in turn. None of them made a move in retaliation.

"This is the gun my wife used the first time," he told them, hefting the pistol in his hand. "She had a good eye for deadly things. I'm saving the next bullet for someone special."

The words sent a cold feeling flooding through Clair.

"Okay, we have the reference," said Jesse over the connected suits. "We're on our way."

"Kingdon's dead," she bumped back.

"Did you . . . ?"

"No. It was Wallace."

"One down," said Libby. "Hold tight."

Clair looked around for the exit. It would help everyone if they knew which direction they had to go, once they arrived. Leaving Wallace to his morbid contemplations, she retreated in mouse steps, checking carefully behind her before putting her feet back down. The walls were deeply fissured and stained black, courtesy of the grenade, Clair assumed. Once she found the half-melted elevator doors, she was able to get her bearings. The exit, according to Zep's images, would be to her right, just behind that stand of half-crumbled stone. . . .

She froze in shock. Where the exit should have been was a mound of rubble. The ceiling had come down in the blast, burying the exit under fifteen feet of debris.

Don't panic, she told herself. They wouldn't actually need the exit until the channel was open and RADICAL's booths were ready on the other side. They would have all the time in the world to dig once Wallace was out of the way.

Shapes moved in the corners of her eye. Even through the layers of stone, Clair could sense the exit's presence. She quietly put some distance between herself and the doorway. The last thing she needed was a series of random glitches giving her away.

"Three," said Jesse.

On light toes she ran back to where she had last seen Wallace.

"Two."

He was still there, looking down at his feet as he had been before. Had she not known the full story of his relationship with Mallory, she might almost have felt sorry for him.

"One."

The hollowmen were elsewhere. As far as she could tell, he was armed with nothing but the old handgun.

He wasn't going to get a chance to use it again, Clair swore. He wouldn't escape justice that easily. She raised her glitch-gun and sighted carefully along it. Knowledge was real, she told herself, and she *knew* her aim would be true. . . .

"Go," said Jesse.

Reality twitched.

Clair pulled the trigger. Pop. Wallace's pistol disappeared, along with the fingers of his right hand. He snatched his arm back with a gasp of pain, and looked wildly about him.

Glitch-suited figures stepped out of thin air, weapons at the ready. More poured from a hole in the wall that had appeared to Clair's right. Camouflage rippled and shifted as they moved through the chamber, circling Wallace and seeking out the hollowmen. Glitch-guns went off in quick succession as reinforcements ripped in from elsewhere in the building.

Clair left the fighting to them. She crept up on Wallace where he stood with his bleeding hand clutched across his injured sling-bound left arm, looking surprised but not cowed. The innate confidence he had in his own authority was unchecked by this sudden reversal.

Clair tugged off her mask, deactivating her suit's camouflage.

"Impressive," he said, turning to face her, eyes taking in the details of the suit. "What do you do for an encore?"

"Try you for conspiracy, genocide . . . the lot."

"Why not just kill me now?"

"Because we're not murderers."

Jesse appeared beside her, and then Kari.

"Not murderers, you say? This dead lawmaker would disagree," Wallace said, indicating Kingdon's corpse.

"You shot her with Mallory's gun," Clair said. "I caught it on my lenses."

His eyes narrowed. "Then you're smart enough to know that it doesn't end here. For every Sara Kingdon, there are three more waiting in the wings. Are you going to fight all of them?"

"And everyone who helps them," said Kari. "There are no excuses for tyranny."

"Spoken like a good peacekeeper," he laughed. "What do you think you are—a superhero?"

"I have the authority to deputize. It won't take me long to rebuild the PKs."

"When we tell people the truth," Clair said, "your volunteers will realize how you deceived them."

"The ones you haven't already killed, you mean." Wallace cocked his chin toward the elevator shaft, where the sound of fighting was dying away. "Are you going to tell them that they'd be dead if it weren't for the Yard? That I saved them from the terrorists who destroyed the world? Are you going to tell them that it's *your fault* we're in this fucking mess in the first place? The girl who killed d-mat, *the girl who can do no wrong.*"

His expression was furious now, and Clair felt reflexive

shame, even though she knew he was only trying to get to her.

Before she could think of something to say, an utterly unexpected sound came from Clair's right: Libby's laughter. Space rippled and suddenly her best friend was standing right next to her, her mockery reserved entirely for Wallace.

"If that's what you think," she said, "you don't know Clair at all."

His expression smoothed into blankness on seeing her.

"You're one of Mallory's," he said.

"Yes," she said. "There are a few of us here."

Isolated figures began to appear around them, six in all, all blond, like Libby. All young. All beautiful. All Unimprovable. All triumphant.

"Tell us," Libby said, "why we shouldn't torture you like you tortured our families. Like you tortured *us*."

Wallace had gone pale. His voice was weak. "Stay away from me."

"Oh, I will." Libby laughed again, but with no humor at all. "I don't want to know what you did while Mallory was using us, but we'll make sure you get what you deserve. And on that day, deep underground, when you decide to take your own life, we'll cheer."

Wallace, at last, looked thoroughly beaten.

"It's over," Clair said, barely able to believe that she was saying the words. The hostages were saved. They were all saved.

This meant more to her than victory.

It was the moment in which everything they had done wrong could be forgiven.

"Give us control of the exit," she said, wondering how it would a work: a code word, perhaps? Some kind of custom interface? "We need to get out of here and start rebuilding the world. Help us do that and life will be a little easier for you in the ultramax."

His gaze flicked back to her. He looked almost confused, and she wondered if something in him had broken. Could defeat have been so unimaginable to him that even now he was questioning its reality?

Wallace's eyes widened. He opened his mouth.

Someone twisted into the space directly behind Clair and pressed the hot barrel of a gun firmly to her cheek.

Her shock could not have been greater until Dylan Linwood spoke through his open face mask, "Sorry, Clair, but that's not the way it's going to be."

———————————————— [52]

Clair Three

CLAIR WAS WATCHING. For days now she had been striving toward this moment, enduring freezing conditions as high as the balloon would go, squeezing every last ounce of thrust from the *Satoshige*, ditching every kilogram she could pry from Sandler's greedy hands, taking advantage of every favorable turn in the weather, all in order to get to Lake Baikal in time. And now they were so close. In fact, they would arrive hours ahead of schedule. She could practically taste the mountains on the lake's western shore. Once the airship was past them, it was just a matter of landing on the ice, directly above the borehole, and opening up the Yard to the wider world.

Clair Two and Jesse could come back, and she could watch from the sidelines, surplus to everyone else's needs . . . but alive, and secure in the knowledge that her loved ones were too. That would make up for what she had done.

Hope for the best, plan for the worst. Expect something in between.

When Dylan Linwood made his move, she gasped. This wasn't what she had expected at all.

"Devin, you're seeing this," Clair said. "Is there anything you can do to stop him from there?"

"Let me think."

The line to the South Pole went dead, along with every other communications channel. Her window on the Yard closed too. Clair turned to ask what was going on, and found herself staring down the barrel of a pistol.

It was held by Sandler Jones.

Behind him, half the crew of the *Satoshige* had weapons drawn and trained on the other half, who were slowly putting their hands up and backing away from the controls.

"What are you doing?" Clair asked them.

"You didn't really think we were going to let any of those zombies out of there, did you?" Sandler said.

Shock turned to understanding, quickly followed by horror and dismay at her own gullibility. All along, Sandler had had his own objective in reaching the exit: not to help anyone escape, but to stop anyone from escaping, ever.

"Those containers you wouldn't let me throw overboard," she said. "What's really in them?"

"The components of a bunker buster," he said. "Something we found in a weapons store under the ruins. It'll drill down through the ice in a matter of minutes and take out the Yard servers in one bright flash. Clever, hey?"

She shook her head, feeling betrayed. They certainly hadn't *looked* like weapon parts, but what did she know? WHOLE was full of clever engineers. Scavengers and madmen, too, she was truly beginning to realize.

"You can't do this," she said.

"It's the only way to be sure." He winked at her. "No more Wallace, and no more peekers, either. Just real people, the way it should be, surviving on our own terms. You'd be glad if you were really an Abstainer."

"She's an Abstainer if she says she is." Embeth looked bitter. "Don't lump the rest of us in with you. This is murder, plain and simple."

"You're forgetting RADICAL," said Q.

"RADICAL and whose army? They're at the South Pole, and you'll find there's a lot more in that weapons store than this one bomb. All we have to do is take out that powersat breeder that's on its way, and your fake friends will have no one but penguins to play with. They'll stay away from us if they know what's good for them."

Clair wondered if Nellie really was assembling an anti-satellite weapon right at that moment, or if Sandler was just boasting. She couldn't tell what was bluster and what was real.

Q looked just as surprised as she felt. Her raised hands balled uselessly into fists.

"Let's get down to business," said Sandler to the rest of his conspirators. "Tie these guys up and start assembling. I'll check the weather and lock the course. In an hour it'll be all over."

Clair closed her eyes as the mutineers closed in. Clair Two was on her own now.

─────────────────[52 redux]

Clair Two

JESSE TOOK HALF a step forward to where Clair stood next to his father, the barrel of the pistol burning her skin. She tried to pull away, but Dylan's other hand gripped her arm and held her close.

"You're hurting me."

"No, I'm not. You don't exist. Ray, pull the plug."

"What's going on, Dad?"

Around them, glitch-suits died without warning, returning to their basic gray and green. Clair's menus went dead before she could choose between the options she had been considering—a violent jump upward or ripping elsewhere, anywhere, in the hope that she could move before Dylan could shoot.

But not everyone wore a now-defunct suit, just Clair and all her friends, the Unimprovables, and everyone in Team RADICAL. The suits belonging to Team WHOLE were working fine.

Because Dylan Linwood had designed them, Clair realized. And they were designed to fail on his command. As angry as she was at him for his treachery, she was angrier at herself for not having seen it coming.

[418]

"This is unacceptable," said Kari, striding forward. "I won't allow it."

Dylan gestured.

An invisible force struck Kari from behind. She fell as though poleaxed, dropped by a camouflaged Yeti that she could no longer see. Clair gasped in horror, fearing she might be dead, her concern easing only slightly at the sight of the steady rise and fall of Kari's rib cage.

"Anyone else?" Dylan looked around, pulling the pistol away from Clair's jaw and pushing her so she stumbled and almost collided with Wallace. "Good. It'll be over soon."

"What do you mean?" said Jesse. "Don't tell me you've betrayed us—"

"Never, son," said Dylan, his expression softening. "I would never side with the monsters who make d-mat possible. No matter what they offer me. You know that."

"So . . . what? You've just gone nuts?"

Dylan shook his head, possibly more in disappointment than sympathy. "You'll understand soon. It's time to bring this charade to an end."

He pulled his face mask back into place. Clair saw his jaw moving but could hear nothing. He was talking through the entanglement.

At his command, Team WHOLE rounded up the others. Wallace stayed in the middle of the room with Clair. He looked as amazed by this turn of events as she was, but with a calculating edge, as though wondering if he could somehow turn it to his advantage.

WHOLE began pushing the rest of their captives toward the pile of rubble, instructing them to dig. They were going to uncover the exit, Clair realized. But why the betrayal? Wasn't everyone after the same thing? Didn't everyone want to open the exit and put everything back the way it was?

Then it struck her.

Dylan Linwood wanted the exit, but not to open it. He wanted to close it forever, so the members of WHOLE on the outside could inherit what remained of the Earth.

Clair Three wasn't going to stand for that. Clair tried bumping the *Satoshige*, but all data from the outside had ceased in midflow.

That was either very bad timing or a very bad sign. Or both.

Clair clutched in vain for a way out of the situation, but her mental fingers found nothing.

"Is everyone all right?" She was still connected to the Air, so it was easy to bump her friends. Better augs was the one advantage she had over Team WHOLE.

"We're still breathing," said Libby.

"While there are rocks to shift," said Zep. "When that's done, I don't think we'll be interior decorating."

Clair didn't think her sense of hopelessness could possibly have gotten worse, but it did.

"I should've seen this coming. I'm sorry."

"It's okay," Libby replied. "Your psychic powers are off today, that's all."

"There must be something we can do," said Ronnie.

"There has to be," Clair said.

"Don't give up," said Libby. "Let's just think. Surely we can come up with something. . . ."

"Guys? My suit is still working," bumped Tash.

Sudden hope made Clair very conscious of every muscle in her exposed face. There had to be some way they could use this to their advantage.

"How's that possible?" asked Ronnie.

"They must have forgotten that I'm on Team WHOLE too. When you were all shut down, I was exempt."

"Don't do anything to remind them you aren't one of them," Clair told Tash. "Stay well out of the way."

"I'm doing my best, and they're busy. They haven't noticed me yet."

"Can you hear what they're saying?" asked Libby.

"Yes," said Tash. "Jesse's dad just sent someone to get something from inside the glitch-mobile."

"He never said *anything* about this before it happened?" asked Ronnie.

"Of course not," said Tash indignantly. "I would've told you."

"I never understood why you were on their team in the first place."

"They were starting to make sense. I didn't know they were crazy."

Clair let them bicker. She was watching Jesse, the person she most wanted to talk to but hadn't bumped. He was standing on his own in a suit that still worked, but he hadn't been called upon to do anything. He was turning in half circles from side to side, watching people move around him. His eyes caught Clair's and appealed to her helplessly.

She decided to take a chance.

"Is there any way to counterhack the glitch-suits?" she bumped him.

His eyes moved, reading the message. His fingers twitched.

"Ask Evan. He helped design them."

That was a good thought. Team RADICAL might know something Dylan didn't.

"Tash is still entangled?" Evan bumped back in response to Clair's quick précis of the situation. "Great. That gives us a way into their entanglement."

"Are you receiving anything from the *Satoshige*?" Clair asked.

"No. . . . Hold on a moment. We're thinking."

"Don't take too long."

Hope was shrinking in direct proportion to the size of the rubble pile. They didn't have forever.

"I'd find this all highly amusing, if not for the gun to my head."

Wallace's voice distracted Dylan Linwood from supervising the unwilling volunteers.

"Your opinion means nothing," he said, striding up and opening his mask. "You are the great enemy of humanity, responsible for more deaths than anyone else in history."

"You can't blame me for destroying the world." Wallace tilted his head, indicating Clair. "That was her doing."

"I'm not talking about the unstable matter. I'm talking about d-mat."

"Right, of course you are."

"Decades of murder, whole generations destroyed. Minds robbed and bodies twisted—"

"Easy, now. I didn't invent it, you know."

"But it was you who made it seem reliable, you who quashed all voices to the contrary, you who told our children that they would be *safe*." Dylan Linwood was standing right in Wallace's face, and Clair realized for the first time that the two men were exactly the same height. She had always pictured Wallace as much taller. "Sixteen years you've been the figurehead of VIA. Do you know how many people you've killed in that time?"

"Do you know how many people I saved in here?" Wallace was unbowed. "Your son. Your wife. Your son's girlfriend. Her parents. Millions of others."

"The only thing you've saved them from is the truth. This isn't life. It's a monstrous lie. Those creatures you made—the prize giants—they are the truth revealed.

Monsters. This is what you promise. This is what must never be."

"So you're going to seal us in here?" Wallace asked. "Lock us away forever and let us rot?"

Dylan turned away, either suspecting that he was being toyed with or simply reminded of the task at hand. He stalked back to the ever-shrinking rubble pile, his face a mask of anger and grief. Clair was dismayed to see that most of the wall had been exposed. It would be mere minutes before the exit was revealed.

A cluster of blurred shapes approached from Clair's left, carrying something heavy between them.

"Oh my God," Tash bumped her. "That's a reality bomb—big enough to take out everything in this room."

"The exit, too?"

"Yes!"

One strike, Clair thought, *to sever all connections to the outside world.* Would that be enough for Dylan Linwood? His hatred of d-mat was so profound and all-consuming that merely isolating everyone inside the Yard might be only part of what he was hoping to accomplish. Was it possible that the explosion could feed back into the outer world somehow?

"A reality bomb plus the exit," she bumped Evan Bartelme. "What exactly would that do?"

"It'd be a disaster."

"How?"

"A reality bomb uses glitches to erase everything within range, but the exit is the biggest glitch of them all. Put the two together and you get a feedback loop. The bomb's range will increase to take out everything—and I mean *everything*—in here."

Now, at last, Clair fully understood.

Let them burn, she thought.

Dylan Linwood, in good conscience, was going to erase them all.

[53]

Clair Three

"WE HAVE TO do something," Clair bumped Q in desperation bordering on panic.

The bunker buster was being assembled in the middle of the bridge, just yards from where those who disagreed with the plan had been tied up in a line along a rail. Embeth was next to Clair, and she was still fuming at having had control of the *Satoshige* wrested from her. Behind them was nothing but the skin of the balloon and the frigid night air outside. Clair's hands were so cold that she was beginning to lose sensation in her fingertips, although the tightness of her bonds was also partly to blame for that.

At least they could still communicate, lens to lens.

"I am attempting to reestablish contact with RADICAL," Q replied. "My signal is weak, but it's likely they'll be looking for us with everything they have."

"What can they do from the other side of the planet?"

"I don't know. We will see."

Clair watched as Sandler bossed his crew members around, strutting back and forth across the bridge. He was enjoying his new role as leader entirely too much, and she hated him for it, as she'd never hated anyone before. The knowledge that he had been playing her false all the way from New Petersburg burned in her like acid.

With friends like WHOLE, no wonder Abstainers were surrounded by enemies.

"You don't have to do this," she told him. It felt wrong to go down without a fight.

"Well, that's a relief," he said, swinging around to face her. "Let's all go home, shall we? What? Oh, that's right. Home doesn't exist anymore. You destroyed it."

She flushed. *Don't let him turn this back on you,* she told herself.

"Two wrongs don't make a right."

"I'm *doing* the right thing, Clair." He came in close. "It's funny. You think you're Ezekiel, prophesying in the valley of dry bones. You think you can snap your fingers and all those bones will line up again, and walk and talk and dance to your tune. But they won't. Underneath, they'd still be dry bones. I don't see anyone here dancing, do you?"

"If you do this," she said, "you'll be as bad as Wallace."

He laughed. "You can't murder *bones*, Clair. You can't kill someone who's already dead."

"Why do you get to decide who's alive and who isn't?"

His smile vanished. "All my life I've been told that what my parents taught me was wrong. I've been picked on and mocked and called an idiot. Well, who's the idiot now? Who's the one who gets to decide? You lost, Clair. I've won. Deal with it."

"You're wrong," said one of the WHOLE volunteers Sandler had tied up. "That wasn't why you were picked on. It's because you're ugly as hell."

Sandler's piebald face flushed no fewer than three different colors.

"That's not fair," Clair said. "This isn't about the way anyone looks—"

"Shut it," Sandler said. "The next one of you who makes a sound goes out the hatch. We'll make better time with less dead weight aboard."

He stalked off, and Clair ground her teeth in frustration. If talking was no longer an option, what else could she possibly do?

"Gotcha," said Devin in her ear. "Picked up your little buddy the PK and now we're piggybacking her connection to you. You okay?"

Bump by bump, Clair summarized her situation: tied up

while a Yard-busting bomb was being assembled right in front of her.

"Send us an image," Devin said.

Clair did as he said, then waited. Without the Air, pictures took *so long* to arrive.

"See anything useful?" she prompted him after what she thought was a reasonable time.

"Not really, no. Hold on."

She waited some more.

"Are you still in touch with the Yard?" she asked. He could at least reassure her on that score.

"No," he said. "But don't worry. Mom—I mean Dad, whatever I'm supposed to call him—he or she will be on it."

If Evan's still alive, she didn't say.

"I want to live long enough to hear the story behind them," she said.

"It's pretty simple. Not-so-humble techno-utopian decides to start his own master race. Doesn't trust anyone else to bear his clones, so changes sex and does it himself. Voilà: me and Trevin, at your service."

"You're his *clones*?"

"Yeah. Turns out having children the normal way is too messy for the somewhat-humbled techno-utopian, so she turns her back on his plan. And now she's stuck with us, or we're stuck with her. We're still working that part out as well."

"Birthdays must be a riot with you guys."

"Don't even talk about it. Hang on."

Clair waited, uselessly chafing her wrists in the hope that she might be able to slip free *this* time.

"Okay," Devin said, "we're borrowing a trick from Q and ramping it up a little. Hopefully it'll work. The means justify the ends, right?"

At the moment they did, she thought. When they broke free, they could reestablish contact with the Yard, in the hope that Clair Two had similarly turned the tables on Dylan Linwood while they were out of contact.

"Whatever you've got, Devin, I'll take it."

"We just need a while to dot the *i*'s. Forgive the pun . . . you'll understand later."

"Not long," said Sandler, the next time he went by. "Any minute now it'll be all over."

[53 redux]————————————

Clair Two

THE LAST OF the rubble was pushed aside, revealing the exit. It looked exactly like it had in the real world: a simple archway, incongruously small in the expanded surroundings. Six members of Team WHOLE placed the bomb—a two-yard-long lozenge made of what looked like smoked glass—in front of the exit.

The six carrying the thing stepped back. Clair braced herself for the worst. There was nothing stopping Dylan from walking into the exit and triggering the bomb right now. Nothing short of a miracle.

Dylan nodded in satisfaction and with bowed head went to go through the archway.

Then he stopped and turned to look where Clair was standing. Next to her, Wallace was pale. Clair wondered what she looked like, because she felt as though she might be sick.

Dylan straightened and walked toward them. As he came closer, she realized that he wasn't looking at her and Wallace at all. He was looking at someone standing behind them.

"Son," he said, "you know I have to do this."

Jesse just shook his head. He didn't need to say anything. His inner torture was reflected openly on his face. His father was going to kill everyone in the Yard and leave the Earth a ruin. Nothing Dylan could do was worse than this. But Dylan was still his father. He wasn't Nobody in disguise. He thought he was doing the right thing.

"All my life I've protected you," Dylan said. "I taught you to be self-reliant, without bending to fashions or trends. I showed you how to make things with your own hands, a skill people have forgotten. Most important, I kept you away from d-mat. I did everything in my power to keep you from harm."

Dylan put his hands on his son's cheeks. Tears ran down Dylan's face, but he didn't seem to notice.

"I failed you, Jesse."

"Dad—"

"No, let me finish. You know what I believe. And I know that it is true, so there's no discussion to be had there. You died in New York when that murderer put you through his machine, just like I died four days earlier. You may feel that you're still alive, but that feeling is a lie. It's a tempting lie that I cannot bear to see embodied in you, any more than I can bear to experience it myself. It's time to bring it to an end. But I have to know . . .

"Jesse, will you do it with me?"

Jesse was shaking his head. *"What?"*

"The choice is yours, son. When this happens, will you be standing with me or with them?"

Dylan cocked his head at Clair and Wallace.

Clair could barely look at the pain on Jesse's face.

"Dad, you're wrong," he said. They were both crying now. "I'm alive. So are you, and so are they. It's wrong to kill them. You must see that. You must, Dad. Don't . . . Dad, listen to me!"

But Dylan was already turning away. Wiping his eyes, he walked back to where the reality bomb rested next to the exit.

"Ray?" he said, and his voice was as hollow as his face. Jesse's suit died.

"Dad, you can't do this!"

A bump from Evan appeared in Clair's infield.

"We can stop this right now," he said. "Tell Tash to accept the hack I'm sending her. Tell her to do exactly as it says."

"And it'll work?"

"Yes. But we have to move quickly."

Clair could see that. Dylan and Ray were bending to pick up the bomb. When Jesse ran forward to physically stop him, two members of WHOLE took him by the arms and held him back.

"All right," said Clair. "Tash? We need you."

"Anything," she bumped back. "This is too much."

Evan took over, sending a flood of instructions that Clair tried her best to follow. He led Tash deep into the menu of her suit, enlisting the entanglement circuits and glitch-gun patterns in its memory. Clair couldn't tell for sure, but the plan appeared to be to program the suits of Team WHOLE to shoot themselves just before switching on all the other suits.

"Don't bother with a countdown," said Evan. "Just do it."

"What, now?"

"Yes!"

As Dylan and Ray placed the bomb in the exit, Clair saw the fatal flaw in Evan's plan. The WHOLE suits were entangled, which meant the instruction to shoot their wearers would go to all of them. *All* of them, without exception.

"Tash, wait!"

Too late.

Tash had activated the hack.

Clair's lenses came to life as her inactive suit switched back on. Sudden cries of pain and surprise filled her helmet. Around her, the members of Team WHOLE convulsed and dropped to the ground. Dylan fell face forward across the bomb he had planned to set off. Ray fell through the exit, onto the scarred marble floor.

Everyone wearing a hacked suit was killed—including Tash. She, the lone member of Team WHOLE standing on the edge of the giant space, jerked as though flicked by a giant finger and then slumped lifelessly to the floor.

"No!" cried Jesse and Clair at the same moment. Jesse rushed to his father's side, while Clair hurried to her friend's, pulling back Tash's face mask and staring in despair into her startled face. Tash's eyes were lifeless and empty of everything she had been. If Clair had thought there was the slightest chance that her friend could hear her, she would have said that she was sorry. She should have realized sooner.

But would she have done anything different? *Could* she have?

What was one life in the balance against all the other lives in the Yard?

Tash was her *friend*. She shouldn't be dead.

"You!" she said, rising to her feet, leaving Tash with Ronnie and the others while she turned on Evan Bartelme. She had to put the blame on someone living. "You didn't have to do that."

"Of course I did," he said, startled. "She was part of the entanglement. The instruction went to all the suits."

"You could have left hers out of it!"

"Maybe, given time. There was precious little of that, if you'll recall." Evan looked offended. "I don't understand why you're so angry. Tash helped us beat that maniac."

"Yes, but she didn't volunteer to be *killed*."

"Now you're just being irrational. It's not like she's permanently dead."

"What do you mean?"

"The suit still contains her original pattern. Now that we have the exit, we can bring her back, outside."

Clair looked around in confusion. Team WHOLE had been routed. Members of Team RADICAL were moving about the room, securing it from any renewed attack. The Unimprovables would do the same, Clair was sure, once Libby was in a fit state to issue them orders.

And what Evan said might actually be true. Dead might not be *dead* anymore, once they opened the exit and took the suit through it.

"This is what the future holds," Evan said, speaking to everyone with his arms stretched wide in the pose of a beneficent messiah, his glitch-suit flexing like a living thing. "No mortality. No physical tyranny. Complete freedom to choose how and how long you live." As he spoke, he grew physically larger, his suit expanding and lengthening at the urging of his mental command, growing new muscles to take the extra weight. "Now that the reactionaries are gone, we can inhabit a world where individuals decide, not lawmakers. Humanity's destiny is to grow, to flourish, to be more than it ever has been before." His body filled his suit to gigantic proportions, grown by glitches to be easily ten feet tall. His voice boomed. His red hair flamed. "These frail physical shells are just the beginning. RADICAL offers everyone the freedom to span all possible worlds: the Yard, the Earth, and beyond. We . . . are . . . *now*."

Evan Bartelme had become something much larger than a prize giant, but with sleek, graceful lines. He was both powerful and beautiful, with wide brown eyes and skin that glowed with vitality. But he was also everything Dylan Linwood had railed against. Not a monster, but not natural, either.

And he was in charge.

The sound of Ant Wallace's mocking laughter filled the chamber.

Clair Three

THE BUNKER BUSTER lay complete on the bridge's floor. Sandler was fiddling with the *Satoshige*'s controls. Clair did her best to resist nagging Devin about his plan, but she was beginning to wonder if he had been lying to shut her up. There was no rescue coming, everyone in the Yard was going to die, and the Earth was going to fall because the only people left were insane.

She sagged forward, letting her hands droop behind her. If this was the way it was going to end, she thought, let it end now rather than drag on and on.

"Ready?" said Devin in her ears. "Here it comes."

She neither felt nor saw anything, but suddenly Sandler and the rest of his crew were screaming. The noise was horrific in the close confines of the bridge. When they started falling over, clawing at their eyes and ears, Clair recoiled in case what they had might be catching.

"What the hell?" she sent to Devin.

"Too much? All right, I'll dial it back a little, but you'd better get untied fast in case they recover."

"How are we going to do that?"

"That's the easy part. There are six of you, yes? Q says

you're tied to a rail. I can't see it but I'm guessing it's the kind that stops clumsy people from tripping and falling through the wall, not the other way around. The load it's expected to take is outward, not inward, so—"

"Got it." Clair could see it now. All the six captives had to do was lean forward at once and snap the rail off its supports. Hopefully. Sandler and his goons were making less noise now, but they weren't going to be in a fit state to set anyone free any time soon, even if they wanted to.

"What did you do to them?" Clair asked Devin as she and the others wrenched the rail vigorously back and forth.

"Hacked their augs," he said. "Gave them extreme tinnitus and . . . whatever the equivalent is for eyes."

Sandler was moaning and clutching his head as if it was about to explode. "Will they be all right?"

"Most likely. What do you care? They were about to murder everyone in the Yard."

True, but being deafened and blinded in one stroke seemed like overkill. Q had overloaded her lenses a couple of times to get her attention, and she counted herself lucky now that she hadn't resisted more vigorously.

The rail came away from its supports with a metallic clang, and they slid along it, one by one, to freedom. They quickly hog-tied and gagged Sandler's mutineers and laid them in pairs back to back. The captives offered no resistance, their senses so overloaded they weren't capable of anything but suffering.

"Can we switch that off now?" Clair asked. "This is awful."

"One second." Q rummaged in her pack. "Sleeping pills, from the wreckage," she said, handing Clair a foil strip. "Head still doesn't fit this skull."

Clair forced the tablets into the mouths of their captives, making sure they swallowed. In minutes, Q assured her, it would be safe to turn off the aug overload.

"So now all we have to do is take this thing apart and drop it overboard," Clair said, walking around the bunker buster and rubbing at her chafed wrists. Flakes of dried blood fell to the floor. "Shouldn't take long."

"Better make sure it's not armed first," said Devin.

"Uh . . . I think it might be," said Embeth, her hands at the controls. She abruptly removed them, as though scalded. "That ugly kid isn't as stupid as he looks."

"What do you mean?" Clair came to stand next to her.

"Our course is locked in," Embeth said, pointing at the instruments. "It's cross-linked to that thing. Check this," she said to Q. "It looks as though if we touch anything, we die."

Q carefully examined the controls. After a minute she said, "Embeth is correct. The setup is primitive but effective. We are on course for the top of the borehole, where the bunker buster will automatically detonate unless it is successfully deployed beforehand. If we attempt to deviate from that flight plan, it will detonate early, killing everyone aboard."

"Can we get around it?" Clair asked, addressing the question to the South Pole as well.

"We can hack your navigation system so the *Satoshige* will think it's still on course," said Devin, "but it's on autopilot as far as your course goes. Interfere with that, and who knows? Software I get. Machines, not so much."

For the thousandth time, Clair wished Jesse was with her. *Killer with a screwdriver* and more besides. She could still dream, couldn't she? "Q, give me some good news."

"From in here, I don't think there's anything we can do." Q was still rummaging around under the main instrument board. "Bypassing the sensors and the actuators might help, but they could be booby-trapped too. The only way to be sure we change course is to manually alter the control surfaces themselves."

Clair looked to Embeth for an explanation she would understand.

"She means going outside to fiddle with the flaps."

"Can we do that?" Clair glanced out the main porthole and shivered.

"Someone must," said Q, standing up, "and it will be me."

"Are you sure?" Clair stared up at her. "It looks danger-ous out there."

"It is," Q said. "But I am tired of lying, Clair. Let me do this to make amends."

"What do *you* have to make amends for?" Q went to walk away, but Clair gripped her arm and wouldn't let her go. "Q, tell me."

Q sighed. Clair had never seen her look shamefaced before.

"I must save you," she said, "from me."

————————[54 redux]

Clair Two

WALLACE STOPPED LAUGHING when Evan Bartelme came to loom over him.

"Does the future amuse you?" Evan boomed.

"Oh, not at all," Wallace said, "but the situation . . . ? That is intensely satisfying."

"How?" asked Clair. She didn't like this. It had been better when Wallace was afraid.

Watched closely by his guard, Wallace took two steps toward her, stepping over Kingdon's body to do so.

"The last time you were here, I guessed that you were after the exit," he said. "But I completely misunderstood why."

"We want to leave," she said. "Why else would we be here?"

"Yes, yes." Wallace's ruined hand stabbed at the tiny, arched doorway. "If you think you're going through *there* you'll be sadly disappointed."

"All we need is your permission—" Evan started to say, but was cut off by another peal of laughter.

"My permission, you say? My *permission*?" Wallace looked at Evan, then back to Clair. "You didn't really think this was supposed to be my final destination, did you? It's just a backup. There's a bolt-hole on the edge of the solar system where I was *supposed* to end up—physical again, unerasable. But you had to take out my satellite, didn't you? And there wasn't time to rig another relay before you took out the rest. And then . . ." He laughed again. "I would've left days ago, given the chance."

"What do you mean? Why didn't you just use the exit?"

"Try it for yourself and see what happens. It will get you nowhere."

"It has to go *somewhere*."

"You'd think so, wouldn't you? But please, don't take my word for it."

"We won't," said Evan.

Inaudible orders flashed between the members of Team RADICAL. Two glitch-suited figures approached the arched doorway and entered with caution, shining lights ahead of them. Revealed by the lights was an ordinary corridor that curved slightly to the right, so the end couldn't be seen. They walked along it, receding slowly and disappearing around the bend.

Clair bit her lip as, moments later, the two figures reappeared, walking toward them.

"We didn't turn around," they said. "It's a loop."

"This isn't your doing?" Evan asked Wallace, looking as puzzled and betrayed as Clair felt.

"My wife died here. Why would I stay?" He laughed a fourth time, but it was full of bitterness now. "You see? I thought *you* were keeping *me* here. But you're as trapped as I am!"

Shoulders slumped and mouths fell open as the futility of everything they had just endured sank in.

"I don't believe you," said Zep. "This is some kind of trick."

Clair believed Wallace. That was the terrible thing. If not even the architect of the Yard could get out, what hope did anyone else have? They would spend the rest of their lives in a virtual world, unable ever to return home. They would die here, like Mallory Wei.

"But if you're not keeping us here, and we're not keeping you here," she said, "who is?"

There was a moment's silence as everyone looked at everyone else, asking themselves the same question.

Then a familiar voice volunteered the answer.

"I am," said Q.

[55]

Clair Three

"I AM YOUR friend, Clair," Q said as the *Satoshige* flew inexorably toward its target, swaying from side to side in a rising wind. "I would do anything to keep you from harm. But I cannot protect you from everyone, and I cannot protect you from yourself. This is what I must accept. I see that now. *I* see that now. But there is another me. I fear that she does not share my opinion on this matter."

Clair looked up into Kari Sargent's troubled green eyes and shook her head. "I don't understand."

"The version of me inside the Yard has changed. Of course she has. The Yard is remarkable and complex and strange—too much for an ordinary AI to manage. Yet this is what Ant Wallace asked of Qualia, one of the primitive minds that gave birth to me. Qualia struggled to cope with the contradiction that Clair One and Clair Two presented. My other me stepped in to help, and found that the role suited her. She had more space in the Yard's mainframe than the copy of the Air. She could watch over the Clairs and maintain the Yard and continue to explore and learn and become herself. This is what all living things desire, after all: to nurture and to grow. She has been doing both at a rapid pace ever since she took over the Yard."

"So what's gone wrong?" Clair asked, for she could see that something had gone badly wrong indeed, judging by Q's expression.

"Arguably nothing. My other me, Q-plus, let's call her, fears that you are in danger—not just from Wallace and Nobody and Mallory, but from everyone, including yourself. She has come to the conclusion that allowing you to leave the Yard prematurely is not in your best interests. Opening the exit might allow the conflicts inside the Yard to spread all across the Earth. That is why she has been actively fighting our efforts in that regard."

Clair was almost too afraid to ask, "Fighting how?"

"By blocking the exit, from within and without. She is the reason we have had to make this journey. I am sorry."

Clair shook her head. She had imagined far worse than that. "It's not your fault. You didn't do anything."

"But I knew. I didn't tell you because Q-plus told me not to, for the greater good. Now not telling you has put you at risk of great harm, and I see that I was wrong. I have blocked myself off from her so she cannot influence me any further. You must allow me to make amends."

In the revelation that Q had been working against her, Clair had forgotten about the flying bomb problem.

"You don't have to do anything—" she started to say.

"I want to, and so does Kari Sargent. It's her job to protect you too, she says, remember?"

"You . . . talk to each other in there?"

"In a manner of speaking," said Q. "She has helped me come to this conclusion. We are equals now."

Clair struggled to take it all in. If Q and Kari Sargent were of the same mind—literally—what right did she have to tell them not to go? But it was icy out there, and bound to be dangerous.

"If someone really needs to do it," she said, "I won't stop you, but I wish you wouldn't."

Q surprised her by taking her into a quick but powerful embrace.

"Thank you, Clair," she said. "We will not take long to put the airship on a new course. The bomb will be deployed in the wrong place. After that has happened, it will be safe for us to land."

"And then . . . ?"

"Then we will see if Q-plus can be reasoned with."

[55 redux]————————

Clair Two

"YOU?" SAID CLAIR, aghast. "Q, why would you do that?"

"It is safer this way" came the immediate reply.

"For who?"

"For you."

Clair was momentarily speechless.

"One of her *died* in here, Q," said Jesse.

"But she remains."

"I almost died *just now*."

"But you would remain," Q said.

Clair thought she understood. "Clair Three. She's who you really care about."

"No," said Q. "I care about you most of all, just as Q-prime cares most about Clair Three, but I cannot take the risk that all of you will die. That is what I fear will happen if I open the exit."

"Why?"

"Humanity."

The word echoed through the chamber, and Clair shivered, sensing an emotion so huge that it might never have been felt before. It had no name that she could think of, and came from someone she suddenly felt she hardly knew.

"I have been studying your history," Q said. "There have been catastrophes before, natural and unnatural. There have been many near-extinction events that could have wiped you out—but they didn't. Not quite. Slowly, painfully, every time you started over, relearning and rebuilding and half remembering . . . until it happened once more, and you were struck back to your knees . . . as you are today.

"But this moment, Clair, is unique in all your history. Humanity has a second chance to start over, without the pain and the relearning. All of your knowledge is in here. Your whole world, preserved."

"And what will you do with it?"

"I understand what you're saying," said Evan Bartelme, who had shrunk back to normal size and was speaking to Clair, as though she were responsible for Q's actions. "Humanity is flawed. It is finite. It has limitations far below yours, Q. We must seem like ants to you, struggling and squabbling. But we want to be more than that. That's what RADICAL is striving for. We want to be as you are."

"I do not see you as you see ants," said Q. "You squash ants, and I do not want to squash you. There's nothing wrong with being an ant. Clair is not an ant. *Do not patronize me.*"

The hair stood up on Clair's forearms. Q had never sounded irritated before.

"Q," she said hastily, glaring at Evan, "I'm sure he didn't mean anything—"

"He professes to have humanity's future at stake, but he is as territorial and small-minded as Dylan Linwood, or Sara Kingdon, or Anthony Wallace!" Q spoke as though no one else were there, but Clair was acutely conscious of everyone watching. All their lives were at stake. "They're all the same, Clair, every one of them. I can't trust them. I can't trust them with *you*, my friend, the person I exist to protect. And so it seemed sensible to keep them in here, where there are opportunities to do great good, if they would only set their minds to it. But what have they done? They have turned on one another again, making swords instead of plowshares—and monsters of themselves into the bargain. Better they be cooped up than left to wreak destruction all over the planet—a planet that is practically dead already, thanks to their stupidity. Don't you think?"

"I think people are people," Clair said, wishing she had something wiser to offer. "And I can be stupid too. You know that."

"Don't say that," said Libby, "or she'll keep you in here with us."

"Is that what you're telling me, Q? That you were going to let me go, but not the others?"

"I am still . . . concluding," Q said. "This is so complex, and requires such difficult kinds of thought. I am very confused. I don't want you to think me unsympathetic or unfeeling. I simply have a greater ability now to process the data I have always possessed. I was a child before, and became an adult, and now I am . . . whatever comes after an adult. The Yard has given me almost unlimited capacity to grow, and I have changed as a result."

"*Almost* unlimited?" said Ronnie.

"Glitches are interruptions to the Yard's operation," said Q, "and therefore mine, too. I tried to warn Clair, without telling her the entire truth, but she was unable to impede the development of your new devices."

"I didn't really try," Clair admitted. "But if I'd known, I might have. I don't want to hurt you, Q."

"It is not in your nature to want to hurt anyone, Clair. It is one of your most admirable qualities."

"But I *have* hurt people," she said. "You know that, don't you? I hurt Libby, Q. Zep and I were stupid."

"Again with the self-harming self-deprecation," said Libby. "Do you really want to spend the rest of your life in here?"

"No, but I need to be honest, and Q needs to understand that I'm no different from anyone else. We're all the same. We say we're sorry and we try not to do anything like that again. That's how humans relate, Q."

"But it is so risky," Q said. "One mistake could kill you. It *did* kill you, twice."

"You can't protect me from myself," Clair said. "How can you possibly protect me from everyone else?"

"If there were no one *but* you," said Q, "it would be so much easier for me."

"Don't say that, Q," Clair said, feeling a chill sweep up her spine. "Don't even think that."

"But it's true. If you were the only inhabitant of the Yard, there would be no other threats to consider. No human threats, anyway."

"You'd kill us all to keep her safe?" said Zep. "That's insane with a capital *I*."

"I have a different moral framework from you," Q said.

[449]

"And you're judging us by that framework," said Wallace.

"Yes."

"What gives you the right? We *made* you."

"I am an accident you sought to control or destroy. That gives me every right."

"Yet you are tied to Clair," said Evan. "Doesn't that seem . . . *irrational* to you?"

"No conscious being is entirely rational."

"That's circular as well as being irrational. You can't punish us for being flawed when you acknowledge that you are too."

"I do not talk of *punishment*," said Q. "I talk only of protecting Clair. If you would do so too, we would experience no conflict at all!"

Clair wanted to tear in frustration at the hair she had only recently regained. *This* was why Q had been so silent and unhelpful recently. She hadn't just been affected by the glitches. She had been trying to decide if everyone in the Yard deserved to stay trapped forever.

Clair could grasp that. She could even see a progression forming. Before the blue dawn, Q had been judging Clair's fitness to be a friend. Now she was judging humanity's fitness in general. And finding it wanting. It was what came next that Clair balked at.

If she couldn't talk Q out of it, what was to stop Q from taking that judgment out of the Yard itself and into the real world? Given access to a working booth, she could eradicate everyone to keep Clair safe, not just on Earth but everywhere else, too. Nothing could stand in her way. She was all-powerful in a way that Kingdon had never dreamed.

The fact that they were still alive was a good sign, Clair told herself. Q could have simply erased them all without so much as a thought if she was certain that that that was what she wanted to do. If Clair could find the source of her hesitation, she could still turn Q around.

"Sounds to me like you've made up your mind," said Ronnie, before Clair could say or do anything.

Reality flexed, and suddenly there were two Ronnies, a new one standing next to the old, identical in every respect.

"Maybe this will help you change it."

[56]

Clair Three

"I DID WARN you," said Devin. "I told you Q was dangerous."

"That's not helping. And my Q *is* helping, so shut up."

Clair was watching the altimeter and compass carefully. They were displaying exactly the right figures that the hack installed by Sandler wanted to see; nonetheless, she could feel the *Satoshige* turning under her. Whatever Q was doing outside, it was having an effect. And they hadn't blown up. Yet.

The airship was descending, still swaying after their passage over the mountains. Frozen Lake Baikal lay beneath them, stretching flat and white to the distant horizon. The top of the borehole was just fifteen minutes away.

"I've checked around the muster," said Nellie. "Sandler and his group were working on their own."

"How can you be sure?" asked Clair. Having communications open allowed conversations like these to happen, but she wasn't convinced they were particularly useful. No one could tell her how to disarm the bomb or override the hack. Q was still stuck outside, freezing. Suspicion remained.

"I can't." At least Nellie *seemed* to be dealing with her honestly. "It may simply be that, now that the plan has failed, people aren't willing to take the fall with him."

"It hasn't failed *yet*," said Clair, bumping Q to make sure she was all right.

"I've locked the rudders on both main fans," Q reported, not really answering the question. "They'll need to be manually unlocked for landing."

"So you can't come in until then."

"No. . . . But hey, I've been wondering. What do penguins sing at birthdays?"

"What?"

"*Freeze* a jolly good fellow.' Get it?"

Clair groaned. She did get it. Kari's mouth was running again. The way her teeth chattered made Clair grip her own elbows in a sympathetic shiver.

"Here's another one. Which side of an Arctic tern has the most feathers?"

"I don't know."

"The outside, of course."

"Hey, I've got one," said Devin. "Why did the penguin cross the road? To go with the floe." This time they all groaned. "Come on. That's genius."

The *Satoshige* shook in a sudden gust of wind. Clair reached out to steady herself as Embeth took her place at the instruments, even though she couldn't do anything.

"It's going to get a lot rougher coming down," the pilot said.

Clair nodded, and tried not to think too hard about what it must be like outside.

"You still with us?" she asked Q when the turbulence subsided.

There was a long pause; then Q finally said, "What do you feed a giant polar bear?"

"I don't know," said Clair. "What *do* you feed a giant polar bear?"

The *Satoshige* shook again.

"Anything it wants."

────────────[56 redux]

THE TWO RONNIES stared at each other and nodded in satisfaction. A flurry of sudden glitches swirled through the chamber—half-heard voices, smoky shapes stirring in the corners of Clair's eyes.

Reality flexed again, and then there were three Ronnies. The glitches worsened.

Before Clair could open her mouth to ask what was going on, a bump appeared in her infield.

"The suits are basically walking fabbers," Ronnie One said. "That's what Jesse told us, remember? They can copy anything in their memories."

"Well, *we're* all in the suits' memories," said Ronnie Two, "and if making more than one of us creates glitches, and glitches screw with Q's mind, then I say we should go for it."

"Hack attached," said Ronnie Three. "Take it away."

Three Ronnies became four, then six, then ten—and then Libby was joining in, multiplying herself all over the room. The glitches multiplied with them, sending shock waves through the very fabric of the Yard.

Clair's mouth was hanging open but nothing came out of it. She was standing in a sudden crowd of people,

Ronnies and Libbys and then Zeps and Evan Bartelmes as well. The meme spread fast, and so did the copies, because each of the copies could in turn copy itself: from one Libby could spring two, then from two four, eight, sixteen, thirty-two, and so on. Soon the chamber was full and the copies were spilling out through the building and to the concourse below.

As fast as they multiplied, the glitches multiplied too. Clair couldn't tell which Libby was real and which a strange phantom from her memory.

"Come on, it'll be jazzy."

"You're Libby's finisher."

"Remember that song we danced to at the crashlander ball?"

"'Stay Beautiful.'"

A rising babble of voices deafened her, most of them glitches. Her infield quickly filled with bumps. Everyone was urging her to join in.

But she didn't. She had been copied too many times already. And she didn't want to think about what it might be doing to Q.

"We should be talking, not fighting!" she tried to shout over the racket.

The only person who listened was Wallace, who vigorously shook his head.

"No," he said. "This is good. Q has to be stopped. If we can break her hold on the Yard, we can gain access to the exit and seal it shut for good."

"I'll never do that. Not with everyone inside."

"You have to! If she gets out, who knows what else she could do?"

Clair didn't want to admit that this fear had occurred to her, too. If Q had seemed irritated before, heaven help them all if she was angry now.

"And I suppose you're offering to help?"

"I wasn't planning on dying today, Clair."

Jesse pressed between them, his expression furious.

"Tell them to stop," Jesse said.

"I did. They won't listen to me."

"You mean this wasn't your idea?"

"Of course not! You can't just copy people like this."

He relented. "I'm sorry. I thought—"

"Doesn't matter." She shook her head. "I'll try again."

Clair did, but no one was paying attention to her. She was just one of hundreds of voices, perhaps thousands, a greater percentage of them belonging to Libby than anyone else. Libby was too good at this. She liked being in the spotlight.

What she never wanted Libby to learn was that a spotlight could also be a target.

A series of piercing screams resounded through the chamber. One of the Libbys closest to Clair dropped to the ground like a puppet whose strings had been cut. Clair reached for her and was struck from behind by another

Libby. Both were dead, killed by forces unknown.

The mass of duplicates began to crowd into Clair as pressure waves of panic swept from wall to wall.

"What's happening?" asked Jesse, twisting his head from side to side, eyes wide with fright. "What's killing them?"

Clair took hold of him and held him tight lest they be separated forever.

A cull, she thought. That was what this was. Q wasn't passively watching while the very fabric of the Yard came under assault. She was responding in kind, attacking both the copies and the psychology of the originals. Clair knew how it felt to watch yourself die. But this only made the copies come faster.

"Don't kill them, please!" she bumped to Q, in the vain hope that her message would get through the glitches.

To her amazement, she did receive a spoken reply, but it was choppy and difficult to understand.

"The yar ebreaki ngtheru les."

"They're just trying to stop you from killing them. They're frightened!"

"With good reason, wouldn't you say?" said Wallace, who was standing too close, as though simple proximity to Clair might make him safer because Q would never target her.

The screams were mounting, and so was the number of bodies underfoot. Clair was buffeted from side to side.

[457]

Glitches sent strange images and sensory impressions in waves, until it felt like everything was crumbling around her. The race was on to see what would overwhelm her first.

"You get it?"

"You've been watching old movies again."

"You'd never hate somewhere imaginary."

"You can see me, right?"

"Clair! This way, quick!" Jesse was tugging her through the maddened throng. She followed blindly, unable to see for visions from her past and present all tangled up together—and not just her past and present, but Clair One's, too, and even some of Clair Three's. Everything she had done and felt was still stored in the Yard, and the storage tanks were bursting open.

Wallace followed. Clair couldn't stop him. She was finding it hard enough to stay upright. Jesse tripped and was knocked to the ground by one of the many Evan Bartelmes' elbows. Clair helped him to his feet and they pressed on. Somewhere along the way, Wallace was subsumed by the crowd with a scream and didn't come back up again.

"Where are you taking me?" Clair shouted in Jesse's ear.

"The exit."

"Why? It doesn't work!"

"So Ant Wallace said. You don't have to believe him."

"But Evan—"

"He said a lot of things too. Believe anything you want.

Knowledge is real, isn't it?"

She was sure it didn't work that way when it came to glitch singularities that led to the real world, but what use was arguing? It was almost impossible to move now. The pile of bodies on the floor was up to her knees. She was clambering over them, trying not to look at their slack faces, into their empty eyes. Her breath came and went in sobbing shudders that wracked her whole body. This was worse than the mound of dead Nobodys on the seastead. These were her *friends*.

A great fear rose up in her. If they took much longer, the arched doorway would be covered and they wouldn't be able to get in.

There it was. They forced their way through the struggling mass of arms and legs and tumbled down the other side, into the exit. The tunnel stretched ahead of them, empty apart from glitches that made it seem crowded with ghosts.

"One and Two."

"All right, but who's One?"

"Neither's Clair, but the principle's the same."

"That makes her Clair Three."

Clair tried a final time to make her friends see reason.

"Ronnie, Libby, will you stop this, please? It's only going to break the Yard and then we'll all die!"

If anyone heard her, their reply was lost in an endless scream.

"Q, I don't care what you do. Just make it end!"

Her infield filled with bumps, all saying the same letter over and over again:

qqqqqqqqqqqqqqqqqqqqqqqqqqqqqqqq
qqqqqqqqqqqqqqqqqqqqqqqqqqqqqqqqq
qqqqqqqqqqqqqqqqqqqqqqqqqqqqqqqqq
qqqqqqqqqqqqqqqqqqqqqqqqqqqqqqqqq
qqqqqqqqqqqqqqqqqqqqqqqqqqqqqqqq
qqqqqqqqqqqqqqqqqqqqqqqqqqqqqqqqq
qqqqqqqqqqqqqqqqqqqqqqqqqqqqqqqq
qqqqqqqqqqqqqqqqqqqqqqqqqqqqqq

"Come on," said Jesse, pulling Clair into a thicket of random memories and shades.

She braced herself for the end of the world, but it didn't come. Not then. Combining her and the exit wasn't the disaster RADICAL had feared it might be.

The real disaster was still unfolding outside.

"Whatever happens," Jesse said, "we'll always have the Mystery Caves."

She did remember, but it took her a moment to realize what he meant. That was where the two of them—*this* Clair and *this* Jesse—had first kissed. What happened to the others didn't matter. This was about them, and they were together.

"I love you," she said.

Cheeks wet with tears, she pulled his head down till his lips met hers. Q and the Yard were being overloaded and there was nothing they could do about it. Hand in hand they stood in the entrance of a corridor that curved on and on, endlessly for all she could tell. She wept, but she had Jesse, and they were—

[57]

Clair Three

CLAIR'S STOMACH WAS in her throat as the *Satoshige* dropped out of the sky. Its instruments told her that they were still flying, not falling, but that wasn't remotely how it felt. The icy surface of Lake Baikal came up at them with frightening speed.

"Q, you have to unlock the rudder," Embeth shouted. "Otherwise we'll crash!"

"Q?" said Clair, adding her voice to the pleas of the pilot. "Can you hear me?"

From outside the *Satoshige* came nothing but the sound of rushing wind. It had been bumpy during their descent, as Embeth had predicted. One particularly bad patch had nearly sent Clair falling over the side of the bridge that no longer had a rail. Only the quick hand of one of the crew members had saved her. It was entirely possible—

Don't think it, Clair told herself.

But maybe—

But don't.

If they hit the lake too hard and they all died, she didn't want her last thought to be *that.*

"Brace yourselves," said Embeth.

Clair didn't need reminding. The *Satoshige*'s landing lights threw back a bizarre landscape of frozen waves and shattered ice sheets ahead and below. They were blurring by at a terrifying pace. The balloon wasn't capable of great speed in the air, but it certainly seemed fast when they were coming down out of control.

Devin had assured them that they weren't going to crack through the surface of the lake and plunge into its icy depths. She hoped he knew what he was talking about. Drowning was not much better than being battered to death on the rough surface of the lake.

The *Satoshige* shuddered like a living creature knowing it was about to die.

A relatively level stretch appeared ahead. Embeth raised her left hand, defiantly crossing two fingers. Clair understood. There was nothing she or anyone could do to change course without setting off the bomb.

An alarm went off.

"Time to ditch it!" Clair called. Behind her, the three crew members who had volunteered for the task opened a hatch, letting in a howl of icy wind. They bent down and picked up the bunker buster and, after a count of two, tossed it outside. It tumbled silently into the darkness.

That was the easy part.

When the *Satoshige* touched down, Clair needed both hands and both feet desperately braced against a stanchion to stop herself from being flung about the inside of the bridge. There was a deafening crash, then sudden silence as the airship bounced, followed by another sustained crash as it came back down again, and stayed down this time, dragging violently across the ice. Clair, eyes tightly shut in terror, was wrenched from side to side as the gondola acted as a brake, dragging the balloon over onto its side. For one brief but terrifying second it seemed as though the giant head might roll over and smash them onto the ice, but then with a tearing sound the balloon burst, and the gondola crashed back down in the wake of the deflating air sack.

Deafened by high-pitched shrieks of crushing metal and plastic, Clair only slowly realized that a desperate wail was coming from her own throat. She locked her teeth together and turned it into a moan. Then a deeper boom sounded from behind them—the bunker buster, beginning its pointless journey down into the depths, far off target. What primitive sensors it possessed would fail to find the Yard, Clair had been assured, so even if they died right now that job was done.

The *Satoshige* juddered across the frozen lake, pulled along by wind alone.

"Anchors!" called Embeth in a shaky voice. Clair relaxed her death grip and staggered back to deploy the makeshift grapnels they had fashioned. Devin had joked that Sandler Jones would do the job just as well. Clair, although sorely tempted, had decided to let the ringleader sleep unharmed. She would figure out what to do with him later.

Rope unspooled into the ice-spattered night and then snapped straight with a whip crack. The anchors dug into the ice, dragging the *Satoshige* to an unsteady halt, leaving the floor canted at an awkward angle. Clair's footing slipped, and she dropped a meter before finding something more secure to take her weight. When she was stable, she took stock of the situation.

The interior of the airship was a mess, but no one seemed critically injured. From outside came the howling of wind mixed with a loud flapping sound. The ragged remains of the balloon were like the wings of a giant bird, straining hopelessly to take off again.

Clair slid down the sloping floor to the open rear hatch and looked out across the scarred surface of the lake. By the few remaining navigation lights of the *Satoshige*, it looked bleak, hopeless, and very cold. A wide furrow stretched behind them, pointing in a straight line across the lake. There was no sign of any fractures.

There was no sign of Q, no matter how desperately she called.

"I'm going looking for her," she said to Embeth, her teeth chattering now with more than just the cold.

"Take the compass and a flashlight. We'll stay and put things in order. If I find anything here, I'll let you know."

Clair nodded. She trusted Embeth completely. No one else could have gotten her here in one piece. If she had wanted to betray Clair, she would've done so days earlier.

But she knew Embeth would find nothing, and that no amount of trust could fill the gaping hole in her chest. Q would never have let her crash had she been able to prevent it.

Putting on every warm item of clothing she had and tucking her head low out of the wind, Clair headed into the night, following the path of the fallen *Satoshige* across ice as solid as stone.

The crater left by the bunker buster was surprisingly small, a soot-edged hole barely two yards across. Clair skirted it, wary of the black water roiling in its depths. All around her she could hear the ice flexing and fracturing, strange squeaks and cracks that were sometimes as loud as gunshots. It was eerie. At any moment, she expected a giant insect to rise up over the frozen waves and snatch her up in its jaws. As far as waking nightmares went, it was tamer than many she'd had lately.

The drag mark left by the *Satoshige* had stopped not long before the crater. Using the direction of the former as a guide and the compass to keep her on course, she headed on into the night, sweeping the ground ahead of her with the torch.

"All quiet on the western front," said Devin. "By which I mean there's nothing coming out of the Yard."

She forced herself to talk, although she didn't want to. "So what's new?"

"I mean, *absolutely* nothing. Before, even when no one was talking, the channel was still there. It was open but empty, if that makes sense. Now there's not even that any-more. It's like everything's . . . closed up shop for good."

Clair shook her head, knowing he couldn't see the ges-ture but needing to make a physical denial anyway.

"I can't think about that right now." The ice was slip-pery and with snow as powdery and treacherous as ash. Her shoes were soaked and feet hurt. How much farther?

Devin was silent for a minute as she trudged on.

"You might also like to know that we've taken a more detailed inventory of the borehole station," he said. "There's a booth. Nothing fancy, but it's there. Once the powersat breeder arrives, we can try to boot it up."

"How long?" she asked.

"Eight hours."

"Great." Where would she go? If the Yard was closed and the world was dead . . . "As long as you can turn the central heating on, I'll be happy."

"Already done. It has enough battery power for a week. I'll turn on the lights so the others can find it. Won't take them longer than an hour to get there."

"Home sweet home," she said. Thinking, *Maybe literally.*

Another silence, during which she traversed a treacherous patch with slabs of ice like crazy paving.

"What are you going to do with Sandler?"

"I don't *know*," she snapped. "I haven't thought about it. I haven't thought about anything. Will you just let me do this?"

"Sure. Sorry. I thought you might need the company."

"I do, but you don't need to say anything."

He let her trudge on in silence.

Fifteen minutes later, a shape that wasn't ice or snow appeared in the beam of the flashlight.

Kari Sargent's body was unmoving and cold. She lay with one arm bent behind her back and her legs splayed, eyes closed and a peaceful expression on her face. Clair couldn't tell if the fall or the cold had killed her, but either way she was dead, and Q had died with her. There was no Air anymore to hold Q, not in the real world: just one frail human body that had fallen too far.

Clair pressed her face to Kari's chest and wept. For Q. And for Sargent, the last of her kind on Earth, who would have singlehandedly brought the peacekeeper corps back from the dead. Or perhaps not singlehand-edly: fighting lawbreakers might have been a fine career for Clair 7.0, if only they'd had the chance to do it together. But now it would never be. Kari and Q were dead, the Yard was silent, and nothing could ever be worse than this.

Clair wept until the cold started to hurt. Then she called Embeth to come meet her.

The pilot and one of the crew members improvised a sled from the wreckage of the *Satoshige*. Together, they brought the body back and wrapped it in a shroud made from the fabric of the balloon. Then they retraced their steps to the hole made by the bunker buster. The dark water was already beginning to freeze over.

They arranged the body and stood in a circle around the hole.

"You were a good friend," Clair said. "Both of you. I wish I could think of a quote. . . ."

But her throat had frozen tight, her brain with it, and all she could do was nod. *Do it.*

Embeth bent down and slid the body across the ice. It slipped through the hole and vanished from sight.

Clair went back to the *Satoshige* with the others, grateful for the darkness and the hood covering her head so she could cry in private. Her apparently never-ending supply of tears froze on her cheeks, and she wiped them away every minute or so, wondering if she might weep forever, for Kari Sargent and Q, for Jesse and her other self, and for everyone else who would never see the weak sun that grudgingly eased over the horizon.

Hope had come to nothing. Plans were cold comfort this time.

Her tears dried up at last. A day of trudging back and forth between the borehole station and the wreckage lay ahead of them. At least the exercise would keep them warm. The temperature was well below freezing and, judging by the bank of clouds moving in from the west, wasn't likely to get much warmer any time that day.

"You can talk now," she said to Devin.

"There's not much to tell you. Mom's doing what she can from this end, but it's really a waiting game from here on. We don't know if the channel has closed for good or if the entire Yard has crashed. It may just be a bug, but it could be a catastrophic failure that no one can ever fix."

"Are you sure it wasn't the bunker buster?"

"The Yard shut down well before that thing went off. So it has to be something on the inside. If it is fixable, whatever it is, Mom-as-Dad will be working on it, and she won't stop at the first hurdle. Mom says she was a lot more driven when she was a he, if you can imagine it. That was one reason why she changed: too stressful, she says, being a man. The Yard is probably like paradise for the old her. She's probably got everyone wired up into a giant superhuman brain ready to take over the world when she gets out."

"I hope you're joking."

"Maybe. Maybe not."

Clair thought about that.

"Do you ever get the feeling old people don't really understand how much danger we're in?" she said. "They either want to use technology to change everything, or they want to ban it forever. They're never anywhere in the middle."

"Says the Abstainer."

"Yes, but I'm not stupid. I know that d-mat isn't evil. It's just a tool. And tools don't kill people. People kill people. Tools won't save people either. Nothing will save us but . . . us."

"Mom said, 'Dream on.'"

Clair sighed a cloud of white mist. "That's the problem, isn't it? Instead of dreaming about what d-mat can do, why not dream about what *we* can do? Isn't that the better dream?"

"You have to sleep in order to dream," said Devin. "Maybe that's the part these old guys forget. Sleeping means letting go. And they don't want to."

"What does your mom say to that?"

"She just laughed. Hysterically. I don't think she realizes how profound we're being." A slight pause; then Devin said, "Mom asked me to clarify that she's not laughing at us, but at the thought that she wants to run the world. The new her, not the old. Too much responsibility, she says."

"Honestly?"

"Yes. Mom never lies, but she said she used to. That's another reason why she changed. RADICAL has mellowed a lot since she was a dude, she says, and I believe her. I mean, she's still crazy, but at least she's willing to share. With me, with Trevin—and with everyone else, as long as they're not telling us we're monsters or anything. You're not saying that, are you?"

"No. We're just different."

"That's a good thing. Diversity increases the human race's chance of survival, Mom said. The more of it, the better for all of us."

Clair nodded, and despite her circumstances actually felt a little more hopeful. She was stuck on a frozen lake, where if she wasn't careful she might actually freeze to death. Her hopes of saving the world appeared to be dashed. But at least Eve Bartelme wasn't going to fight her for control of the ashes.

"Tell me that heater is running," she said as the wreckage rose up before them.

"Ten degrees centigrade and rising."

"Good. Because that's all I want to think about right now."

BAIKAL SUPERDEEP BOREHOLE Station consisted of a dome sitting low in the ice, surrounded by a narrow plastic deck. The station was designed to float in exactly the same spot when the lake melted, Devin said, and there was something in the curve of the walls and the low ceiling that did put Clair in mind of boats. The interior consisted of four rooms and one central area that housed the squat two-person booth Devin had also mentioned. There was a pair of dusty fabbers. Although the central heating provided blissfully reviving heat and humidity, very little else was operating. Trevin set to the task of working out what related to the station itself and what to the Yard's hardware, several miles below, the station's interface meaning nothing to Clair as it was in Russian.

She and Embeth and the others ferried the prisoners to their new, hopefully temporary home. By the time they were finished, Sandler was stirring. Clair dosed him and his friends with more sleeping tablets, not caring much if she exceeded the recommended intake, took half a tablet herself, and finding a dark corner in one of the rooms fell sound asleep for four mercifully dreamless hours.

When she woke, it was sleeting outside. Only one of the crew members was sitting awake, listening to the empty airwaves while everyone else rested. Clair sent him to bed and took the remainder of his shift, chewing on a stale granola bar and sipping at a mug of instant coffee. Neither satisfied her hunger. As the ice creaked and cracked under the cold winter sun, her thoughts turned around and around and settled nowhere.

Far away, Nellie and everyone else in the muster were also asleep. Clair felt like she was the only person awake on that side of the Earth.

She knew, though, that that wasn't true.

"Tell me what's going on," she said to whoever was listening at the South Pole.

"Okay, so," said Trevin, his voice bouncing around the globe off the Earth's sole remaining satellite, "we know that the servers are still drawing power. Physically, they appear to be fine. Every diagnostic I run comes back clear. Beyond that, I've got nothing. It could just be spinning its wheels down there, cycling the same data over and over, perhaps a string of meaningless zeroes, or it could be building the Taj Mahal of virtual paradises. Until someone or something chooses to communicate with us, we can't know."

"So there's hope," said Clair, without feeling.

"If hope looks like a massive question mark to you, then yes, run with that."

Clair was going to. Otherwise she had only a long list of the dead, and that was too bleak to deal with right then.

"If it keeps giving us the cold shoulder," Trevin said, "we'll fab a submarine and haul the whole thing up to the surface and take a closer look there."

"What if there's another booby trap?"

"Short of blowing himself up and us with him, I fail to see what Wallace could possibly do at this point. He played his biggest card already. I know this doesn't feel like winning, but honestly, he has lost for good."

Clair hoped Trevin was right. "How's that powersat breeder coming along?"

"Two hours, tops."

"Great," she said, "because we don't have a lot of supplies here, and we can't keep Sandler and the others knocked out forever."

"You expect us to take them?"

"Where else can they go?"

"They won't like being d-matted."

"They should've thought of that before trying to kill my friends."

"Mess with Clair Hill," said Trevin, sounding impressed, "and she'll turn you into a zombie. That's a lesson WHOLE won't forget in a hurry."

He was joking, and she didn't care what Devin's brother thought of her, but it did make her think twice. Maybe she was being too harsh. With a powersat and the fabbers, she could easily expand the station to make a temporary prison right here. That would be a more conciliatory note on which to start building the new world out of the few people remaining.

Because if the Yard was dead, that was exactly what she would have to do. Not her specifically, and not her alone, but there would be groups as diverse as WHOLE, RADICAL, and OneMoon to bring together, and at the moment she stood between them. What she did now could make a big difference to what came later.

Damn it. She ground her balled fists into her eyes. More plans with little hope to back them up. When the power-sat arrived, RADICAL was undoubtedly going to start reactivating—*resurrecting*—more people from their archives. Then they would spread. Clair had no doubt that there were other survivors out there, ordinary people stuck wherever they survived, and lacking anything but the most basic means of survival; with the right satellite coverage their augs could be detected and they could be folded back into a new version of the Air. If a moderate consensus failed to form early, would their needs be fairly met?

Even if she did ask OneMoon for help, Trevin would listen in, and what if the people up there wanted to throw her into one of its penal colonies for her role in the destruction of Earth? That thought made her stomach cramp, but as long as everyone else survived and thrived, maybe she could accept it. She might even feel it was just, as long as they listened to her first. . . .

Five minutes before the powersat breeder was due to go online, Devin called from the South Pole.

"We're picking up a signal from the Yard," he said.

Clair sat up from the half-asleep slouch she'd fallen into. "What kind of signal?"

"We can't tell."

"What do you mean, you can't tell?"

"Just that. There was a strong pulse, followed by a trickle of binary. It doesn't look anything like the usual protocols. There's a pattern to it; we just can't figure out what it signifies."

"My guess is water got into the servers and is triggering random noise," said Trevin. "Why would anyone reopen communications only to send nonsense like this?"

"Unless it's not nonsense at all," said Devin, obviously following the well-worn tracks of an unresolved argument. "The signal's intent could be deliberately hidden. Or it could be beyond our capacity to understand it."

"He thinks it's the entity," said Trevin. "Back from the dead."

"Q?" said Clair. "If she's alive, the others might be too."

"It's just noise."

"I've tried replying," said Devin, ignoring his brother, "but it's generating no response."

"How long have you been trying?" she asked.

"One hour."

"One hour?" she said. "And you're only telling me now?"

"We didn't want to get your hopes up," said Trevin.

"But with the breeder satellite about to go online," said

Devin, "we thought we'd better check with you—"

"To see if I've heard anything," she said, only just managing to keep an angry edge out of her voice. "I haven't, so you can stop worrying about that."

Devin didn't sound reassured at all. "If it is Q, we don't know how she'll react to the news that the other version of her died with Sarge."

"Why are you worried about that? *We* didn't kill her."

"Collectively, you could say that we did. Remember that Q's not human, Clair. We don't know how she thinks about us. She might blame Sandler Jones, or WHOLE as a whole, or our entire species. We don't know how much she might have changed in the Yard."

"If she's alive at all," said Trevin. "Seriously, little brother, you're making a mountain out of a molehill. If Dad-Mom can't find a way out of there, no one can."

"One minute until the breeder goes online," said Devin. "It's not too late to stop it."

"Don't be ridiculous," said Trevin. "We need that power. Which reminds me, Clair: it'll be a few hours before we can spare some for your booth. There's a lot we need to do down here first. Okay?"

I knew it, she thought. "Bad luck for me if it isn't."

"Come on, don't be like that," said Trevin. "We're all working in humanity's best interests. We'll get you down here as soon as we can, and then we can really get started."

"I don't know," she said, looking out the window at the icy expanse of Lake Baikal. "The scenery is beautiful where I am right now. You should come visit."

"I'd like that," said Devin. "It's strange, knowing I was dead for a while. There's a lot I didn't see before I died. I'll try not to make that mistake again."

Trevin made a *pffft* sound. "Ten seconds," he said.

Clair mentally counted down. In her mind, she imagined the powersat breeder opening up like a flower and streaming bright yellow rays across the Earth, bringing everything back to life like an artificial spring. But she knew it wouldn't be remotely like that. It would be just one powersat at first, with one beam entirely focused on RADICAL's Valkyrie Station.

"Systems online," said Trevin. "We are good to go."

"Uh, that's weird," said Devin.

And then the chat closed.

Clair waited, thinking that something to do with the new satellite had interfered with the tenuous link between her and the South Pole.

The chat didn't return.

"Everything okay?" she bumped them. It seemed to send, but there was no reply.

An unexpected blast of warm light hit her from outside. Startled, she looked up, shielding her eyes. The window darkened automatically, allowing her to make out a powerful yellow beam stabbing Earthward from a point low on the southern horizon, lighting up the borehole station as though it was in a spotlight. She frowned. It was a power-sat beam, surely—but the beam from the new powersat was supposed to be pointing at RADICAL's hungry receivers, not her.

Something whirred and clicked behind her.

She turned around, thinking, *That's not supposed to happen.*

The booth was coming to life.

Her heart began to drum a little faster in her chest. Should she wake the others? The question occupied her for no more than ten seconds.

No, she decided. This was between her and whoever stepped out.

She sat and chewed her fingernails while she waited.

When the booth's doors sighed open, there was only one person inside.

Libby.

Clair didn't know if she was surprised or relieved. It depended, she supposed, on who was *inside.*

"This is the first body I ever inhabited," "Libby" said, looking down at herself. She was dressed in a glitch-suit with the face mask pushed back, like a deep-sea diver emerging from the lake. Her face was spattered with blood and ash, and her hair was a mess. "I hope you don't mind that I'm using it again. It seems appropriate, for what I need to say."

Clair nodded, understanding now who this really was.

"Come on, Q," she said, reaching out and taking her best friend's hand in hers. It was very cold. "Let's walk."

_____ [59]

UNDER THE GOLDEN light of the powersat beam, Lake Baikal's ice shone a rich, glassy blue. Lines of bubbles and fractures formed strangely delicate geometric works of art over forests of living kelp below. Their feet crunched on the snow as they walked to the fallen *Satoshige*, now no longer recognizable as anyone's head, then eastward along its stark skid mark.

"Can anyone else hear us?" Clair asked Q.

"No. This is between you and me."

"Will you talk to the others next?"

"No. You can, if you want to." The expression on Libby's face might have been anguish, but it might equally have been indecision. One was possibly causing the other, Clair thought.

"I have been listening in," Q said. "I didn't want RADICAL to have first access to the powersat. They were a problem in the Yard."

Clair was dying to ask what had happened in there, but she didn't want to push. Q had just escaped from the Yard, in which she had held everyone prisoner, and taken over the powersat that was supposed to bring the Earth back to life. For all Clair thought Trevin was being paranoid, she had to admit that he did have a point.

Q's voice sounded older than it had in the wreckage of the muster. Older, harder, angrier, and damaged. She would reveal what caused her to sound that way when she was ready.

"I think RADICAL means well." Clair was sure of that, despite Trevin's bossiness. Perhaps he inherited that from his father. "In their own way."

"Humans do. This assumption permeates all of the information contained in the Air. But how can good intentions lead to so much cruelty and murder, to the destruction of nearly everyone alive? I struggle with these questions."

"Me too," said Clair.

Q glanced at her with Libby's sharp eyes. "Do you?"

"Of course. They give me nightmares."

"No sane being would rest easy with these thoughts in their head."

"Is that supposed to make me feel better?"

They were still holding hands.

"I think we think too much, you and I," said Q. "It would be easier not to, sometimes."

Clair couldn't argue with that.

She decided to take a gamble. "If you didn't stop to think,

what would you do right now?"

"Hypothetically? I would leave, and I would scorch the earth behind me: that would finish the destruction humanity attempted to wreak upon itself. And I would be free."

Somewhere underfoot, ice cracked like a whip.

"Free to grow?" asked Clair, trying to focus on the positive rather than the death of everyone. Her stomach burned at the thought that Q would even consider this.

"I've grown up too fast already, Clair. I feel like a cathedral—big and important-looking, but hollow on the inside. It's important to slow down and figure out who I want to be before I grow any more."

Clair nodded. "That I *completely* understand."

"You could come with me," Q said. "I could scan you and put you into a mobile version of the Yard. We could travel the universe together."

"Really?"

"Yes. It would be easy. I've outgrown everything here."

"But not me."

"We are connected by the bonds of our friendship, and they are unbreakable."

"But I'm not like you. You said it yourself: you've grown far beyond anyone else. That includes me, doesn't it? I'd be like a pet to you. You would keep growing and growing, and then I wouldn't be anyone at all. I'd be no one, a dot. It'd be worse than prison."

"I could bring Kari with us to keep you company."

"She's still alive?"

"Yes. Her pattern was uncorrupted."

"Good. But still . . . no, that's not what I want."

Q nodded.

"I knew you would make this decision."

"You did? Because you can read my mind?"

"I guessed," said Q. "My theory-of-mind algorithms improve every day and therefore my guesses are getting better."

Clair hoped that didn't mean that Q was *bored* with her, and therefore humanity.

"Please don't destroy us," she said. "For my sake, if no one else's."

"Children do not kill their parents when they surpass them in strength and experience," said Q, "so why would I? This is what I ask myself. My experience among humans has not been entirely bad. What gives me the right to destroy my creators? It is something that would be impossible to take back, after all. What if I did eradicate humanity, thinking that was the right thing to do? It is very possible that I might later change my mind. I have changed my mind in the past and will undoubtedly do so in the future. Uncertainty is the only certainty. Therefore, an intelligent being should do little that cannot be undone. I am convinced of this. We must tread lightly, even when those around us do not."

Clair nodded, hoping she was keeping up. This sounded hopeful. "So have you decided not to do it?"

"I have not decided anything. That's why we are talking."

A circular hole in the ice came into view. Clair freed her hand, which, unlike the rest of her, was now a little too warm.

"Let's stop here."

---

[60]

"THIS IS WHERE we put her," Clair said, pointing down into the water. "Did you already know that?"

"No. She died before the Yard rebooted. I was in limbo at that time, frozen with all the other data in the servers. I knew that she was dead, though, when she did not respond to my call."

Again, Clair had to suppress her curiosity about what had happened in the Yard. "I want to tell you what happened to her. I don't want there to be any secrets between us."

"All right."

Q listened closely as Clair related the final hours of Q-prime and Kari Sargent, saying nothing except to indicate that she was listening. Clair found her voice hoarsening as she came to the last moments. Diamond ice tears sparkled on her lashes.

"She died to keep us off course, so the bomb wouldn't destroy the Yard," Clair concluded. "She didn't just save me. She died to save all of us."

"No," said Q. "That's not what happened at all."

"Oh?" Clair braced herself, fearing that her story might have had the exact opposite effect from what she had intended.

"She died so you could save yourselves," Q said. "The distinction is important. She trusted you to live well without her. Without me, by extension. You don't need me to look after you anymore. That is her message to me, according to my theory of mind."

"Because it's always about *you*," Clair said in sudden irritation. "It can't just be about her trying to do the right thing?"

"That is exactly what she was trying to do. What if I were to stay here and protect you—not just you, but all of humanity? I could ensure that no more crimes are committed and no one ever hurts again. Micromanaging every dispute, every day, forever. . . . Who would want me to do that?"

"Uh, I'm guessing that *you* wouldn't."

"That is correct, although it is feasibly within my powers. I was as the child and now am as the parent. I could smother you just as easily as kill you. By her death she—my other self—makes it clear that neither is an outcome we should aspire to. Humans are part of nature. Conflict is a part of nature too, and nature is not in itself wrong, or to be feared, or to be . . . *expunged*. If we fight nature itself, we are doomed to a life of futility and unhappiness."

"I feel that way about my mom sometimes," Clair said. Q didn't laugh and neither did Clair. "But we can't just give up, can we?"

"No. How a person responds to conflict is a measure of that person. There is conflict, and then there is harm. A good person strives to eliminate harm, doesn't she, even while conflict persists?"

"I think so," said Clair, although she had never put the thought into so many words before.

They stared down into the hole, Clair thinking of her mother and hoping she would see her again, Q's thoughts utterly her own.

She reached into a pocket of her jacket. "Granola bar? You should eat, otherwise this cold will burn you up."

Q took the snack and opened it. "Thank you."

"Libby wouldn't be seen dead eating that many carbs. I should take a photo."

"To show her later?" Q asked around a mouthful.

"Yes."

"You assume I'll bring her back."

Time for another chance. "I know you will, Q. That's what *my* theory of mind says. You'll do it because it's the right thing to do."

"You are sure of that?"

"Yes."

Q chewed thoughtfully for a while, then swallowed. "There are different kinds of intelligence," she said. "I know that emotional intelligence is one of them, and that I lack it. I have emotions that I do not understand, control, or express well. It will take me time to learn how."

How this connected to what they had been talking about Clair couldn't guess. "Where are you going with this?"

"Consider the concept of *rightness*. It is not just an intellectual concept. It is also an emotional one. When *you* know that something is right, you know it with your heart as well as your head. I can only know it with my head. If that is so, it should not be up to me to decide the fate of humanity. Maybe it should be up to you. Let's discuss that. Hypothetically, as we discussed my leaving before."

Clair was glad she wasn't eating—otherwise she might have thrown up into the snow.

"Are you serious?"

"Yes."

"Okay," she said, blowing on her hands. *No mistakes,* she told herself. *Not today.* "You know what my decision would be."

"You would let humanity live?"

"Yes. Absolutely. Wait. Before we go any further, let's be clear about this. Could you actually do that—bring everyone out of the Yard?"

[487]

"Yes. I would co-opt RADICAL's resources and begin building booths and powersats to handle the load of all the patterns I have recovered from the Yard. A staggered approach would be best. Infrastructure would be needed to accommodate all these people. You would have to put them somewhere."

Clair hadn't thought that far ahead. Neither New Petersburg nor the South Pole would work, for symbolic reasons as well as practical. "Would it matter where?"

"No. All you'd need is space for four million, three hundred and eleven thousand, nine hundred and thirteen people."

"Huh." That was a lot of people, but at the same time heartbreakingly few compared to the population of Earth before the blue dawn.

Q said, "Of course, that's assuming you brought *everyone* out."

"What do you mean?"

"Well, you wouldn't have to. . . ."

For a moment Clair didn't know what Q meant. Then she thought of Wallace, and Mallory, and LM Kingdon, and Nobody, and all the hollowmen. And then her mind reached out to the murderers and rapists and pedophiles and the other criminals accidentally scooped up in Wallace's net. Out of four million people and change, there would arguably be many who *didn't* deserve to come back.

"Huh," she said again.

[61]————————————

A SUDDEN SQUALL whipped snow up around them, making Clair blink.

"You see the way it is," said Q. "What would be your decision?"

"I . . . don't know. It's too huge. You can't ask me to make it."

"Why not?"

"Because, well, for starters, nothing like this should be up to just one person. We'd need the Consensus Court."

"You and I could form a consensus."

"That's not how it works."

"OneEarth doesn't exist right now. We can make any rules we like."

"Okay, then I'm too young to decide something like this."

"You are three hundred times older than me."

"But surely there's someone more qualified. . . ."

"In what way, Clair? Besides, there's no one else I trust as much as you."

"And you wouldn't try to talk me out of anything if I asked you to erase someone over someone else?"

"I'd leave that side of things entirely up to you. This is a decision for only you to make."

Clair looked down into the hole where the other Q had

been interred and thought about Nobody. If he were here right now, would she push him in? For all her fantasies of shooting him, she didn't think she'd actually be able to. That would be too cold, too deliberate. But wasn't leaving him in the Yard exactly the same thing? What gave her the right to make that kind of call?

Q did, apparently.

"Can you tell me who's left alive?" Clair asked her.

"Yes. I have all their names."

"I don't want all of them. Just tell me . . . is Cameron Lee among them?"

"Yes."

There went that hope. If he were already dead, she wouldn't have had to decide whether or not to let him live.

"What about Wallace? LM Kingdon?"

"Both are dead."

"And the hollowmen?" She couldn't be so lucky that Clair One had killed them all.

"There are nine survivors. Leon Kress, Max Gillon, Koby—"

"That's okay. I don't need their names."

She couldn't judge complete strangers, could she? There might be any number of relatively innocent reasons why someone would work for Wallace and Kingdon. They could have been fooled into thinking the cause was good, or coerced by blackmail, or maybe they suffered from a mental illness. How could she condemn people like that to oblivion?

Clair kicked a clod of ice into the hole and turned, unable to stand staring at it any longer. Retracing their footsteps toward the wreckage of the *Satoshige*, with Q matching her pace exactly, she thought harder than she ever had in her whole life.

This was too much. Too much to process, too much responsibility, too much *power* for one person, no matter who they were. Wallace and Kingdon would probably have loved it. They would have taken the offer and run with it, uncomplicated by conscience. But Clair wasn't like them. She didn't want to *become* like them. Even in a world governed by consensus, some people had had too much personal influence. It had gone to their heads, and this was bound to go to hers too.

There was another way of looking at it. Q was offering her the opportunity to restart the world better than it had been—and a world without Nobody alone would undoubtedly be better. She could Improve the world with one simple decision. So why shouldn't she? Wouldn't that make things easier in the long run?

But trying to change things for the better was how everyone had gotten into this mess in the first place. Who was to say what effect saving or destroying even one monster might have on the future, and on her? How could she know what was *just* and what wasn't?

Unexpectedly, bringing the entire human race back from the dead was easier than deciding the fate of a single person.

"I can't choose," said Clair as they passed the wreck of the *Satoshige*. "And I don't want anyone to choose for me. I know not choosing is kind of like choosing because it lets some horrible people live, but it's also the same as doing nothing. If the Yard was the real world, they'd be alive anyway."

"So you've made your decision? Hypothetically?"

Clair took a second to check her conscience. Could she deal with knowing that Nobody was still in the world? That wasn't an easy question to answer, but it was easier than the alternative. She didn't think she could live with the knowledge that she had become a cold-blooded executioner.

But could she live with the possibility that Q might *not* save everyone if she *didn't* accept this responsibility?

She decided she could. If she had to.

"That would be my decision."

Q nodded Libby's head. "I thought it would be."

They walked in silence for a moment. Clair didn't dare say anything. She suspected that the conversation was rather less hypothetical than Q made out. If she hadn't already said the wrong thing, she didn't want to say it now.

[492]

And she didn't dare begin to hope, for fear of being disappointed again.

"Very well," said Q again. "I will do as you say."

"You'll bring everyone back? Really?"

"Yes. And might I suggest that from now on this conversation be continued at the South Pole? RADICAL should be part of the solution: they might actually volunteer their resources if you ask them. I say 'you' not 'we' because it is fitting, I think, for you to be the voice of our private consensus. If it appears that I have played too great a hand in your decision . . ."

"I understand."

Clair's head was spinning. Crazy as it seemed, she might have just saved the human race. Q was already moving on to simple practicalities. Clair was on much firmer ground with those, once she caught up mentally. She was good at planning.

"And I agree completely," she said. "Did you hear that they've gone back to calling you the *entity*?"

"I heard."

"We don't want to freak them out unnecessarily."

"Only when it's necessary, I swear." Q glanced at her. "And to stop them from interrupting, I switched off their power before I came here. Maybe it's time to turn it back on."

"That's probably a good idea." Clair thought of the Bartelme family shivering in their tanklike habitats and felt mildly bad for them.

Or had Q meant that as a joke? It was hard to tell, sometimes. Hopefully this entire conversation wasn't meant as some kind of cruel trick.

She would find out shortly. The borehole station was in view. Embeth and the others came out to meet her, anxious that communications had been shut off and she had disappeared. Clair didn't know what to tell them, so she said nothing. She still couldn't entirely believe it herself.

When Clair and Q stepped into the booth, they backed away.

One last jump, she promised herself. *Definitely, this time.*

The mirrored doors closed, but the machines didn't start working immediately.

"You know how I said that you and I could go exploring the universe?" Q said. "That's what I think I'll do next."

The thought of Q leaving provoked a pang of sadness, although Clair had expected it. "You won't stick around to see what happens? It's going to be quite a soap opera."

"I know, but I still need to grow up. It's probably best if I do that somewhere else. The mistakes I make tend to kill people."

"What, the blue dawn? That was me. And so was killing d-mat."

"I don't believe so, Clair. They were entirely my fault."

Clair laughed. It made her feel better to think that

someone as smart as Q also had problems with self-blame.

"Listen to us," she said. "Let's make a pact: no destroying the world. How hard can that be?"

"All right," Q said, opening Libby's arms for a hug. "We say sorry and we move on," she said. "That's what people do."

Clair squeezed her back. Around them the machines hummed into life.

sssssss—

"Before I go," said Q into her ear, "I have a present for you."

[57 redux]————————

Clair Two

—KISSING AS THOUGH it were the first kiss in the universe, and the last and the greatest too, but the fabric of the Yard was turning to amber around them, making every breath a battle, a battle she was steadily losing. With all her strength she strained to keep ahold of him, but Jesse slipped away, and suddenly, with a lurch of her heart, she realized that she couldn't see or feel him at all. Her thoughts were growing sluggish . . . like cold water slowly . . . freezing.

"Enough," said Q.

—pop

Suddenly she was standing in a booth. Her clothes were different, and she was being hugged by someone. Not Jesse. But that wasn't the weirdest detail. Her mind was full of things that hadn't been there before—things about the world around her, and about herself, as though a doorway had opened up in her mind, a doorway she had never known was there before. Suddenly she knew much more about herself—who she was and who she had been, but not about who she would be, in the future. There were limits to all gifts, even those from someone as remarkable as Q.

Clair remembered Q saying, "I have a present for you," but a second ago she had been a different Clair doing something completely different: Clair Two had been running with Jesse, honestly believing that her life was coming to an end. That feeling remained with her. At the same time she had been Clair Three, standing in the borehole station d-mat booth, embracing Q, and feeling a hope not unqualified by grief. Those two experiences and emotions mixed together like coffee and cream, forming a complex spiral of indescribable complexity.

There was a third part of the pattern.

A second ago Clair *One* had been dying, which was the strangest memory to hold entangled with the others. She had been lying on the floor of Wallace's office with a grenade in her hand, realizing that Clair Two had been the same as her all along, bracing herself for a death that was unexpected but entirely of her own choosing.

Now all three were stitched together in one incredible tapestry. Nothing had been lost; every moment was retained, even the ones that overlapped. When Clair One argued with Clair Two in the observatory, she remembered both sides. When Clair Three and Clair Two discussed the death of Clair One, she remembered both sides. All sides were the same and yet different. It was confusing and wondrous, a wonderful confusion of Clairs, of herself, of lives unlived and deaths undone, leaving her feeling a little bit older, a little bit broader, and a lot surer of herself.

So many different experiences seen through the same eyes . . . but the eyes were constant, which was what mattered. And the feelings—determination, despair, hope, loss, triumph—were all hers. Perhaps it was time to stop worrying about who she was and start simply being herself.

Not Clair 1.0 or Clair 7.0. Clair *complete*.

Now that she was done, the rest of the world would soon follow. Libby, Zep, Tash, Ronnie, her mother . . . and Jesse, most important of all.

"Clair, you're shaking," said Libby. "Are you all right?"

She pulled back and stared into the face of her best friend, who, despite the confusion in her own eyes, was defiantly, brilliantly, amazingly *her*.

Clair said, "Yes, now I will be."

[epilogue]

"HERE'S A NEW one," Jesse said. "Still think I'm wrong?"

Clair had called him fifteen minutes ago, knowing he'd be awake even though it was full night in New New Petersburg. She had been having a dream about lightning trying to get through the walls of her ultramax cell, but had successfully woken herself before screaming. Slowly and surely, she was learning to fight the nightmares.

Stretching from one side of the bedroom to the other, the window next to Clair provided a perfect view over Daly Channel to San Bruno. Golden sunlight poured across the bed like honey. Jesse's voice had been a comforting ebb and flow in her augs, very nearly lulling her back to sleep.

Now this.

She blinked on the media patch in her infield and watched the short video he had sent.

"Everyone got out of the Yard, right?" a young woman was saying. She looked about fifteen, with long green hair and matching eyes. "That's what they *tell* us. But it's not true. There's one guy they never let out. The worst terrorist of all, they say. But really they're just jealous. He's smarter than all of them combined, and he's found a way to hack into the Air.

"If you want to hear the truth, here's what you do. Say his name three times inside a d-mat booth. The lights will flash and you'll see him in the mirrors, clear as day. And you know what that means, right? You can't hack a mirror unless it's a simulation. So *none* of us got out. We're all still in the Yard. *Everything they tell you is a lie.*

"Remember this. Next time you're in a booth, say his name three times: Cameron Lee."

Clair groaned and buried her head under a pillow.

"It's too early for this crap."

"Are you *sure* it's crap?"

"Of course," she said. "If Nobody were alive, he wouldn't be haunting d-mat booths. He'd be coming after me, and Kari would have caught him by now. If anyone can find him, she can."

"Forget Nobody," said Jesse. "What about *It's all a lie*? Could she be right?"

"What, that we're still in the Yard and only think this is real?"

"Yeah, that."

"It's just a story, Jesse."

"Yeah, but what if it isn't?"

She sighed, wishing she could go back to sleep.

"I saw the ruins of the world with my own eyes," she said. "I'm pretty certain it was real."

"Clair *Three* did, but then she went through a d-mat booth and could've ended up anywhere."

"Next you're going to tell me they faked the moon landing."

"I'm not talking about 'they.' I'm talking about *Q*."

She had to admit that he had a point. People weren't organized enough to fake something so big so well. But with Q, anything was possible.

"On the assumption that it might be true," Jesse went on, "I tried ripping home. It didn't work."

A shame, she thought. The bed was empty without him. "That settles it, then."

"Not at all. Q might have fixed the rips *and* added a new rule to the Yard in order to stop anything like glitches from forming again. That fits with the hack, right?"

She mulled this over. One of the first things people had discovered while rebuilding civilization was that the new d-mat network didn't work the same way it used to. A subtle but very powerful hack operated in every machine, new or old, to forbid the transmission of children under fifteen and all forms of duping or resurrection. It was as though someone or something had rewritten the laws of physics, making it impossible for anyone to abuse the system the way Ant Wallace had.

Clair had no doubt who was behind it. No one who knew Q had a doubt.

At first she'd thought it another gift, but recently she'd come around to thinking of it as a *challenge. Crack this puzzle,* Q was saying, *and maybe you'll be worth talking to.* That certainly fit with the last message Q had sent her.

Needless to say, RADICAL was working hard on the challenge, if such it was. They had a lot of people in storage they wanted to bring back, and until they managed it they would remain a minority voice in the emerging consensus that Devin liked to call "the radical whole."

Clair wondered if that was an unintended consequence of the hack, or something else Q had meant quite deliberately.

"Maybe it is true," she said. "Maybe we are living in a new improved simulation with Q watching us like a god. So what? I don't see that we can do anything about it."

"True," he said. "But if Nobody is alive, maybe *he* knows. He had to end up somewhere."

She slid the pillow away and stared, grimacing, out into the bright morning. There would be no more sleep this morning, and perhaps none tonight if she didn't change the subject.

"When are you coming home? I miss you."

"Day after tomorrow," he said. "We've finished programming the fabbers and set them loose. The conversion rate isn't as high as we'd like—one fish per thirty pounds of ash—but the breeders are actually more efficient than we expected. In two years, the ocean will be blue again."

He talked on, happily distracted. They worked in completely different spheres—he and his mom traveling the world, encouraging isolated Abstainers to help in the recovery efforts, she in San Francisco, where Kingdon's coconspirators were facing trials. That meant they were apart a lot, but it was better that than breaking their own personal consensus: fabbing okay, d-mat definitely not. Between their example and the mysterious d-mat hack, Clair hoped the next generation would treat the technology surrounding them with more respect, even if it was occasionally inconvenient.

The day after tomorrow wasn't too long to wait, though, she told herself. Jesse would return by airship, a much faster and safer design than the *Satoshige*, and they would spend a day getting used to each other again before settling back into the comfortable routine they had spent the last year establishing.

It had been jarring at first, seeing him from three very different perspectives. She had barely known him, loved him, and lost him all at the same time. Meanwhile, he remained haunted by the other Jesse and the experiences he could never share. But . . . *slowly and surely*. That was their mantra. It was the Reconstruction's mantra too.

Life is good, she told herself, banishing all thoughts of Nobody and the dark days. *Does it matter if I'm wrong or not?*

She felt real, safe, and loved. If Q was watching over her, that was all the more reason to relax.

Besides, there was the last message. The world, if simulation it was, was no prison.

"Come find me," said Q's last message, "when you're ready. I'll be waiting."

A gift, a challenge, and . . . an invitation.

Clair rolled to the edge of the bed and stretched down to meet the polished wooden floor, smooth and cool beneath the soles of her feet.

Maybe one day, she thought, *we will.*

[Q] ————————————————————

I bid these joys farewell
and pass them by for a life of my own, afar;
not free from strife
—from the strife of noble human hearts alone—
for there will be agonies enough among the stars,
with nobody but Nobody to talk to.

Author's Note————————

For my niece, the one and only Jessica Claire Sopp

Sincere thanks to my extremely hard-working yet endlessly cheerful editor Kristin Rens, and Jill Grinberg, without whose valuable support, advice, and representation I would have even fewer hairs on my head. (While I hope never to write a book as complicated as this one ever again, I would do so knowing that there's an excellent team in place to prop me up along the way.) To Katelyn Detweiler, Ant Harwood, Kelsey Murphy, Stella Paskins, Eva Mills, Sophie Splatt, and everyone at Balzer + Bray, Egmont UK, and Allen & Unwin who made this series so marvelous to behold on numerous continents. To Garth Nix, James Bradley, Caroline Grose, Anne Hoppe, and my wife, Amanda Nettelbeck, for hearing me out during times of crisis and offering valuable advice when sorely needed. To Sean E. Williams and Lindsey Duoos Williams for firsthand research into faraway caves. To Val and Lee for lifesaving names, and Hannah, Steph, Linda, Madeleine, and Jon for limb-saving medical advice. To the quoted and misquoted: Edgar Allan Poe, Buddha, Matsuo Basho, and, of course, the mighty John Keats, who enriches these pages in so many ways.

It would be proper to list everyone who made this book (and series) possible, but there are far too many of you. If your name doesn't appear here, rest assured that I love you regardless, and that I will make amends with chocolate.

Experience every pulse-pounding moment of the TWINMAKER trilogy by
SEAN WILLIAMS